Acting Like
A Killer

Patsy Collins

Chapter 1

Honestly, how could anyone be too ill to die? And where on earth was she going to find someone else willing to be bashed over the head with a blunt instrument in twelve hours' time?

"Next year will be very different," vowed Amelia Watson, duty manager of Falmouth's largest hotel. Rather than devise an interesting scheme to boost the usual pre-festive season slump in business, and avoid mid-November tinsel, she would embrace Christmas starting early. Why wait until next year? She immediately made New Year's resolutions. "I'll avoid everything to do with crime of all kinds, particularly murders and dead bodies. And if I get any more brilliant ideas I'll keep them to myself," she promised, very quietly, whilst printing an itemised receipt. It didn't count unless you wrote it down or said it out loud.

As Amelia processed the fidgeting queue of guests checking out, she allowed her attention to drift to the man waiting patiently at the back. Partly because he was pleasant to look at. Mostly to avoid thinking about the impending disaster which would begin with the far longer queue who'd soon attempt to check in.

"We hope to see you again soon," she told a departing guest, then, "How can I help you?" to the next in line.

He didn't want to be helped. He wanted a discount for not having a sea view, because gulls existed, and the fact it had rained on Wednesday. Amelia, politely but firmly, charged the price he'd been quoted for the room he'd booked. Thankfully there were just seven people left for

1

Amelia to deal with, and the attractive man at the back wasn't a complainer. She could always tell.

Although it was great that The Fal View was fully booked, it would have been better if they were also fully staffed. Increased bookings proved Amelia's idea had been excellent. Had, past tense. A quarter of her staff getting colds was inconvenient, but not a complete shock during November. Amelia had just about cajoled enough people to take extra shifts when the real snag arose – one which was in no way her fault and which she simply couldn't have anticipated. No corpse.

"There's lots of information and a map here," she told the lady wanting advice about local attractions. Usually she took the time to give personal recommendations; today it was a smile, a fistful of leaflets and, "How can I help?" to the next person.

At last the patient man stood before her. He was average height, with a lot of glossy reddish-brown hair, a body which suggested he exercised and face that looked as though it often smiled. Amelia felt oddly hopeful as she asked, "Can I help you?"

"You really, really can."

The deep voice and slight Irish accent had Amelia's stomach attempting a jig. His grin reached his eyes, which were lighter than his hair. Almost the colour of caramel coated popcorn. Amelia felt hungry and not just for her favourite snack.

"All you have to do is avoid saying, 'Sorry, we're fully booked'."

"Ah."

"Please, just don't say it, Amelia. I know what the sign says, but I'm desperate for somewhere to stay for the next fortnight."

She liked that he'd used her name. A lot of men glanced at her bust, but they weren't all reading her name badge. "We can do two weeks starting Monday."

"I need somewhere from today. Perhaps you have a room which is being decorated, or has no heating, or no bed? Anything." He gave a persuasive smile.

Amelia suspected it usually got him what he wanted. Or maybe she'd made that assumption because she was very keen to help him. She had a brilliant idea which could solve both their problems at once. Glancing round to ensure no other guests were within earshot, she leaned closer and asked, "How do you feel about dying tonight?"

'Shocked' was clearly the answer. "You're offering to book me into the local morgue?"

He had a wonderfully expressive face, especially his eyebrows. Somehow they combined horror, desperation and even a hint of amusement. Amelia couldn't help imagining how he'd look when experiencing entirely pleasurable emotions.

"How about you let me sleep in my car in the car park and come in for breakfast and use a bathroom, just until Monday?"

"I'm offering a genuine room… complete with bed."

"Sounds perfect, apart from the dying bit."

"Obviously I don't mean you have to actually die."

"Obviously not." He didn't sound, or look, entirely convinced. In fact he looked intrigued.

"You just need to be a bit dead for a little while. OK, there's slightly more to it than that, but mostly it's eating dinner and talking to some people and then lying really, really still. That bit's very important."

"It is a classic behaviour in dead bodies."

"Exactly! Once you've been declared dead you get the rest of the weekend to yourself, then on Monday you can book in like a regular guest."

His easy smile returned. He gestured to the sign advertising the murder mystery weekend, with 'SORRY WE'RE FULLY BOOKED' pasted across it. "You want me to play the victim?"

"Exactly!"

"Tease."

"No!" Amelia grinned. "OK, maybe a bit." Surely he'd been teasing her too? The murder mystery weekend signs were everywhere, which had to be a clue that non-permanent deaths were a possibility. "Misleading you wasn't entirely deliberate though. This weekend is my big project and I've been thinking of nothing else lately. I forget it's not the same for everyone."

"I know what that's like," he said. "I can get wrapped up in things and… Explain how this gets me a room."

"The person who was supposed to play the victim hasn't arrived due to illness, which means there's a spare room, but only for someone willing to die."

"I've never done any acting before. And my experience of being dead is equally limited, but if someone explains exactly what I need to do, I'll happily give it a try."

"Great. And actually you'd really, really be helping me out too."

"Then I'm very willing to do this."

"Brilliant. I'll call Sonia. She's the lady in charge of the actors." Amelia got an engaged tone. "I'll try again in a minute. While we're waiting, let's get you booked in. Can I take your name?"

"Patrick Homes."

"Holmes? As in Sherlock?"

"No, Homes as in houses." He produced a business card.

"Seriously, you're an estate agent and your name is Homes?"

"Yep."

"And you're a local estate agent who has absolutely nowhere to stay?"

"There is a good reason. Perhaps I could explain over a drink, once I've finished being dead?"

That sounded like an excellent plan. Amelia finished checking him in and gave him a key. "Check in isn't usually until three, but I know that room is ready, so you can go up. I'll have Sonia or one of her team contact you about how you die, as soon as possible."

"Thanks, Amelia."

His back view was almost as good as the front. After watching him walk out, presumably to collect his luggage, Amelia again called the lady in charge of the actors. "I've found a victim for you, Sonia. He's not an actual professional actor, but he's keen." Keen was a synonym for desperate, wasn't it?

"Oh, right. Is he a friend of yours?"

"Sort of, yeah. And like I said, he's here now, so there shouldn't be a delay in getting things started."

"I'll come right down."

Sonia's arrival in reception coincided with Patrick's return with his luggage. Amelia introduced the two, ordered coffee, then left them to it. Things took a turn for the better from that moment on. Two of the casual staff she'd called to ask if they'd do an extra shift rang to say they'd be in soon. Even better, Bianca, their newest receptionist, arrived so Amelia could leave the lobby and

5

get back to the duty manager's office where she only had her own job to do.

"Sorry I couldn't come in this morning," Bianca said. "But I can do tomorrow and stay until six from now if that helps."

"It certainly does. Thanks."

Half an hour later Sonia tapped on Amelia's office door. "You were right, your friend seems more than capable of playing dead for us."

"Oh, thank goodness! I was dreading having to cancel the weekend."

"We were never going to do that to you! An agency we use would have provided a replacement."

"Oh. I didn't realise…"

"That explains you taking the news so badly. Sorry, I should have explained more clearly."

And I should have listened to all you said, not begun to panic at the first part, Amelia thought.

Amelia was back on reception at three, helping process the guests checking into every one of the hotel's eighty-seven rooms. She provided those taking part in the murder mystery weekend with a timetable of events and some background information on the story they'd see enacted then try to solve. Once all those packs had been given out she left the other receptionists to deal with the last few guests and headed for one of the reception rooms.

"Everything ready, Jasper?" she asked the head barman, although she could see for herself it was.

"It's perfect. The room is ready, the drinks are ready, me and my boys and girls are ready, your actor people are ready, so don't you worry."

"Thank you," she said with feeling.

"No, sweetie, thank you." Jasper, who was always reliable and enthusiastic, was delighted to be playing the part of a 1920s barman and to have been given little clues and pieces of misdirection to offer the guests. "I've always fancied myself in garters." He snapped one of the armbands which made up part of his costume.

"You do look very… " He looked twice as much like himself as usual, as though he were a dramatic actor playing the part of Jasper. In a way she supposed he was.

"Suave? Sophisticated? Hints of Noel Coward?"

"Absolutely," Amelia said.

"Isn't it time you popped on your frock?" He'd almost persuaded Amelia to wear a tasselled flapper dress.

"Wouldn't my uniform be better?"

"It would not. Go dress."

Whilst changing, Amelia got a text from her best friend Nicole. 'Wishing you luck for your big weekend, not that you'll need it or have time to read this. xxx'

'Thanks! You are right about no time! x x x' she texted back.

When she returned to the, by then crowded, reception room, Amelia was glad she'd done as Jasper suggested. Her outfit tied in well with the actors' costumes and some of the guests were also dressed in 1920s styles. Feeling she was playing a part helped her confidence as she gave a formal welcome on behalf of the hotel. The way some of the male guests, especially Patrick, looked at her did wonders for her ego too. The way Patrick looked, in a vintage suit and with his hair centre parted and oiled didn't have much impact on her. It was just curiosity about how it would feel which made her want ᴐᴜooth back one of his only partially tamed curls. Well, mostly that anyway.

Disappointingly she didn't even get a chance to speak to him, nor any of the official actors, so didn't have any details to add to the background information she'd barely had time to skim through. Amelia couldn't stay for the entire reception as she needed to get back into her office and uniform and rejig the rotas to account for the staff going off sick and others returning to work. It was worth the sacrifice as she was able to get all positions covered. She might even get some sleep and a chance to walk Bongo, the border terrier she co-owned with a colleague, if nothing else went wrong.

The phone on Amelia's desk rang. "Miss Watson," a receptionist said. "A Mr Patrick Homes would like to speak to you. He's in reception now."

"I'll be right down." As she'd ordered coffee for Patrick and Sonia when they'd been talking, and she'd not yet had a break that day, Amelia did the same again for her own conversation with him. With that accent to listen to, I don't want to rush the conversation, she thought as she locked the office door.

"I hope this isn't an inconvenient time to talk?" Patrick asked.

"Not at all. I was going to have a coffee anyway. I hope you'll join me?" Actually work was so busy that any hour with minutes in was a bad time to take a break. On the other hand it was important to stay hydrated and Patrick's enticing smile made his eyebrows look like happy caterpillars. It had an effect on parts of Amelia's anatomy too.

A tray of coffee and biscuits arrived just as they'd got settled at one of the small tables in the lobby. Chocolate caramel biscuits – her waiting staff knew her well.

"Is everything OK?" She hoped so, partly because she didn't want another problem to deal with, but mainly because she hoped Patrick had asked to speak to her just for the pleasure of her company.

"Perfect." As they added cream and stirred their coffee, Patrick thanked her for all she'd done, and the bonus of free drinks and dinner.

"It's no trouble. As I said you're helping me out and the actor you're replacing would have had that room and all his meals as part of his payment, so it's only right you get them. Is everything OK with your role?"

"Yes. I'm…"

"No spoilers, please! I'm hoping to have a go investigating this myself."

"No problem there as I don't know myself who the guilty party is. I was going to say the chap I'm playing is called Max Gold, but everyone else except Sonia is using their real names. All I've had to do so far is mingle at the reception, talking to as many people as possible and drop in a few clues."

"I missed most of that. Can you give me a few hints?"

"Clues to the clues?" Patrick grinned.

"I know it's cheating to just tell me which parts are clues. It's supposed to be mixed in with your cover story, and the other guests don't know you're the victim so won't be paying extra attention to you – but then I'll miss other stuff, because of working. Shouldn't a good detective use every means possible to gather evidence?"

"Yes, they should. And to be honest I'm quite interested to know which of the people who've been so nice to me are going to kill me this evening."

"It's happening that soon?"

"I don't know the exact time, but I'll be dead by breakfast. The things I guess are important are that I'm very rich and I didn't think I had many blood relatives as I was adopted, but have recently learned I have a half-sister. She's staying at the hotel so we can get to know each other. I was married, but my wife mysteriously disappeared nearly seven years ago."

"Oh, so will be presumed dead!" Amelia declared, wondering how that clue could be useful.

"Thought you didn't know the story?"

"I don't, but that's what happens if someone vanishes. I think it can be quicker if there's some kind of evidence of what happened to them – but if they just disappear then it's seven years before they can legally be declared dead."

"Right." He said that as though humouring her.

"Are those all the clues?"

"From me, yes. We're all supposed to introduce ourselves to each other and of course the actors are giving cover stories and clues. I probably overheard some, but I don't know which bits are actual clues."

"What's your cover story?"

"I've been living abroad, hoping to find my missing wife. I've given up on that and returned to England hoping to rebuild my life and connect with my family. I've found a home that I've got cheap because it needs doing up. That's rubbish by the way, the ones needing work seem to be the most expensive! Anyway, I can't move in for a couple of weeks so am staying in the hotel, where I've invited the sister I've never met to stay."

"All very mysterious!"

"Indeed. I think there might be someone waiting to speak to you."

Amelia turned to see her fellow duty manager, Gabrielle, had arrived early. "You're right," she told Patrick. "I have to go. See you at dinner I hope."

"I'm looking forward to it."

"Is everything OK?" Amelia asked Gabrielle. "You've not caught the bug, have you?"

"No, don't panic."

"Thank goodness. If you couldn't do tonight's shift..."

"I can and it will all be perfectly fine." Gabrielle smiled. "It's not as though anyone's going to be murdered, is it?"

"Don't say that! In books there's always a real murder at these things."

"There won't be tonight, but if there is I promise faithfully to bury the body at sea and cover the whole thing up." Gabrielle gave what might have been a Boy Scout salute.

"Thanks, I think. So, why are you in early?"

"Because you haven't taken a break today, and you'll be staying until eleven at least, for your murder party."

"I ate some lunch." She was certain that must be true, though she couldn't remember what it was. "And I stopped for coffee."

"You mean you drank a coffee, in the hotel, while sorting out a hotel problem or talking to a member of staff." Gabrielle didn't ask it as a question.

"You know what it's like." They both did. Once at the hotel there was always something requiring their attention, even if it was listening to the concerns or ideas of a staff member. Not being at the hotel wasn't easy, either. With only three duty managers, they even slept there one day in three.

Amelia, Gabrielle and Jorge hardly ever saw each

other, except when one handed over to the next, but got on well when they did and were determined to work as a team. It was that team spirit which had led to Gabrielle and Amelia sharing a dog. They'd both wanted one, but felt it wouldn't be fair for it to spend so long alone. Technically he belonged to Gabrielle, but she referred to him as their dog and he spent a lot of his time in Amelia's flat.

"I haven't taken Bongo out today, so you're going to have to go and walk him."

"Sneaky! Thanks, Gabrielle." She knew it would do her good to get away for a bit, even if most of the time would be spent getting ready to come back. Amelia walked up to the office with Gabrielle, giving a speedy handover on the way. She grabbed the rainbow-coloured cloth backpack she took everywhere with her and got out before anyone could waylay her with 'just a quick question'.

Amelia returned to The Fal View in time for the dinner, wearing not just the flapper dress, but also half a pound of smoky eyeshadow, deep red lipstick, high heeled dance shoes, seamed stockings and a bejewelled headdress. Strictly speaking she didn't need to talk to Patrick as she'd already got his clues, but she did anyway. Her own cover story was the truth – that she was a manager of the hotel in which the participants had booked, apparently coincidentally, and in that role she needed to be polite to everyone, didn't she? Besides ignoring one guest might mislead the thirty who were trying to solve the mystery.

Patrick wore a tuxedo. The sick actor whose place he had taken must have been a slightly different shape, as it was tight across his shoulders, loose at the waist and a little long in the legs, but he still looked very smart. The suit had satin trim and facing on the lapels. Amelia had to fight the temptation to see if it felt as luxurious as it looked.

Instead she offered him a tray of canapés.

"Gorgeous," he said. "And these snacks look interesting."

But not as tasty as you, Mr Flatterer, Amelia thought.

"Do you know what all this stuff is?" He lifted the herb decorations from a swirl of salmon mousse on cucumber, and a skewered shrimp.

"That one is dill and the other is flat leaved parsley."

"I'm impressed. I can do fish fingers and things like spag bol, but I'm not an adventurous cook. I'd like to learn more."

"Don't be too impressed. I'm a lot better at telling the chef what to prepare than I am in making it myself."

Getting back into character, Patrick told her he left such matters to his staff, then launched into details about his Saudi oil wells and South African diamond mine.

"Oh, Mr Gold, you sound like you could become this girl's new best friend. You really must tell me if there's anything we at the hotel, or I personally, can do to make your stay more comfortable." She gave in to temptation and stroked his arm flirtatiously.

"I really do appreciate the personal touch, Amelia."

"Anytime, Mr Gold."

"Please, call me Max," Patrick said.

An elderly guest joined them. "I'm going to be keeping my eye on you, young lady."

"Because I'm behaving suspiciously?"

He chuckled. "No. You work here so I don't think

you're really going to be the killer. I just like looking at you because you're so pretty."

"You're very perceptive, sir," Patrick said. "I'll be doing the same for exactly the same reason."

Amelia, feeling herself blush, batted her eyelashes at each in turn. "Why thank you, gentlemen." Addressing the guest, she said, "Tell me, Mr...?"

"Hudson. John Hudson."

"Tell me, Mr Hudson, do you own oil wells and diamond mines, like Max here?" She stroked Patrick's arm again.

"No," Mr Hudson admitted.

"Actually it's just the one diamond mine," Patrick said.

"Oh? In that case, you'll both excuse me while I circulate? I *may* be back."

Both men laughed as she moved away in what she hoped could be described as 'sashaying in a provocative manner'.

Amelia talked to as many people as possible, but felt she'd collected more admirers than clues. A good-looking man called Trevor paid her compliments on her appearance. That's if you considered, 'That dress would look great on my bedroom floor,' and presenting her with one of the glasses of complimentary champagne and saying getting closer to her was worth every penny of the drink's price, to be compliments. She definitely preferred the friendly gallantry of Patrick and Mr Hudson.

Amelia thought Trevor was one of the actors, but wasn't sure as she didn't recall seeing him during her brief appearance at the initial reception. He was very intense and seemed to be trying to back her into a corner.

"What do you do?" Amelia asked, whilst trying to

think of a tactful means of escape.

"I'm an investment advisor. If you have any savings I could be of real interest to you, if you catch my meaning."

"I don't actually, but why don't I introduce you to Max Gold? He's very rich."

"No, I don't think so." He vanished and Amelia didn't catch sight of him for the rest of the evening, not that she was trying.

When they were together again, Patrick asked Amelia if there was any way he could stay on as a mystery weekend guest after he'd been declared dead. "It's more fun than I thought and I feel involved now."

"Maybe if you wore a disguise or pretended to be Max Gold's twin brother? We'll ask Sonia."

On Saturday morning Amelia, who had taken the dog home with her, took Bongo out for a walk up to Pendennis Castle. She intended getting to the hotel early. She didn't want to miss any clues – nor the chance to spend time with the corpse. As she hurried the little terrier along she received another text from Nicole. 'What's the body count? xxx'

Amelia called her back. "It better be only one. I think it's already happened."

"Think? Why don't you know? And what's with the heavy breathing."

"I'm walking my half of a dog up a really steep hill."

"Oh good, I thought you'd be madly busy and never leave the hotel."

"We are, but Bongo's other owner said I needed a break."

"She obviously knows you well. But you need more

than dog walking. Come up to Lee-on-the-Solent."

"I'm definitely coming in May. I won't let you down over that. I've written it in my diary and everything." She'd have been happy to look after her friend's B&B anyway, but had the distinct impression that Nicole's planned week in the Canaries was more than just a much needed break.

"I know you won't, but that won't be much of a holiday for you. You need something other than work in your life."

"I'm investigating a murder."

"Which makes it an especially good idea for you to come up here for a rest afterwards."

"Solving crime is fun for me, you know that."

"My point exactly. Your detective brain will be warmed up."

"Oh?"

"Didn't I say?" Nicole asked, all fake innocence. "There's a real mystery to solve here. A local celebrity, one I think you might actually be interested in, has gone missing in *very* suspicious circumstances."

Chapter 2

"Who's missing?" Amelia slowed down so she wasn't puffing into the phone.

"Angus McKellar," Nicole said.

"Never heard of him."

"Really?"

Why would Nicole doubt that? Only last month Amelia received a huge bouquet from a guest, thanking her for her tact and discretion during his stay. 'It's a rare treat for someone in the public eye to be treated as a member of the public,' he'd scrawled. She still had no idea who he'd thought he was.

"Suspicious how?" Amelia demanded, when she properly had her breath back. "Were there strange lights in the sky and crop circles spelling out, 'we've got your man, love the Martians'?"

"Don't be daft. That'd be no mystery at all, would it?" Nicole said.

"No, it would be a clear case of you eating brie before bed. Remember when you dreamed there was chocolate stashed in the house and had me looking for it?"

"Only because you mention it at regular intervals! This is different. Angus McKellar really existed before he disappeared. He started his business in Falmouth."

"McKellar doesn't sound like a West Country name."

"He was Scottish originally, as I'm sure your brilliant deductive powers have deduced, but moved to Falmouth for a few years before coming up here. Did I mention he runs marathons? I know how you like a fit man and nice Celtic accent."

"I do, but if he's missing I'm not going to hear it, am I? Anyway, I prefer Irish to Scots."

"Since when?"

"About 11 yesterday morning. He's our body. Actually they're probably doing the post mortem now. I'd better get back."

"Wow! This guy must have something, you've not asked anything about the real mystery."

"It doesn't sound particularly mysterious. It's probably just a publicity stunt… But yes, there's definitely something about Patrick."

"Aaaw, sweetie. I hope it works out."

It was odd that her two closest friends, who'd never met, both called her 'sweetie'. Nicole had started it as a joke when they were kids, to remind Amelia she had caramels in the tartan backpack she'd had then; a not very subtle hint she'd like one. Jasper used endearments for almost everyone he'd met more than once and didn't hate, but it was usually darling, sugar or pal. As far as she knew Amelia was the only person he called sweetie. Maybe it was that which had first drawn her to him? What Jasper saw in her was anyone's guess, but he'd proved to be a good friend as well as a reliable colleague.

Amelia returned the phone to her backpack and took out a few treats for Bongo. "Yes, you heard that right – I do have a slight crush on a curly haired Irishman. Doesn't mean I don't love you though."

She sighed and retrieved her phone. The call to her parents was answered by the machine. Brilliant timing! "Hi, Mum and Dad. Just called to say hi and sorry I've not phoned recently. We're still mad busy at work. Hope you're both OK?"

Duty done, she dropped the phone back into her bag and enjoyed the walk round the castle's dry moat. It was only as she and Bongo crossed the castle's still empty car park she realised her parents probably hadn't answered as they were still in bed. Hopefully she hadn't woken them. "I'll try again later, if I get the chance and actually remember. Come on, boy. Let's get you home."

Amelia returned to the hotel before breakfast. "You relieved me early, so it's only fair I do the same for you," she told Gabrielle. "I took Bongo for a short walk this morning."

"Thanks. It's all been quiet here. Your murder has all gone to plan – I've had the message saying the body has been discovered and the police called. They're having bacon butties now, ready to burst into the red dining room once everyone is there."

"Brilliant."

"The lady running it wants to see you. She said to tell you it's not a problem, just about your idea for Max. Who is Max?"

"The dead guy. I was thinking…"

Gabrielle grinned. "Whatever your plans for a dead guy are, I don't want to know."

When her colleague had left, Amelia called Sonia. "You asked for me?"

"Yeah. I've agreed with your friend Patrick that he'll come back as his character's estranged younger brother Lester."

"Not twins? Oh! Max Gold and Less Gold! Very clever."

"Glad you like it. I keep the actors' real names most of the time, just to simplify things, but I like to invent a

19

few. Lester won't know much about Max, or anything connected with the murder, so Patrick doesn't need to learn a part. He'll just confirm some of what the victim has already said. That will fit in with the storyline."

"Don't tell me, I'm hoping to solve this," Amelia reminded her. "I've sorted out my own staffing problems now, so should be able to get to the rest of the events. And if I can't, I can get Patrick to tell me."

Sonia laughed. "Yeah, I doubt you'll have any trouble getting information from him."

"So, you've noticed my incredible powers of persuasion?"

"I have. But I was more meaning young Patrick has noticed your neat figure, sleek hair and big blue eyes."

As arranged, Amelia entered the red dining room halfway through breakfast and remarked that one place was vacant.

"Max Gold hasn't come down yet," one of the actors said. "No one has heard from him since dinner last night."

"I did," Arnold, another actor, announced. "About four this morning. He was out there on the lawn."

"And what were you doing out?"

"I wasn't. I… er, I couldn't sleep and just happened to look out," Arnold claimed.

"And you're sure it was him?"

"Positive."

That was Amelia's cue. "If he was up late perhaps he won't want to come down for breakfast. I'll send someone up with a tray." She left the room, returning very swiftly with another actor dressed as a maid.

"Mr Gold won't be joining you this morning," Amelia said, in as dramatic a tone as she could manage.

The maid yelled, "He's dead! Murdered!" She then ran out, to do a quick change into police uniform.

She, and the rest of those acting as police officers, soon returned, to confirm Mr Gold was indeed dead.

A little later the actors playing hotel guests, and some real guests, were questioned in a corner of the Pendennis room, which had been used for the welcome drinks the previous evening. It was partitioned off so as to resemble an interview room in a police station, whilst allowing all participants to listen in.

Everyone but Arnold claimed to have been in their rooms sleeping soundly at the time of the murder. As far as Amelia could tell they were all telling the truth, except Arnold. She knew he couldn't have seen the lawn from his room. That could just be artistic licence except that Lucy, another of the guest actors, did have a view of it. Wouldn't Arnold have been given that room, to make his statement seem true?

Amelia mentioned this detail to Sonia.

"Well spotted. Perhaps you should inform the police?" Sonia suggested.

"Brilliant! I got a clue!" Amelia said. Then in a more professional tone added, "Sure. Just about Arnold's room, or Lucy's as well?"

"Just Arnold's, until you're asked for more information, then tell anyone who asks."

Feeling rather silly, but still pleased with herself, Amelia approached the detective. "Excuse me, sir, but I think Arnold must be... um... mistaken. His room doesn't have a view of the lawn."

"Thank you, Miss Watson. Mr Telford, what do you have to say to that?"

"I did see him, I tell you!" Arnold insisted.

"Describe him please."

"Everyone here knows what he looks like. We had drinks and dinner with him last night."

"What was he doing? How was he dressed?" the police detective asked.

"He was walking around and waving his hands about. He wore ordinary clothes."

"Not nightclothes?"

"No, and not the tux from last night either. I couldn't see the colours, but it looked like white trousers and panama hat, and a striped blazer."

In groups, guests and actors were escorted up to see the 'corpse'.

The police surgeon, played by Sonia, pulled back the covering sheet to reveal the body was dressed in white trousers and a striped blazer.

Sonia then declared he'd been killed by a blow to the head approximately six hours previously – about the time he was apparently seen outside. Sonia wore a man's suit in place of her usual long dress and cloche hat, but was so good at altering her voice, mannerisms and expression the costume was barely needed.

Patrick looked very pale, and the lurid wound to his head stood out clearly. It was rather too realistic for Amelia's liking. She didn't consider herself squeamish but, even though she knew it was fake, it was unsettling to see an injury on someone she knew and liked.

There was an actor in each group. The one with Amelia's bunch asked about the panama hat. She wondered if the same thing happened in each group, or if they helped reveal other clues.

"No hat has been found," a policeman admitted.

After that there were no formal murder mystery events

until everyone returned to the red dining room for lunch. On her way to her office, Amelia went up to Patrick's room. OK, it wasn't exactly on the way, but she wanted to thank him for doing such a good job and a couple of extra flights of stairs would be good for her thighs.

Thankfully he'd begun removing the makeup and looked very much alive.

"It was easy," Patrick said. "Just lying really, really still, as promised."

"I discovered a clue. Arnold claimed to have seen you outside about four this morning, but if he did it wasn't from his room as you can't see the lawn from there."

"Interesting. Reckon he killed me?"

"No. That would be too easy and Sonia had me tell her police detective straight away."

"Hmm. Any other suspects?"

"No, but I'm going to ask as many questions as I can before lunch. I suppose you can't do that, what with being dead?"

"No, and in any case I have to go out for a couple of hours this morning."

"Oh, I..." She'd been hoping they could discuss theories, and forgotten he worked locally and would have friends in the area, not be at a loose end with only her for company.

"I'll be back during lunch, making a grand entrance in my new character, which should be fun. Good for finding things out too, because it's natural my brother will ask lots of questions. If you have any free time after lunch, maybe we could get together and pool what we know?"

"I'd like that."

Amelia raced through her work so as to be free to

attend the lunch as she'd always planned, and to join forces with Patrick for as much time as possible afterwards, which now seemed equally important.

As anticipated, Patrick bursting into the dining room just as people were finishing dessert got quite a reaction. That was nothing compared with people's shock when he declared who he now was, swore he'd avenge his brother's death and pointed at an actor called Jill. "Did you kill our brother?" he demanded.

Jill looked shocked. "How did you know?"

There were gasps from other diners.

"I don't mean I killed him! Of course I didn't," Jill said. "I only learned myself last week that I have two half-brothers. Max contacted me and asked me to come here. How did you know about me?"

"When my dear brother changed his will to favour 'all living relatives' rather than just me, I did a little digging."

After that, questions and accusations came thick and fast. Jill denied having known until the previous day exactly who she was related to. "But he did say he had a brother he'd fallen out with and not seen for months, and who might not be pleased to know of my existence."

Patrick aka Less Gold refused to say how he knew Max had changed his will. Arnold said he'd been thinking about Max's behaviour early that morning and thought maybe he'd been arguing with someone. Several people reminded Arnold he couldn't have seen that from his room and wanted to know where he'd really been. One of those was his wife.

"OK, I'll come clean," Arnold said.

"No!" Lucy shouted. "Don't let them bully you."

"Don't let him cover up the truth!" creepy Trevor the

investor said.

"Don't tell anyone but the police," Lucy insisted. "One of these people is a killer."

"Arnold, what were you doing and where?" his wife yelled.

"Smoking under that entrance gate thing," Arnold said.

"You quit," his wife stated.

"No, I've just done it in secret to avoid your nagging."

"Nag! How dare you? How many times have I told you not to show me up in public?"

"Many, many times."

After that the guests were left to their own devices until they assembled again in the red dining room for afternoon tea. Many chose to stay where they were and question each other.

Amelia sought out Patrick. "I've got a few things to do. Can we meet in an hour and see what we can work out?"

"OK, I'll ask around and see if I can discover more clues."

On her way to her office, Amelia was accosted by a couple who clearly thought she knew far more than she did. They took some persuading that she really was on the hotel's management team and not part of the cast.

"But we saw you talking to that Max character several times – including just after the reception and you seemed very pally. That was a clue, wasn't it?" the man asked.

"No, honestly."

"You'd have a key to all the rooms, wouldn't you?" the lady asked.

"I can get into them all, yes. But I didn't kill… Max. I wasn't even on duty last night."

"Hmm. Could that Arnold guy have gone out smoking in the middle of the night, like he said?"

"Yes," Amelia told them. "But he'd have been seen by reception."

"And was he?"

Amelia, concerned that her answer might lead them astray, promised to find out.

"While you're at it, can you find out if any of our lot have a room where you could see that lawn from?"

"I already know that. Lucy has." Then remembering some genuine guests might also have such a view, Amelia added, "Of course several other rooms do too."

"Thanks for the tip," the man said.

"And I hope that Less likes you just as much as Max did," the lady said, giving Amelia a dig in the ribs and a squint which was probably intended to be a wink.

Everything in the hotel was running smoothly so, despite the interruption, Amelia arrived at the bar before the time she'd agreed to meet Patrick. She'd barely sipped the mineral water which Jasper served her, garnished with fruit in a cocktail glass, when Patrick arrived.

"Any developments?" she asked him.

"It's now common knowledge that Lucy's room has a view of the lawn. Apparently the couple who are telling everyone that say they have it on very good authority!"

"Don't listen to them – they think I seduced and then killed you."

"I thought you truly cared, and you were just after my diamond mines all along!"

"Don't exaggerate, it's just the one mine. And actually I'm after your clues. Can I get you a drink while you tell me?"

"I'd prefer seduction."

"Not while she's on duty," Jasper said, having responded to Amelia's subtle signal she was ready to order.

"In that case I'll have a pint of Doom Bar," Patrick said. He attempted to pay, but Amelia assured him it was part of his deal.

"Only problem with that is that you'll have to talk to any guests who want to question you," she said.

"Question? It's gone way beyond that! Some of your murder mystery guests are inappropriately enthusiastic."

"Yep, a few are worse even than me. Talking of which, do you have any theories?"

"Lucy?" he suggested.

"Based on…?"

"She's been acting jumpy. Really acting, I mean. Sonia had a quick word with us and she wasn't like it then, or when I've spoken to her before. She's only nervy when in character."

"Maybe, but I'm not convinced she did it," Amelia said.

"So, who else could it be?"

"Less Gold. I know it isn't, because he wasn't going to be part of it until we asked if you could stay on, but he knew about his brother changing the will and I was thinking maybe there wasn't time for that. If Max had a massive fortune his affairs wouldn't be simple would they? And he wouldn't be doing his own will."

"No, but if he's got a solicitor on hand they could do it quickly – that's if he'd decided to change it. He'd only discovered the sister very recently and hadn't met her."

"And he had no reason to think there was a rush. So, he was only thinking of changing it, if he liked the sister, and his brother killed him while he'd still get the lot?" Amelia suggested.

"Excellent deduction. Except for the fact I didn't kill myself."

"At least we've narrowed it down. It's not either of us!"

"I'll drink to that," he said picking up the pint Jasper had just delivered. They clinked glasses.

"Do you think we'll solve it?" Patrick asked.

"I hope so. I may as well confess that I'm a bit obsessed with crime. The fictional kind, I mean. That's why I set up this whole thing."

"And why you assumed I was Holmes as in Sherlock – wishful thinking?"

"Sort of."

"And you're Watson"

"That's right."

"We're a natural team, aren't we?"

"Yep, should have no trouble solving this. I wondered if it could be the investor guy. He's creepy."

"Trevor? I like him. Mind you I've not seen him in character. I suppose as I'm part of it he thinks I don't need any clues and has kept out of my way."

"I wouldn't mind him doing the same to me!" Amelia said.

"Bad as that?"

"Worse."

"I'm sure it's an act."

"Then he's a brilliant actor. Perhaps he's embezzled your funds or something?"

"Maybe. I'll see what I can get out of him."

"I know your fictional reason for wanting a room here," Amelia said. "But why were you really so desperate to book in on Friday night?"

"Long story." He shrugged. "Like Max, I have been away, but only as far as Totnes. Like him I needed somewhere to stay until I moved into the property I've bought. Getting away from where I was staying probably wasn't life or death, but it was beginning to feel that way. Then I stepped in here, and you know the rest."

That wasn't a long story at all, and was definitely missing the beginning and end, but there was no doubting his desperation to get away from where he had been staying prior to The Fal View.

"I'm so glad we were able to sort something out," she said gently.

"Me too." He held her gaze until Amelia blushed, then he drank more beer.

In the awkward pause which followed, Amelia glanced at her watch and discovered it was later than she'd thought. "You're going to be late."

"Late for what?"

"There's a meeting for all the actors. Just to check everything is going to plan, and decide if the audience needs more clues or a few red herrings, Sonia said."

"In the dining room we've been using?"

"Pendennis, I think." Then seeing his frown, "Where we had the reception on Friday."

"See you later then."

Amelia was left reflecting on their conversation. Much as she wanted to concentrate on the murder clues it was what he'd not said about the real him which filled her thoughts. It had to be a person he was getting away from, as an estate agent wouldn't leave himself homeless mid sale. And why had it been so important to book into this particular hotel? Could seeing her on reception have played a part?

She was tempted to call Nicole to discuss the matter, but what kind of a detective did it make her if she couldn't decide whether a bloke fancied her or not?

Thinking of difficult relationships prompted her to try calling her parents again.

Dad answered. "We got your message. It's your murder thing this weekend, isn't it?"

"That's right. I've been really busy setting it up. That's why I haven't called."

"We understand. Is it going well?"

"Yes, great. Now anyway." She briefly explained about the staff shortages and finding a replacement victim.

"I hope your boss appreciates your resourcefulness."

"He's appreciating every room being full and the bar staff rushed off their feet!"

"I should imagine so. Don't let him forget why that's the case."

"I won't."

"I'll give your mother your love, shall I? She's at her pilates class at the moment."

"Yes, please do."

"Goodbye then."

Gosh, not only had they had a genuine conversation, he'd actually demonstrated support! Six o'clock on Saturdays was clearly an excellent time to phone her parents.

Amelia gave a quick handover to Jorge, the duty manager who was doing Saturday's night shift, and told him that although off duty she would be back in an hour to attend the dinner, so there was nothing he need do for the murder mystery weekend. Then she put her backpack over one shoulder and went for a quick walk round to check all was well before heading home.

On her way to the Pendennis reception room she paused. She was off duty and everything was under control, so her motivation wasn't work related. Overhearing any of the actors' meeting would definitely be cheating when it came to solving the murder so she abruptly changed tack and headed for the bar.

Patrick was sitting at the table where they'd been talking earlier.

"Couldn't you find the others?" she asked. "I can ring…"

"I found them, but they didn't want me."

"Oh. I suppose your current role is extra, so they're not relying on you to reveal anything important."

"I got the impression there was more to it than that. Sonia was nice about it, but she wasn't happy to see me and got rid of me quickly. There's definitely something they're not telling me."

Chapter 3

On the Saturday evening there was a 1920's gala dinner for the murder mystery actors and guests. Amelia had researched food and drink popular in the twenties and worked with the head chef to concoct the menu for the entire event, but she was especially proud of the dinner. They started with Mimosas, Bees Knees and Sidecars, or convincing non-alcoholic versions for those who preferred. The cocktails were served with a selection of hors d'oeuvres including olives, radishes, salted nuts, and devilled eggs. Sonia moved people around between the courses, which featured a choice of appropriate period foods extravagantly garnished with plenty of aspic, as well as contemporary favourites for less adventurous guests.

Amelia wore another flapper dress. A shorter one this time, but far heavier due to being covered in metallic sequins. Her headband was in the same bronzy colour and decorated with a, presumably fake, gemstone as big as a lemon. She'd thought of asking Jasper where he acquired her clothes and how he'd found some which fitted so perfectly, but decided against it. When Jasper wanted people to know things, he generally told them.

From both a culinary and collecting clues point of view the evening was a huge success. Amelia learned that Arnold had been asked by several guests for a light, but never had matches or lighter on him.

"It was him then?" someone suggested. "He made up the story of going out for a smoke, to cover up having been seen outside."

"Why? And what about his wife?"

Nobody could think of a motive, and everyone agreed that Arnold's wife wouldn't have covered up for him, not unless she was in on it too and in that case wouldn't she have said he smoked?

"She sort of did though, didn't she? By saying he was supposed to have quit and then making sure everyone thought she was such a nag he might have continued just to spite her."

Other guests reported that Lucy, despite being alone, had no idea how much it cost to stay in the hotel and had at various times claimed she'd won a weekend away in a competition or got a special offer because there was renovation work going on. Amelia was able to say that neither were true. She agreed that Lucy's stories and manner were suspicious, but privately remained convinced she wasn't the murderer. There was no hint of a motive and although it was odd she was the only person who'd had a view of the lawn, Amelia couldn't see how that tied in, as Max hadn't been killed out there.

The couple who'd assumed Amelia knew more than she did, asked if she'd found out if Arnold was seen going out that night. Amelia, now briefed by Sonia said, "No, Arnold wasn't seen to leave the hotel."

"But somebody else was?"

"Yes. Trevor!"

"Do you think it was him?"

Amelia did, but didn't reveal the fact. Instead she commented on Lucy's inconsistent stories and blatant lies.

When she sat at the same table as Amelia, Lucy pointedly said that hotel staff should be discreet and not talk about guests. Trevor the investor tried to interest several people in a 'not to be missed' financial opportunity. Some guests suspected Less had killed his brother Max for being cut out of part of his fortune, others thought his sister Jill was responsible.

Amelia found it all fascinating, yet disappointing too as at no stage was Patrick seated near her.

Sunday's breakfast, like that of the previous day, was a buffet. Although the foods provided were exactly the same as offered in the main dining room, they were given a period look by being served in silver dishes with domed lids. The arrangement meant it would have been easy for Amelia to approach Patrick, but she didn't have to as he came straight over to her.

"Sorry I didn't get a chance to say how wonderful you looked in your outfit last night."

"You've made up for it now." The fact he'd wanted such an opportunity was as pleasing as the compliment.

As they helped themselves to fruit and yoghurt in Amelia's case, and a full English in Patrick's, they went over the clues they'd so far gathered. During the meal there was general speculation about who the culprit could be and what their motives were. Nobody, Patrick included, seemed to know more than Amelia did herself.

Afterwards they were invited back to the Pendennis room, where a scene from the police station was enacted. A few more clues were revealed to those who'd not yet worked them out and confirmed for the rest, including the fact Max hadn't actually changed his will, only asked his lawyer to arrange it, just as Amelia had guessed.

That really did give Less Gold, the man Patrick was now playing, a very strong motive. Amelia would have been absolutely sure it was him, were it not for the fact she knew he couldn't be. Patrick was to have played dead and fade from the story. He was only still part of it at their request, which meant Less couldn't be an important character. She wondered what the original actor would have done from Saturday morning – he'd been scheduled to have meals and keep his room until Sunday afternoon.

Once the police station scene ended, the audience's attention was diverted to the other side of the room, where Trevor the smarmy investor was invading the personal space of Lucy – and attempting to blackmail her! Lucy was discovered not to be Lucy at all, but a woman called Miranda Simpson.

Part of this was 'overheard' by another actor, who informed everyone else. That news led to a dramatic gasp from Arnold's wife and a loud wince and stricken look from him.

After this the guests had a chance for further discussion and were then to submit their theories, ready for the big reveal over lunch. There wasn't much time for Amelia to talk to Patrick, although he readily agreed to have coffee with her.

"How long have you worked here?" he asked.

"About a year as one of the three duty managers, but I was head of housekeeping for a couple of years before that."

"Do you live in?"

"No. There's a room for whichever of us is on the night shift, but I have my own flat."

She was pleased he was interested in her, especially as it seemed he was tactfully trying to discover if she were single, but he was booked into The Fal View for another fortnight. There would be plenty of time for that kind of thing. Solving the murder was, if not more important, certainly more pressing.

"Obviously neither of us can be declared winners for solving this, but I still want to submit a written answer," Amelia said.

"You really are taking this seriously, aren't you?" He didn't look thrilled.

"I think I mentioned I'm obsessed?"

"So you did. I don't know anything. Sonia's not given me any more information since Friday night. Sorry."

"Neither do I. That's the point, isn't it? I'd like us to work it out properly, not rely on insider knowledge. I suspect several different things. If I don't commit to something in writing it will be easy to tell myself I guessed correctly. I want to see if I really have."

"OK." This time his smile looked genuine. "I suppose Lucy must be the culprit, or possibly Arnold actually did it, and she was involved somehow."

"It seems a bit too obvious."

"I know what you mean, and they don't have any motive as far as I can tell. They're definitely up to something."

She sipped her coffee. "Arnold's wife reacted badly to hearing Lucy's real name, didn't she?"

"Yes, and Arnold was none too pleased," Patrick remembered.

"I think they're having an affair. Lucy, or Miranda as she's now called, is Arnold's secretary or something and his wife recognised the name and worked out what was going on. Yes, I reckon that's it! And Arnold really did see you just before you were murdered... well not actually."

"I know what you mean. His character saw mine, but

the scene wasn't acted out as all the guests were asleep then... Except he couldn't see from his room, and he didn't go out."

"He saw it from Lucy's room!"

"Of course! But if he was there with her he wasn't killing me."

"No, that was a total red herring. It has to have been Trevor, doesn't it? He's a blackmailer and well dodgy. I reckon he'd embezzled Max's money and thought killing him would cover it up."

"My sister Jill is out of it?"

"Yes. She'd have no motive until the will was changed in her favour, and no reason to think it would be before they'd even met."

Amelia, helped by Patrick, wrote out her solution and passed it to Sonia. Between courses at the lunch, various people's theories were read out. Almost everyone seemed to have come under suspicion, including Amelia herself – because she was in a relationship with Less Gold, and gave him access to Max's room on the night of the murder.

Had her interest in Patrick really been so obvious? That wasn't very professional. She'd better tone it down a little. Or a lot. He'd been her only possible ally in solving the murder and it was far more fun having someone to discuss it with. That meant she'd sought him out far more than she would have otherwise done, and as he was as pleasant as he was attractive, she wouldn't exactly have been avoiding him.

Before lunch, Sonia asked for a quick word with Patrick. Amelia was not invited to join them, and got no answers to her questions as they ate.

After the meal the actors carried out another scene, in

which Arnold's affair was revealed.

"You rat!" his wife said, and slapped his face. She turned to Lucy, "You're welcome to him, but nothing else. I'm going to take him for every penny!"

"Serves him right," Patrick said. "Got to go, I'm on."

Patrick, playing the part of Less Gold, approached the police detective and handed him a sheet of paper. Then he turned to the audience. "I have something terrible to confess..."

There were gasps from many around the room, Amelia included. Had he killed Max?

"I told you to keep your mouth shut!" Trevor yelled.

"And because I did, my brother is dead."

The police moved closer to Trevor, and one put a hand on his shoulder. He pushed them off. "You've got nothing on me!"

"Yes, they have. My signed confession! You tricked me into getting hold of some of Max's money, and then threatened to expose me for fraud. You thought that hold over me would give you access to my brother's fortune when I inherited."

"I only wanted a fair share! And I'd have earned it. Without me you'd have had to wait decades and even then you'd have been sharing it with your sister. Getting it all now would have been worth my twenty per cent fee."

"No, it's worth twenty years, at least," the police detective said. "Trevor Styles, I'm arresting you for the murder of Max Gold. You do not have to say anything, but anything you do say..."

There was a round of applause, plus champagne and a set of detective stories for those guests who'd solved the mystery. Then more applause for all the actors.

Patrick congratulated Amelia on getting it pretty much right and said how much fun it had been. "If I'm ever mixed up in a real crime, you'll be the first person I call to solve it!"

Amelia who'd rather been hoping he might want to call her for another reason said, "Thanks, I think."

"No doubt I'll see you around over the next couple of weeks."

"Of course. Are you happy with the same room? There will be others free from tomorrow."

"That one is fine. All I'm interested in is somewhere to sleep."

Well, that told her! How silly to think she might have been of interest for any reason other than to provide him with a room.

Sonia came to see Amelia, just before leaving the hotel. "Thanks for everything. I hope you enjoyed it yourself?"

"I did, yes. I was wondering, did you rewrite it to allow for Patrick wanting to stay involved?"

"The opposite. Originally Max, the real one who is off sick, was to play both parts. I was going to amend the script a bit, but as Patrick was doing a good job and keen to continue, I kept him in the role."

"Ah. Maybe I'd have got it completely right if I hadn't known Patrick was a stand in, not expected to take part beyond Saturday morning?"

"Quite possibly. You did very well under the circumstances. Sorry about misleading you a bit, but if I'd explained that would have given the game away. I knew you wanted to try and solve it and as your friend Patrick was helping you, I had to keep him in the dark too."

"That explains his feeling something was being kept from him. He's not really my friend though."

"No, I'd say he wants to be more than that. He was very keen to get extra clues, I think he wanted to impress you."

"Don't think so. He's just someone who really wanted a room and taking that part was the only way to get one. I said I was keen to solve the mystery. He probably thought helping me do that was a way to pay me back for letting it happen."

"It could be that, I suppose."

"This weekend has been so successful I'm sure the boss will agree with my suggestion to make it a regular event. I'll be in touch about the next one as soon as I can – and I'll solve that one."

"That would be great, but don't give up the day job!"

"Are you suggesting I'm not a brilliant detective?" Amelia asked, in a mock hurt tone.

"Perish the thought! I just think that you're even better at all this," she gestured around the hotel lobby." Her laugh rather spoiled the praise.

After work, Amelia took Bongo for a walk up to Little Dennis, round the castle moat and back home via Swanpool, and then crashed out. She'd really enjoyed the murder weekend, but the extra hours involved, stress of the responsibility, not to mention all the deductions, had exhausted her. She put off calling Nicole for a couple of days. She had time off work and knew her friend would suggest she came up. It was almost a five hour drive from Falmouth to Lee-on-the-Solent, assuming there were no holdups and she didn't get lost, both of which were entirely possible. Much as she'd love to see Nicole she simply didn't have the energy.

Amelia avoided the hotel too, despite the temptation of seeing Patrick. Nicole was right, she did work too many hours and going in on her day off wouldn't help that. She knew if she did, her boss would want a chat about other ways to increase business, or someone wouldn't have turned up and she'd be persuaded to stand in for them, or a colleague would have some kind of crisis she'd get involved in.

There was also the fact Patrick hadn't made any attempt to arrange another meeting with her. She wanted to delay discovering that wasn't simply because he felt sure of seeing her around, but because he had no interest in her at all.

As though she needed reminding what that was like she called her parents. They were out, so she left a message. "Just ringing to say my murder weekend went well. I hope you're both well. Um, well... Talk later."

That was imaginative! It was no surprise at all that neither of them rang back. Still, Bongo loved her and she had him almost to herself for two days, as Gabrielle was doing a double lot of nights to partially make up for Amelia covering some of her shifts the previous week.

Both days Amelia and Bongo drove out and explored the coastal path at Penwith. The sight of that huge sea crashing repeatedly onto the dark, jagged rock formations wasn't exactly soothing, but it somehow eroded a little of her stress. One day she started at St Ives and walked toward Pendeen and back. On the second she also went into Pendeen, but made the walk several miles shorter by approaching from the opposite side at Sennen.

On both occasions she had a delicious and much needed meal at The North Inn. Although she carried her phone with her the whole time, she had it switched off and buried deep in her backpack. The walks were long, often steep and totally exhausting, but it felt good to be physically tired, not mentally worn out.

When Amelia switched her phone on she discovered several missed calls from work, and even more texts from the same number. She read the last one which said, 'Don't worry all sorted now' and deleted the rest unopened. There were a couple of missed calls from Nicole too, and one text saying 'Hope it all went well and you're now doing bad things with your sexy Irishman. Call me when you come up for air. xxx'.

"Come on, Bongo. Time to take you home." The border terrier scampered off and returned with his lead.

"Oh, alright then, we'll walk." Her leg muscles felt stiff, but it was probably a good idea to stretch them rather than risk cramp at work. Walking to Gabrielle's would also mean she couldn't stay long, as she'd need to walk home and get ready to take over from Jorge at The Fal View. It wasn't that she disliked Gabrielle, as she didn't, just that they had little in common other than the job and the dog. There was nothing which needed to be said about Bongo, and she didn't want to think about work again until she was back there. She couldn't recall the last time she'd had two days off in a row, and was determined to make the break last the full forty-eight hours.

On her return from Gabrielle's, where her colleague had been too tired to tell her about whatever catastrophe had led to all those calls and texts, Amelia's phone rang. It was Nicole.

"Did it go so badly you got arrested?" she asked.

"What? Oh, no. The whole thing went brilliantly, and I worked out who did it!"

"Great. And worked loads of extra hours too no doubt."

"I have, yes. Sorry, I was bushed and…"

"Then come up here for a break, and solve our local mystery."

She didn't sound like her usual jokey self and immediately Amelia felt bad for deliberately being out of contact. "Nicole, are you OK?"

"Yeah. I just meant about Angus McKellar going missing. Why?"

"You keep asking me to come. I worry about you," Amelia said.

"Worried enough to come and check up on me?"

"Worried enough to come if you need me."

"Well…" She laughed. "No, honestly I'm fine. It's you I worry about. I really thought the disappearance of Angus McKellar would be right up your street, even I'm intrigued, but you've not shown a flicker of interest."

Maybe Nicole was right to be worried. Somehow the fictitious murder had been more appealing than the real mystery. That was understandable for several reasons, the main one being Irish, but didn't explain why she'd almost completely forgotten about the Lee-on-the-Solent disappearance. "Sorry."

"There's nothing to be sorry about. I just thought you'd like to look into it, but no worries if not. Oh… Does your reason for wanting to stay down there have anything to do with a gorgeous man with a sexy accent who's willing to play detective games with you?"

"Sadly not. You're right, I've been working too hard and have no life."

"Then come up here. Go on."

"I'd love to really," That was true now she wasn't so tired. "But I'm simply not going to have time before Christmas."

"And it won't involve a nice man at all?"

"I've no idea. Actually it's possible he's interested, but I'm not sure and... I've avoided him since Sunday afternoon."

"Playing hard to get? Good idea – let him chase you."

That advice was the closest Nicole ever came to reminding her that being the proactive one in a previous relationship had got her a broken heart. Usually whenever Nicole referred to the time Amelia was dumped shortly before her wedding day, she just pointed out that most men weren't like James. Nicole was always optimistic and often right. And now she thought she had a mystery Amelia would enjoy solving.

"Go on then, give me the details of the missing man."

"He's Angus McKellar."

"So you keep saying. You're going to have to give me a bit more than that."

"Angus McKellar is the owner of McKellar's confectionery."

"He's an actual person?" Amelia wouldn't go so far as to say he was a hero of hers, but she had been known to go into McKellar's now and then. The company's first English store opened in Falmouth, so it seemed right to support it, especially as they sold rather nice caramels.

"Yep. I only made the connection recently, but I've known of him for quite a while. He runs marathons and does all kinds of daft things for charity. Seems he'd do just about anything to get his face in the paper or on TV. Just local ones I mean, but I doubt that's his choice."

"So I could be right about this being a publicity stunt?" Was it horrible of her to sort of hope it was more than that?

"I think he's too nice to worry his family like that."

"He sounds annoying."

"Actually he's totally charming."

"You didn't say you knew him! If I'd known that..."

"I don't really, but we've met a couple of times at chamber of commerce things. Most people who talk to me at those events are trying to sell something, but he asked about my business and was encouraging."

"So not a massive ego?"

"No. His attempts to get publicity are to help raise money for a couple of local kids' charities. Actually he set one up, Salterns Support, which is the main source of funding for The Salterns respite centre. He'll do things directly too. A really badly disabled kid wanted to go to sea and he took him and his family out on his yacht. Even hired nursing staff so the parents could relax. When the clown didn't turn up for an open day at The Salterns, he dressed up and let people throw plates of squirty foam at him."

"Oh, OK. An actual nice guy. So what happened?"

"He was due to be interviewed for Outlook South, that's our local TV station, last Thursday. The guy interviewing him is a friend of his, Sean Underhill. Angus didn't show, and when Sean tried to contact him, he got no reply. Sean says he'd been acting strangely recently and seemed worried about something."

"You told me on the Friday he'd gone missing. If it was public knowledge by then, the police must have been concerned."

"I'm not sure about that. It was Sean who made it

public and put out an appeal for information. He's one of those 'do anything' reporters for the local news, covering sports, cats up trees and interviews with local people who've done anything vaguely interesting. Last night it was a chap who can knit with his toes."

"That's actually pretty impressive. I have two working arms and don't do anything creative."

"This man has two working arms, he was a submariner."

"Right. So, back to Mr McKellar. He's been missing nearly a week now – and no word?"

"Nothing at all. The local news is full of the story, but it's just rehashing what happened and speculation. People have been paying tribute as though he's dead."

"That's not likely, is it? If he'd had an accident or something I'm sure he'd soon have been identified. The police must cross check with missing persons reports."

"Unless it was murder and the body has been hidden?" Nicole suggested.

"I thought I was the fanciful one!"

"It seems unlikely, but so does any other theory. Who would want to kill such a nice man? And why would a nice person make his friends and family worry like this if he was OK?"

"No idea. Does he have a wife and kids?"

"No kids. His wife claimed he was fine, nothing out of the ordinary at all until he didn't come back from meeting someone about possible funding for a sensory garden at The Salterns. She hasn't seen him since and didn't know anything about his TV interview."

"Hmm. What about the person he did meet?"

"Nobody knows who that was."

"Interesting." She could totally see why Nicole had

thought she'd be intrigued, and the fact her friend had met him, the link between their two home towns, and his manufacture of caramels made her feel it was her duty to investigate.

"Told you."

"So you did. I'll check the news reports and things when I get a chance and call you back."

During her meal break, Amelia looked online for the Outlook South news. It was easy to find information on the disappearance. Predictably a reporter stood outside a branch of McKellar's confectionery, to give the little information he knew. There were several clips of the missing Angus McKellar and he seemed as annoyingly upbeat and enthusiastic as Amelia had imagined, but also as likeable as Nicole had suggested. His accent helped with that, as well as his modesty.

"I didnae do much," he said after being involved in an extensive home makeover which allowed a teenager who'd been severely injured to return to the family home and have some measure of independence. "These people did all the work," he said gesturing to various tradespeople.

The reporter revealed 'these people' were all paid by Mr McKellar, who'd also bought the necessary equipment.

Even without the constant references to his chain of sweet shops, it was clear Angus McKellar was wealthy. His yacht in particular was fabulous. Amelia would love to have the chance to steer something like that out to sea. Or perhaps just sit on the deck sipping a gin and tonic while someone else did all the work. She guessed Mr McKellar would drive it himself, if drive was the correct term. He was obviously an active man and his expensive purchases seemed to be for things he used rather than to show off. He wasn't stuck up, or dressed in designer labels, or reported to buy valuable pieces of art only to lock them away.

In every clip, whether he was finishing a marathon, attending a charity dinner for The Salterns or being interviewed, he wore clothes in bright contrasting colours, making it seem he'd be very hard to miss. Otherwise he was unremarkable. Early fifties probably. Medium build, perhaps a fraction taller than average. His fair hair was so neatly kept in place whatever the situation it must have mousse or spray. Other than the Scottish accent Nicole had mentioned, he made little impression. If the man chose to vanish, then he could probably blend in pretty much anywhere.

His wife, Heather, seemed colourless and quiet. Possibly that was partly due to worry, but Amelia didn't notice her in any of the clips she'd watched until she took another look, searching for the woman. She was often there supporting her husband, but very much in his shadow.

Something, or rather someone, which added to Amelia's interest in the case was Sean Underhill, the friend of the missing man. He was really good looking in a slightly artificial way. He reminded Amelia of a robot designed to look human. Perhaps he actually looked like a character from a film she'd seen, or maybe it was because he seemed to be trying a bit too hard to appear caring. There were several reports from Sean about the disappearance, and he was interviewed as a friend of the missing man, and the person to raise the alarm. He spoke very warmly of Angus and praised his Salterns Support charity events, perhaps a shade too enthusiastically. He referred to Angus 'fixing' people's problems, mentioned how much he loved kids and said, "This much loved public figure was often seen running locally, in his distinctive tracksuits." Somehow, although every word was positive, added together they made him sound a bit creepy. Amelia's instincts told her something was wrong.

She called Nicole back. "That Sean... are his interviews and news reports usually straightforward?"

"I'd say so. He's a bit gushing and fancies himself a bit, but no worse than that. Usually."

"But not over Mr McKellar?"

"Now you're getting to it... Some of his reports made me a bit uncomfortable. As though he was implying something he couldn't say. That's one of the reasons I thought there was a mystery for you to solve."

"Think: what seemed out of place?"

"Sean Underhill made more of being the man's friend than seems justified, and although technically he was really nice about Angus it somehow came across as though he was too good to be true."

"Reminds you of Jimmy Savile?" suggested Amelia.

"Urgh, could be it. I don't mean Mr McKellar is really like that. He wasn't the slightest bit creepy in person and doesn't come across that way when I've seen him on TV."

"You'd think his friend would be more careful when talking about him."

"Yes, you would."

"I don't know what's going on, but I agree with you – there's more to this than him just having fallen over a cliff."

"Agreed. Especially as we don't have any round here."

Chapter 4

In a rare break at work, Amelia called her parents.

Mum's, "Are you well?" was followed by a pause for her to answer, but otherwise sounded as disinterested as the 'How are you?' of casual acquaintances who wanted to get that part over with quickly and move on to the more interesting topic of the weather.

"I'm fine. What about you and Dad?"

"The same as always," Mum replied.

"The murder mystery weekend I ran went well."

"We did get your message."

Good of Mum not to overdo the congratulations and embarrass her! "And we've got good levels of bookings from now into next year."

"I suppose you will be too busy working to spend Christmas with us?"

Amelia was tempted to call her bluff and say she had a fortnight off and would love to spend it with her parents, but didn't feel they deserved such a horrible shock. Instead she said, "Sorry, but I won't be getting a single day off. I knew when I took on the duty manager role that I'd be working longer hours, but when I signed the contract the owner was still working full time. We're gradually taking on most of his shifts too."

"If you're hoping for that promotion then taking on additional responsibility is probably a good idea."

"I don't remember telling you about that." She didn't, and was even more amazed Mum had paid enough attention to recall it herself.

"That's why you organised that murder event, isn't it?"

"Not really. I've always been interested in mysteries."

"That's why you chose that particular event, but the reason you did anything at all was to show your boss that you're creative, willing to go beyond your regular duties to help the hotel succeed, and that you're the best person to become the new deputy manager."

"I suppose." She hadn't thought of it like that, but Mum was right. It sounded as though her parents had been talking, and therefore thinking, about her recently. "I'm sorry about Christmas."

"Your career is important to you, we both know that. We'll be fine, and look forward to seeing you when you can spare the time."

From anyone else that would have sounded like a complaint, but Mum wasn't like that. She might not be warm and emotional, but neither was she overly critical and she'd never use passive aggression or guilt trips.

"Is there anything in particular either of you would like as a Christmas present?"

"That hamper you sent last year was very nice. It must have taken time to put together, but something similar would be very welcome if you can manage it."

Actually it had been really easy. The hotel had hosted a kind of upmarket craft and food fair and Jorge who'd organised it came up with the brilliant idea of getting participating businesses and artists to agree to a combined mail order scheme. Customers could order from any number of them and have everything sent in one package. All Amelia had to do was fill in a card with her contact details, walk round giving the registration number to each seller saying what she'd like, and then try not to hyperventilate when the credit card bill arrived. Everything had been nicely packaged and sent with no further effort from her. For her parents she'd mostly chosen really nice food and drink – hand made chocolates, fancy liqueurs, smoked nuts. Nicole had got chocolate too, plus some lovely organic toiletries.

The event was to be repeated in just over a week's time, so problem solved.

The following day Nicole called, suggesting Amelia watch a news segment in which Angus McKellar's wife had given an appeal for information, in an interview with Sean Underhill. Heather McKellar quietly read a bland statement asking anyone who had any idea what might have happened to her husband to please come forward. As she spoke her voice wavered and she paused to collect herself several times. Either she was a brilliant actress, or she found the experience an ordeal she'd only agreed to because she was desperately worried.

Sean Underhill, with a great show of compassion, gently questioned Heather, teasing out a few details about Angus. During this Sean did nothing to suggest his friend was dodgy in any way. In fact he went to the other extreme, saying he couldn't possibly have any enemies and that many people owed their lives to his charity work.

"Regular viewers will know my own involvement with the respite centre, but Angus's efforts and generosity totally eclipse mine," he said.

He continued his praise for Mr McKellar, stressing how his business provided hundreds of people with employment on good terms, and created an affordable source of pleasure to many more through his confectionery shops. Sean claimed, "Angus himself spent little money, preferring to give it to good causes rather than spend it on himself."

That suggestion was slightly undermined by Heather's surprised reaction. The fact the interview was being conducted in the McKellar's obviously large and expensively furnished home, an image of Mr McKellar's luxury car which Sean reported had been found properly locked and with no sign of damage, and mention that Angus's yacht was still on its mooring didn't add credibility either.

"Please do contact the police, or us here at Outlook South, if you have any information at all which could shed light on this disappearance, which is entirely out of character for Angus McKellar."

Heather's expression showed she did agree with that. "He'd never deliberately do anything to hurt me, or cause worry to his family and friends."

"That's very true. He is such a reliable man. Never lets charities or anyone else down, always turns up on time," Sean said.

Not surprisingly all this got a reaction online. There were comments from people saying they'd like to be half as hard up as he was, or recalling incidents where he had let people down. There were only a few of those and they didn't seem to be his fault. He'd not taken part in a marathon for which he'd got a lot of sponsorship because he had a stomach bug and he'd had to lay off a few employees from one of his shops located in a mall which closed. Amelia could understand that people might feel aggrieved, but not how either could be relevant to his disappearance.

A couple of people suggested Angus had gone missing as some kind of insurance scam, or to cover up a misdeed of some kind, but they just seemed to be anonymous trolls intent on causing trouble. Amelia tended to ignore opinions expressed entirely in capital letters and devoid of punctuation.

She searched the internet and watched the local news for Lee-on-the-Solent, but learned almost nothing new about the disappearance of Angus McKellar. Some people thought he'd seemed worried about something in the days before, but his wife said there was absolutely nothing out of the ordinary in his manner or behaviour. The only further fact to emerge was that his car, which was found locked and undamaged as Sean reported, had been discovered on a housing estate in Winchester. Mr McKellar wasn't known to have a connection to anyone living nearby.

Watching the clips of Angus, Amelia realised he often tugged at his ear lobe. She'd read that was a sign a person was lying. It could just be nerves though, as he did it most frequently when being talked about, rather than speaking himself. It was most noticeable whenever he was praised for his charity fundraising efforts. On those occasions he was quick to say the credit was due to his sponsors, or people buying from the Salterns Support charity shops.

Nothing she'd found brought Amelia any closer to solving the mystery of Angus McKellar's disappearance, but it did convince her it wasn't just a question of miscommunication or a publicity stunt. There really was something to investigate.

A different kind of problem Amelia wanted an answer to was where she stood with Patrick. He'd flirted with her and helped her solve the fictitious mystery. Was that because he really liked her, because he was trying to repay her for getting him fixed up with a room, or as a distraction from whatever or whoever had made him need one? He'd not contacted her, but then they'd not exchanged numbers, so he could only do so via reception, which he might well be reluctant to do even if he was keen to ask her out. It would make a bit of a drama out of it and despite his stint as an actor, he didn't seem dramatic. Either he wasn't interested, or he was hoping to bump into her in the hotel.

Amelia could look up his number, as he'd provided it when he checked in, but it was hardly professional. She wouldn't like it if she'd given her number in such a situation and it was used to try and chat her up. Not unless she really fancied the man in question and he had no other possible way to contact her. Patrick was still staying in the hotel, so she didn't need last resort measures. Not yet.

She'd not seen him for four days, but then she'd not been trying. At least not very hard. He wasn't eating in the hotel, or using the bar in the evenings, as far as she could tell. As it was more expensive than most local places, and he wasn't a tourist, that wasn't particularly surprising and didn't imply he was avoiding her.

Maybe he thought she was keeping out of his way? He'd first met her when she was working on reception – something she'd not done since, and he'd spoken to her during meals in the restaurant and drinks in the bar. Those were places she now only visited briefly to check all was well and demonstrate to the staff that she was taking an interest in their departments. Most of the time she was too busy to leave her office when on duty.

Nicole called in mid-November, exactly a week after

she'd first mentioned her local mystery, and advised Amelia to watch the late evening news for Lee-on-the-Solent area.

"I don't think I'll be able to. I'll still be at work. I'm overdue a break now – can I grab a sarnie and call you back?"

Once she had her food, Amelia returned the call. "I assume the mystery has been solved?" She took a big bite and sat back ready to hear the solution.

"Not exactly. Angus McKellar has been found wandering about in the New Forest. He was in a terrible state; half starved, dehydrated, dirty, confused. Even he doesn't know where he's been or why. All that seems certain is that he'd drunk a huge amount of whisky."

"Odd. Is he a big drinker?"

"There's been no suggestion of it. He isn't teetotal either, so probably not a former alcoholic."

"Then most likely he's a current one, but has been good at hiding it until now."

"Yeah. That would account for him sometimes being unreliable," Nicole said. "Bet you're glad you didn't come up especially to investigate."

"When I come, and I will, it will be to see you and nothing whatsoever to do with solving mysteries."

"Aaaw, thanks, mate. How are things there?"

"Fine, except I hardly leave the hotel."

"Because your Irishman is in residence?"

"Because we're understaffed."

"Thought that was sorted?"

"We've got more people on flexible contracts we can call on now, which is better. The problem is a duty manager has to be on duty at all times. That seemed OK when the boss first suggested it, but there must have been a decimal point in the wrong place in our calculations or something, because it's not working out."

"Oh dear. Guess you need to tell him."

"I don't want it to seem I can't cope. He won't promote me then, will he?"

"Are you coping?"

"Jorge had to swap shifts for a dental appointment so I've done three nights in a row and something happened on every one. The guest who set off his smoke alarm twice by smoking is really lucky he was only on the second floor – it didn't seem worth throwing him out the window from there!"

"Oh dear, sweetie. Bad as that?"

"Not really. Just having a moan. You know what I'm like when I'm tired."

"A right whinger!"

Amelia laughed. "Thanks, mate. I'll talk to the others, see if we can rejig the shifts a bit. How about you? Have you had any luck contacting your Spanish cousins?"

"We've exchanged a few emails. Still don't know if they really are cousins, but they're as interested as I am in finding out."

"Maybe you'll know by the time you go over."

"Possibly. Progress is slow, especially as we're doing it in two languages, but Google translate gives me a good laugh."

As Nicole talked about their research in the UK and Canaries, Amelia was able to finish her sandwich and drink a coffee slowly enough not to give herself indigestion. That left her feeling far more positive. She really must make an effort to take proper meal breaks. How odd that it actually seemed easier to carry on answering queries and tapping away on the computer while eating whatever she could grab quickly, than go to the restaurant and be served something tasty and nutritious.

Angus McKellar turning up after a drinking binge was an anti-climax, but probably just as well as it had been frustrating to be interested and unable to spend any time getting involved. The same was true with Patrick in a way. One reason she'd had no contact with him for several days was that she'd lacked the time to do anything about it. That wasn't good enough. She'd keep her promise to Nicole and get together with Gabrielle and Jorge to sort out their shift patterns. Maybe they could do what the police did and have a week of nights, followed by the same of early, then late, shifts. That should make it easier to plan their lives away from the hotel.

Buoyed up by the possibility of having time for a love life, she tried to think up a pretext for contacting Patrick. Nothing that would justify the duty manager of the hotel contacting a guest came to mind. Pity she was happy with her flat, or she could ask if he did lettings. Of course! Patrick had given her his business card when he told her what he did for a living. That wasn't needed for check in, and she'd kept it. Surely that meant it wasn't unethical to contact him?

She still couldn't think of a plausible reason to call. Did it matter? Either he was interested and would welcome her contacting him, or he wasn't and wouldn't. If the latter she'd be better off knowing sooner rather than later.

Despite it being after normal people's working hours, he answered with a businesslike, "Patrick Homes, how can I help you?"

"Hi, it's Amelia your friendly detective here."

"Hi, Amelia. Nice to hear from you."

"I'm just checking if you need any bad guys unmasked?"

"Not right now, I don't think. Actually, I'm not expecting to be involved in any major crimes anytime soon."

"Oh. Right, well that's good I suppose."

"I know it's a bit dull, but will you settle for just a drink one evening?"

"I'd like that."

"Is tomorrow evening too soon?"

"It wouldn't be except that I'm working. I'm free Sunday evening."

"I'm not. How about… What's that?"

"Smoke alarm. We get an alert in the office if there's a problem. Sorry, I have to go and drag someone up three flights of stairs and throw him out of a window."

"Okaaay. Shall I call you back another time?"

"Please. This is the work number, let me give you mine."

Although the smoke alarm was sounding in the same room as had been occupied by the smoker, he was no longer in residence, luckily for him. The current guest had done nothing wrong. Thanks to his predecessor the battery was now running down. The poor man had to put up with intermittent high pitched beeps whilst Amelia contacted someone to replace the unit. She felt bad about not having done that the previous evening. If she'd thought of it then she'd have saved the current guest the disturbance and have had an excellent reason for waking up the smoker just as he'd drifted off again.

"I'm so sorry about this," she told the innocent guest.

"Can I offer you breakfast tomorrow morning as an apology?"

"It's not your fault, love, but I won't say no. I do like a fry up... That would be OK would it? A full English?" His tone was hopeful, rather than greedy, which made a change. So many guests expected compensation for things which were in no way the hotel's fault, and sometimes hadn't even happened at all.

"Of course. I hope you enjoy it."

Back in her office, Amelia made a note that he wasn't to be charged for breakfast, no matter how much he ate, and he was to be given a ten percent discount on his overall bill.

When Gabrielle took over from Amelia in the morning, she asked if she could come in a little early for her next shift. "Jorge says he'd like to speak to us both."

When the three met, Jorge said they were all being pushed into longer hours than it was reasonable to work. "When the boss came up with the idea of having a duty manager to cover at all times I worked out that was 56 hours a week each. As we'd be here on average two and a bit nights and get to sleep for most of it, unless there was a problem, that seemed doable. It didn't allow for any holidays or us getting sick though, and I think we were all under the impression he was going to keep working at least enough to cover those."

Amelia and Gabrielle agreed they'd thought so too. Of course the boss being increasingly absent was why they weren't coping when it had seemed the new hours wouldn't leave them with any less free time.

Gabrielle added, "And that's not the only way we're working longer than expected. If we come into the hotel for any reason when we're not on duty then we end up working."

"True," Jorge said. "I came in for a drink with a couple of friends last night and ended up in the cellars changing a barrel. Not Jasper's fault, and it wasn't your fault the other day when I had to stay on an hour and sort out those marketing emails because you had to go straight over to housekeeping because of the laundry problem – but there's always something."

"True," Gabrielle said. "My mum loves coming here for coffee, but almost every time I end up doing something, even if it's just sitting on reception for a minute while someone nips to the loo. I suppose it's the price we pay for such a generous staff discount."

They were saying the things which had been at the back of Amelia's mind, but which she'd not logically thought through. "It was my choice to come in for almost the entire weekend when the murder mystery was on, but I do think that as I was running it, and I helped serving and things that it should have counted as work hours."

"Did the boss say it couldn't?" Jorge asked.

"No. I didn't ask," Amelia admitted. "But if it had then I'd have been owed time off this week and you two would have had to cover."

"Which would have been impossible. We're not going to see our friends and families this side of Christmas as it is."

"Do you have a plan, Jorge?" Gabrielle asked.

Jorge suggested they tell the boss they would be claiming half an hour handover time per shift as overtime. "It won't make much difference, but it's the principle of the thing. We all work hard, we shouldn't be doing it for nothing."

"Good idea. And maybe we should be paid for any other extra time we do, rather than being owed it and never getting to take it?" It wasn't ideal, but money in the bank was better than the frustration of trying to get someone to cover when she took time off, knowing she was just passing on the problem to them. How had she not seen quite how impossible and unsustainable it was? "Who is going to tell the boss?" Amelia asked.

"I will if you like," Jorge said.

They thanked him.

"And I think we should avoid visiting the hotel when we're not working. It's too difficult to say no to friends and colleagues who need help."

"Yes, but I like to bring Mother…"

"Just for now, Gabrielle. In the long term we need another person in a supervisory role. It's easy enough to call in those people on zero hours contracts to do an extra shift, but not so easy to get cover for one of us if needed."

"Are you going to tell the boss that too?" Amelia asked. As she'd apparently told her parents, the boss had already hinted that a new post of deputy manager might be open to her. If that were to happen it would solve the current problem, provided a replacement were found for her.

"I am if I have your backing?"

They both assured him he had.

Jorge was right that they'd have no free time until the new year. That was partly Amelia's fault as the usual pre-Christmas slump might have allowed them to catch up on routine tasks and take holiday owed to them. The hotel being full to capacity for her murder weekend had put a stop to that. She apologised.

"Don't be daft," Gabrielle said. "It was great for business and besides, who wants days off in November?"

Amelia might, if Patrick called her back. Other than that the lack of time was no problem for her. She wouldn't get to see Nicole over Christmas anyway, she wasn't close to her family and Gabrielle, Bongo and Jasper were her only other friends.

Nicole was right about her working too hard and having no life! But that didn't mean it had to stay that way. She'd take the initiative and call Patrick again. She brought up her work schedule to see when she next had a free evening.

The simple answer was that she didn't, not that year. She wasn't working every single night shift, but had agreed to doing more than her fair share to give her colleagues time with their families. She was also hosting a handful of Christmas events which she'd organised at the hotel, had invited Muriel, her widowed downstairs neighbour for a meal, accepted a couple of invitations to drinks with others in her building and there was Jasper's birthday party. How could a person with no life be so busy?

She debated calling Patrick anyway, but 'I'm sorry, I can't come for that drink' wouldn't send the right message. Oh well, he might be good looking, charming and fun with adorably expressive eyebrows and a really sexy accent, but she had her pride and wasn't going to chase him!

Leaving Patrick to get in touch and Jorge to solve the work problem were both sensible plans, but hardly proactive. She should at least try to do something positive. Amelia rang her parents' number.

"Amelia, what a surprise to hear from you again so soon," Mum said.

A nice one? Mum would never say either way.

"I'm taking a break at work and just thought I'd call to see how you are."

"We're fine, thank you. I hope you're well yourself?"

"Yes thanks, Mum. Busy with work of course."

"Yes, of course. I won't keep you then. Goodbye."

Well, that had made a world of difference!

There was a tap on her office door.

"Come in."

It was the newest receptionist. "Amelia, I… Hey, are you OK?"

"I'm fine, Bianca. What's up?"

"I'm really sorry…"

"About what?"

"A delivery came for you yesterday and I forgot."

"And now it's gone missing?" she guessed.

"No."

"Then it doesn't matter."

"It does a bit." She produced a wilted bunch of what must have been gorgeous flowers the day before. "Sorry."

"I hope you've learned the importance of noting everything down and not relying on your memory?" said Amelia, who'd instructed the girl on that very point.

"Yes. Sorry."

Although it was probably too late, Amelia put the poor flowers in water. Amongst the limp daisies, sagging roses and collapsed lilies was a card saying 'guess who?' In much smaller writing underneath were the words 'need a clue?' and a tiny drawing of a house.

Chapter 5

Obviously the flowers were from Patrick. She was rather pleased he'd assumed any number of people could be sending her bouquets so felt the need to identify himself. It was brilliant that he'd done that with a clue. They might not have known each other long, but she'd found him really easy to talk to and felt he was something of a kindred spirit.

Amelia typed out a text. 'Thanks so much for the lovely flowers. I'm really busy at the moment, but hope we can find a suitable time to go for that drink'. That wasn't too pushy, was it? No. Didn't sound like she was nagging him about calling her back? No, it was more of a gentle reminder about the offer. She sent the message.

The flowers, despite their sad appearance, had completely restored Amelia's usually cheerful mood. What a good thing Bianca had been brave enough to admit her mistake and bring them up. Some people might have disposed of the evidence hoping nobody discovered what they'd done, leaving Amelia thinking Patrick didn't care about her at all. It was easy to make such assumptions when there was no evidence to the contrary.

Amelia dialled her parents' number. When Mum picked up, she cut off her greeting with, "I was wondering how you'd feel about coming here for Christmas. To the hotel, I mean, there isn't room in my flat."

Silence.

"Mum?"

"Yes." Then a faint clunk, as though she'd put the receiver on the little table which held the phone, TV remote and sudoku puzzles.

Aargh! What did that yes mean? Why was every conversation so hard?

"Mum?… Mum?"

"Sorry, I was talking to your father. Are you sure it won't be too much trouble?"

"It won't be any trouble, Mum. I won't be able to spend all that much time just with you as I'm working most of it, but I can arrange it so I meet your train and we have our meals together and… things."

There wouldn't be many things. If they wanted to, her parents could take themselves off to 'see the sights' and if they didn't do enough of that to avoid any difficulties, she could arrange for Jasper to summon her for an emergency cocktail. Dad would enjoy the food, Mum would enjoy showing off to the neighbours that her daughter could arrange such a holiday for them, and all sides would feel they'd done their duty.

After a muffled conversation, Mum came back on the line. "Thank you, Amelia. It's very thoughtful of you. We'd both like that very much."

There was another long silence as Amelia processed the fact the last sentence hadn't started with 'but' and ended with a polite refusal.

"Amelia? Dad here."

"Hi, Dad."

"You sure this will be alright?"

"Of course, Dad."

"We'll pay the going rate naturally."

"There's no need."

"Well let's not worry about that just now," Dad said.

"The important thing is that we shall come."

"That's brilliant. I'm looking forward to seeing you. Bye!" She hung up before emotion choked her voice, and made her parents worry something was wrong.

The next time Amelia's shift coincided with that of Bianca, the new receptionist, she went down to work with the girl for a couple of hours. That's what she'd done with any new recruits to her department prior to being made duty manager. Recently Amelia hadn't had the time, and left Bianca to the care of an experienced colleague. Clearly that wasn't good enough and she must make time. "The reports will have to wait – probably forever," she told her office door as she closed it.

Jorge had tackled the boss about the need for another member of staff but got little response. There had been a vague 'I suppose that's fair' to the suggestion they be paid for any extra hours they worked, rather than building up time in lieu which could never be taken. There was no promise of action to solve the problem long term. They'd agreed to still come in early for a handover, as they couldn't function efficiently without, but wouldn't work any extra hours unless absolutely vital to the day to day running of the hotel. Any reports, planning of new events, form filling, advertising, updating VAT reports and filing which couldn't be done during their regular hours would remain undone. Let the boss deal with all that, proper staff training was more important.

Amelia had only been on reception for a few minutes when a guest came to say she was disappointed her room had no sea view.

Bianca looked the booking up, and said, "You are in

the grade of room you requested, madam."

"Yes, but… You have such lovely pictures of the coast on your website. I'd rather got my hopes up and was looking forward to saying on Trip Advisor that I'd experienced them for myself. Would it be possible to move us, do you think?"

"Um, well… I'm not sure…"

"Of course," Amelia cut in. "That's no problem at all. The upgrade will be £35 per night." She gave a beaming smile.

"Ah. I see. Right. I'll tell my husband."

"Just let us know if you'd like to go ahead. You might like to take into account that your current room is in the quietest part of the hotel."

"That makes a difference. And we've already unpacked… I think we'll stay where we are."

"Of course, if that's what you prefer." Amelia gave a much more genuine smile. "By the way, if you'd like to explore the coastline round here, there are some lovely walks and boat trips. Bianca, can you find some leaflets for the lady?"

"Certainly, Miss Watson."

Amelia turned back to the guest. "You're right, the coastline round here is stunning. I'm so lucky to be able to walk my dog in such a lovely area." She went on to direct the guest to easily accessible vantage points and the least challenging of the walks, declaring them to be especially worthwhile.

The guest thanked them profusely. When she'd gone, Bianca commented on Amelia's handling of the situation. "I'd have been worried that if I didn't give her a free upgrade she might have given us a bad review. You completely won her round."

"There will always be guests who try to push their luck. You need to be polite but firm. We'll always do what we reasonably can to make guests happy, but if it's a service which comes at a cost then they must pay for it. Most understand that and the few who don't won't be happy whatever you do for them."

"I think I see. Can I ask about the leaflets? You didn't give her them all..."

"Someone unwilling to pay for the sea view most likely won't be interested in the more expensive trips and did she look to you as though she had hiking boots with her?"

Bianca grinned. "No, not really. So, I suss them out a bit and only give them info on what I think suits them best?"

"Exactly. Anyone can hand over a fistful of leaflets, it takes intelligence to select the most appropriate ones." Amelia was certain Bianca was clever enough to quickly pick up the skills to be a very good receptionist. "You won't always have time, but when you do, give as personal a service as you can. Preferably recommend places you know personally."

"I wish I could personally recommend the sea safaris," Bianca said, indicating one of the leaflets Amelia had decided not to give the unadventurous looking guest.

"It does look like fun," Amelia agreed. She loved taking the short harbour tours or the crossing over to St Mawes when she got the chance, but they were very sedate experiences.

Between dealing with guest queries and booking in a few late arrivals, Amelia passed on the phrases she'd found useful for soothing annoyed guests, made sure Bianca understood what she could offer as a goodwill gesture herself, and what required authorisation from the duty manager, and reminded her of the importance of checking anything she was unsure of. "And make a note of everything right away. We think something is so big or important we can't possibly forget, but trust me it's all too easy."

"Like your flowers. I really am sorry."

"I know. It's a shame they wilted, but you did remember in time for me to save most of them. More importantly you admitted your mistake. I'm sure you'll learn from it."

"I will." Bianca called up the booking of the guest who'd asked about changing her room for a sea view and noted she'd done that, been advised of the cost, and was considering the matter. "I don't think she'll come back, but if she does when someone else is on duty, it might help them to know what happened."

"It will. Well done."

"Thanks for all your help, Amelia. I really appreciate it."

"I really should have done this on your first week," Amelia said.

When Patrick eventually called Amelia back he apologised for not doing so sooner. "Things have been a bit hectic with moving in and… all kinds of things."

"I understand. I've been busy myself."

"Are you working tonight?" he asked.

"No, but I have something else arranged, sorry."

"Tuesday?"

"Working. Sorry, I'm not trying to fob you off. Honest."

"If evenings are difficult, would meeting in the day be

easier? I'm out and about doing valuations and viewings, but perhaps we could have lunch, or even just a coffee?"

"Tomorrow? I have a meeting early in the morning, but don't have to be at work until three." She didn't start until three-thirty, but needed to change into her uniform and get there, and wouldn't want it to seem she was rushing off early.

"That's perfect. Lunch at the Star and Garter?"

"Lovely."

"I've got a viewing at eleven, but should be free by twelve I think."

"Shall we say twelve-thirty then?"

The early meeting was between their boss, Amelia, Jorge, and Gabrielle. The other two would be there anyway handing over and Amelia had been asked to come in specially.

"I'll keep this short. I know that one way or another I've taken too much of your time recently," the boss said. "Yes, you will be paid for small amounts of that, such as staying for this meeting and what you call your handovers if you need these."

"We do," Jorge said, with the others adding their agreement.

"And if you cannot take the days off you are now owed, these will be paid for, or you may take them next year. That's in the short term. I've been working on a long term solution."

"Could you tell us what you've decided?" Amelia asked.

"I'll make someone my deputy. This will be someone new, or there'll be a new extra someone."

"I don't understand," Gabrielle said, probably because

it didn't make a lot of sense.

"Are you saying you'll either get in someone completely new to be your deputy, or you'll promote one of us and then replace that person with a new duty manager?" Amelia asked.

The boss looked uncomfortable. "Yes."

"When will this happen?" Gabrielle asked.

"At the beginning of next year."

The three duty managers glanced at each other and nodded. It seemed they all realised that little could be done before Christmas, and as anyone new would need some training it wouldn't help their workload anyway.

"Is everyone happy with that?" Jorge asked, once the boss had left.

"Yes," Gabrielle said. "We need another person and with the boss not here so much, it would be best to have one person in overall control."

"I agree," Amelia said. "We've done a good job sorting things out between ourselves, and I hope we continue with that, but I think it does need someone who can have the final say if that's ever needed."

"I... There's something..." Gabrielle said. "The boss... He said to me before that I was the most senior of the duty managers."

"You want... I mean, are you being considered as the deputy manager?" Jorge asked. He sounded less surprised than Amelia felt. Gabrielle was a good duty manager, her only fault being an occasional lack of confidence. Whenever an important decision could wait, she would confer with either Jorge or Amelia and do as they suggested. If it couldn't wait she'd often text Amelia to ask advice. That was never really needed, she just wanted reassurance that her solution was a good one.

"No. I want to stay as I am, and for one of you to get the new job. I will tell him that if you agree?"

"Thanks, Gabrielle," Amelia said.

"Yes, please do," Jorge added.

"And you two will not fight over this, promise? Fight for the job, but more important, fight for it to be one of you, not someone else who isn't our friend."

Jorge offered his hand which Amelia shook. He'd make just as good a deputy manager as her. One of them might soon be working for the other and, like Gabrielle, she hoped to retain their current harmonious relationship.

Amelia arrived early for her lunch date with Patrick, to find he was already waiting.

He stood and stepped toward her as though he might hug or even kiss her, but seemed to change his mind. "What can I get you to drink?" With his accent even that simple query sounded seductive.

"Mineral water please. I..." She spotted his pint just before saying she didn't drink in the day. "I'm really thirsty."

There was another awkward moment when he returned with her drink and she had to stand to let him squeeze back into his seat. If she'd moved further out of the way it might have helped. She probably should have done that.

"Did you sell the house?" she asked after a few moments of silent sipping.

"I think so, but they've not put in a formal offer. Did your meeting go well?"

"The same really! It seems things will get sorted out, but it will take time."

"What things, or is that commercial in confidence?"

"We've been very short staffed on the management side and finally persuaded the boss to take on someone else."

"Ah. Yes, I suppose it takes time to find the right person."

She decided not to mention that it might be her. "And then there will be training. By about March I should have time for a life!"

He nodded, but for once she couldn't read his expression. Oh dear, did he think she was already making excuses not to see him again? "My friend Nicole is always telling me I just work and have no life. She's had a point lately, but I'm determined to put that right."

"I'll drink to that." They clinked glasses. "Do you have time for lunch at least? The food is pretty good here."

"It's certainly popular, and I make it a rule to get through at least one meal a week without being interrupted by a call to alert me to some kind of crisis."

Patrick produced his phone, switched it off, returned it to his pocket and picked up a menu. Amelia did the same, except her phone went into the rainbow backpack hanging off her chair. They discussed the lunch options, deciding on a sharing platter of mini pub classics, so they didn't have to make too many decisions. That led to further talk of food and suddenly it was as easy to talk to him as it had been when they'd attempted to form a crime solving duo.

Patrick made her laugh by telling her about a lady who excused the mess in her house by saying it was the work of a poltergeist and was then surprised by the lack of offers.

"Crikey. What did you do?"

"Arranged a viewing for when she was out, arrived early and shoved as much junk as I could in cupboards, under beds and behind the sofa. It was still a mess but at least potential buyers could see the house under the debris."

"Did you put it back?"

"No. I told her the poltergeist seemed to have had a change of heart!"

"Maybe I need to start a rumour The Fal View is haunted. I'm sure that could come in useful."

After they'd eaten their way through miniature toad in the hole and battered fish, tiny chicken pies, the cutest little burgers and regular sized onion rings, garlic mushrooms, and chips Amelia, asked him something she'd been wondering about.

"Why were you quite so desperate to book into The Fal View that day?"

"A long story," he said as he had before. Then he shrugged. "But perhaps now is a good time to tell it."

Amelia tried to look encouraging, understanding and sympathetic all at once. It probably just came out as nosy, but seemed to do the trick.

"I think I said there were some similarities between my role as Max Gold and my real life?"

"You did."

"Like him I'd moved away for a while. He was looking for his lost wife, I was getting away from mine. Ex-wife, I should say. We're not yet divorced, but it's just a matter of time."

"OK."

"We'd been... not rowing exactly, but things were very tense and we were making each other miserable. The agency was opening a new branch in Totnes, so I decided to relocate there while I got it off the ground and see if it was true about absence making the heart grow fonder. That was only slightly successful." He took a long swallow of beer. "I missed my girls more than I missed Meghan and she didn't miss me at all. Still, cooling off meant we could discuss things properly. We made the split official, sorted out the finances and agreed I should spend as much time as possible with the children."

"You have children?" Somehow, despite the internal reaction, her voice stayed quite normal.

"Isla's eight and Ava's six." He showed her a photo.

"They're cute." They certainly looked it with their fair hair in bunches and beaming smiles, but appearances can be deceptive.

"They can be when they want to! Actually, I know I'm biased, but they're very good most of the time, despite everything."

"And you needed to book into the hotel because…?" There was now only one thing she was sure she wanted from Patrick – the answer to that question. A not quite ex-wife was off-putting and two children were frankly alarming, even if they were sometimes well behaved.

"I bought a house back here. I was my own worst customer as I wanted somewhere near my girls, but not too close to my ex-wife, big enough for my daughters to stay, but not so huge I felt lonely there alone. Anyway, I found somewhere and got things moving swiftly, but there was a month before I could move in." He took another drink. "Meghan and I were on good terms again, so she said I could sleep in the spare room. I'd been there three days and it started getting tense again, not helped by the fact Meghan has found someone else who understandably wasn't thrilled I'd moved back in. We just about managed to keep it polite, but the kids picked up on the tension. They were both upset and poor Isla was getting physically ill. I decided to get away, rather than start rowing again."

"That sounds sensible. But…"

"But not quite urgent enough to be prepared to die for?"

"No."

"For a long time we'd both been telling the girls everything was OK, when really it wasn't. That morning we'd explained that I'd be moving out again, but would be staying nearby and see them often. Ava asked where I would live. As their grandparents had recently taken them there for afternoon tea, I said The Fal View. I thought it would help if it was somewhere they could picture and liked."

"Makes sense. And you couldn't then say you'd be somewhere else as they wouldn't have believed you about everything being OK."

"Exactly. I'm so glad you understand."

"And is everything OK now?"

"Much better. Which reminds me." He gave her an envelope. "Invite to my combined housewarming and Christmas party."

"Thank you." She checked the date. "I'm really sorry, I'm working then. There's no way I can swap shifts as none of us have got any free time left."

He looked suitably disappointed. "Can I persuade you to look at the dessert menu?"

"As I spotted caramel sundae on the specials board there's no need for that."

Patrick opted for sticky toffee pudding, which was a

bit unfair as she didn't feel she knew him well enough to help him eat it.

They chatted easily until Patrick said he would have to leave soon to collect his daughters from school. As they walked out together he said, "I'd really like to see you again, Amelia. I think it's going to be difficult for a while though?"

"Very. There's work and Christmas."

"Perhaps we should wait until the new year?"

"That might be best." She'd have preferred him to be a little more eager, but his suggestion was the most practical thing to do, and would give her time to think how she felt about dating a man with kids. What if they hated her? What if she took after her parents and cared little for them? Obviously Patrick loved his daughters and she wouldn't want to spoil that relationship. Him ending the time they'd spent together because of his responsibility to the girls was probably only a small demonstration of the impact they'd have on his everyday life – and hers too if she became seriously involved with him.

"Can I call you or text?" Patrick asked.

"Of course."

Just as he had when she'd arrived at the pub, he stepped towards her. This time there was no doubt that he was considering a kiss or hug. She solved his dilemma by placing her hands on his shoulders and pecking his cheek. "Thanks for lunch."

The next couple of weeks seemed to flash by in a series of texts. She and Nicole always communicated that way when one of them was busy. It meant they avoided adding to the pressure the other was under, and they could read and reply when they actually had a moment to pay enough attention for messages to make sense.

'Had lunch with Patrick. He's got a nearly ex-wife called Meghan and two cute little girls called Ava and Isla. x x x'

'Boo for Manky Meghan. Cute kids OK though? xxx'

'Dunno. Not met them. Could be nightmare. x x x'

'Or dream come true. xxx'

Nicole, who'd been brought up in care, thought a large family guaranteed happiness. Amelia, an only child, thought it might be nice in theory but knew that blood relatives didn't always have close, loving relationships. In some cases they could be downright toxic, though thankfully she'd not experienced that at first hand.

Patrick seemed to quickly catch on that texting was the best way for he and Amelia to keep in touch, and regularly communicated that way. Often he sent silly Christmas jokes. She did the same and couldn't help wondering if it was his children who supplied his and laughed at hers.

Even Amelia's parents sent her texts. It was sensible as it meant she had a record of which trains they could catch and was able to work out which suited her best. She was surprised they accepted her suggestion of a four night stay. Although it would have meant longer waits for their connections, they could have made the visit shorter. She was surprised too that they didn't opt to communicate by text all the time. That seemed perfect for Mum's preference to get whatever the call was made for said as soon as possible and then hang up, but she did make two actual calls. Once she was chatty enough to make completely unnecessary comments about Christmas lights.

On the day of Patrick's party, Amelia called at his new home on her way in to work. She'd bought him some potted plants as a housewarming gift.

"Amelia! Come in," he said when he answered her knock.

"I really can't, sorry. I just came to bring these."

"That's very kind. Oh, they're herbs aren't they?"

"Yep. That one is dill. It's good with fish, so might work with fish fingers, and that there is basil. That's the one you want for your spag bol."

"You remembered my specialities! I'll have to cook them for you sometime."

Amelia could hear children's voices from inside the house. He must cook for his daughters. How would they feel about her literally getting her feet under the table? She continued as though she'd not heard him suggest it. "Basil is really good on pizza, too. So is the rocket, especially with black olives."

He laughed. "If you're not willing to risk indigestion, just say."

"It's not that." But she couldn't say she was anxious over meeting his daughters before he invited her to do that. "OK, maybe it is!"

"I'll have you know that almost everyone I've cooked for has survived."

"You've no idea how reassuring that is."

From inside the house a little girl's voice called, "Mummy, someone is here already! Can we eat the cake now?"

Great sentiments, but why was Meghan there? "I really must go," Amelia said. Then she did exactly that. At speed.

Chapter 6

The arrival of completely the wrong bulk drinks order on Christmas Eve meant Amelia was late and stressed leaving to collect her parents at the station.

"I'm so sorry," she said on seeing them waiting outside in the icy wind. At least the lack of taxis proved she'd been right not to text them to say she was held up and to make their own way to the hotel.

"Knew you'd get here as soon as you could," Dad said. "And luckily it's not raining."

"You did say you were busy," Mum said. "We guessed something had cropped up at work."

As Amelia took the case from her, their hands touched. "Mum, you're freezing!"

"It is cold, but I'll just appreciate the log fire you mentioned all the more. Will it be lit tonight?"

"If it's not, I'll put a match to it myself. Come on, get in the car." Once they and their luggage were settled, Amelia added, "It's great to see you." Actually she was quite pleased they'd all be together over Christmas, especially as it would be in short bursts and her parents seemed determined to be cheerful.

Despite it being dark, or perhaps because of it, Mum said how nice Falmouth looked. Amelia remembered her mentioning the Christmas lights in a phone call, saying they must be lovely reflected in the sea. She'd meant to ask Bianca to check where would be the best place to see that and then forgotten.

As Amelia guided her parents into The Fal View, she began to wonder why she'd ever considered them distant and critical. They were impressed she had her own parking space and looked delighted when staff addressed her as Miss Watson, took their bags to the room without them having to join the check in queue, and said variations of, "We're delighted you're joining us for Christmas, Mr and Mrs Watson."

The VIP package of fresh flowers, exotic fruit, local artisan chocolates, and champagne had been set out – not something Amelia had requested. She had meant to ask for flowers, but couldn't recall if she'd ever had a moment to do so. Propped in front of the ice bucket was an envelope addressed to Mr and Mrs Watson.

"What's this?" Mum asked, opening it. "Oh." It was a Christmas card from Amelia's boss wishing them seasons greetings and hoping 'these few trifles will add to your enjoyment of your stay'. Stressed out by the long hours she'd been working, Amelia had forgotten what a nice man he could be.

Dad lifted the bottle from the ice bucket, revealing it to be the most expensive champagne on the hotel's wine list. "You really are appreciated here," he murmured, as he ran his finger over the vintage date.

Amelia had become convinced that although appreciated in her current position, she wasn't about to be promoted. More than anything it was the way Jorge's manner had changed towards her and Gabrielle. He was actually less bossy and took more obvious care to be tactful. Not that he was ever rude, but in the past he'd sometimes made decisions and informed them afterwards rather than consulting them first. They were good decisions and often better for being made quickly so that small issues were solved before they became problems, so there had never been conflict over it. Now he explained such things far more fully. If she hadn't realised he was doing the same to Gabrielle she might have thought he was adjusting to the idea of her being his boss. As it was, she was sure he'd been offered the promotion and was trying to keep them onside by showing he wouldn't lord it over them. The fact he'd bother showed how suited he was to the position. Still, she'd not been informed officially, so wouldn't have to disappoint her parents before Christmas.

"Sorry, Dad. You were saying?"

"Just remarking that, quite rightly, there are three glasses. I suppose it's too early…?"

"It's not yet five, David," Mum pointed out. "And Amelia probably has hours of work ahead of her." She sounded almost wistful.

"I do. Actually…"

There was a tap on the door. Amelia opened it to see Bianca.

"Good evening, Miss Watson. I have that map you requested… For the lights?"

"Oh! Yes, thank you."

"Mr and Mrs Watson, I've taken the liberty of booking you a late dinner, so that Amelia will be able to join you towards the end. I do hope that's acceptable?"

"Perfect. Thank you."

"Our chief barman suggested you might like to go down for cocktails a little after eight. He's created a rather special Christmas Eve drink, which is complimentary for all guests staying with us tonight."

"How lovely. Thank you."

Once Bianca had left, Dad said, "Looks like the champagne will have to wait."

"In that case, I promise to make time to share a glass

with you," Amelia said.

"Perhaps when we give you your gifts tomorrow?" Mum suggested.

"Perfect." Amelia glanced at the map Bianca had given her. The clever girl had marked out a circular route, highlighting places of interest, suitable venues for snacks and drinks and vantage points to see the tree, lights and decorated buildings. She gave it to her mother.

"This map has been marked up with the best places to see the Christmas lights. Just here," she indicated a spot, "is where you'll see them reflected in the sea."

"Oh, Amelia! How thoughtful of you."

"I didn't do anything."

"You arranged for it to be done, which amounts to the same thing."

Did it? Even when she'd completely forgotten having done so?

"That's our evening sorted then. We'll look at the lights, unpack, dress for dinner and hope to see you later," Dad said.

"I will eat with you, but please don't wait if I'm not there for starters."

Amelia did manage to get to the table just as the first course was served. Her parents seemed impressed the waiter had known what to select for Amelia. She didn't burst their bubble by explaining that she, and any other staff, would be given whichever dishes were least in demand that day.

Conversation was easy. All Amelia had to do was smile while her parents discussed how lovely everything was, how proud they were of her, how kind she had been, and how delicious Jasper's cocktails were. Perhaps the fact they were referred to in the plural helped account for her parents' unusually warm, chatty and buoyant mood. Or perhaps it was Christmas spirit rather than cranberry gin?

Amelia had saved Nicole's gifts and both the card and gift Patrick had left for her, to open on Christmas Day. The card was a cartoon of reindeers kissing under mistletoe. Inside he'd written 'if I keep some mistletoe, can I take a *rein* check on this?'

"Yes, you definitely can." She was still a long way from certain that dating a man with children was what she wanted, but a kiss or two might help her decide if it was worth trying.

The gift was a large box of caramels. She didn't recall giving him reason to think she liked them, but must have done. She was impressed as it wasn't easy to buy boxes of caramels and nothing else – not that she'd ever been overly bothered about being 'forced' to eat chocolates and truffles too, if they were in with the sweets she was given or bought for herself. The gift was just right, not only were they her favourites, but they were in line with the cook book she'd given him – not very expensive, but not just a meaningless token either.

As Amelia had guessed from the size, one of Nicole's gifts to her was a cd. She hadn't anticipated it would be 'the best of' The Ruffled Raspberries. It took a moment to recall the band. She might not ever have done so had it not been for a note saying, 'in the very unlikely event they ever make it big this could be valuable, so I strongly advise you not to open the cellophane! P.S. if you don't come and visit me soon, I might have time to track down a ticket to one of their gigs for whenever you do make it, and as I'm such a good mate I'd insist on you having it and waiting in the car myself. xxx'

The Ruffled Raspberries had been playing in a pub the last time Amelia and Nicole had spent a few days together. They had been really, really dreadful. Amelia and Nicole admitted they weren't great singers themselves, but the few times they'd done karaoke they'd sung the same song as each other and that was playing on the backing tape. To be fair the Ruffled Raspberries might have all been attempting the same song most of the time, but they didn't all start simultaneously or pick the same key.

After a quick lap of the hotel, checking everything was running smoothly and exchanging festive greetings with her staff, Amelia went to her parents' room. She took with her a plate of pastries and a bag of small gifts. She'd not stopped for breakfast, so was taking her break with them. Even so, she couldn't stay long.

"Happy Christmas," they chorused as she came in.

"And to you." She kissed them each in turn and was pleased they both hugged her briefly. Perhaps not seeing her for almost a year had made them miss her.

Dad made a performance of opening the champagne and encouraging them to drink a toast to Christmas, then in turn to his wife, Amelia, her boss, and all the staff.

"To Blitzen," Mum said, taking another sip.

"And Dasher," Dad said.

"And Prancer!" Amelia contributed.

The glasses had to be topped up by the time they'd named all the deer they could think of, including Rudolph, Bambi and The White Hart pub. Amelia couldn't recall the last time they'd shared a moment of silly fun.

She laughed again when her parents gave her exactly the same caramels as Patrick had. "Wonderful! Thank you."

They also gave her a teach yourself Spanish kit which was less appreciated, and a huge waterproof poncho. "So you can walk your dog without spoiling your hair and clothes in the rain."

Wow. Mum had remembered about Bongo and was actually being supportive of an arrangement which was entirely about making Amelia happy and of no conceivable benefit to her career.

Even more astounding her parents expressed an interest in seeing the dog. She did wonder if it was a ploy to see her flat, but they were undaunted when she explained he was at Gabrielle's home.

"She's working tomorrow too, so I was planning on taking him out. You're welcome to come."

"We'd like that," Mum said.

"I'm not sure what time it will be, but will give you as much notice as I can."

"Anytime is fine with us," Dad assured her.

"These are for you." Amelia gave them the shiny red bag decorated with snowflakes.

"But we've already had that lovely hamper. It arrived just before we left," Mum said.

"I know, but I wanted you to have something to unwrap today. It's not much."

Dad put on his musical socks right away, and Mum said her holly patterned scarf looked very cosy and, "It's not at all prickly!"

Amelia didn't see them again until lunch, which she was hosting so had to divide her attention between her parents and the other guests on their table, who were all there alone. The atmosphere was festive and everyone chatted to whoever was sitting nearest.

She next met up with her parents when they all shared another late dinner.

"We've had a splendid day," Dad informed her.

"Such lovely music," Mum said. "It's a shame you missed that."

"I did hear some while I was working. It seemed very popular."

"Oh, it was. They had to bring in extra seats."

Amelia knew that as she'd had to negotiate to get porters to shift them and persuade the Maitre d' the chairs would be back in time for dinner.

When her parents met her by the car on Boxing Day, Mum was wearing her holly scarf. A tinny blast of Jingle Bells as they travelled to Gabrielle's home told her Dad was still wearing his socks.

"Sorry, Mum. I hope the battery doesn't last long."

"I have a very strong feeling it won't survive their first wash."

"Probably for the best."

Dad declared himself horrified they could be so cruel. "I'd better make the most of them while they still work!" and set them going again.

Bongo seemed delighted to have three people walk him not just one and his enthusiasm, while not precisely mirrored by her parents, was faintly echoed.

"I can see how you keep slim, " Mum said. "All these hills!"

"We won't go too far."

"I don't mind, Amelia, really. You take the route you would have if we weren't here."

"I suppose your pilates keeps you fit?"

"It helps a lot." She moved closer. "I've got your father doing it. He won't come to the class, but we have a dvd."

"Are you talking about me, Christine?"

"Just saying what a good idea it is to get some exercise after all that eating."

"Yes indeed. I want to be able to do justice to the beef Wellington tonight. My favourite. Did you order it especially, Amelia?"

She admitted she had. "And the pavlova. What is it about that anyway?" Mum rarely selected it, but always remarked when she saw it on a menu, or pointed it out when it was seen on TV or in a magazine.

"It's what we had for our wedding reception. Prawn cocktail, beef Wellington and pavlova."

"I didn't know what it was," Dad said, "but your mum agreed so enthusiastically when the caterer said we should have it that I didn't like to ask. Afterwards I found out she didn't know either!"

"Who could have ever guessed that decades later our daughter would have us to stay in her wonderful hotel and recreate that exact meal for us?"

As she'd not appeared until they'd been married for ten years Amelia had always assumed they'd not expected to have a daughter to do anything, but hadn't liked to ask. Maybe that reticence was a family trait?

They were so nice about Bongo, and Amelia's practical arrangement in sharing him, that she suggested they go back to her flat for a cup of tea. "It will be so busy later I doubt I'll have much chance to talk to you."

She took Bongo so he too had company for a bit longer. Her initial reason for inviting them to accompany her when walking him was that as well as allowing her to spend time with her parents his presence might reduce any tension between the three of them, but that hadn't been needed. She was starting to wonder if they really were always as cold as she thought them, or if some past incident was colouring her judgement.

Once back at the hotel Amelia seemed to only stop working to eat, take her parents back to the train station, and hug Jasper at New Year.

In early January Amelia heard about a fire at a nearby hotel. Thankfully nobody was badly hurt and the damage was mostly superficial. Her boss told her the other hotel was due to host a conference for a company called Hearts and Diamonds which would now take place at The Fal View.

"Hearts and Diamonds sounds romantic. What are they? Wedding planners, jewellers?"

"They make adult games."

"Oh!"

"Chess, quizzes, cards, things like that. They make real sets and online versions."

"That sounds OK then."

"I am glad to hear you say so. As your murder mystery weekend was so successful I would like you to run with it."

"OK, I'll do it but… I've been thinking…"

"Yes?"

"About the deputy manager position. I'm not sure I'm really ready for such a role. Jorge is and I think he would be a really good choice."

"It's generous of you to say that."

"Just the truth." It was. She'd realised it was really unlikely the boss would choose her. She'd been certain he'd decided on Jorge before Christmas and was waiting for a suitable moment to inform her. When the realisation came she wasn't disappointed. It was brilliant doing the murder weekend, but really stressful too. She didn't mind organising the event for Hearts and Diamonds, especially after discovering everyone involved would be taking part in a marbles championship, but wouldn't like to be in the position of having to take on every such task.

Once they were fully staffed, the duty managers would be able to book days, even whole weeks, off occasionally. They'd be able to say no to tasks which weren't strictly part of their role. They'd get to have a life outside work. Jorge, or whoever got the deputy manager job, would have to take on whatever the boss suggested, have to cover any hours the duty managers couldn't, and as that was likely to be due to illness or personal crisis it would usually be at short notice. They'd have all the responsibility and the stress which went with it and only an increasingly absent boss to turn to. Jorge was very ambitious and would enjoy the challenge. Amelia wasn't and wouldn't.

There was also the possibility the boss hadn't yet decided. By giving her support to Jorge she made it more likely he would be promoted. She'd much prefer to work under him than someone new, and it would be much easier to replace a duty manager than recruit for a position which didn't yet exist. It would still take time for that and the training, but with luck her words to Patrick would come true and she'd have time for a life by March.

Amelia called her parents. "Thought I should tell you

that I didn't get that promotion I mentioned," she told her mother after exchanging greetings.

"Oh, I am sorry. Are you very disappointed?"

"No. I'm not sure I was quite ready."

"Then it's for the best. You're so young still, there will be other opportunities."

Amelia heard her dad speak and Mum reply, but couldn't make out the words.

"Your father says the same. You are doing a very good job, Amelia. We're proud of you and you should be proud of yourself."

"Thanks, Mum."

"Well, I won't keep you."

She'd let them down, but at least they'd tried not to make her feel bad about it. Perhaps one day she'd want to accept one of the 'other opportunities' which would come her way and make them truly proud.

To cheer herself up she called Nicole.

"Sorry, mate, can I call you back?"

"Yeah, sure. It's nothing important."

"OK then."

Great. For once she had a bit of time to herself – and her parents and best friend were too busy to speak to her. She considered phoning Patrick, but knew he'd suggest a date and she'd have to say no. Instead she sent a text, saying she would be even busier for a while as she'd be helping train the new duty manager, when one was appointed, but really would have some free time eventually.

She'd only just sent it when Nicole called back. "Sorry about that. I was just loading the dishwasher. I wanted to get it switched on so we can talk properly. Come on then, give me all the gossip!"

Amelia explained about her work situation.

"Excellent. And then you'll be able to come and see me. You definitely need to work less and get a life."

"Why did you never mention this to me before?"

"You know me, never like to tell my friends what to do, and definitely wouldn't discuss anything personal. Talking of which, are you getting it on with that Patrick bloke, or not?"

"Not."

"Oh dear, sorry. You need to sort yourself out. Start by getting away from the hotel sometimes. You'll never meet a man there."

"Actually a lot of people meet their partner through work."

"Any prospects among your colleagues?"

"Not really."

"They all like your mate Jasper?"

"Most are women. We do get the occasional guest though, you know."

"Yes, but just passing through."

"Or playing the part of a corpse while moving into a property in the area," Amelia said.

"And having a sexy accent?"

"Always a bonus!"

"So it *is* happening between you two?"

"Sort of. Trouble is he's busy with his work and kids, and I'm always at The Fal View, so we hardly see each other. You know, a good friend might have warned me about overworking and not having a life."

"Yeah. Pity all you've got is me!"

"And what about you? Are you meeting any eligible bachelors?"

"Not really, but it's different for me. I'm not wanting

to settle down with a husband and kids."

"And you think I am?"

"I know you, remember?"

Nicole was right, she did know Amelia better than anyone else did. Which meant it was probably true that Amelia wanted a loving family. Of course it was... Her problem with Patrick being a father wasn't that he had children, but her fear they wouldn't want her in their lives any more than her own parents had when she'd unexpectedly arrived. Why had it taken her so long to realise that?

As Amelia had predicted, Jorge was offered promotion to deputy manager. As she'd also guessed he proved to be an excellent choice. One of his first decisions was that it should be he, Amelia and Gabrielle who decided who would join their team as the third duty manager. He advertised immediately and set an interview date for the first week in February.

It was a hard task whittling down the number of applicants to interview. Selecting from those they did invite in for a face to face meeting was surprisingly easy. They'd all liked Charles immediately and been impressed by his experience and references.

"Why did you leave your last place?" Amelia asked.

"I'm sixty and thought I was ready to retire. By the time I realised I was wrong, my place had been filled."

The clincher had been when Jorge asked, "When can you start?"

Charles had swallowed the last of his coffee and said, "Ready when you are."

Nearly four months after first meeting him, Amelia

finally had a proper, uninterrupted and unhurried date with Patrick. He'd met Bongo and joined her on a couple of short walks. He'd sent her flowers for Valentine's, and they texted and called each other frequently. They'd met numerous times for a quick drink, even a quick meal, but she was usually grabbing a bit of time before going in to work. Sometimes she'd had to cancel or cut short a date because of work. More frequently he'd had to cancel on her, or was called away because one of his girls wasn't well. Always the same one. Isla apparently was subject to urinary infections, which showed how little Amelia knew about children. She'd thought that was something only suffered by old ladies.

A couple of times Patrick had suggested she come with him to pick up the girls from school or have a meal, but she'd declined. She wanted to be sure how she felt about their father before meeting the girls, and it felt like their relationship was marking time, not progressing.

That night was different. They were meeting for a drink, then going out for dinner. His children were spending the night with their mother. Amelia wasn't due into work until the following evening. Her preparations for the date hadn't stopped at making sure she looked her best; she'd done the same with her flat.

Patrick greeted her with a kiss on her cheek and said all the right things about her appearance – both in words and with his eyes. They talked easily. Not about anything much, but with a lot of laughter and the realisation they shared many opinions and were very quick to pick up each other's meaning. Even though it was no longer a novelty, her reaction to the lilting sound of his voice hadn't worn off. Over the phone she barely noticed that wonderful accent, but in person it affected far more than her ears.

The table he'd booked was in a quiet corner and lit by a candle.

"Very romantic," she said.

"Not too much?"

"Is there such a thing as too much romance?"

"I guess it depends on who is directing it to who, and possibly the situation."

"Fair point. This here, right now, is most definitely not too much."

They held hands between courses, gazed into each other's eyes during intimate silences, and made plans about things they'd do together. It was both clichéd and wonderful.

They weren't the only couple to be sharing a romantic evening. "There's a man behind you looking nervous and he keeps putting his hand in his jacket pocket," Amelia said.

"So you were gathering clues, not ignoring me?"

"Sorry, I didn't mean…"

His laugh cut her off. "You glanced over my shoulder a couple of times is all. I did wonder who or what you were looking at and why. I gather from your tone he's not about to tell us to put our hands in the air and relieve us of our valuables."

Amelia grinned. "I think he's going to propose."

As Patrick turned to see who she meant the man left his seat, got down on one knee and presented the young woman with a small box. They didn't hear what he said, but her delighted squeal and the way he jumped to his feet and kissed her made it clear how she'd responded.

Amelia and Patrick joined in the cheering and clapping.

They ordered coffee and talked as it went cold without them taking a single sip. As they prepared to leave, Patrick helped her into her coat. Outside he took her hand as they walked towards the taxi rank. On the way they stopped to admire the moon, reflected in the sea.

"So beautiful," Patrick said. He was no longer looking up, but right at Amelia.

She moved nearer. He gently pulled her closer still, and she placed her arms around his waist. For a while they just held each other, with her head resting on his shoulder. She felt him kiss the top of her head, and raised her face.

Patrick kissed her. First very tentatively, but then he tightened his hold of her and kissed her with a great deal of enthusiasm. She responded eagerly until he stopped and abruptly pulled away.

"Sorry, it's been a long time. I've not been involved with anyone since Meghan."

Great. A romantic meal, witnessing a proposal, Amelia in his arms, and he thought of his ex. They returned to their different homes in separate taxis.

Chapter 7

"How was your big date?" Nicole asked as soon as Amelia answered the phone.

"What's that egg phrase?"

"There must be loads. I'm guessing from your tone you're not expecting to be wearing a meringue of a dress anytime soon."

"Nope."

"Are you thinking of not being able to make an omelette without cracking some eggs?"

"No. The thing about it being good in parts, but the not good bits spoiling everything."

"Oh dear. Come on then, tell me all."

Amelia did. As she described the evening she was reminded of how perfect it had been, right until the end. "I know I overreacted, but it had been going really well until he mentioned her. It's not like he can just wipe her from his memory, but it's so frustrating that Meghan seems to be always be in his thoughts, or on the phone to him, no matter what we're doing."

"Yeah, I can see that."

"Do you think it means he still likes her?"

"From what you've told me he does *like* her. That's a good thing for them and the kids and doesn't need to be a problem for you."

"I suppose not. But…"

"But you need to be sure he only likes her, nothing more, and that he feels differently about you."

"How is it you're so good at this stuff?" Amelia asked.

"Because it's not my stuff. Like you with Steve. You

saw right through the charming front he put up. I couldn't see it even after he put me in hospital proving it was all a lie."

"Oh, Nic…"

"Just promise me your Patrick isn't like that."

"I'm certain he isn't. Would his ex still be a friend and want him around the kids if he was?"

"Most likely not."

"So, what do I do now?"

"Some really kinky sex act his ex would never have done, to blow all thought of her from his mind?"

"And plan B?" It wasn't that she was against mind blowing sex, but a relationship based on nothing but that wasn't what she wanted.

"Go out with the bloke again. Talk, hold hands, see how it goes."

"Yeah, but it's not just how he feels I'm worried about. I'm not sure how I feel about a man with kids. Perhaps you were right when you said I wanted a family, but this is different."

"It is. Same thing applies though. Spend some time with him. See how it goes."

"He hasn't asked to see me again."

"He didn't ask to get killed for you, did he?"

True. She'd asked him to die. "Alright, alright!" Amelia hung up on Nicole and rang Patrick before she lost her nerve.

His, "Hello, Amelia. Lovely to hear from you," sounded genuine. If she was being optimistic and wanting to read too much into a phrase he'd used several times before, she might even have thought he sounded relieved.

"The weather forecast is good for the next few days

and I have Wednesday off. I thought I'd take advantage and go for a long walk with Bongo, and on the off chance that you could swing a couple of free hours, I thought I'd see if you fancied coming." The advantage of making it up as she went along, was that she managed to sound nicely casual about the whole thing.

"I would like that. I do have some appointments on Wednesday, but I should be able to move at least some of them. What time were you thinking, and how long for?"

"Bongo is very flexible. You let me know what you can manage, and we'll pick a route to suit."

"I'll call you back as soon as I can."

Patrick picked them up in his estate car. Bongo needed no persuasion to jump in the back where Amelia had placed his bed.

"Are we going to park at Pendeen or somewhere else and walk there?" he said once they were on their way.

"I was thinking of walking to the pub from somewhere else. I've done that a few times. The path is quite steep in places, so it's good to have a rest halfway."

"You've done it on your own?"

"No." She paused for what she hoped was just long enough for him to get a hint that talking about exes wasn't the most fun they could have. "I always take Bongo. He might not look scary, but he's very protective."

"Good for him. Has he eaten many bad guys?"

"Not whole ones! A man scared me once. Not on purpose I don't mean. He… well he was having a wee. Neither of us realised the other was there until I came round a corner and nearly bumped into him. I thought he was a flasher and yelled. Bongo was all snarling outrage."

"I shouldn't laugh, but…"

"I don't see why not. The guy should have been more thoughtful of others. Luckily for him I had Bongo on a lead because it's slippy there and I didn't want him to startle anyone and cause a fall. Talking of which, it might be a bit muddy still."

"That's OK. I brought an old blanket in case the dog needs to be rubbed clean, and I've got a change of shoes."

When she'd put in the bag containing Bongo's towel, bowl and bottle of water, she'd noticed an ice cream tub and water bottle, which she guessed were for the dog. "Were you in the boy scouts?"

"I was actually, why?"

"You seem to be prepared."

"That comes from having kids. They're always getting dirty, needing a drink, change of clothes, favourite toys."

"Oh. A bit like having a dog then."

"Very similar, I should imagine."

Amelia got Patrick slightly lost with her directions as, although she'd passed the car park several times before, she'd always reached it on foot. Annoyingly roads were all pretty much the same colour, so it wasn't always easy to identify one from the end you'd not previously seen. Patrick accepted the wrong turns with good humour, despite having to turn round where there really wasn't room.

Bongo's excitement about being let out of the car on arrival was obvious and as he thought Patrick was playing a game when he tried to catch hold of him, the poor man was spinning round in circles.

"Dead dog!" Amelia called.

Immediately Bongo slumped on the ground.

"Here, you can put his lead on now."

Bongo didn't so much as twitch while Patrick attached the lead and stood back up.

"He's alive!"

Bongo resumed his excited bouncing, until they set off and he obeyed the instruction to walk nicely.

"He's great isn't he? Isla and Ava would love him."

"I don't know what he's like with children."

"No. Of course not."

She'd spoken too quickly and made it seem she wasn't prepared to find out. "He's a big softy with everyone except flashers and other scary people though, so would probably be fine." And in any case, she knew Patrick would be careful and not risk them getting hurt.

Odd that although she'd never seen the children she knew that for sure. What she was less certain of was whether she considered them scary people. Of course she wouldn't want them to get hurt, but it wasn't how the dog and the girls would react to each other she was really worried about. Although a little unsure how she'd take to them, even that wasn't the problem really. She could put on a good act of liking them if she had to, but quite possibly she'd find them OK. If they took after their father in any way they'd have some good points. They might even be nice – but they might not like her. Amelia could easily imagine them hating her, yelling 'you're not my mum' and trying to destroy her relationship with Patrick. The problem pages of the magazines she read were full of things like that.

Amelia hadn't fully realised how narrow the coastal path was in places, until it became obvious they couldn't walk side by side.

"Do you want to lead?" Patrick suggested.

"OK. I really do know my way now we're on the path, although I admit that's partly because there is only the one path."

"Is navigation not a strong point?"

"If you ever meet my friend Nicole, and want to keep her talking for hours, be sure to ask her that."

"I hope to meet her soon."

"Honestly, her stories about me getting lost are wildly exaggerated and still not that thrilling."

"You're close to her?"

"Like sisters." Was that his reason for wanting to meet her? "We've known each other since school. She's an orphan and… and I'm not all that close to my parents."

"Does she live locally?"

"Unfortunately not. She runs a B&B near Portsmouth. We talk a lot though and I'm going there for a week in May." She added that to reassure herself she'd see her friend soon. Mentioning their childhood had made her miss Nicole.

They didn't talk much more after that, but it was a companionable silence, interrupted by occasionally pointing out things of interest. Other than the view, that was mainly birds, which Patrick knew the names of. Or claimed to. Some sounded unlikely and she was tempted to call his bluff by asking one of the several birdwatchers they passed.

"I only know two things about birds. One is that I can recognise a seagull."

"And the other?" Patrick asked.

"That there's no such thing as a seagull! They're all different types of gull and terns and, I dunno, lesser spotted storm ousels or something."

Lunch at the North Inn was just as welcome and just as delicious as before but, as Amelia had on her previous visits, they'd sat outside because of Bongo and the cool breeze meant they didn't linger.

"I assume we go back the way we came?" Patrick asked.

"Safest, I think. Unless you know an alternative route or want to end up going round in a circle all night?" She rather liked the idea of having to cuddle up to him for warmth during a night under the stars. It sounded so romantic, but the reality probably wouldn't be very comfortable.

"Perhaps not today. I do have to get back by five."

Please, just for once, don't say because of the children or Meghan.

"I put back a couple of viewings until this evening."

"Oh, sorry."

"It only took a phone call, and I think it suited the clients better. I was thinking I might do more in the evenings if… if it fitted in with my life better."

They didn't speak again for a little while, then Patrick pointed out a man dressed in bright orange who'd stopped with his back to them up ahead. "I hope for his sake he's just admiring the view!"

"I think he's safe. We're not likely to catch up with him."

She was wrong as they overtook him about half an hour later. He was a twitcher not a flasher, if the binoculars, flask of tea and notebook were anything to go by.

"Do you think he's seen any seagulls?" Amelia asked once they were passed.

"Two at least, plus your spotted ousel and a dozen rock-climbing, crested flamingos in the time he's been there."

"You sound sure. Are you going to reveal a tell-tale pattern of sea spray which proves what time he arrived?"

"Sadly not. I was just going by the fact that we passed him on our way out."

"You can't blame me for not noticing."

"No, that luminous tangerine blends so well into the landscape."

"What I meant was it dazzled me so much, I couldn't see his face."

"I almost didn't see him, dazzled as I was by your beauty."

"Good answer!"

Bongo, who'd been let off his lead again once they'd passed the orange coated twitcher began to bark excitedly.

"Bongo, no! Come on!" Amelia ran after him.

When she reached him he was still barking – at a thick, spiky bush.

"Is he OK?"

"Yes, I do believe he's learned his lesson." She attached the lead and coaxed him away.

"What was that?"

"There will have been something disgusting and smelly in that bush, most likely a long dead rabbit. Bongo, the monster, likes nothing better than rolling in things which are disgusting and smelly. He's thrown himself over cliffs to do so, and once dived into a thicket of thorns and cut his nose open."

"Makes me glad I have girls."

"Do boys roll in stuff that's disgusting and smelly?"

"I expect so. Horrible creatures boys. You stay well away!"

"You do know I'm older than eight?"

"I had noticed that, yes."

She giggled at his silly leer, then recalled Nicole's mention of kinky sex acts and laughed so hard it was difficult to breathe.

A cloud passing in front of the sun suddenly plunged them into relative gloom. The previously blue sky had turned a brooding purple without her noticing. "That looks ominous."

"Don't worry, we're almost back at the car. Besides, I feel really safe," Patrick said.

"You do?"

"It's always dog walkers who find the body, but nothing ever happens to them, does it?"

"Oh crikey. I often take Bongo around the Pendennis moat walk. There are some really eerie shadows there, which seem to leap out at you as you round the corners. Next time one startles me, I'll remember your reassuring comment about finding bodies."

"Ah. Sorry about that. Is it really creepy?"

"No, just teasing you. It's lovely. Especially this time of year when there are so many wild flowers on the banks. The moat walls are smothered in primroses now and soon there will be red campion and bluebells. The old castle's really nice too. I know of course that it was built for defence and the site used in both world wars, but it's so sweet, it's easy to imagine it as the fairytale sort of castle. "

"OK, you can stop with the sales pitch, you've convinced me. My girls might like it, do you think?"

"I'm sure they would." Only then did she wonder if

that was the very idea she'd been trying to give him. She really should try to sort out what was going on in her own head, and heart, before sending him clues.

The way he kissed her goodbye outside her door gave her plenty of clues to how he felt about her. Patrick only had one thing on his mind – a game for two in which she'd have the starring role. Maybe she was mixing up her metaphors, but it was hard to think with his soft warm lips and hard lean body doing his talking for him.

As she hurriedly removed her clothes she wasn't quite sure whether it was a good or bad thing she was doing that alone because she needed to get ready for work. It was certainly disappointing, and she was in no doubt Patrick had felt the same way. He hadn't been at all pushy, but moments after he'd left he was back tapping on her door again.

"We didn't arrange when I'd see you again." He pulled her into his arms.

She made a token effort to wriggle free. "Because I have to go to work."

"Promise me I'm going to see a lot more of you very soon."

She answered with another lingering, knee dissolving kiss. "Call me later. Now go!"

When he did call, he suggested they meet for coffee and cake to arrange their next date. Amelia would have pointed out the illogicality of that, except that by going along with it she got to see him again very soon, to eat cake and then have a proper date later. Perhaps he was implying the next date would also bring their relationship to the next level?

She'd convinced herself that must be the case until

over cappuccinos and strawberry shortcake Patrick suggested Amelia came to his place for a dinner party. "I have a couple of friends who'd like to see you."

"Oh. Who do you want me to meet?" He'd occasionally mentioned people he worked with, but not any special friends. A couple of times they'd bumped into people one of them knew when they were out together. Introductions were performed, but as far as she knew the only people he was close to were his brothers in Ireland, his children and his ex-wife. "Please don't tell me it's Meghan."

"Why would you think that?"

"You do talk to and about her quite a lot."

"Do I? Yes, I suppose I must or you wouldn't have said it. Sorry…"

"It's OK." It wasn't really OK and her tone said as much. She completely understood him talking about the girls and enjoyed his stories about funny things they'd said. Him caring about them so much was one of his attractive features. Of course he and Meghan needed to communicate sometimes to arrange childcare, but Meghan did have a tendency to call at inconvenient times. It was good the girls' mum loved them too, and coped so well when Isla was sick, but Amelia could have done without her being constantly lauded as a new and improved Florence Nightingale.

But her wasting part of her time with Patrick by thinking and talking about his ex wasn't any better than when he did it. "Who are these friends then?"

"You know them already. In fact you introduced us."

"I don't… Sonia and her actors?"

"No. Couple of chaps called Basil and Mr Rocket."

"The herbs! You still have them?"

"Sort of. Sadly poor Dill is no longer with us, and Mr Rocket has gone a bit peculiar, but Basil is fine."

"I'd be very happy to see them again."

"I could make you dinner."

"You could, or we could cook it together?"

"I'd like that."

They exchanged frequent texts and calls devising a menu, eventually opting for antipasti in which basil would play a part, a spicy ragout, and strawberries and cream. The meal appealed to Amelia because the ragout required a long cooking period, and none of the courses would spoil if they got distracted.

Amelia got ready by taking two shopping trips, one to a greengrocer and the other to the lingerie department of her favourite clothes store. On the day, she took Bongo for an earlier and faster walk than she'd usually have done, so she had extra time in the bathroom for final preparations.

None of her efforts were wasted. She did have to be very firm with Patrick so they got dinner in the oven before he discovered the cream silk camisole and matching knickers. By the time he did get to see them the colour was the only surprise as he'd given them a thorough inspection by touch as she tried to concentrate on dicing vegetables and grinding spices.

"How long did you say that will take to cook?" Patrick asked.

"An hour and a half at least."

"Just time for us to work up an appetite."

She attempted to look naively innocent. "I can't go jogging in these shoes."

"Then I'll have to get creative and think up something else energetic, won't I?" he said before simultaneously kissing her and unbuttoning her blouse.

"What about our starter?" Amelia broke away to ask.

"I'm trying to start, but someone keeps interrupting with food."

"This is a dinner party, remember?" She teased him for a while by repeatedly making him stop what he was doing to take a sip of wine and nibble on an olive, or other tasty morsel. Her willpower didn't last as long as the antipasti but she did have the presence of mind to turn the oven down before being led out of the kitchen diner.

The ragout was perfectly cooked by the time they got to eat it – Patrick wearing his dressing gown and Amelia in the shirt he'd had on when she arrived.

"This is delicious," he said. "I like a bit of spice with my food."

"In that case how about we save the strawberries for breakfast?"

"I really like that idea."

"Thought you might. Strawberries and just a little cream?"

"You don't need to watch your figure, that's my job." He gave her the silly leer which always made her giggle.

"I wasn't suggesting we didn't eat all the cream, in fact I think we should have some of it right now."

"What are we going to put it on?" he asked, delighting her with his puzzled expression.

"Come on, Mr Homes, use your imagination."

His reaction to that was surprise, but very definitely in a good way. He even left his phone downstairs.

Chapter 8

"That you, Patrick?" Amelia said into the intercom the moment it buzzed.

"Good evening, Watson," a tinny version of Patrick's voice replied. "That was well deduced."

"There were a few clues." Like this being when he said he'd be there.

"I have something I think you're going to like," Patrick said.

"Now there's a promise!" She buzzed him in.

There was a lot she liked about Patrick Homes. More than liked. It was time to decide what she was going to do about that.

"My dear Watson," Patrick said as Amelia opened the door for him

She ignored his daft hat which, despite the flaps, was not a deerstalker and the liquorice pipe sticking out of his shirt pocket and kissed him. Then she seized the huge bag of toffee popcorn. "You're almost right to think I'd like it, but actually I love this stuff."

Amelia used to eat a couple of packs a week, but when Nicole was trying to give up smoking, she'd made a pact with her. If Nicole didn't buy another cigarette, Amelia wouldn't buy more popcorn.

"No you don't, you love the caramel it's coated with."

"Ah, you've got me there!"

Thankfully Nicole hadn't seen through that. Although Amelia got her caramel fix in other ways, she'd managed to quit the popcorn – or at least stop buying it, which was all she'd promised. Amelia didn't feel the slightest bit guilty over her minor deception. The point was to protect her friend's health, not to deprive Amelia of a comparatively harmless pleasure.

"Actually, I was referring to this." Patrick produced a dvd. Not just any random film but a murder mystery set in the 1920s.

She recalled her flippant 'love me, love murder' comment a few days previously and was sure this was his response. "Great choice. I've not seen that one."

She tipped the popcorn into her mixing bowl, poured them both a drink and settled herself on the sofa. She didn't pull away when he sat close and draped an arm round her shoulders. At least not until she recognised an actor in the film. Something about the girl polishing glasses unsettled Amelia.

"What's up?" Patrick asked.

"I thought… " At that moment the character came into view again. Amelia realised almost simultaneously who the person playing the waitress reminded her of, why the sight of her in the restaurant had been disconcerting, and that it wasn't really anyone Amelia knew. "No, my mistake."

The waitress had reminded her of a chambermaid who'd once worked with Amelia, before she transferred to The Fal View. What she'd seen seemed wrong, because that young woman had no business being in the restaurant, nor anywhere else in a hotel, as she'd been sacked for theft. As it wasn't her, but an actress playing a part, maybe she had every right to be there. Maybe not. Amelia grabbed another handful of popcorn and snuggled back against Patrick to enjoy the film.

Not long after that, the victim, an unpleasant character who seemed to bully his wife and made offensive remarks about everyone else, died. At first it was assumed to be a tragic accident, but Amelia knew better. "Murder, definitely."

"I'm amazed at how you always work these things out," Patrick said, sounding impressed.

Amelia was unsure if he was teasing her or not, this was a murder mystery after all. She decided to give him the benefit of the doubt. "The waitress did it," she said.

"Which waitress?" Patrick asked.

"The pretty blonde one."

"I can't say I noticed her," Patrick said, not entirely convincingly. "But if she's the killer, I'd better keep my eye on her."

"You do that," Amelia said. He was definitely teasing her now, but she wasn't rising to it. Instead she grabbed more popcorn, carefully placing the bowl just out of his reach.

That didn't bother him, he just pinched some from her hand.

Gradually it emerged that the victim was just one in a spate of poisonings.

"Maybe they all had investments with that smarmy banker bloke and he was swindling them all?" Patrick suggested.

That did seem plausible; a bit too plausible. "No, it was the waitress." Actually she was slightly less sure about that now, as she couldn't see any possible motive, but thought she may as well stick to her theory. The alternative was to name every character in turn. That would be cheating and Patrick would definitely see through that. Better to be wrong with confidence and integrity.

"The blonde one who, although quite pretty, is

nowhere nearly as lovely as you?"

"That's the one." Amelia reached for the popcorn bowl, took another big handful and nudged it closer to Patrick.

He took no notice and continued stealing hers. It was a nice feeling to be sharing like that, until she wondered if he used to do exactly the same with Meghan.

In the film, the police discovered the chef who'd prepared the meal the dead man had eaten was his ex-wife. Although it wasn't her job, she'd washed up both the pan she'd used and the plate he'd eaten from. Not only that, but she'd known one of the previous victims.

"It's her then, obviously," Patrick said.

"Too obvious."

Amelia was right. The chef confessed to tampering with the victim's food, but she'd only added a laxative to the sauce. It was evidence of that and nothing worse she'd been attempting to hide.

Patrick was almost smug when it was revealed that several of the victims had used the services of the smarmy banker. "Are you going to admit I'm right?"

"Nope."

Finally, after several other people had come under suspicion, the killer was revealed to be the blonde waitress. The clues were there all along. She'd pretended to polish glasses, an odd thing to do when they were already on the table and guests were being seated. That was so she could slip poison into the victim's glass. She'd also been in a position to remove it before the victim showed symptoms and replace it with a fresh one. She'd used a similar tactic on all her victims, in various places.

Amelia's instinct that there was something wrong

when she first saw the waitress had been exactly right – she'd just been temporarily distracted by the fact her appearance was similar to that of another guilty person.

"OK, you win," Patrick said. "Your prize is the rest of the popcorn."

"There's none left."

"Ah, so there isn't. Shall I ring for pizza then? I don't fancy eating in a restaurant tonight after watching that."

"Not even if there are pretty waitresses?"

"Especially not in that case."

"OK, pizza it is."

"With all your favourite toppings?" Patrick suggested.

"Which are?"

He didn't answer other than to place the order. "An extra large, thin crust with red onions, roasted red peppers, black olives, rocket, sweetcorn and extra cheese, please."

"How did you know?"

"Elementary, my dear Watson." He laughed much more than she thought was justified by the remark.

"You found out what I like on pizza just so you could make that frankly terrible joke?"

"Yep." He looked extremely pleased with himself.

It wasn't just that though, Amelia was sure. Patrick would have amused himself just as much and far more easily by guessing the answers and wouldn't have minded being proved wrong in his deductions. Unlike her ex, James, he didn't have to be right about everything.

The reason Patrick had proved he knew what she liked on pizza was to show how well he knew her. That he listened to her and remembered what she'd said, or took the trouble to find out.

"Stalling for time?" he asked.

"Sorry, I was miles away."

"I asked how you knew who the killer was."

"I deduced it, using Miss Marple's method."

Patrick pulled a face which may, or may not, have been intended to look as though he was impressed with her detective abilities. "Remind me of Miss Marple's wonderful method?"

"She works out who did it because they'll remind her of the butcher's boy who once teased a cat, or something."

"Right." He sounded sceptical. "And how does that apply in your case?"

"The killer reminded me of a chambermaid who we'd had to let go, because she'd been stealing cleaning supplies.

"That makes no sense, you do realise that?"

"How do you mean?"

"Being a thief isn't like being a killer and…"

"Cleaning supplies could easily be used to poison someone."

"Do you think your chambermaid was planning a murder?"

"No, she was selling stuff on the local market, almost within sight of the hotel. That's how we found out."

"Not too bright then?"

"Definitely not. It was all stuff she could have bought from the same wholesaler we used. If she'd said she'd bought it then I think I'd have believed her. I certainly would have had to give her the benefit of the doubt, but she gave no explanation and then stole more the next day. I caught her at it."

"Is that what got you interested in detective stuff?"

"No, I've always liked reading mystery stories. I suppose they're what made me keep an eye on her."

"And run a murder mystery weekend?"

"Exactly."

"Maybe we could go on one where all we'd have to do is enjoy ourselves solving the crime?"

"I'd love that!" Had she really said so out loud? Of course she would like to attend one, but was she ready to go away with Patrick? It would definitely be moving their relationship on a level.

"Wouldn't be too much of a busman's holiday to stay in a hotel?" he asked.

"Not at all." At least she had no doubts about that.

"OK, I'll look into where and when we could do it. Talking of fitting things in, I'm taking the girls ice skating over Easter. Would you like to come?"

"I haven't been skating for years," she said, fully aware that wasn't answering his question. "I'm sure it would be fun." The skating part might be, but meeting his children? If she was ready to go away with him for the weekend then she should be ready for that. So far she'd found it really easy to put it off, but she couldn't do that for the entire Easter holiday without being obvious.

This was it – decide if this was a serious proper relationship, where she'd be part of his life and future, or if it wasn't. How she reacted to yet another attempt to get her and his girls together would send that message.

"It would be a big help actually, to have someone else with me," Patrick said.

Good tactic playing down it being a big deal for them all to meet. If only Amelia could do the same. She had an image of holding onto a small child and towing her round on the ice. Was that a good idea if they were unsure of each other? No. No, it really wasn't.

"I'm not sure that would be a good idea. You know, for the first meeting. Skating takes concentration and the child would need to trust me and they don't even know me so obviously they don't like me and…" In her panic she was burbling.

"Would it be better if you met them before?" He sounded so hopeful.

If she was to meet them at all then yes, it would be best if it was before the skating. The longer she left it, the more time she'd have to fret about it.

"How about we meet somewhere with Bongo? You could take them somewhere and we could, you know, just bump into each other." She could handle a quick chat and a game with Bongo.

"That's a pretty good idea. You said you often do the Pendennis moat walk, how about we go there?"

"That sounds fine."

"I haven't been for years. I think there's quite a lot to see, so it might be best to get there quite early. Half ten on Saturday?"

A complete day out? Nooo. "Umm… Yes. Yes, OK." She could always fake an urgent call back to work.

When he'd gone, Amelia analysed how she felt about what had happened. Patrick would understandably consider they'd moved their relationship on. Clearly that's what he wanted. She needed to be sure she wasn't doing what James had, getting pushed along by other people's wishes and not stopping to properly consider her own.

How odd, in all her soul searching after James left her, practically at the altar, she'd never understood how someone who cared about her could hurt her so deeply.

Finally she saw that much of the problem had been a desire not to hurt her. A proposal was expected of him so he proposed. Then everyone expected a date to be set and plans to be made, so he'd allowed that to happen. Then, being James, he couldn't admit he'd made a mistake, that he wasn't ready, that perhaps they weren't suited to a lifetime together. Instead of coming to the rehearsal two days prior to the wedding he'd written her a note and gone into hiding for a week. At the time it felt like the worst thing ever to happen to Amelia, but now she could forgive him and see that to go through with it would have been far worse.

Maybe one day she'd also forgive him for marrying a former girlfriend less than six months later.

Amelia rang Nicole and asked if she'd call her at eleven on Saturday, in case she needed an escape.

"Escape from what?"

"Children."

"What children? How would I be helping?"

Amelia tried to explain everything, but that wasn't so easy when she didn't totally understand herself.

"It's very simple," Nicole said. "Do you love Patrick and want to live happily ever after with him?"

"It's not simple at all. He's got kids. They might hate me. I might not like them or we might row all the time. You know families aren't really my strong point. He's got an ex-wife who expects a lot of him, we might row over that. We might have habits which annoy each other that we don't know about…"

"Excuses, excuses. I didn't ask if you were sure it would work, but if you want it to."

"Oh."

"Was that an oh or a no?"

"An oh." Amelia realised she did want that very much and the doubts were just to protect herself.

"So you do?"

"Yes."

"So the next step is to find out if it will work. Get to know the kids and see if you can get along with them. Spend more time with Patrick and see if he squeezes the toothpaste tube in the middle or freaks out that you often get so lost you end up in a different country."

"Once that happened. Once." Despite Nicole's usual exaggeration, her idea did seem very sensible.

"How about getting him to come here with you in May? Working together in the B&B would be a bit like playing happy families. Bet you'd learn a lot from doing that."

"You're right, I would. Thanks, I'll do that assuming everything goes OK with meeting the kids. It would be great for the two of you to meet too. You both getting on is important."

"Vital! If I don't like the look of him he's history."

"Not even that. It'll be as though he never existed."

"Talking of which, remember the man who vanished?" Nicole asked.

"Angus McKellar? I thought he didn't really?"

"I don't know, we never heard any more about it. Nothing official that is."

"And unofficially?"

"Just odd little things. Rumours really."

"Saying?"

"I don't know how to describe it. I suppose they're saying he's dishonest and leading a double life, only it's not put as strongly as that."

"Aaaargh, Nicole! It's like trying to have a conversation with my mother! Just tell me what you've heard and if you know if any of it's true."

"A couple of people have said that he's ignored them. Not close friends, but he's the sort of person you feel you know because he's been on the telly and you see him about and usually he speaks to everyone and is really friendly."

"OK, that's out of character, but there could be reasons. He might be avoiding publicity."

"He's not that big a celebrity. Besides, at other times he's kind of pushed himself into conversations with people who've never spoken to him and been a bit 'don't you know who I am?' He wasn't the slightest bit like that when I met him."

"I suppose there's no doubt it's really him – not somebody taking his place after he went missing in November?"

"If it's an imposter, they've fooled his wife, colleagues and friends. He's been living at home, working, playing golf, hosting fundraising parties, doing all the things he'd be expected to do. But he's been seen places he shouldn't be."

"Perhaps he's having an affair?"

"I hate to think it of him. He seems so nice. His wife too. And that's not quite what I meant by being where he wasn't supposed to be. He was seen miles from the TV studio at the same time as being seen on what was supposedly a live show. Another time he was walking the coastal path just before he was due to run a marathon – and he did run it."

"A segment might have been recorded, people could have been mistaken and just seen his bright tracksuits.

When we went for a walk the other day, Patrick recognised a birdwatcher. I didn't. Maybe Patrick only thought he was the same man because he was dressed the same?"

"I see what you mean, but there's more. If guests want anything a bit extra, like filling a flask of tea, or using the oven to heat up a pie, I don't like to charge, but I don't want it happening too often, so I suggest a donation to Salterns Support."

"The charity Angus McKellar set up?"

"Yeah. I took the cash into their charity shop a while ago. The woman there took my details and said the B&B would be listed as a donor. I wouldn't have checked, except Mike who has an ice cream van on the prom mentioned his donation wasn't listed. Mine wasn't either."

"Did you report it?"

"Yes. And the list was corrected, sort of. It actually said more than I gave."

There were so many oddities Amelia knew something was wrong, but she played devil's advocate. "The money could have been overlooked, then when someone realised their mistake, they added to it as an apology."

"What, 47p? I remember that when I handed it in I said it was almost £50. It was actually £49.21, but on the statement it showed as £49.68."

"One or other of you counted it wrong then. Did the lady count it in front of you?"

"No. A man from the charity happened to come in while I was there and he took it, along with other collection boxes."

"This is bothering you, isn't it?"

"Yeah. Angus always seemed such a nice man.

Actually it was more than that. He made it seem that other people were nice too. That's a lovely message to get from the evening news, which is usually so depressing."

"Yeah."

"When Angus McKellar was praised for raising a lot of money he always said it wasn't him, it was the people who sponsored him, or bought or donated anything at the charity shop. When I took in a book I'd read, or a blouse I didn't wear I felt like a good person, doing the right thing. Now I don't know what to think."

"You are a good person."

"Sure. And there are lots of good people about – but are we also gullible fools who've been lining his pockets instead of helping kids? I don't really think that, but I have a few doubts, you know? Any of the things I've heard could be people making a mistake or have some other innocent explanation, but not all of them."

"Exactly what I was thinking. I can't promise I'll find anything, but I'll ask around when I come up, see if I can find out what he's up to."

"Thanks, mate. You're a good person too. Sometimes anyway!"

Amelia decided not to spend nearly a week dreading meeting two small girls and so rang Patrick.

"I've been thinking, going to Pendennis Castle with the girls might be a bit much for a first meeting. They wouldn't have time to process what they thought about me before having to spend hours in my company, and share you." As that was exactly what worried her it seemed reasonable to assume it would be the same for them. Nicole, who'd grown up surrounded by them in the home, had assured her children were a lot like people.

"It doesn't take them long to decide if they like people and I know they'll like you."

If their relationship was going to work, she needed to be honest. "It's not just them I'm worried about. I'm sure they're lovely and everything and it will all be fine, but I find the idea of the children slightly scary. I'm not close to my parents and it's difficult for me sometimes, the way you're always there for them. I… Like I said, it might be a bit much for the first time."

"I see. What would you suggest?" He sounded really tired, maybe this wasn't such a good idea? Still, saying she didn't like his plan whilst not providing any alternative wasn't helpful.

"When are you next picking them up from school?"

"This afternoon."

"On foot?"

"I could."

"That'll be about four?"

"Three."

"Even better. You tell me where and I'll be there with Bongo. Just to say hello and maybe, if they like each other, play for a few minutes, and then we'll go our separate ways."

"OK. Yes, that's good." They arranged a location. "I can't be precise on time, sometimes they chat to friends, but we should get there about quarter past."

"Shall we synchronise our watches?"

Patrick approached, on the opposite side of the road, with a small girl holding each hand. He was striding out with them skipping beside him. She'd have taken them for twins if she didn't know. They were the same size and dressed in matching school uniforms. The only difference she could see as they got nearer was that one was very pale and thin. Presumably that was Isla, the sickly one.

"They're just small people, Bongo. We can outrun them if we need to, right?"

The dog didn't seem convinced, but that was because he'd picked up on her anxiety, not because he knew how this would go.

"Play nicely. I'm relying on you, boy."

Bongo wagged his tail at that. If Patrick had given the girls a similar instruction, it would be OK. She waved when they drew level, and crossed over.

Amelia thought Patrick's surprised, "Fancy meeting you here!" sounded false, but the girls didn't seem to see through it.

"Girls, this is my friend Amelia. Amelia meet Ava and Isla."

"Hello," the three of them said pretty much together.

"Who is that?" one child asked, pointing at Bongo.

"My dog Bongo."

"Does he bite?"

"Not usually."

"How does he eat his dinner then?" both girls said through giggles.

"He slurps it up through a bright pink straw." Why the heck had she said that?

"Really? Can we see?"

Rats. Lesson learned, don't make up mad stuff Amelia Watson, or you'll be sussed. "He can't really. He can do other things though."

"Show us!"

Patrick guided them onto a grassy area where Amelia

had the dog sit, lie down and roll over. Then, when satisfied they would realise it was a game, demonstrated 'dead dog'.

"Poor doggy," one girl said. They both crouched down and stroked him.

Bongo didn't move, except for his tail. She thought he was trying to keep it still, but it was definitely wagging.

"I wonder if your daddy can make him better?"

"Quick, give him the kiss of life, Daddy," the skinny kid said.

"Or do defriberlatering on him"

"OK. Stand clear!" Patrick knelt and patted Bongo's chest.

"He's alive!" Amelia cried, sending dog and children into a delighted frenzy.

"Thanks, Amelia," Patrick said as the children and dog ran around in a game which made no sense to Amelia, but seemed to amuse them all.

"It's all down to Bongo."

"I meant suggesting we meet like this. You did before and I didn't listen. I should have."

"No problem."

"Isla's getting tired, we'd better go."

The girls said goodbye nicely, showing considerable reluctance to leave Bongo.

Amelia watched Patrick stride away, carrying one girl on his back and with the other skipping beside him.

On the way home from watching an am dram whodunnit, which Amelia had no trouble solving, Patrick praised her powers of deduction. "How do you feel about real crime?"

"Are you suggesting our next date involves masks and

handcuffs?" Amelia asked.

"I wasn't, but if it would make you happy…"

"Actually, I think I would like that. No, not that!" She slapped him playfully as he gave his funny leer. "OK, maybe that, but I meant being a real detective. I wouldn't want to be in the police or anything like that. I'm sure there's lots of boring parts to it and you couldn't get to pick and choose your cases. Being a private detective appeals though."

"That probably has boring bits too and it might not be so much fun if that's what you had to do, and keep doing, to earn a living," Patrick said.

"I agree, but I'd be amateur and part time and I'd just take interesting cases."

"What would you find interesting? Murder?"

"I suppose so. There's a lot at stake, isn't there?"

"For your poor victim there is."

"I'm not quite so hard hearted I actually want people to die in order to provide entertainment for me, I'll have you know. Actually I meant that there being so much at stake could be a downside. It's too dangerous. I prefer unexplained oddities, like the disappearance of Angus McKellar. "

"Should I have heard of him?"

"He owns McKellar's confectionery."

"Suppliers of that necessity of life, caramel?"

"That's the one. He vanished from a spot 200 miles away, just when you were getting killed."

"And you're interested because…?"

"He lives where my best friend Nicole does."

"Portsmouth."

"Oh, yes, I told you about her didn't I? Actually she's in Lee-on-the-Solent, which is nearby and she told me about Mr McKellar. He was missing for a week, turned up really drunk and apparently had no idea where he'd been or why."

"Didn't Agatha Christie do that? Not getting drunk I don't mean, but vanishing for a bit and turning up with no explanation to get herself in the papers?"

"That's what I said to Nicole!"

"That he was impersonating Agatha Christie?"

"No, that it was probably a publicity stunt. Trouble is, I don't see why he needed one."

"Why did Christie?" Patrick asked.

"She didn't. I read that her husband was having an affair and she tried to kill herself, but failed or changed her mind. Then when she saw what a big fuss her disappearance had caused she didn't want to talk about any of it so said she couldn't remember."

"That sounds more plausible than it being a publicity stunt."

"Maybe that's sort of what Angus did? Took off for what he thought was a good reason, then saw he was all over the news and it took a while to get up the nerve to come back."

"So, are you going to investigate?"

"I will when I go up there. Nicole has a B&B and I'm going there for a week in May."

Annoyingly his phone rang before she could drop in a casual comment about it being more fun not to go alone. Doubly annoyingly as the caller was Meghan, saying one of the kids was sick again. Poor little Isla seemed to be ill more than she was well.

"Sorry, I have to go," Patrick said.

"Of course you do."

Chapter 9

There had been some big changes at The Fal View since Christmas. As well as the management changes, it had gained another twenty rooms thanks to taking over an adjacent building. The boss had dealt with converting and fitting those out.

"That's what I like to do," he explained. "Take on new buildings and projects. Once it's a success I start looking for something new. That is why I'm promoting Jorge again. He's no longer deputy, but the manager."

Everyone congratulated Jorge, despite the fact they were all aware he'd effectively had that role from the start of his last promotion to deputy.

Jorge had started holding weekly management meetings. He timed them for when one duty manager was handing over to another, and invited the third to attend if it was convenient. By varying the timings he ensured Amelia, Gabrielle and Charles attended at least every other one. A representative of each department was also present.

These were a chance to mention any potential issues and suggest improvements for staff, guests or the business overall. At the last meeting in March, Bianca said, "I've had several enquiries about whether we'll be doing another murder mystery weekend."

"If you do, make sure you have agency staff on standby," said a young man from housekeeping.

"Why?" Charles asked. "Is there a high body count at these things?"

"Half the staff!"

"They didn't all die," Gabrielle kindly pointed out. She explained there had been a huge number of staff off sick while the hotel was fully booked.

"You were fully booked in early November?" Charles asked. "That's good going!"

Amelia had provisionally agreed with the boss and Sonia to repeat the event, but the staffing issues with the first and Jorge's promotion had made her reticent about mentioning it since. The conversation showed that her colleagues weren't against the idea in principal.

"Jorge?" she said a few days later. "I wonder if we could talk about another murder mystery weekend."

"Of course. Have a seat."

She made her case, including citing the number of emails and telephone calls they'd received, enquiring about the subject. "The last one went well in the end, and I learned a lot from it. Sonia, the lady who dealt with all the performance aspects, is eager to do another and could organise something suitable for a larger number of attendees, and I'm sure we'd have no trouble filling the places."

"If you do it, you'd be responsible for the whole thing. Every detail."

"Fine with me." Last time, taking on extra staff hadn't been her responsibility, and she'd not realised until almost too late that it hadn't been done. They'd all been far too frantic to check up on anybody else back then.

"And of course you'll need to work around anything we already have booked."

"Of course."

"OK then, it's all yours." Jorge made a big deal of picking up his pen and ticking off something on his notepad with a theatrical flourish.

"What's that?"

Jorge grinned and turned the pad towards her. It was a list of tasks. 'Talk to Amelia about another murder weekend' had a large tick against it.

"I'd love to," Sonia said, when Amelia contacted her. "The same date as last year?"

"Or earlier. We're pretty full over the school holidays, and there's not time for me to do all the promotion for anything before that, but it's quieter afterwards, and we'll have more rooms available by then."

"Early September would suit me, and it would be something for grandparents to look forward to after kids are back at school. From what I remember, most of the guests probably were grandparents."

"I think you're right and I expect some of them to come back, so I'd want a different murder. Actually I want that for myself too!"

"I guessed as much. That's no problem."

"Do you have lots of murders worked out?"

"A few, yes. We usually do the same one for a few months, then rehearse a new one. We do more single day or evening events than whole weekends, but I can extend them for longer periods."

"That sounds complicated."

"To be honest it isn't. People don't want it full on the whole time, unless it's just for a few hours, so I space things out and add a few more characters and red herrings. The main plot stays the same. And we repeat some, using different time periods, or switching motives or whatever."

"Having a specific time period was great, really added to the whole thing. I'm glad you talked me into that."

"Do you want the same, or a different era?"

"Different, I think. I'm not sure when…"

"I'll have a think. What about the time frame? Same again?"

"Yes. That worked well and repeat guests will expect the same number of meals and everything. I'll email you with details of which public rooms will be available when, and the capacity of each. I was thinking, if we're doing a themed weekend maybe we could include a dinner or party or something for non-residential guests. I don't know if that could be worked in?"

"It's a possibility. Maybe as background for something else."

"That's what I thought."

"Leave it with me, I'll see what I can do."

"Excellent." Sonia had said exactly the same thing when she'd asked if Patrick could stay involved after being killed off as Max Gold. It wouldn't surprise Amelia to learn the other woman already had a scheme in mind.

"There's something else," Sonia said. "If you'll forgive a personal question?"

"Probably. Might not answer it though!"

"It's about Patrick. I had a feeling you'd still be seeing each other after he'd checked out."

"You were right. Actually I'm spending the day with him tomorrow. Him and his kids."

"Oh, I hadn't bargained on kids."

"Neither had I!"

"But it's OK?"

"Yeah. Yes, I think it's going to be."

Amelia told Patrick she'd wait for him and the children

outside Pendennis castle, rather than in the car park. That way she'd see them walking towards her as they had before and she'd have time to get her nerves under control and tell her anxious face to smile.

At least, that had been the plan. Children it seemed didn't always read the script, as one of them came running towards her.

"Hello, Melia!"

"Hello." Which one was it? The pasty looking one feeling better, or the other one?

"Is Bongo at home today?"

"Yes. I share him with another lady and he's with her today."

"He will be sad not to play with me and Isla."

"Yes, Ava, he will."

When Patrick reached them with his other daughter, who was still just as pale, he kissed Amelia's cheek, which didn't seem to bother the girls. "I'm a lucky man, getting to spend all day with you," he murmured in her ear. That did bother her and not because of the reminder the girls too would be with her for hours. Mostly it was the effect of that gorgeous accent, but it was a little bit because she couldn't help thinking about him getting lucky all night.

Patrick released her and turned to Isla. "You remember Amelia, don't you?"

"Yes. Course. Hello, Bongo's mummy."

"Hello, Isla."

"Isn't Bongo here?"

Simultaneously Patrick reminded her he'd said he wouldn't be and Ava explained he was sad at home.

"Poor Bongo."

"He misses us."

133

Feeling the conversation had already got away from her, Amelia said, "Perhaps you can play with him another day and cheer him up?"

"We will, Melia."

"We promise."

"We will make him better like daddy did with the defibileraterer."

Although curious, Amelia resisted asking why a six-year-old was so enthusiastic about defibrillators. Maybe she was just interested in everything? Ava was definitely the liveliest of the two. Avid Ava, Amelia mentally nicknamed her, to help her tell the girls apart when the other one got over her latest illness. If she wasn't so pale and skinny the two would look identical.

Each of them had their hair adorned with a liberal selection of pretty clips and scrunchies. Both girls wore knitted sweaters. Ava's was powder blue with pink flowers and Isla's the reverse. Each girl had a scarf and gloves matching their knitted flowers.

"Granny made them for us," Ava said, when Amelia admired them.

"They're lovely. You're very lucky."

"Mine is itchy," Isla said, pulling at her scarf.

"Leave it on, you'll get cold," Patrick told her.

"It's really itchy, Daddy and it makes my head hurt."

She sounded petulant and Amelia hoped she wasn't about to witness a tantrum.

"Why don't we swap? Just for now?" Amelia suggested. Her own scarf was a silky one, chosen more for how it looked than any warmth it might provide, but on the little girl it could be wrapped round several times and do a good job without being at all itchy.

Isla agreed, and Amelia put on the small, soft wooly

one as Patrick wound the silky one around Isla's skinny neck. Everyone laughed at the change. Isla wanted to swap gloves too, but the size difference made that impossible.

They decided to start by walking around the outside of the castle, so they could see it from all angles.

"I need a wee," Isla said at the exact moment they were as far as possible from the toilets.

"It's OK, Melia can take us," Ava said in a reassuring tone. "Do you know where it is, Melia?"

"Ummm." Help! She could see that with her being female it seemed more logical for her to go with them than Patrick, but she had no clue what was expected of her. Then she remembered they both went to school, so would be able to manage OK. They just wanted someone to walk in with them. She could do that.

"It's on the map." Amelia produced the leaflet they were given when they bought their tickets. "That way, I think."

It was fine. All she had to do was stand outside the cubicle doors assuring them she was still there, then lift them to reach the soap dispenser when they washed their hands. It had been daft of her to panic – caring for children wasn't really so hard.

Over the next two hours Amelia forgot to think of them as strange alien creatures and saw them as small people with distinct personalities. The girls were full of random questions about the castle and impressed Amelia knew so much. She couldn't actually answer all their queries, but they seemed just as pleased if she gave any vaguely connected fact instead. Her lifelong love of castles ensured she had plenty of those.

Avid Ava was super enthusiastic, manically energetic

and delighted with everything. That joy was infectious. She frequently raced ahead, calling, "Come on, Melia!"

Amelia was happy to follow and see what had captured her interest, or discover whatever was around the next corner. Seeing the castle from the little girl's point of view was almost like seeing it again for the first time.

Isla was more restrained and thoughtful. She wanted to know what things were used for and who by, not just what they were called. She also seemed something of an attention seeker. Isla had to be taken to the toilet again, carried up any steep slopes and tended to lag behind, meaning Patrick was often waiting for her and coaxing her to keep going. At first Amelia thought she was trying to keep her dad to herself.

When Ava said, "Isla is tired again. She needs a rest," it became obvious this behaviour wasn't something directed against Amelia, but normal.

When Ava ran back to encourage her sister to keep going, Patrick said, "Would it be OK if I gave Meghan your number? Just in case of emergencies?"

Meghan never seemed to have any trouble getting hold of him, quite the opposite, but Amelia supposed it could happen and presumably she'd only be called if it really was important. She wouldn't want to be the reason Patrick couldn't get to his girls if he needed to be with either of them. "I suppose so."

When Isla and Ava rejoined them, Amelia suggested, "Shall we stop for a picnic? I have cake."

Both girls were unsurprised that Amelia just happened to have not only drinks, crisps and sandwiches, but a pack of millionaire shortbread, and a caramel flavoured cake easily big enough for four, in her backpack. It was as though they knew her already. Isla only nibbled her food but she did say 'thank you' politely as Amelia divided everything up. Ava ate far more enthusiastically, finishing her sister's share as well as her own.

The nearest exhibit to their picnic spot was about WW2. It offered the chance to blow up enemy ships. The girls had a go, but Amelia could see it wasn't totally capturing their imaginations. Isla got cross when she didn't do well.

"That's a good thing, Isla. You've scared them off so they'll go home and nobody will be hurt," Patrick said.

His attempt to make her feel better backfired as the girls' questions quickly revealed that wars didn't usually involve everyone going home without getting hurt.

"Come on, I want to show you something." He took them to a gun emplacement and got them to look for enemy ships. The lack of them reassured the girls a little.

"The war was a long time ago. Before I was born. But when it happened, soldiers stood here just like us to keep a look out. That wasn't because they wanted to hurt anyone. They were trying to keep their friends and family safe."

"Did it work, Daddy?" Ava asked.

"Yes it did. This castle has helped with that lots of times."

"It scared bad people away?" Isla asked.

"That's right. Sometimes, just because it was here, the enemy decided not to attack."

"Because the soldiers did scaring them!" Ava raised her arms and curled her fingers like claws. "Graaarghhh graaaargh, go away baddies!"

Isla and Amelia joined in with the ferocious lion routine and Patrick pretended to be terrified.

"Don't be scared, Daddy," Isla said. "All the baddies have gone now."

Soon the girls moved on from defending the country to being princesses looking out for pirates bringing them treasure. That was far more in Amelia's comfort zone than the ethics of war, and she joined in speculation about what would be in the holds of the imaginary ships. The cargo mainly comprised teddy bears, pretty clothes, and vast quantities of chocolate. It wasn't historically accurate, but it had done as Patrick intended and cheered them up. Amelia loved their imaginations and how sweet and girly they were.

"Lots of cake," Ava declared. "And shiny jewels."

"And magic storybooks, that never end," Isla said.

"And rainbow coloured parrots," Amelia added.

"Talking ones?" Ava asked.

"Oh yes."

"Do they say rude words?"

"Probably, if they've been listening to the pirates."

"Like what?" Isla asked.

"Ummm." Amelia glanced at Patrick for help, but he just grinned at her.

"Bum?" Ava said it, but both girls giggled.

"Probably."

"You do it, Melia."

Patrick was still of no use, this time because he had his mouth clamped shut in an effort not to laugh.

"Bum!" Amelia squawked. Their reaction was so gratifying she flapped her arms like wings and squawked some more. "Bum, bottom, fart, wee-wee!" That was the first time she'd actually seen anyone roll on the floor with laughter. Patrick's daughters were almost as amused as he was.

When they'd recovered, Amelia said, "Let's climb back to the top of the castle for an even better view." Climbing the spiral stairs was her own favourite part of visiting castles, so she thought the girls might be keen. Avid Ava was, but not Isla.

"Why don't you two go up and try sending secret messages to me and Isla?' Patrick suggested.

Amelia was touched that Ava grabbed her hand and dragged her off like a friend would. Ava was definitely Amelia's favourite, but she liked quiet Isla too. The children seemed very close, so if one had taken to her then the other might well be won round soon.

At the top of the tower, Amelia and Ava went in different directions around the little circular path, looking for the other two.

"There they are!" Ava called.

Amelia joined her in time to see Patrick blowing kisses.

"That means he loves me."

"It does," Amelia agreed.

They both made heart shapes with their fingers back down to the other two.

They all tried acting out other messages. Not very successfully as far as Amelia could make out – phoning to ask whether they'd got anything right would have ruined the game.

Patrick put Isla on his shoulders and skipped about.

"What do you think he's doing?" Amelia asked.

"Being a silly billy!"

No doubt they looked equally silly trying to convey that opinion via mime. It was fun being a kid, but exhausting too. Amelia was relieved when Patrick mimed drinking a cup of tea. Ava and Amelia mimed back eating. Both Patrick and Isla gave a thumbs up signal.

Ava held Amelia's hand again as they climbed back down, and didn't let go as they walked across the grass to meet her sister and father.

Isla raced up and took Amelia's other hand. "Me and Daddy were sailors come to save you and we have!"

"Thank you, that's very kind."

"You have to do kissing us now because we are heroes!"

Amelia gave Isla loud air kisses near either cheek. Both girls, giggling madly, copied her.

"And Daddy!"

"No time. Amelia will have to reward me later." His grin suggested the reward would involve some part of her body actually making contact with his.

During hot chocolate all round and shared chips, mostly eaten by Ava, Amelia said the girls might like Lanhydrock House. "It's as beautiful as a palace and you can visit where the children lived and where the staff worked, and the gardens are really pretty. About now would be a great time as the camellias and rhododendrons would be coming into flower." She'd thought of suggesting to Patrick that they go there together, but it might be even more fun with the girls.

Amelia didn't think the day could have gone any better and was surprised at her reluctance to say goodbye to the girls. If she continued to be as fond of them as she was, and they came to like her half that much, then some of her fears for the relationship had been unfounded. And she really did think a genuine affection was growing.

This was confirmed during her next date with Patrick. Over dinner he said, "The girls talked about you all the way home. They asked if you could come and play."

"Good to know they appreciate my mature personality."

"Not to mention your knowledge of parrot vocabulary. They've recreated that several times."

"Excellent."

"Yes, their… teachers were most impressed."

"Ooops!" Then she realised he was teasing. "Hang on, the Easter holidays aren't over yet."

"No, but you're going to feature heavily in the 'what I did in the holidays' essays."

"Maybe it's not too late for me to replace that memory with something more educational."

"We needn't worry too much about the educational part, but I know they'd like to see you again. And I'd like that too."

"So would Bongo, I think. What about going for a walk with him?"

"Sounds good. First though, don't you owe me for saving you from whatever it was I saved you from while you were safely up that tower?"

"I suppose I do. If only I could think of some way to express my gratitude."

Patrick leered and waggled his eyebrows. "I have a few suggestions."

Chapter 10

The way Patrick kissed her outside the restaurant, halfway back to her place, outside her front door and then again even more passionately once they were in her flat, prompted several ideas from Amelia too. They explored them all, before falling asleep.

The next morning Patrick suggested Amelia join him and the girls for lunch. She readily agreed.

Stopping on her way to the café, Amelia bought the girls colourful clips and scrunchies to go in their hair. They'd been wearing a selection both times she'd met them, and Patrick had expressed no surprise they had far fewer by the time they'd explored Pendennis castle.

They both thanked her nicely.

"Will you plait my hair, Melia?" Ava asked.

"Sorry, I don't know how."

The little girl shrugged away her disappointment. "Mummy do it in a minute."

Patrick explained Meghan was taking them shoe shopping after lunch.

"You can come, Melia."

"No. I can't. I have work." She was working that evening, but could have fitted in a few hours shopping with Patrick's ex-wife had she wanted to, which obviously she very much didn't. "And I have to take Bongo for a walk." Amelia chose a sandwich for lunch, ate half and wrapped the rest in her serviette. "I have to go, see you all later."

"Everything OK?" Patrick asked.

"Yes, fine." Just as long as she avoided meeting

Meghan anytime soon it was. "Bye girls. See you later!"

"Thank you for our presents, Amelia."

"Bye, Melia!"

An hour later Patrick texted, 'Everything OK?'

'Yep. Great.' Then because she didn't want him getting the idea she was avoiding his kids sent 'When girls back at school could walk them home with you and Bongo?'

'Good idea. Still on for tomorrow?'

'You bet.'

During their next date, neither of them mentioned her sudden departure. As they went to the cinema they didn't talk much about anything. And as Amelia was on earlies the next day, and Patrick had morning viewings booked, he didn't stay over.

"It's no coincidence that most of your viewings and things are booked for when I'm working, is it?" she asked.

"One of the perks of being my own boss. As you sometimes have time off in the day, it seems sensible to make the most of it."

"It does. Especially as I didn't really have any free time when we first met."

"I take it the new manager is working out OK?"

"Yeah. When he applied I wasn't sure about having someone much older, and who'd been the sole manager elsewhere, but Charles is great. Hardly needed any training and is happy to go along with how we do things. He says he's enjoying not having to make every decision and having colleagues he can blame!"

"Sounds perfect."

"Except he'll probably only stay a few years. I'm thinking Bianca might make a good replacement. I've had her shadowing me when she can be spared and she's learning fast."

"Is that what the sea safari was about?"

"Not really. A little bit of it was for me – I can never resist a boat trip. But I knew she liked the idea too. When I was talking to her about advising guests on things to do during their stay, it occurred to me that we're offering a service to any businesses we recommend. I got in touch with some and wangled a few freebies, so we can do a really good job of that."

"Clever."

"Yes, I am."

"And modest," Patrick said.

"That's true. And very, very lovely."

"I admit it. Talking of which... Isla and Ava have been asking about seeing you and Bongo."

"Are they back at school now?"

"They are."

"We could walk them home together sometimes?"

"Definitely, if you'd still like to." She had wondered why he'd not taken her up on that suggestion before. Maybe he'd forgotten.

It became a regular routine for Amelia to walk Bongo to somewhere near the school and wait for Patrick and the girls. They played games in the park on the way home once or twice a week. The girls liked getting Bongo to perform his tricks and trying to teach him new ones. As this involved the liberal use of dog biscuits, Bongo was more than happy to oblige. They were convinced they'd taught him to bark on command, but really he was just echoing their excitement. He really could make dog biscuits vanish, but Amelia suspected he'd been born with that ability.

On the occasions Patrick walked the girls back to his

home, Amelia came too when she could. If they turned in the other direction, towards Meghan's home, she unfortunately never had the time, and left them before they reached their destination.

Several times Isla was at home unwell.

"Poor thing. What's wrong?" Amelia asked the first time.

"She just says it hurts," Patrick said.

"Her stomach?"

"It seems to be all over the place."

That was so vague Amelia half wondered if Isla didn't like school and was faking, but quickly dismissed the idea. She seemed to love learning. "Could it be her appendix? When Dad had problems with…"

Patrick abruptly cut her off. "It's not her appendix."

Twice more Isla had urine infections. Amelia looked online and discovered she'd been right to think it was usually far older people who suffered from that, but she didn't say anything to Patrick. He seemed sure that's what it was and, as the doctor prescribed antibiotics which solved the problem, it must have been.

Amelia and Bongo got so used to walking in the area around the school she sometimes headed in that direction without thinking, even when she wasn't going with him to meet the girls. One Saturday morning she was startled to see them right in front of her. They were each holding an adult's hand, but instead of it being Patrick's broad back between them, it was that of a petite blonde. Obviously Isla got her small frame, and both girls got their fair hair, from their mother.

Before Amelia could think what to do, the three of them stepped through a gateway in front of a row of terraced houses. Amelia abruptly turned around, in case one of the girls spotted her as they waited to be let in, or Bongo noticed them and barked. No doubt she'd meet Meghan one day, but Amelia didn't want that to happen until she was prepared for the encounter – and it didn't look as though she might be spying on the other woman.

Amelia was genuinely unable to attend Ava's birthday party, but as it would be hosted by Meghan she didn't regret that too much. It would have been nice to see the child open her gift though – Amelia had bought her a pirate outfit, complete with luridly coloured parrot.

"We had a fab day today," Amelia told Nicole in a phone call. "We went to the Eden project."

"You and Patrick, I assume."

"And the girls. It was great, but the very best bit happened before we got in. We got a family ticket!"

"Makes sense."

"It lasts a year, so we can keep going back as a family. We had to have our pictures taken for it. Patrick and I both carry around little bits of card saying we're a family. Me and him, not him and his ex."

"I told you, didn't I? Play happy families and it'll work out."

"That's not what you said. You wanted me to wait until you go away in May and do it at your place without the kids."

"You can bring them here too, if you want."

"They'll be at school. To be honest, I'm looking forward to us having some time together. Just me, Patrick and plenty of time, but I reckon I could handle a trip with Ava and Isla too sometime."

"So, apart from Manky Meghan, it's all going perfectly?" Nicole asked.

"Brilliantly. Being with the girls is almost like being a kid again. It's not quite as fun as a day out with you obvs, but not bad. Going to the cinema is tricky though."

"Oh, why?"

"Deciding which girl to let sit next to me is a dilemma. Ava is my favourite."

"You're not supposed to have a favourite!"

"I haven't told them, and there's not much in it."

"Hmm. Anyway, go on."

"As I say, Ava is my favourite, but she's as bad as you for nicking my popcorn."

"You're not supposed to be eating popcorn!"

"Oh. Well, actually I only promised not to buy it."

"You sure about that?"

"Yep, I was very careful with my wording."

"Hmm, anyway, the girls?"

"That was my point. Ava eats it, Isla doesn't, so I always say I want to sit with her in the pictures. That's not showing favouritism to Ava, is it?"

"Maybe not. Isla is the one who's sick a lot?"

"Yeah, poor thing. It's odd, the girls are so alike in every other way, but Ava's never ill. Isla gets everything that's going round, plus loads of other stuff. Actually she's never what you'd call healthy. She must have a weak immune system or something."

"Is she really ill as often as all that?"

"Yes. Or maybe it seems that way because she's usually sick when it's going to mess something up. Patrick's cancelled a few dates because of it – we never got to go ice skating and he was actually on the way to pick me up to go to Lanhydrock when he had to take her home again. And if she's feeling poorly when Patrick's not there Meghan often phones him – always picking the most inconvenient time – and expects him to come running."

"Which he does?"

"Yeah. Every. Single. Time. Of course it's good that he cares so much and I know it's not Isla's fault, but... You know, I sometimes wonder if Meghan makes her worse."

"What? Not that thing... something German, where people make kids sick to get attention themselves?"

"No, not as bad as that. Crikey, I hope not... No, I'm sure Patrick would know. He has the girls himself quite a lot and sometimes she's poorly then too. I just think maybe Meghan makes the most of it to get him coming back to her, and the kid picks up on her satisfaction over that and exaggerates any symptoms."

"It's not about you then? You thought at one time it might be?"

"I'm sure it isn't. She's quieter than Ava, but just as affectionate and just as likely to suggest I come with them on days out and things. Did I tell you they came to tea at mine?"

"You said they were going to and how you were getting loads of goodies in, to tempt her to eat."

"I did and it worked brilliantly. I made everything really little, so she could try lots of different things even if she wasn't very hungry. She had less than half what her sister did, but Patrick said it was loads for her. Even better, there was no call that evening saying she was sick."

"Sounds like a success to me."

"I'm sure the kids like me. I was worried they wouldn't."

"I know you were, but not why."

"Because of Mum and Dad. I mean they don't dislike me, I don't think, but…"

"Of course they don't. What you've been saying about having fun with Isla and Ava like we did on days out, I expect you have to work at it a bit sometimes, to make it fun?"

"Yeah, but it's definitely worth it."

"We didn't go on our own trips all by ourselves, did we?"

"No, of course not." Her parents had taken them. "Oh."

Everything seemed to be going perfectly for Amelia. Work was great. Her boss, noticing the change in his management staff, belatedly realised how much pressure he'd put them under and apologised. He explained he'd become enthused in another project and not paid enough attention to the hotel. He'd always intended to take on another manager, but took too long to do anything about it. He was forgiven even before he declared that Jorge, Amelia and Gabrielle would each receive a bonus and they, and the new duty manager Charles, would all be awarded a small share of the profits each year.

Her parents' manner had changed a little since Christmas, and even more so after Amelia paid a flying visit for Mum's birthday.

"How lovely," Mum had said when she opened the door to Amelia holding a huge bouquet. Then just as Amelia was wondering if she meant the flowers added, "and these are beautiful. I assume they're for me."

"They are."

"Thank you. How long can you stay?"

"Overnight, if that's OK?"

"Of course. I'll just put these in water. David, can you ring the restaurant and ask them to make it a table for three?"

"No need," he said.

"Why not?"

"Because I made the booking, and it's already for three."

"And you didn't tell me?"

"Just in case Amelia couldn't make it. We know how important she is at that hotel and I didn't want you to be disappointed."

It took Amelia a moment to process the fact her father had kept her visit a secret, not because he considered Amelia likely to let them down, but because he knew her mother would have looked forward to her coming and been saddened if it didn't happen. This was the woman she had to practically drag a conversation from to stop her ending phone calls in under a minute.

That wasn't an issue during her stay. Her parents asked questions about Bongo, the hotel and the staff they met, and were interested in hearing about Patrick and his daughters.

Even better in terms of life going well, was her relationship with Patrick. They were as compatible physically as they were mentally, and whilst they always had fun, things were becoming more serious in the best sense of that term. One day when she'd very cleverly spotted the twist to a drama they were watching he's said, "You know, you should really be Holmes, not Watson."

"You think?"

"I do, but I'd prefer it if you'd become Homes."

"Oh, would you?"

"Something to think about, anyway."

His phone had rung, just at that moment. She'd hoped he'd ignore it, as he often did when he was with her, but the ringtone was Meghan's. Her calls were always answered.

Amelia walked away so he wouldn't see her irritation. Meghan seemed to expect him to come running whenever she called. She was right to expect it, as he always did.

"Sorry, I have to go. It's Isla."

"Another nightmare?"

"Maybe."

He'd just had a conversation about the girl, which convinced him he must leave. Not just leave a date, but leave during a conversation in which he'd been hinting at the possibility of marriage, and he didn't even know what was wrong?

Would Meghan try to summon him away when they were up in Lee-on-the-Solent? Or even prevent him from going? Come to think of it, he hadn't said one word about it since he'd agreed to the trip and he'd joked that he'd look for somewhere to open a branch of his agency up there and see if he could emulate the success of McKellar's confectionery.

"Before you go, remember I said I was going to Lee-on-the-Solent next month?"

"To stay with your friend... Nicole, isn't it?"

"Yes." That wasn't quite what she'd said, but close enough. "You are still coming with me?"

"Um... sorry, what day?"

"From the twelfth of May, for a week."

"Right, yes."

"You'll come?"

He nodded. "Maybe not the whole week, but yes, it would be good to… I'd like that."

"Go on then, and give my love to the girls."

Amelia felt bad over her resentment when she saw Isla next. Poor thing looked washed out and when they stopped to play with Bongo she sat on a bench and held herself in a way which reminded her of Nicole when she had period cramps.

Ava was trying to make Bongo bark again. Isla's role was to reward him with biscuits, but she just dropped them on the ground instead of holding them for him to take. She didn't giggle once, not even when he licked her hand.

"She really isn't well, is she?" Amelia whispered to Patrick.

"No. One doctor thinks it might be M.E. but if it is she'd be the youngest ever case."

"Poor thing." And she'd been cross he'd gone to her bedside the other night!

Later she wondered about the chances of Isla really having M.E. if it was so rare in children. If it wasn't that, what could it be?

Two days later Amelia and Patrick again collected the girls from school and Isla was back to normal. She greeted Amelia with the loud air kisses they still exchanged and announced a new trick for Bongo. The plan was to get him to lie on his back, furiously peddling his legs in the air, just as he sometimes did when asleep.

"How will you teach him that?"

"We'll do it and he can copy us."

Of course it didn't work, but it was fun to watch, then hilarious as she and Patrick were persuaded to join in.

Out of breath, they sat together on a bench telling knock knock jokes. Then Ava patted Bongo on the head, said, "You're it," and ran off.

She didn't get far before falling over and letting out a high-pitched wail. She lay still sobbing.

Patrick picked her up. "You've grazed your knee. Why did you do that?"

The crying stopped immediately. "Because I'm a silly billy, Daddy!"

"Yes you are."

"Oh no!" Ava pointed to where a button had been ripped off her skirt.

"I can fix that," Amelia said. "But first we need to clean that knee." She rummaged in her rainbow backpack then dabbed gently at the grazed knee with an antiseptic wet wipe which she promised would magically make the knee stop hurting.

"It worked! It is magic."

"Told you. Now, where's your button?"

All four of them looked, but couldn't find it. Fortunately Amelia's little sewing kit had a spare button in it, which she quickly sewed on.

Ava was delighted. "Can you fix anything?"

"I try."

"You're like Stuart. He's good at mending things. He mended my bike," Isla said.

"That was nice of him," Amelia said, wondering who Stuart was and if she could ask.

"Stuart is Mummy's boyfriend," Ava confided. "Is Amelia your girlfriend, Daddy?"

"She's my friend and I like her a lot."

"She is, she is!"

Of course she was his girlfriend, so why didn't he say

so?

Amelia thought she had the answer when he arrived late after she'd gone to quite a lot of trouble to make him dinner. It wasn't totally ruined, but her mood was when he apologised by saying, "We took the girls to Lanhydrock House. You were right about that, they loved it and we had a job to get them to come home."

"We?"

"Meghan and I."

"Of course. It's always Meghan, isn't it?"

"She is their mother."

In theory it was good he spent some time with his ex and the children together, so the split wasn't too painful for them, but she hadn't bargained on whole days out to places she'd suggested and had hoped to take them to. "I know that. And she's your wife. You remind me every single day."

"Meghan and I…"

"Just once, I'd like us to have a conversation that didn't involve bloody Meghan!"

"Right."

"Is that too much to ask?"

"Not at all. In fact I'm sure it's happened."

"It doesn't feel that way."

"Sorry."

Amelia tried to accept his apology and changed the subject. "I was thinking about Isla. When she's sick, it's usually after she's eaten, isn't it?"

"Yes."

"Maybe she has an allergy, or is coeliac or something?"

"Bloody hell, Amelia!" he yelled, startling her. She'd

never heard him raise his voice before. "Do you think we've not been doing all we can to find out what's wrong? We've sat up all night holding her when she cries in pain, taken her for test after test, coaxed her to take medicines which she hates."

Poor little Isla. Amelia hadn't realised things were quite so bad, but how could she if he hadn't told her?

"I hope Meghan is going to be able to manage without you when you come to Lee-on-the-Solent." She'd meant it as genuine concern, but it came out far more snarky than she'd intended.

"That's if I come."

"You don't want to now?"

"It's not that I don't want to be with you, but she needs me at the moment."

"Surely her mother can look after her for a few days?"

"It was Meghan I meant. This is so hard for her."

"If you don't want to come on a break away with me, maybe we should have a different kind of break?"

"Yes, perhaps we should."

"That's it? We're finished?"

"No, no. Not that. But I think it might be best to cool it for a while. Why don't we see how things are when you come back from visiting your friend?"

"Right, fine." She didn't bother explaining Nicole wouldn't be there. If he'd not been listening last time she told him, why would he listen now?

He didn't stay for dessert. Amelia cried into hers.

It seemed Patrick wasn't the only one who couldn't stop thinking about Meghan, because once again Amelia walked past her house without consciously intending to. Early on the Saturday she was going down to Nicole's, she gave Bongo a last walk before leaving him behind for a week.

It wasn't until she saw Patrick step out of the house and walk down the path that she realised it was Meghan's home. The early hour suggested he'd stayed the night. The way Meghan waved when he turned back to blow kisses at her suggested a whole lot more.

Chapter 11

Amelia thought she had herself pretty much under control by the time she returned Bongo to Gabrielle, but her colleague's concerned, "Are you OK?" proved she hadn't.

"Just a bit tired, and I'm really going to miss Bongo."

"OK. Well, have a good week away... and Amelia? I'm here if you want someone to talk to."

"Thanks, Gabrielle. I appreciate that. I'm OK really. Nothing a quiet week away with no shocks and no responsibilities won't put right."

"We all need something like that now and again."

Wondering what it was Gabrielle could be needing a break from helped distract Amelia from her unhappiness, but not for long. Her tears would have meant she missed the package waiting for her in the lobby, had her concerned elderly neighbour not pointed it out.

"I think it might be books," Muriel said.

Under normal circumstances Amelia would have made deductions about the fact her neighbour had nothing better to do than study other people's deliveries and then loiter in the lobby until they were collected. That time she barely registered the lady's existence. Usually her mind would have been trying to guess what was in the parcel, but it had switched off at the sight of Patrick's handwriting.

'Thought you might like these' was written on the back of one of his business cards. Nothing else, not even a signature, but then there wasn't room.

"You OK, dear?"

"Hay fever."

Amelia headed straight for the shower – she could do without being asked if she was OK every ten minutes of the seven hour train journey down to Nicole's. Surprisingly the hot water followed by soothing eye gel not only made her look better, but feel it too. Either that or she was in shock.

As she lathered herself with moisturising body lotion, she realised her downstairs neighbour must have hoped for a chat. Amelia knew Muriel was lonely and invited her up for a meal sometimes, and used to pop in for a cup of tea quite frequently, making the time even when she'd been so incredibly busy with work. She'd done so more regularly after Charles's training was far enough advanced he was taking on some shifts himself, but when things had really got going with Patrick, Muriel, and everyone and everything else, was almost forgotten. She must do better.

What was in that parcel? She couldn't go away for a week without knowing. Amelia rang for a taxi, then ripped open the large padded envelope. Inside were five books, second-hand just like the envelope. They were old detective books, including three she thought she'd previously read, the one of Margaret Allingham's she'd got in her backpack to read on the train and a Rex Stout she'd never seen. Those last two were perfect for different reasons. She shoved both in her backpack, picked up her case and went downstairs and rang Muriel's bell.

"Amelia!" her neighbour said when she opened the door. "Oh, are you going away?"

"Just for a week. I was going to get the bus to the station, but decided I didn't want to lug my case on and off, so rang for a taxi. Is it OK to wait for it here? We'd see the driver from the window, so I could go right out, saving him ringing the buzzer and waiting for me to come down."

"Of course. You don't want the meter running any longer than you need."

"Thanks."

"The kettle's just boiled," Muriel added hopefully.

Amelia glanced at her watch. "Go on then, but put plenty of milk in mine."

The neighbour made Amelia's tea, then refilled the kettle to make her own.

"You were right about my package, it was books."

"From your young man?"

"Um… yes."

"Sorry, dear. I didn't mean to be nosey. I just like to work things out. Trying to keep my mind active you know?"

"Do you like detective stories?"

"Oh, I do, yes."

"Have you read this one?" Amelia produced the Albert Campion book she'd bought to read on the train.

"No, I don't think I have."

"That's good as I've got two. I'll leave this with you and we can discuss it when I get back."

"Oh, yes. I would like that. Thank you."

Amelia had relieved the lady's curiosity about where she was going and drunk her tea by the time the taxi arrived.

The books gave Amelia something to think about on the journey. When had Patrick bought them? If he'd ordered them before they argued then perhaps they didn't mean anything. He wasn't a vindictive man so if he'd bought them for her he'd still have let her have them. A parting gift perhaps. "Oh what do I know?" She'd thought he wouldn't cheat and been proved wrong. For all she knew he'd bought the books to make her feel bad about their argument. She didn't believe that, but then neither could she quite believe what she'd seen him doing.

"Get a grip, Watson, and think." The envelope they'd been left in had been addressed to his office. It seemed more likely he'd picked that as something suitable to carry them in than it being how they'd arrived. If he'd had them posted, wouldn't he have sent them directly to her?

Studying the books for clues, she saw £1 and a date pencilled into the front. They were from a charity shop then – a good place to find such books. He hadn't mentioned them to her, despite them discussing favourite books and films the day before they argued. "So, he got them recently." What did that prove? That he still thought about her in the kind of way which prompted him to spend a few pounds on something he thought she'd enjoy. "But what does *that* mean?" Maybe the man was just really keen to stay friendly with his exes. Really, really, friendly in Meghan's case.

Amelia knew she had a tendency to let her imagination run away with her, but surely there was only one interpretation to what she'd seen? Patrick, who was supposed to be her boyfriend, even if they were having a sort of break, had been blowing kisses to Meghan, who was supposed to be his ex-wife. Patrick hadn't completed divorce proceedings. And he'd taken Meghan, not Amelia, out twice in the last few days. And although he'd initially promised to spend the whole week with

Amelia in Lee-on-the-Solent, he'd changed that to, 'a couple of days, if I can' and then to not going at all. The kisses were definitely the worst part though. That wasn't helped by her memory of him at Pendennis castle, blowing kisses up to Ava and the little girl saying it meant love.

Amelia rang Nicole and explained the whole story. "I don't think I'm being overly dramatic in thinking not everything is absolutely perfect with our relationship,"

"Sorry, sweetie, but neither do I. Shall I cancel my trip?"

"No! There's totally no need for that. I promised I'd run your place for you and I will."

"You're really sure?"

"Honestly I'm OK, although I was hoping you'd say I've got it wrong somehow and he really loves me and we'll live happily ever after."

"That's possible I suppose, but I think it's him who needs to say so, if that's the case."

"Yeah, you're right. Should I call him?"

"And say what?"

"I don't know. Thank him for the books?"

"You could do that, but…"

"But that's not the issue and I can't just talk about that and pretend I didn't see what I saw. I don't want him to lie to me, or tell me he's back with Meghan, and I'm not sure I'd believe him if he said it didn't mean anything. Maybe we should do what I said and have a complete break. Give us both a chance to think about what we really want."

"I hope I'm not being selfish in thinking that's a good idea."

"Of course you're not. You deserve that holiday, and

when I first said I'd take over for you while you were away I expected to come on my own, so it's no problem that's what I'll be doing. I'd better go, I need to change trains any second."

"You're absolutely sure that…"

"Hanging up now!" Amelia ended the call, mostly to stop Nicole talking herself out of the trip she'd been looking forward to.

It wasn't as though Amelia hadn't broken up with boyfriends before. She'd learned, through painful experience, that if things weren't working in a relationship then it was better to end it than struggle on until both parties were miserable. It was a good thing she'd realised now that Patrick wasn't the man for her, before she fell in love with him. If that had happened splitting up would have broken her heart. It wasn't breaking, that feeling of loss was just a bit of disappointment, mixed with annoyance at being strung along by a man who didn't know what he wanted. And as she'd told her neighbour, her eyes were streaming because of hay fever. She couldn't have handled being a stepmother and didn't want to try, besides the girls would be much better off if their parents got back together. She'd just keep telling herself all that until she believed it.

How could she have been so wrong about Patrick? She'd known there were many potential obstacles to their relationship, but his cheating on her seemed so out of character. If anyone, even Nicole, had told her they'd seen it coming she wouldn't have believed them. She had to believe her own eyes though.

There were three changes on Amelia's journey from her

home town of Falmouth to Fareham – the nearest station to Nicole's B&B in Lee-on-the-Solent.

"Did you know we're the largest town in the country without a train station?" Nicole had said, when Amelia decided against driving up.

"I didn't even know Lee-on-the-Solent was a town."

"Actually it is, but I meant Gosport. That's just a couple of miles down the road."

"Okaaaaay."

"Sorry. I've got used to throwing stuff like that into conversations. My guests like interesting facts about the area."

"Ours too. And directions. They're always asking me for directions."

"Oh dear."

Remembering that made Amelia smile. It would be so good to see Nicole, even though they wouldn't have long together. And it would be good for her to have a break away from work and other stresses. Deciding not to drive up and spend the whole journey worrying she'd get lost on the way had been such a sensible idea. She'd explore the area on foot and via local transport, like a proper tourist.

It took a few attempts, but Amelia did eventually manage to concentrate on her book enough not to keep thinking about Patrick, and not so well she missed any changes.

Nicole met her at Fareham station. Once they'd hugged Nicole said, "I can't believe that rainbow bag is still going."

"It's because you gave it to me as a sign of our friendship which will never end."

"I gave it to you because the one you had before gave

me the creeps."

"Which one was that?"

"With animals on."

"That was nice."

"It was not. The different bits weren't matched up properly, so some animals were cut in half, or had an elephant's head on a tiger."

"It was just a pattern."

"The rainbows are better."

"True."

When Nicole had put Amelia's case in the boot she said, "Maybe you were mistaken about Patrick?"

"Ha! Bit late, but nice try."

"No, listen I've been thinking. Maybe it wasn't him. Didn't you say he has brothers?"

"He does. They're in Ireland, don't look all that much like him, and aren't sleeping with Meghan."

"Right. So it was him, but it might not have meant anything. Maybe it was just habit or something?"

"No, it's over between us and that's for the best. I'll have a nice uneventful week here, then get on with my life without any unsuitable men. Now, tell me more about your place. I can't believe you've been there nearly two years and I've never seen it since the day you put the offer in. I'm a terrible friend."

They'd agreed to never mention the fact Amelia had talked her parents into helping Nicole buy Wight View. They'd taken out wedding insurance and, when that paid out, they'd offered it to Amelia for a holiday or anything else which would cheer her up. Nothing which could be bought would have done that, so she asked them to wait until it could be put to good use. They'd invested it and she knew Mum and Dad had added more still, but that was something else never discussed.

"Terrible? No, you're way worse than that. But you're about to make it up to me. I've got nine guest rooms, six of which are currently occupied and although some people are leaving, two more couples are due to arrive."

Amelia, used to over ten times the number of rooms, was unfazed. "What should I do if anyone else wants to book?"

"Up to you. Accept if you can manage, but I don't want to put pressure on you. I really appreciate you helping me out like this, especially as you're not getting the holiday with Patrick you were hoping for."

"It's no pressure. I think I'd like to be busy, as long as I have some time free to look at your local castles." Portchester was the one she was most keen to see, but there were others fairly near.

"That shouldn't be a problem. Obviously breakfasts are first thing in the morning. You can do any housekeeping stuff soon after and that's when people check out, so you'll have from say eleven o'clock onwards free, except for the two check ins."

"Perfect."

"If you don't want to take anyone else, just say you're fully booked. When I genuinely am, I give them contact details for other B&Bs in the area and they do the same for me. The numbers are by the phone."

"No problem. We do the same thing at the hotel, the few times we are completely full."

"Talking of phones, my mobile number is on the website, so if existing guests need anything while you're out, they'll use that. Rarely happens but I think either I should divert my calls to yours, or you can just use mine."

"You're not taking it?"

"I've got my old one for emergencies, but don't plan to use it. I want to switch off from the internet for a while."

"Fair enough. I'll use yours then – and be selective who I give the number to, so I get a proper break." And avoid the temptation to check every five minutes to see if Patrick had called with a convincing explanation for what he didn't know she'd seen.

When they arrived, Nicole took her in through the back door.

"It's easier for anyone with wheeled luggage than the steps at the front, and of course anyone with a wheelchair or pushchair uses this entrance, so I give all guests a key to both." Once in, Nicole showed Amelia to her room, gave her a quick tour to point out the improvements she'd made and then poured them both a glass of wine.

"By the way, I've discovered there's technically a castle within walking distance."

"Technically?"

"It's just a bit of a hill, apparently. No walls or anything. Motte and bailey or something? That of any interest?"

"Any kind of castle is better than none. Where is it?"

Nicole produced a map of the nearby nature reserve. "Round here somewhere," she said indicating what seemed like quite a large area.

"I'll see if I can find it, as well as seeing what I can find about the mysterious Angus McKellar. Anything new there?"

"No, but I've made a few case notes for you. I've put them in a proper file and everything."

"Brilliant."

One glance at the ornate handwriting of the title 'the case of the vanishing, reappearing and being in two places at once man' showed Nicole had created the file more as a joke than anything else.

"If you're going to go off exploring, I need to tell you about some useful navigational points." Nicole pointed to an image of a pointy landmark on a picture map. "You can look out for The Spinnaker Tower. It's in Portsmouth, on the opposite side of the harbour to Gosport, four miles down the road from here. That'll tell you if you're headed in the right direction. Right by it is The Hard interchange. From there you can get buses, trains and ferries, including one to this side of the harbour." She explained how Amelia could get back to her B&B from there. "If you forget, those exact directions are on my website."

"You don't have much faith in my ability not to get lost, do you?"

"Not much, no. The other thing you need to watch out for is a wet wobbly thing called The Solent. If you reach that you've gone far enough."

"Now you've gone too far!" She gave her very best indignant scowl.

"I'm still in the same country!"

"If you're going to start on that again, I'll need more wine."

Patrick phoned before Nicole had finished pouring.

Amelia showed the caller display, took a deep breath and answered. "Hello."

Chapter 12

"Hello, Amelia. Are you with your friend now?"

"I am." She couldn't help enjoying the sound of Patrick's voice. It was just the accent though – she didn't care much about the man.

"That's good. I just wanted to make sure you got there OK."

"I did."

Under normal circumstances Patrick would have asked her if she was in the right place, or accidentally ended up on the Isle of Wight, so his polite inquiry sounded very odd. Still, he hadn't really needed to call and if he could do polite, so could she. "How are the girls?"

Nicole pointed to the door and raised her eyebrows, offering privacy, but Amelia shook her head. It would be easier if Nicole heard the conversation, rather than repeating it afterwards.

"Isla is still poorly. Ava isn't her usual self either."

"Oh dear. I'm sorry about that. I hope they feel better soon." Weirdly it seemed a good thing that whatever it was they were suffering from affected them both. That sounded like a normal childhood bug, not a more serious condition which Patrick had clearly thought Isla must be suffering from.

"I'm sorry about… about the last time I saw you," he said.

She didn't want to talk, or think, about that, but it was a better subject than the last time she'd seen him. "Don't worry, it takes two to make an argument."

"It was my fault. I realise now you were disappointed about the trip. I was worried about Isla, but sort of in denial there was anything seriously wrong, so didn't share it with you."

If there was anything to share which wasn't in Meghan's head! But there was no doubt Isla really wasn't physically strong. Amelia could understand Patrick not wanting to think and talk about that – especially to someone as unsympathetic as she'd apparently been at times. There didn't seem any point now in explaining her resentment over Meghan's calls were really to do with jealousy that she could get him to come running whenever she asked. Amelia didn't blame little Isla for getting sick, or wanting her dad when she was.

"Amelia?"

"Still here."

"I messed everything up, didn't I? Pushing you into meeting the girls. I'm like one of those annoying dog owners who think just because their dog is friendly and they love them, then it's OK to let them jump up and slobber over everyone. They forget that some people don't share their enthusiasm."

"No, it's not like that at all. You didn't let them bound up to me when I wasn't expecting it. And they hardly slobbered at all!" Actually Avid Ava had sort of bounded up to her unexpectedly at Pendennis castle, and they both kissed her, but their attention wasn't unwelcome.

"I'm glad to hear it."

What was the point of this call? He'd made it clear with his words to her and then his actions towards Meghan that it was over between them. Was he sorry about that? It didn't matter if he was. Not if he was back with Meghan. After a pause Amelia said, "Thanks for calling. I'd better go."

"OK. I'll ring you again soon."

"OK. Oh, let me give you the number I'll be on this week." She did that. "Speak later. Bye."

After she'd hung up, Nicole gave an inquiring look.

"He just talked about his kids. Maybe. I don't really know why he called."

"Perhaps not, but as you gave him my number, you obviously don't mind if he does it again."

"Actually I don't know what to think about any of it."

"This won't help at all," Nicole said continuing the refill of their wine glasses. They sat chatting and laughing, mostly about their shared schooldays, until Nicole's expression became serious.

"Um, Amelia?"

"What?" Horrible thoughts that Nicole was ill or in trouble flashed through her mind. "Nicole, whatever it is, just say. I'm your best friend. Practically your sister."

"You are. You always will be. It's just… I do have relations on La Palma."

"The people you told me about, they really are cousins?"

"Yeah."

"That's great, and it proves me right once again."

"It does?"

"I knew this wasn't just a holiday and there was more to it."

"You don't mind?"

"Of course not. Would you mind if I discovered a cousin I'd not met and went to say hello?" Actually Amelia was a tiny bit hurt Nicole hadn't shared her investigations and might become slightly jealous about not being the closest Nicole had to family, but that was something she'd deal with on her own.

"This all feels very strange," Nicole said.

"It must do. Maybe it'll make more sense when you meet them. And whatever happens, you've still got me."

They hugged, then talked about Nicole's trip until her taxi to the airport arrived.

Amelia enjoyed cooking the guests' breakfasts and talking to them as she served their food. Washing up, cleaning the bathrooms and hoovering around the large house were less fun but, after years of doing that kind of thing in various hotels, doing it for just six rooms wasn't much work. There were no guests checking in or out that day, so she'd finished by ten and was free until breakfast the following morning.

She opened the box containing Nicole's case file. On top of the documents were samples of merchandise produced by McKellar's confectionery – and a few empty sweet wrappers proving Nicole's research had been thorough.

Amelia read through the contents. A map was marked with the locations of the McKellar home, the nearest Salterns Support charity shop, the Salterns respite centre which benefitted from it, and other places mentioned in the notes. Nicole had also highlighted the nearest bus stops and marked the appropriate route numbers.

Clipped to the back of the file was an envelope marked 'travel essentials'. Inside Amelia found a ticket entitling her to ten trips on the harbour ferry, a weekly First bus ticket for the area, a timetable booklet and a label saying, 'Please look after this geographically challenged individual. When lost, return to the Wight

View B&B Lee-on-the-Solent'.

Although she didn't know how often she'd need to cross the harbour to get wherever she wanted to go, Amelia was going to use the ferry ticket to the full. Maybe she should do a little investigation first though, as Nicole had gone to so much trouble to help her get started. She was just pondering where to start when her own phone alerted her to a text.

It was from Jorge. 'Hope you're enjoying your holiday. We had a group of 30 try to book for your murder in Sept. Thought you'd like to know.'

Brilliant! They must be close to fully booked already. With four months to go, that was very reassuring. The number suggested a coach load, which would please Jorge. He'd been making efforts to get the hotel included on the regular route for west country touring holidays. Odd that he'd contacted her while she was away though. It had been him who'd been the most insistent they not do anything work related when not actually working a shift. Perhaps Gabrielle hadn't been fooled by Amelia's claim her red eyes were due to the hay fever she'd never previously suffered from and thought she needed cheering up.

Not wanting her colleagues to worry about her, Amelia called Jorge. "Don't panic," she teased. "I know it's a big booking, and you're not used to actual work these days, but reception can deal with it."

"They could, if we had 30 places left."

"And we don't?"

"Nowhere near. I think I'm right in thinking that you can't increase the numbers?"

"You are. Any more and people won't be able to see and hear the action." They were already relying on the layout and excellent acoustics of the Pendennis room to help all guests get a decent view and good chance of hearing everything. To do that in the main dining room they'd need microphones and TV screens, which would totally spoil the atmosphere. "There's the disco on Saturday though. We did think that could be opened up to outsiders."

"OK, I'll let them know. I kept their details and said we'd contact them as soon as the dates for the mystery weekend in November are confirmed."

"There's going to be one in November?"

"There is if you'd like to organise it?"

"I would." Her attempts to investigate a real mystery had never really got started, but she could make things happen with a fictional one. "The same as last time – first weekend in November?"

"Ideally, yes."

"I'll call Sonia and see if she can do that."

"Thank you. Sorry to interrupt your holiday, but you've got the contacts and I thought you'd like to handle it all yourself."

"You're right. Besides, I'm going to keep a note of the time I spend on this and claim it back." He didn't need to know she no longer had much reason to need time off work.

"Fair enough."

Amelia called Sonia immediately, and explained the situation.

"That's excellent. Of course I'd like to do another one with you. To be honest, I was hoping this might happen and kept the date free."

"Crikey! You have a lot of faith in my ability to sell tickets."

"I do of course, but don't worry, I haven't turned down jobs, just suggested alternative dates."

"I'm glad you did. I'm actually away at the moment, so can we just confirm this all verbally and I'll sort out the paperwork when I get back to Falmouth next week?"

"That's fine. There are a couple of things I want to talk to you about for the September one, but that can wait. I guess I'll have to wait until then to hear how things are going with that man of yours too?"

"You will, yes," Amelia said.

She quickly gave Jorge the good news and then got back to the Angus McKellar case file to stop herself thinking about the fact her relationship with Patrick wasn't going, it had gone.

There was no branch of McKellar's confectionery in Lee-on-the-Solent, but Amelia had no trouble finding the Salterns Support charity shop. Once there she realised how difficult it would be to make casual enquiries about Mr McKellar. She contented herself with buying another book and explaining to the assistant that she was staying in the area for a week. Who knew, building up some kind of relationship with her might be useful later.

The lady was happy to talk and Amelia learned a lot – which was the best chippy, that if Amelia wanted to do any shopping she'd need to go to Portsmouth and that the lady supposed 'there is a lot of history stuff round here if you like that sort of thing'.

The early May weather was lovely, and from what Amelia could make out from her various maps the bus to Portchester castle took her past Angus McKellar's home, so she decided to go there. On the journey she called her parents.

"Hello, Nicole," her Mum answered. "How are you?"

"It's me, Mum. Just wanted to let you know I'm going to be using Nicole's phone while I'm here."

"Oh, I see. How is she?"

"She's fine, Mum. Just like me."

"I'm glad to hear it. Do give her our best, won't you?"

"Yes…" Her mum had rung off.

Thanks to slow moving traffic, Amelia was able to identify with reasonable certainty which of the large houses belonged to Angus McKellar. There was an expensive looking car outside. Not the one which was mentioned in the news report of his disappearance, but that could have been in the double garage. No people were visible.

The castle was great, but Amelia would have enjoyed it more if she'd been seeing it with Patrick, Isla and Ava. She bought postcards to send to the girls and then wondered if she should do that – and to which address. "Oh why shouldn't I?" They were lovely kids and she hadn't fallen out with them, even if it did seem likely their parents were on the way to a reconciliation. For Isla she described the wildflowers she'd seen, beady eyed black capped gulls, smart black and white birds she'd been informed were oyster catchers and busy little brown things pecking at the seaweed. On Ava's card she wrote that the castle had been there since Roman times and about the beautiful heiress who'd once owned it and married the handsome Sheriff of Hampshire. Of course Amelia had no idea what that pair had really looked like, but the ease with which she was able to write to the girls made her realise she knew them quite well.

On the return journey, she was on the right side of the road to get a clear view of the McKellars' home and again the slow traffic helped. Amelia counted nine windows, including four bays, two chimney stacks and two stone animals which were probably lions guarding the steps to the front door. There were no cars on show, no people, and nothing to mark it out from the other houses on that road. They all looked like perfectly normal homes, if your normality involved owning a yacht and at least two expensive cars.

Amelia felt unsettled that evening. She almost called Patrick. There were several things she could claim were reasons for doing so, but they wouldn't tell her what she needed to know. She could demand to know the truth about Meghan, but preferred to indulge in the fantasy that she was somehow mistaken over what she saw.

Rather than sit and brood, Amelia decided to search for the motte and bailey castle Nicole had mentioned. Finding the Alver Valley nature reserve was easy. From the entrance a well-worn path took her up a hill, where she had great views of The Solent, Isle of Wight, Portsmouth, and Southampton. She easily recognised The Spinnaker Tower. Everything looked so close – probably deceptively so. She doubted she'd be able to manage a trip to the island. A shame as she'd have loved to look round Queen Victoria's holiday home, Osborne House. Still she should be able to get to Portsmouth and Southampton OK. That gave her a chance of visiting Southsea and Calshot castles, which she'd read were similar in design, age and purpose as her 'home' castles of Pendennis and St Mawes. She'd have to look up how far they were from the city centres before she made up her mind to see them, or she might find that without a car it would be impossible and then she'd be disappointed.

Being realistic was one of Amelia's strong points, recently. After getting dumped by her fiancé she no longer got her hopes up about anything unless she was certain she wouldn't be disappointed. Maybe she was carrying it too far? Had that been the problem with her and Patrick? She knew relationships could end, hers had with James and Patrick's had with Meghan. Maybe.

Had she let thoughts of what might go wrong stop her risking being happy? Perhaps. In fact she'd probably been looking for signs that things wouldn't work out. When Patrick said he couldn't come away with her and she'd seen him blowing kisses to Meghan she'd almost welcomed the proof she was right and no longer had to wait for things to go wrong.

Amelia hadn't paid attention to where she was going in the woods and totally lost track of her bearings. Nicole had mentioned there was a lake near a children's adventure playground at one end of the nature reserve and had drawn a quick sketch map, showing how to get back to the B&B from there. Once Amelia got to the lake she just needed to return to the road, walk along Cherque Way, then turn right at the junction, and walk along the seafront road back to Wight View. She could see water ahead of her. "This is going to be easy!"

She crossed the bridge. Nicole hadn't mentioned one, but maybe it had seemed obvious. Amelia continued on, and after a few wrong turns reached a children's play area. It wasn't what she'd have called an adventure park, but Nicole did have a tendency to talk up the local amenities. She hadn't done that about the motte and bailey castle, and rightly so. The best thing about it was Amelia's satisfaction in having located it. There was nothing to see but a small mound, a bit too regular in shape to be natural, but so covered with trees she wouldn't have noticed it, had she not set out to look for it, walked straight by, got to the road, retraced her steps and seen what she deduced was the remains of a rotting sign. After a quick look she returned to the play area.

From there The Spinnaker Tower wasn't visible, but she could see a road. She'd walked along it for quite a while before realising it wasn't Cherque Way. She successfully retraced her steps, to where she'd first got lost, and set off in the opposite direction. By then it was getting dark and she hadn't seen anyone for quite some time. Just when she was wondering if she'd ever find her way out of the woods she saw lights and heard voices, and eagerly rushed towards them.

She was quite close before she realised the men were arguing – something to do with money and paperwork. It seemed an odd time and place for a business meeting. Amelia had the impression they wouldn't welcome an interruption. At least some of the lights were coming from a car's headlights. She must be near a road. She could walk along it until she recognised where she was, or saw someone less angry to ask for directions. Amelia tried to pick her way through the undergrowth to walk unseen behind the vehicles.

"Don't be ridiculous, you'll never get away with it," a man with a Scottish accent said. There was such desperation in the voice that Amelia spun round. Now, at a different angle, she wasn't so dazzled by the lights and could see the scene more clearly. One man had the arm of another twisted up behind his back as though he was arresting him.

A third man walked up close to the other two. Was he going to read the culprit his rights? Or maybe he'd done that already.

The third one held something up. Evidence perhaps? It wasn't a notebook to take down a statement, Amelia was fairly sure of that. Did the police still do that? She had an idea it was all on tape and computer now, but of course that would be difficult in a wood. Something like a smart phone might do it. What the man held was too long and thin for that. As he moved, it glinted in the headlights. It looked just as though he was holding a knife. A really big knife.

He thrust it into the man who was being held. Amelia screamed. Her throat was so tight and breath so short only a thin sound escaped, but it was enough for the men to hear. The one who'd been stabbed looked in her direction, then slipped down through the arms of the man who'd been holding him. The third discarded his knife and ran towards Amelia.

She was close to the path and he had to fight his way through brambles, so she thought she had a chance to get ahead. He'd soon catch her on the path. Her best chance was to try to hide. She set off across grassland towards the trees – and tripped.

The man grabbed hold of her arm and hauled her back, just before she went sprawling.

She tried to kick at him, but he pulled her close and hissed, "Stop right there."

Chapter 13

"Let go of me!" Amelia yelled. Probably the only person she'd alert to her plight would be his accomplice, but she had to try something.

He put his arm over her mouth. If it had been his hand she'd have tried to bite him, but she wasn't going to make much impression on the sleeve of his heavy waxed coat.

"I will let you go, but first you have to promise me you'll be careful. Running along here in the dark you could easily hurt yourself and it's going to be a cold night."

Those didn't sound like the words of a killer. She nodded and he let go. As Amelia tried to step away from him she realised her feet were entangled in a patch of brambles. If he'd not grabbed her she'd have gone flying face down into it.

"Now, what was all that yelling and running off about?" her attacker-come-rescuer asked in a teasing tone. "Sounded as though you thought you'd seen a murder." He laughed.

"It's not funny."

"You're right. Sorry. And of course that's what you thought you saw. We're filming." He shone a torch on his face. "Recognise me now?"

"No." Actually he did look familiar, but she couldn't place him.

Clearly he'd expected her to know who he was and wasn't happy to be disappointed. "Are you not from around here?"

"No. Falmouth."

"Falmouth? In Cornwall?"

He made it sound as though having beamed down from Jupiter would have been more likely. "Yes. They do let us leave you know."

"Yes, of course. Sorry, it's just that… It's a long way. That explains you not recognising me."

"Who are you?"

"Sean Underhill."

The friend of Angus McKellar who'd reported his disappearance on TV!

Sean explained he was a news anchor and often on local TV in various capacities. By keeping quiet about having heard of him, Amelia had the satisfaction of knowing he was exaggerating his position on the local news, and that she wasn't pandering to his ego.

"Actually I'm an actor, although I'm not so well known for that," Sean added.

Not known for it at all then. "I didn't see any camera crew."

"We're shooting a demo. Come back and see, that should reassure you."

Amelia didn't want to go anywhere with him, but he'd taken hold of her arm and she wasn't sure she had much choice. If he really was a killer he wouldn't let her get away just because she said, 'no thanks'. And if he really had been acting then he was right, seeing that for herself would be reassuring. The scene she'd witnessed had been so dramatically lit, and had scared her so thoroughly that she'd probably have nightmares about it, even if she wasn't left wondering if it was real.

As they walked back, Amelia was surprised at how far she'd run before Sean caught up with her.

"It's OK, I've got her!" Sean called out as he pushed

his way back through the undergrowth. "Poor girl thought she was witnessing a real murder."

Sean introduced his accomplice as Corey and the victim as Tony. Corey, who was holding the torch, gave her a cheery wave and then turned his attention back to what Amelia guessed must be the film cameras. With the vehicle's lights shining straight at her she could only see silhouettes.

The corpse too raised an arm in greeting. His body shuddered as though he were having some kind of fit, although probably it was just theatrical shivering. It must be cold lying there like that.

"What's up, Tony? I can't hear you," Sean called.

"Forgive me for not getting up, but with all the blood I've lost…"

It wasn't a great joke, but she laughed with relief. "You've done a great job, it all looked so real," she said.

"I think that's a wrap for tonight?" Sean called out. "Can I leave you to clear up here, while I make sure our audience gets home safely?"

Corey gave a thumbs up. The corpse played dead.

Amelia wasn't sure she wanted Sean to walk her home. She'd not warmed to him in person any more than she had when watching him on TV, reporting about the missing, and then found, Angus McKellar. Of course being worried about his friend might not have brought out the best in him, but Nicole had said he fancied himself before that, and he'd certainly expected her to recognise him. No doubt his good looks often made up for any lack of charm, but they failed to work their magic in the dark.

"If you could direct me to Cherque Way, I'd be very grateful."

"It'll be a lot easier to show you."

He was right. If there were paths back to the road she couldn't see them. Neither could she spot anything she recognised.

Sean apparently took it for granted Amelia would be fascinated by anything to do with acting and cameras and explained, at length and in far too much jargon filled detail, what he'd been doing when she stumbled across him. From the bits she listened to, the whole thing could have been summed up with, 'I'm marvellous. The not marvellous people with me were doing stuff to show how marvellous I am. Soon everyone will realise I'm great and I won't have to endure the horror of women screaming because they don't recognise me and how marvellous I am.'

"It's lucky you have friends with technical expertise," she said when he paused for breath. That was a mistake.

Sean talked about cameras and how they were now so clever it was possible to film in almost complete darkness and that they were so easy to operate they could even be set up by people less clever than him, so those people could also act, though not as marvellously as him.

Or maybe she was being unfair. Sean's chatter might simply be an attempt to distract her as he could see she was still shocked by what she'd thought she'd seen. He seemed the type not to realise a subject he was passionate about was of no interest to others.

"Here we go, this is Cherque Way. Where are you staying?"

She wasn't sure she wanted to give him the name of Nicole's B&B, but there weren't many other places she could be staying so he could work it out, or even follow her if he really wanted to know. Besides, if he'd wanted to do her any harm, he'd had plenty of opportunities whilst she was lost in the wood. Guiding her safely to a well-lit and quite busy road was surely proof of his good intentions.

"Wight View. It's on Marine Parade East, between Queens Road and Ryde Place." She was pleased with the confident way she said that – just as though she actually had some idea where she was going.

"This way then. You said you're not local?"

"No, I live in Falmouth," she reminded him.

"What are you doing up here?" Sean asked.

"I'm on holiday."

"Staying with family, or…?"

Although it was natural of him to ask, Amelia was reluctant to tell him much about herself or Nicole. Perhaps that too was natural – she had just seen him kill someone, even if it was all an act. But was that any reason to imitate her mother's conversational style?

"I like castles. We have St Mawes and Pendennis near me, so I thought it would be interesting to see Calshot and Southsea."

"Henry VIII fan are you?"

"Sort of." She couldn't explain she wasn't really that interested in the history, just liked a good story and looking round interesting places, especially if they had a spiral staircase leading to a great view. At least, she couldn't explain that without it seeming odd that she'd travelled hundreds of miles to do it.

What she could do was take advantage of his local knowledge. "Can I get to them on the bus? I don't mind walking some of the way."

"For Southsea your best bet would be to get the bus to

Gosport and catch the ferry over to Portsmouth. The Hard is just the other side and you could get a bus from there, I expect, or even walk if you're feeling energetic. It can't be more than two miles."

Him mentioning travel details Nicole had talked about, and the thought of walking round a castle in daylight were both very reassuring. "Is it easy to find?"

"Yes, just go along the seafront."

"Great. And Calshot? I guess I'd need to go into Southampton?"

"That part is easy enough, but it's at least as far out the other side. You have to go past the edge of the New Forest. I think you'd need a car to get there. How long are you going to be around? I could take you."

"Oh no, I couldn't ask you to do that!"

"You're not asking, I am."

Did he mean he was asking her out? It did sound that way, but Amelia didn't want to sound as though she'd made that assumption and reject an advance which hadn't been made.

"That's kind of you. It would be good for me to have someone local to help me find my way round. Patrick often teases me about getting lost."

"Patrick is?"

"My boyfriend."

It seemed her doubts had shown. "You don't sound sure. Where is he?"

"Back in Falmouth. Something happened just before I came up here."

"A row?"

"Not exactly." She wasn't going to explain. "Look, the thing is, I'm not looking for a holiday romance or anything like that."

"No problem. I'm still happy to take you. After scaring you like that I'd like to prove I'm a nice guy and I'd quite like to see the castle myself. I haven't been since I was a kid. I get to see a lot of interesting places and events through work, but we tend not to appreciate what's right on our doorsteps."

"Maybe that's true if you've always lived in the same place, but I've moved several times and I've always been interested in history."

"Any particular period?"

"Tudor and Victorian. Quite a mix I know. I've read lots of books by Philippa Gregory and CJ Sansom, people like that, and got hooked, and Queen Victoria is absolutely fascinating." She just stopped herself mentioning Osborne House and her disappointment at not going there. She didn't want Sean to think she was fishing for an offer to be taken to the island.

"We've got lots of interesting places round here. I'm doing something at QA hospital tomorrow. If you like, I could pick you up about eleven and drop you off at the Royal Armouries while I'm doing that. The fort is Victorian so I'm sure you'd find it interesting."

Amelia was tempted. Her adrenaline levels had returned to normal, and it had occurred to her his local knowledge would be even more useful for finding out information on Angus McKellar than it would for directions.

"Say yes," he coaxed.

"That would be great if it's really not putting you to any trouble."

"Absolutely not."

When they reached the B&B Sean gave her his business card with his phone number on. "See you tomorrow then."

"Yes. Thanks – and for getting me safely back."

"Least I could do."

Amelia went in and made herself a milky drink. She was glad there were other people staying in the B&B. Seeing the murder scene had definitely unsettled her. That, added to the way she and Nicole had talked themselves into thinking there was something odd in Sean's reporting of Angus McKellar, had coloured her impression of him.

Of course he was who he said he was, and doing what he said he'd been doing. Why else would he have had cameras and a business card? He'd been very kind to her. Even if stopping her running away terrified her at the time, she was glad he had.

Amelia laughed almost hysterically at the image of her dialling 999 and calling police to the scene of a film shoot. Then to give herself something pleasant to look forward to, she Googled the Royal Armouries. It looked pretty good, and it was free.

Amelia saw Sean again much earlier than she'd expected the following morning. One of the guests asked if she'd put on the TV so they could see the local weather forecast. Sean's good looking face filled the screen as soon as she did. He gave the local news, handed over to the weather presenter and then finished off by saying to switch back on that evening as he was presenting a special report from Queen Alexandra hospital.

Despite a slight suggestion that it was him and not the subject of the report which would entice viewers, he came across as charming and friendly, just as he'd been the night before, once she'd stopped trying to get away from him. Amelia felt much better about the day's planned excursion after that. She would make a real effort not to be so suspicious of people in general, and handsome men offering to take her to historic buildings in particular.

She quickly washed up, wiped round the bathrooms, and got a vacated room ready in case anyone should want it. Whilst she showered and changed, Amelia thought about the murder mystery weekends planned for The Fal View. The last one hadn't been scary at all. She'd been slightly upset to see the corpse, but that was because it was Patrick lying still on the bed. She'd not have been at all bothered if an unknown actor had taken the role.

Of course she didn't want to terrify guests, but a brief thrill of something close to fear might add to the experience. It was partly the darkness and dramatic shadows which had made Amelia so frightened. Maybe Sonia could write in a brief power cut?

Sean arrived on time and greeted her pleasantly.

"I do hope you've got over the shock of seeing us filming last night?"

"Totally."

"As I knew what we were doing, and know I'm a nice guy I knew you had no reason to be scared. It wasn't until I left you I realised how awful it must have been for you. You really thought I'd stabbed Tony, didn't you?"

"It did look very realistic."

"You must have been so relieved to hear him speak."

"I expect I gave you a fright when I screamed?"

He grinned. "I'll say! I dropped the knife on Tony's foot. Good job it wasn't a real one, or he'd have been missing some toes!"

"Ooops. Sorry."

"Don't be, it was a completely natural reaction. It was caught on the recording and we were thinking of leaving it in. Would you mind if we did?"

"Um, no, I suppose not."

"We could credit you. Additional dialogue by… ?"

"Oh, that'd be cool. I'm Amelia Watson."

"Don't get too excited. Like I said, it's just a demo and not very likely to be seen publicly."

"Yeah, but I've got a bit of a thing about crime. Fictitious crime, I mean. I love mystery books and crime dramas and things and it will be nice to think my name is associated with one."

"In that case I'll definitely add you to the credits. If we edit out your scream I can put 'with special thanks to' because, awful as it was for you, your reaction showed how convincing the scene was and that's helped our confidence."

Amelia doubted Sean ever had any problem with confidence. As he was driving her somewhere she wanted to see, and would otherwise have had difficulty reaching, she kept that thought to herself.

"I guess I'll be about two hours filming my report, but you can never tell exactly how long these things will take. If you give me your number, I'll call when we're done."

She gave him Nicole's.

Amelia looked around the outside of the fort, enjoying views of Portsmouth, Gosport and across to the Isle of Wight. The main exhibition inside was of hundreds of weapons, from small handguns to huge canon. She wasn't bothered if Sean was ready to go before she'd seen all those. The parts she was most interested in were the kitchen and hospital for the Victorian garrison, and the tunnels which had allowed soldiers to move around the fort in safety. She enjoyed those, though couldn't help imagining the games Ava and Isla might play in the tunnels and silly messages they'd send using the signalling flags available for that purpose. Amelia refused to think of their father.

The guns were more interesting than she'd expected. Some of the really old ones were very ornate and a couple were almost cute – if you didn't realise their true purpose, that was.

When Sean called to ask how she was getting on, she replied, "I've seen the bits I was most interested in." Hopefully that showed she was ready to leave if he'd finished, but didn't mind waiting if he wasn't.

"In that case, how about meeting me in the café? It's lunchtime and I managed to avoid hospital food."

"OK, see you there." Amelia intended to buy the meal to thank him for the lift, to politely ask if the report went well, and promise to watch it on TV.

It didn't take her long to rummage in her backpack and find her purse. Certainly not long enough for Sean to reach for his wallet, but he was busy telling her in great detail what a good job he'd done of his report. After that she didn't feel the need to watch it, or even say she would. Clearly he took it for granted she wouldn't have had enough of him in person and would eagerly grasp every opportunity for another glimpse.

"Have you really seen enough here? I don't want to rush you."

"Yes. Thank you." Why did he have to be so nice, just as she was enjoying thinking bitchy thoughts?

"Shall I take you back to the Wight View?"

"If you're going that way, otherwise drop me off somewhere I can catch a bus from. I quite like exploring as long as I don't get lost."

"Or stumble across a murder scene?"

"I didn't like to mention that!"

"I'm going into Portsmouth next. I could drop you near Southsea castle if you like? I won't be able to take you home afterwards, but it really won't be difficult for you to find your way to The Hard where you can get the ferry over to Gosport."

"Please don't say 'you can't miss it'. My brain seems to take that as a challenge."

"I expect you could miss it if you really tried, but I'm sure you'll be OK. From outside the castle, just head for The Spinnaker Tower and then get a ferry from The Hard. There is potential to get lost there, so be sure you get on a small green one. If it's red, white and blue you'll be heading for the Isle of Wight."

"Or France?"

"You'd have to get really lost to reach the international port."

That didn't reassure her very much, but remembering her instructions from Nicole for getting back to the B&B from The Hard did.

On the drive she tried to think of ways to ask about Angus McKellar, but soon realised it was hopeless. As she'd pretended not to know who Sean was, it would seem very odd to admit to having heard of his friend's temporary disappearance. And in any case, he'd given several reports and interviews at the time. If there was anything he wanted made public he'd had plenty of opportunity to do so, and if he wanted anything kept quiet he wasn't going to tell her.

She contented herself with asking Sean about himself. As anticipated, he was very chatty with regards to his favourite subject. When he mentioned anything, such as his running, which could possibly link to Mr McKellar she asked questions. That allowed him to remind her how marvellous he was, but didn't reveal any further clues.

Sean took her right to Southsea castle. "I'm sorry I can't pick you up again."

"No problem. I'm sure you're very busy."

"Always! I'm on air every day and most evenings for the rest of the week."

"Oh, right. Well thanks for the lift." Charming! She'd spent ages stoking his ego and he'd responded by making it extremely clear he had zero interest in seeing her again. Which suited her perfectly, but wasn't exactly flattering.

Amelia's castle knowledge was sufficient to show her that Southsea castle was built at the same period and for the same purposes as Pendennis and St Mawes. Compared with those, there was little to see inside, but it was perfect for looking over to the Isle of Wight, Portsmouth and towards Lee-on-the-Solent. Of course it being somewhere to keep watch from had been one of its intended purposes. Sadly for King Henry, it had given a perfect view of the Mary Rose sinking. That ship was on display in the historic dockyard, along with HMS Victory and other exhibits, according to the leaflets Nicole had left, but that might be too much history for one day.

The Spinnaker Tower, which was clearly visible from the top of the castle, was far more modern. Sean was right, it would be quite difficult for her to miss that!

Below it, according to Nicole, was an area called Gunwharf Quay. As that was a shopping centre with lots of restaurants, and on the way back to the B&B, Amelia headed there.

Although exactly as described, Gunwharf Quay had little to catch her interest. Perhaps that was just because she was amidst crowds of families and couples. Eating alone in a restaurant didn't appeal, and where was the fun in clothes shopping without a date to be buying for or a friend to laugh with?

She still had the postcards she'd written for Ava and Isla in her bag and still hadn't decided what to do about them. She did the obvious thing and rang Patrick.

He asked if she was having fun, just as though there'd never been even a hint of awkwardness between them. He wouldn't know she'd seen him blowing kisses to Meghan, but it seemed he'd forgotten they'd split up.

"I just rang to ask if it's OK to send postcards to the girls." As she spoke, something tugged at her memory.

"Of course it is. They'd love that."

Of course? Was he not even a little surprised his ex-girlfriend wanted to stay in contact with the children of his no longer ex-wife? "I don't want to cause any trouble or upset Meghan."

"You wouldn't be doing that."

"Should I send them to your address?"

"No, it won't be the same as getting them in the post." He gave her the address, unaware she already knew it.

What did that mean? It proved he wasn't keeping the existence of Amelia secret from Meghan, but was that because the marriage was over, or because Amelia didn't mean anything to him? It was a good thing she'd already written the cards, or she'd be tempted to include a message which wasn't primarily aimed at the girls.

"Amelia, you there?"

"Yeah. I'll send the cards today. Bye."

The abrupt way she ended the call reminded Amelia of her mother. That in turn made her understand the flash of memory at the start of the call. She'd used the phrase 'I just called to' in order to show she'd phoned Patrick for that purpose and nothing else. But it was also what she said so often when ringing her mother. Perhaps that was why Mum kept conversations to a minimum.

As an experiment she phoned her parents and was careful with her phrasing. When she said she'd been visiting local places of interest, Mum asked questions about where she'd been, the weather and Nicole's B&B. Prompted by Amelia she then talked about walks she and Dad had been on, and a dinner party they'd attended with people Amelia vaguely recalled.

"They were pleased to hear how well your career is going," Mum surprised her by saying.

It wasn't their interest which was the surprising thing, that was almost certainly just politeness. It was strange to think of Mum boasting of her success, when if anything she'd have expected a mention of the missed promotion. Other than at Christmas, it was the longest and most positive conversation she could recall them sharing. Except for Mum's birthday. And now she thought about it, lots of others in her childhood.

Back in Lee-on-the-Solent, Amelia bought fish and chips from the place the lady in the charity shop had suggested. They were as delicious as she'd promised. After eating, Amelia decided to amuse herself by making another attempt to uncover something about Angus McKellar.

Making good use of her bus pass, she took trips past his home that evening. There was no sign of him or his car.

The following day, Tuesday, Amelia took the bus first to McKellar's confectionery head office and then to the respite centre Angus supported. She couldn't go in, so all she did was establish his car wasn't parked at either of those places. There weren't any cars at his home when she passed, so she got off the bus by some shops near Portchester. She'd intended to just grab a coffee and snack, but seeing two conservatively dressed people next to a leaflet stand gave her an idea. It took her a while to get away from the Jehovah's Witnesses, but she did so with a small collection of literature.

There were still no cars outside the McKellar home when Amelia rang the bell. The instant she heard the chimes sound she wondered what she'd say should whoever answered the door invite her in for a chat, or be a Witness themselves. She wasn't sure it was a good thing nobody was home, as it encouraged her to walk around the side of the house. When she saw the back was almost entirely composed of picture windows and a conservatory she knew it was good the owners were out, or she'd almost certainly have been seen. If she ever did anything similar, she'd make sure she had one of Bongo's leads in her bag and pretend to be looking for him. She'd learned nothing, but achieved her primary purpose of amusing herself playing detective.

Her biggest discovery came as she returned to the Wight View B&B with a take away pizza that night. A familiar figure left a house just a few doors away from Nicole's. Surely he couldn't really be here?

Chapter 14

The man was fair haired and wearing brightly coloured stretch leggings and hooded top. He stopped and gave a self conscious wave to whoever he'd just left. Could she have stumbled across Angus McKellar by accident, and solved the mystery of his short disappearance, after a day of looking for him? Amelia walked slowly, so she could get a good look at the person being waved to, in the hope she could deduce the likelihood of them being involved in an affair.

The person in the doorway, who was turned slightly away from Amelia, was a man, which did nothing to discredit her theory. In fact if Angus was gay, and determined to keep that a secret, his apparently strange behaviour made more sense.

As Amelia passed where the man was still waving outside the house she glanced back. The other man was holding a little dog and moving its front paw so it waved back. It was the dog the Angus McKellar lookalike was waving to. The pizza slid from Amelia's grasp and her knees momentarily stopped supporting her as she realised the implication. Patrick hadn't blown kisses to Meghan, but to the daughter, or daughters, with her.

"You OK there?" the man in the tracksuit asked her. He was older than she'd first thought and had no trace of a Scottish accent.

"Wonderful, thank you."

"You sure?"

"Really, really sure."

He, and the man with the dog who'd come to join

them, took a little persuading she was OK. When she told them where she was going they seemed relieved, and insisted on walking her the short distance to the B&B. As she climbed the two steps and let herself in, Amelia reflected that she was making a habit of being walked home by men who had zero interest in her.

The pizza, despite landing upside down, was still pretty much intact, but a ruined meal wouldn't have upset her right then. "Patrick wasn't blowing kisses to Meghan!" Amelia had absolutely no doubt about that. He blew kisses to his girls sometimes, but never did it to Amelia. It was just something between him and his daughters. If he'd kissed Meghan goodbye, it would have been on her cheek, or even a proper kiss. Of course he might have done that when Amelia hadn't seen, but she didn't think so. No, she was certain of it. Getting involved with a man who had children and wasn't yet officially divorced wasn't straightforward, but the man himself was… wasn't he?

Her jubilation subsided a little as she ate and considered what to say to Patrick. She felt she should apologise for doubting him over the kisses she'd seen him blowing, but was there any point? He didn't know she'd had doubts and the fact he really was just good friends with his ex-wife, as he'd always claimed, did nothing to alter the fact he and Amelia had agreed to take a break from each other. The two telephone calls didn't prove anything either – except he still considered her a friend. Which was fine. Who needed a man with baggage anyway?

She was no further forward with her detection either. Angus McKellar wasn't having an affair with someone living three doors away from Nicole, but that didn't rule out the possibility of him being involved in such a relationship. Maybe he'd run off with whoever he was having an affair with, it hadn't worked out or he'd realised it was a mistake, and gone home. If that's what really happened the chances were that neither he, nor his wife, would want it made public.

Nicole's mobile rang as Amelia was cooking breakfasts on Wednesday morning. She dropped the rest of the mushrooms into the melted butter, turned down the heat and answered before a potential guest gave up and booked elsewhere. "Wight View B&B, how can I help?"

"Good news, the lady shall go to the castle."

"Pardon?"

"I said I'd take you to Calshot Castle if I could, and I can."

She should have guessed it was Sean by the way he assumed she'd have his number saved and be waiting eagerly for him to call. To be fair she had saved the number, she'd just not checked the display, and if she'd thought the offer to take her to the castle was anything more than an empty promise she might have been looking forward to his call. Or if she'd realised he'd not been blowing her off the last time they spoke.

"I don't want to put you to any trouble." Even to her that sounded like an invitation for him to assure her it was no trouble at all, which he duly did.

"I had a visit to Calshot pencilled in for today, which is why I suggested I might be able to take you. I've only just had it confirmed."

"Right. So this isn't a date or anything?"

"No. You said you'd like to go, and I have room in the car."

Oh dear. Now it sounded as though she were chasing him. "When would I need to be ready? I have a few things to do first."

"Two suit you?"

"Perfect."

"We won't be back until about seven. That OK?"

"That's fine. Why is the castle in the news?"

"It isn't. There are five cruise ships going out this evening, and Calshot is the best place to see them from."

"Five? Wow! When we get one in Falmouth it often makes the local news."

"It's not really news as it happens quite often, but lots of people like to go and watch them, the cruise industry is a big money earner locally, and there's very little real news at the moment."

On the way to Calshot Castle Sean asked about her family and job. It was contrary of her, but now he'd stopped talking about himself and shown some interest in her, she didn't want to tell him anything. She turned every question back on him.

"Have you always lived in Falmouth?" he asked.

"About three years. What about you? Always been in this area?"

"I was born here, as were all my immediate family. Do you have any brothers or sisters?"

"No. You?"

"A brother," Sean said.

"Does he work in TV too?"

"No, he's a mechanic."

"Quite a difference."

"It's what my dad does. He works for him. How about your parents? Are they involved in hotel work?"

"No."

"Do they live close by?" Sean asked.

"No, miles away. How about yours? I hope they get to see you on the television?"

That did the trick and he talked for a while about how proud they were of him and then about his TV career and hopes for the future.

"Will the film I saw you making help with that?" Amelia prompted.

He seemed surprised by the suggestion. "Probably not."

"Isn't all publicity good publicity?"

"Not sure it will result in publicity. It's just a demo."

"A means to an end? Bit of practice?"

"Exactly. Did you see my report last night?"

"Yes." She'd only done so to see what was so important that he wouldn't have time to speak to her for the rest of her stay in Lee-on-the-Solent. Litter! Hardly flattering, despite the piece pointing out that something so trivial could have a huge impact on the environment, local economy and even people's mental health.

"What did you think?"

Amelia said she agreed with the person who said litter got people down and made them care less about an area and even the people living there, but soon realised he was more interested in her opinion of his presentation skills.

"Did I come across as caring about that stuff?"

"I'd say so. Not obsessed or anything, but as though you were sure she was right."

"Good. With my job it's important to build a reputation for being compassionate."

"So you aren't really?" she asked.

"Of course I am, but it's not macho to say so, is it? Don't want you thinking I'm a softy."

Hmm. Was he trying to impress her now? She thought he was, although not in the way men usually tried to do that. He'd not told her how nice she looked, or expressed any regret she wasn't interested in romance. His abrupt dismissal of her outside Southsea Castle had been borderline rude. Even his questions about her felt more like an information gathering exercise than an attempt to learn how she thought and felt.

Maybe all that was his default behaviour? He was good looking enough not to have to put in much effort to attract women. As Nicole had said, he was a little big headed and self-centred, but you probably needed to be to get on in TV.

"What about the charity work you do? Does the fact that it's tough to run marathons make up for the softy aspect of helping sick children?"

"Something like that."

A little later Sean's phone rang. To her annoyance he checked the screen and then answered it – completely ignoring the holder which would have allowed him to do so hands free.

"What is it?... I can do that... I see." He sighed. "Yes... Don't panic, I've got it all under control. ... Yes." He ended the call. "Another job for me."

Amelia had no idea what the call could have been about, but she was fairly sure he hadn't just been offered more TV work. His tone would have been considerably less exasperated. She suspected he'd actually lost the chance to do one piece and his abilities to do another were being questioned. Tactfully she changed the subject by asking if he knew where the cruise ships were going.

"I've got a list, so I can tell you later. Med most likely." For the rest of the drive he told her how he'd been a special guest at the naming ceremony for one of the ships they'd see, and from that moved on to mentioning every famous person he'd met. Amelia had actually heard of some of them.

Amelia was slightly disappointed that Calshot Castle was very like all the others built on behalf of Henry VIII she'd looked at. That was silly, because she'd known they were all pretty much the same. They'd been cutting edge technology at the time and built for the same person for the same reasons. It was a complete castle in an interesting location, but it was hard to get really enthusiastic in the company of someone who wasn't doing a great job of hiding their boredom.

The castle roof was better. A huge container ship went by as they got up there, although Sean claimed it wasn't particularly large.

"We get some of the biggest in the world here. There was a period recently where almost every week I was reporting on the latest largest ever ship. They're all the same though, just have room for a few more boxes. In the end we switched to a different presenter just for a bit of variety."

Or someone who could at least feign interest in his subject? No, she wasn't being fair. Just because he was sticking to the facts when talking to her didn't mean he wouldn't have been more animated in front of the camera.

Sean pointed out Lee-on-the-Solent, The Spinnaker Tower, Southampton docks and the Isle of Wight. "The Needles are just a bit further round, and down that way is Osborne House. That's where Queen Victoria stayed when she visited the island. She had her own train which took her through Portsmouth and right up to the jetty so she could get straight onto a boat. It's still called South Railway Jetty today."

Ava and Isla would have loved both the castle and the view. Amelia could imagine them playing guessing games about where all the different boats and ships were going. She'd enjoy that herself. Patrick would tease her for letting her imagination run away with her, and then come up with a really ludicrous idea himself. Sean wouldn't. He probably knew about a lot of them and would just tell her the facts, with heavy emphasis on any he'd ever reported on and what a great job he'd made of it.

"Is that ship coming back in?" Amelia asked, gesturing to the container ship, which was now facing in the opposite direction.

"It's following the shipping channel."

"That's where the water is deepest?" She'd heard about ships in Falmouth having to take the correct route in and out of port or risk getting into trouble, but hadn't realised that applied to all ports.

Sean talked at length about shifting sands, dredging and ship's drafts, all of which amounted to the fact she was right and ships took the route where the water was deepest.

"Over there is Bramble Bank, which is equally famous for cricket matches at low tide, and ships going aground when it's covered in water."

"Do they have something like Sat Nav, to tell them where to go?"

"Maps and a tour guide."

Great. Mansplaining and now sarcasm. "I only asked!"

"They really do. They have charts, which are like maps of the seabed and unless they come in and out regularly, a pilot who knows the waters well will come aboard and help them navigate."

"Oh." Not sarcasm then.

"They do have something a bit like Sat Nav, only instead of telling them where to go, it tells other people where they are. It's called AIS. That stands for automated identification system. Here let me show you." He opened an app on his phone, and handed it to Amelia.

It showed a simplified map of the area. The sea was filled with coloured arrows.

"Tap on that big green one."

When she did an image of the container ship popped up, along with the name of the ship, what speed it was going and where to. "Can I do another one?"

"Sure."

She tried a few more, learning the cruise ships weren't yet moving, the Isle of Wight ferry was going to the Isle of Wight, and a tanker was coming in to Fawley. "What's Fawley?"

Sean pointed out the oil refinery between where they were and Southampton docks.

"Do ships go a different way around the Isle of Wight, depending where they're headed for?"

"I'm sure they used to when ships were smaller, but now it's unusual for anything but small boats to go out through The Needles, even though that's a shorter route depending on where they're going."

Back in the huge car park, Sean was met by a cameraman he obviously knew well. Despite his name being Tony, Amelia didn't think it was the man from the murder film, which was confirmed when Sean introduced Amelia. "She's up from Falmouth and I'm showing her the sights."

It was interesting to watch Sean do a 'piece to camera' about the cruise ships which would be going out later that day. He prepared by speed reading some notes, and then spoke almost wistfully about the different destinations, as though he'd spent time researching them and the attractions to be found there. She noticed a change in him whilst he was being filmed. He actually seemed more real in front of the camera.

"That's a sort of trailer for when they sail," Sean explained. "There's time to nip up the Co-op for a sandwich before that."

The cameraman, who preferred to leave his gear set up, told them what he'd like.

"He's hungry," Amelia remarked as they walked to the car.

"He knows I'm paying! I can charge it to expenses. Yours too. As you're going to be in it you're crew."

"How do you mean I'll be in it?"

"Only if you want to. You'd just need to stand and wave when I do the live bit. It's good to have cheering crowds in the background."

"OK, sounds like fun."

In the Co-op Amelia and Sean saw someone shoplifting.

"Hey!" she said.

The man stared right at her, raised one finger in an insulting gesture, then continued stashing jars of premium label coffee inside his coat.

"What should we do?" Amelia asked. "There's no point calling the police, they wouldn't get here in time."

"It's better not to get involved."

"What?"

"I'm quite well known, so my presence often complicates things. Besides, big companies factor that in and can afford the loss."

"We can't just let him get away with it, and it's factored in by putting up prices for the rest of us!"

"Of course it's wrong, but it's not worth us getting hurt over. He could be feeding a drugs habit and turn nasty. I've reported enough news items about would be 'have a go heroes' coming off badly."

"I wasn't suggesting we rugby tackle him and perform a citizen's arrest – just tell someone."

"Ah."

Clearly such a normal, boring action hadn't occurred to Sean. She was sure he'd weighed up whether something like the rugby tackle action would do his career any good, decided against it and lost all interest in something which wouldn't directly affect him.

Amelia went in search of a member of staff to inform. If it had been someone looking hungry and they were stealing food she might have thought twice, but the young man was well dressed and presumably taking the coffee to sell on. He was running out the door by the time Amelia reported what he was up to.

She remembered Patrick saying she might not enjoy being involved in real crime. He was right – the experience was very disappointing. Again that could be down to the company. Patrick would have teased her about her detective skills as they debated what to do, but he definitely wouldn't have ignored such a blatant crime. Probably in the end it would have come to much the same thing. The assistant she'd told about the incident, later found her to say the man had been caught quite clearly on the CCTV cameras.

"We'll pass the details on to the police. It's not the first time he's done it, but it's the first time he's been daft enough to show his face."

That must have been when Amelia called out and he'd looked right at her. She left her name and her own phone number in case she was needed to give a statement.

They filled a basket with sandwiches, crisps, chocolate, nuts, and canned drinks. After paying they returned to the car park by the castle, which was by then much busier. As they ate the food, more cars arrived. Amelia, Sean and Tony the cameraman weren't the only people enjoying a picnic and the atmosphere felt almost like a street party. Many of the crowd seemed to know someone else, and everyone wanted to talk about friends who were sailing, or ships they'd been on themselves.

The sight of the cruise ships was impressive – all but one were even larger than the container ship she'd seen earlier. It was easy to see why so many people had come out to watch. Amelia wasn't really needed to add to the waving crowd, but did that anyway. She almost wished Nicole was at home to see it, but then if she was, Amelia wouldn't have been there. No one she knew would see it, unless she directed them to find it on iPlayer or whatever. She wasn't quite vain enough for that.

On the drive back, Sean told her about all the jobs he had lined up for the next few days and said he'd call her if she could come along. Clearly she was supposed to be thrilled at the possibility of watching him work, and ready to instantly drop any plans she might have. She wasn't. She'd been happy to accept a lift to the castle, and to hang around after he worked because it was his reason for being there and a novelty to her.

Patrick's attention had always been on her except when he was thinking of his girls and it was nice he cared so much about them. With Sean, she'd been pretty much ignored most of the time and felt all his attention was on himself. When he talked to her it was as though she was being interviewed, pumped for information almost. Then when the camera was off her he lost interest and moved on to the next topic. That suited her fine. No need to worry that she would be breaking his heart when she went back home.

Sean's phone rang again. This time after a glance at the screen he put it in the holder on loudspeaker.

"Hi, Heather. How are you?"

"I'm worried about Angus. Have you heard from him recently?" The lady had a Scottish accent.

"Not since Sunday, but I didn't expect to. Didn't he go up to Scotland?" Sean asked.

"What did he tell you about that?"

"Nothing really, just that he needed some time to think."

"He didn't even tell me. Just sent a text. Sean, he didn't take anything with him, his family haven't seen him and he's not answering his phone."

"Oh, Heather – Not again."

"Should I call the police?"

"I can be there in less than an hour. Let's go through what we know first."

When he'd ended the call, Sean apologised and said he'd have to drop her and go.

"No problem." That's what she'd been expecting anyway, and hadn't been bothered whether she saw him again, but the phone call changed all that. It had to have been Angus McKellar they'd been talking about and she wanted to hear more. "I can see your friend needs you right now, so you'll want to go straight there."

"Yeah. Look, sorry but can I drop you in Fareham? You could get a bus back."

"Right. Of course." She hadn't really expected him to take her with him to the McKellar's home, but it had been worth a try.

"And please don't mention this to anyone, until the news is made public."

She had no hesitation in agreeing, as she didn't have anyone to tell. That didn't mean she wasn't keen to learn more. "I hope you hear from him soon and it doesn't have to be reported."

"So do I, but I doubt that will be the case. The poor man has… issues. Frankly I'm really worried about him."

Chapter 15

As Sean drove her the remaining short distance into Fareham, Amelia tried to think of ways to find out more about Angus's second disappearance. Even if she'd shown huge interest in seeing Sean being filmed again, that wouldn't have been the time to ask when that might happen. The only other reason she'd have for asking him to stay in touch would be to pretend she was attracted to him. She doubted she'd be convincing and it wouldn't be fair to try. The way she'd mentally compared him so unfavourably with Patrick all afternoon showed her how she really felt about both men.

Sean was simply someone she was using for transport and the possibility of clues. He was great to look at, reasonably interesting to spend time with, but also vain, self-centred and a bit annoying. It was unclear to Amelia whether he actually enjoyed her company, thought he owed her after the fright he gave her, or just liked having an audience even when the cameras weren't running. She didn't care much either way.

Patrick was altogether different. She was no more sure how he felt about her, but knew she cared very much. She loved him, and had believed that to be mutual. Her jealousy of Meghan had stopped her showing it and might have permanently spoiled things between them, but she hoped to find a way to show she was over it. Or at least trying to get over it.

If Patrick wanted to get back with his ex-wife and that's what Meghan wanted they'd just do it, wouldn't they? Perhaps they'd take things easy at first, but he wouldn't have been dating Amelia. He wasn't the sort to do that. He'd told her almost straight away about his daughters and made it clear they'd always play a large part in his life. Patrick being so loyal to his girls and able to stay on good terms with his ex were positive things. That wasn't baggage, it was part of what made him the man she loved.

Amelia didn't have long to wait for a bus – just enough time to log onto the bus company's wifi and start looking for reports about Angus. Of course she found nothing new; his wife hadn't even reported the second disappearance to the police.

Back at Nicole's B&B Amelia wrote down everything she could recall of Sean's conversation with Heather McKellar, to update the case file, and made a note of Sean's comment that the 'poor man has issues'. What did that mean? She could hardly ring him and ask... not about that anyway. After what she'd heard it would be perfectly reasonable for her to ring Sean in the morning and express the hope he'd had good news about his friend. She wouldn't get all the answers she wanted, but should learn something.

Was it perfectly reasonable to phone Patrick? One way to find out!

He answered her call, which was a good start.

"How are you?" she asked.

"Me?"

"Yes. Are you OK?"

"I suppose... And you?"

"I'm fine. Having a good look round."

"Did you get to Poor whatever it was castle?"

"Portchester, yes. On my first day. That's where I got the postcards for the girls."

"Yes, sorry. Where was it today then?"

"Calshot castle. I was on the news."

"That's good."

"You're not curious why?"

"Why what? You like castles…"

So much for thinking he paid attention to her! "Patrick, are you even listening to me?"

"I'm trying to. Sorry, I'm worried about Isla."

"Is she ill again?"

"Still, rather than again. I know I didn't say, but we've known for a while something is really wrong."

"If you want to talk about it now, I'm ready to listen."

"I suppose it would be better if you knew."

Despite her concern over Isla, Amelia was pleased to hear him say that. If it was really over between them, there would be no point in her knowing more about his children.

"I know she's often poorly."

"She's very tired all the time, but can't seem to sleep. She has bad dreams and gets up several times in the night for the bathroom. She'll hardly eat and when she does try she's often sick afterwards. She gets thinner by the day. We don't know what to do for her."

Amelia had known most of that, but hadn't really seen it as an ongoing problem. When Amelia saw her last she'd thought she was back to normal, which she was, but only normal for Isla. She was still the thin, pale child, no bigger than the sister who was two years younger, that she'd first encountered. Amelia had never seen her truly well, despite only ever seeing her at her best. When she was particularly ill, she stayed at home with her mother.

"You mentioned M.E. Do you think it's that?"

"That was just one possibility, but the specialist she saw didn't think it likely. Before that we thought it might be diabetes, but the doctor ruled that out. He's taken some more blood tests which he's sure will show what is wrong."

"I'm so sorry, Patrick. I wish I could help." She'd offer to go back home early, except she couldn't let Nicole and her guests down with no notice.

"The doctors are doing all they can for Isla."

"I meant you, Patrick. I wish I could help you."

"Me?" he said again, just as when she'd asked how he was. She guessed he'd not thought about himself for a while.

After a long pause, he said, "I think maybe it might help me to talk to you. That's if you don't mind?"

"Of course not."

"I kept telling myself she was fine. That she wasn't small and thin and tired, it was Ava who was a fast grower and extra energetic. Then when she got worse and kept being sick I assumed it was because she was upset over me and Meghan not getting on. How arrogant is that?"

"Not at all. You saw something was wrong and tried to put it right. You were so determined she shouldn't see you arguing with her mum that you got yourself killed just to stop it!"

"Ha, yes, I did, didn't I?" She could almost hear the smile in his voice, but it didn't last long. "How did I miss her being ill?"

"Same way I did. I saw she was pale and thin and doesn't eat much, but I just thought how different the two of them are, not that she must be seriously ill. You missed it the same way her mum and doctors did. Your ex was with them all the time, and doctors are trained to recognise symptoms. If they didn't spot it, you can't be surprised you didn't."

"That's true."

"And you wanted her to be well. It's natural you'd hope it was nothing serious, that she'd soon get better. I know, because I did that too."

"I just pretended she was OK."

"Hoped, not pretended. You didn't ignore her illness. You looked after her, took her to the doctor, tried to find out what was wrong. And she's having tests now. Once they know what's wrong, they'll be able to treat her and you can look after her and help her recover."

"I was right, talking to you does help."

"Happy to help."

"Was the castle interesting?"

"Very like St Mawes, but a bit smaller I think. No mistaking the connection." She chatted a bit about the places she'd seen, leaving out the fact she didn't go everywhere by bus. Sean wasn't ever going to be important to her and if Patrick loved her he didn't need the worry of thinking he might have a rival.

"I'm sorry I couldn't come with you… and for what I said."

"Don't worry about it."

"We need to talk properly. When will you be home?"

"Sunday evening." It meant a long journey, but she'd always liked reading on trains, mostly because she never felt she should be doing something else instead.

"Shall I pick you up from the station?"

"That would be great."

"And can I call you before then?"

"Of course you can. Anytime." She meant that. She

was sorry he'd not felt able to fully confide in her before, but that was in the past. He needed her now and she would be there for him – and his girls too if she could help in any way. "If you avoid breakfast time, you'll have my complete attention."

After she'd washed up from breakfasts on Thursday, Amelia rang Sean. "I wondered if there was any news about your missing friend?"

"Nothing so far. His wife, Heather, has contacted the police to report him missing and I'll be reporting that and doing an appeal for information later."

"That must be difficult when it's someone you know."

"It is. I had to do it before. Angus went missing at the end of last year."

"Oh. Does that help?" It was too late now to say she was aware of the earlier disappearance, over six months previously.

"No one knows where he went, or why. Not really."

"You have an idea?"

"A few. Do you have plans for today?"

"Nothing much." She'd intended to buy gifts for Isla and Ava, which she could do anytime, and to try to find out more about Angus McKellar. Being with Sean was her best opportunity to do that.

"My schedule's really hectic, but if you don't mind some hanging about it might help me make sense of things if I could talk it over with someone who'd be unbiased. All my friends know Angus, or work in TV, so would be looking for a story not the truth. You seem like the perfect choice. Did you know Angus came here from Falmouth?"

"Really?" Why tell him she knew when he so liked

explaining things?

"The company was started in Scotland, where he's from initially. It was only small, but he brought it to England starting with one outlet in Falmouth and quickly expanded. That was twenty years ago, and I know it's just a coincidence you being from there, but it feels like a connection."

"It does to me too." No need to say she'd felt that way since Nicole first mentioned it.

"After your reaction to that shoplifter I know I can trust you, and as you overheard Heather's call you already know part of the story."

Yes! She didn't want to seem too keen though. For her it was almost a game, whereas he was obviously worried. "I don't mind if that would help. And it would be interesting to see you working." He wouldn't see anything at all odd about someone finding him interesting.

"What time will you have finished with the B&B work?"

"By eleven usually, but I could make it earlier." How did he know she wasn't just a guest?

"I'll pick you up after eleven then."

A few minutes later Nicole's phone rang. On seeing the number wasn't listed Amelia answered with, "Wight View B&B. How can I help you?" She'd done the same when Sean called her the previous morning. She felt uncomfortable that he'd deduced she was working there after she'd pretended to be a guest, but it was too late to do anything about that.

On the way to Sean's first appointment, where he was to interview someone informally to see if there was enough of a story to come back with a camera, he explained about Angus's earlier disappearance.

"Just like this time, he contacted people to say he was going away for a while and cancelled his appointments for the next few days. When he turned up he couldn't or wouldn't say where he'd been, or why."

"You said you had some ideas?"

"Something the police didn't make public is that shortly before he was found, Heather got a text, saying he was sorry. We thought he'd committed suicide."

"How awful." She recalled the news reports saying 'concern is growing for the missing man' but had assumed that was just due to the fact he still hadn't been located. "Was he depressed?"

Sean considered the question. "He had things on his mind. We used to talk to each other about everything. He was a lovely man. Helped so many people, including me. When I was a very junior reporter he introduced me to a lot of people and arranged for me to do interviews I'd never otherwise have got. He was a great support in other ways too. Invested some money for me, boosted my confidence. I owe him so much."

As he talked, Amelia thought perhaps she was seeing the real Sean for the first time. He'd not talked about anyone or anything, other than himself, with anything like the same level of enthusiasm.

"He didn't just help me either. He helped everyone. A while ago one of his employees got pregnant. A single girl with nobody to help her. Nobody but Angus, that is. He really went out of his way too, not just giving her money, but visiting her and arranging for the flat over one of his offices to be refurbished so she was living somewhere he could keep an eye on her."

Sean might think he was demonstrating his friend's kind nature, but he was also adding to Amelia's earlier suspicion that he might have been having an affair. Sean himself didn't seem to see anything odd about it, so maybe he really was a very considerate boss? Or had been. Sean was talking in past tense.

He continued praising Angus's generosity and then listed some of the things he'd done for local good causes, including setting up the Salterns Support charity. "He was just a lovely man."

"Was? You think…"

There was a long pause. "Yes, I'm afraid we've lost him. I think we started to at the end of last year. He grew distant, to Heather as well as me. We knew something was wrong. He wasn't his usual self at all. He'd started drinking heavily and was moody, but he wouldn't talk about it."

"And then he vanished?"

"I think now that he intended to kill himself, but failed. He found somewhere to hide out and thought about it for a long time, then sent Heather the message and took some pills. Sleeping tablets, something like that. They didn't kill him, just knocked him out for a while."

"That fits with the news reports. They said he was dehydrated and hadn't eaten for a couple of days, but wouldn't have survived the whole time with no food or water," Amelia said.

"You knew he'd gone missing before?" Sean's tone was accusing.

Why hadn't she told him the truth from the start? What was she going to say now? 'While you were desperately worried your friend was suicidal, me and my mate were having fun playing detectives'?

"I… I looked it up last night."

"Did you?"

He didn't sound happy, nor as though he believed her, and why should he? Amelia had sounded as guilty as she felt. She wouldn't make things worse with more lies.

Sean didn't speak again until they arrived at what was presumably the home of the person he was to interview. Then he just snapped, "Wait here." Away from the car he made a short phone call, then went into the house.

Amelia had plenty of time to think about what she had and hadn't said already, and what she'd say to Sean when he returned. Having heard nothing about Angus until yesterday and then deciding to conduct a thorough online investigation simply wouldn't sound credible to most people.

She had her story straight by the time Sean returned to the car, having made another call just outside the house.

"I'm sorry, I haven't been completely honest with you. My friend Nicole runs the Wight View B&B. I'm here because I'm helping out while she takes a short holiday." She had no explanation for keeping that quiet, except she hadn't liked to admit she was there alone because he'd so unnerved her by acting out a murder. He felt guilty enough about that already. "I think I told you I'm interested in crime and mysteries?"

"Yes." He sounded tense. Looked it too.

"Nicole knows that, so she told me about Angus McKellar going missing."

"So you decided to come and snoop around?"

"No!" OK, so she had snooped around, but that wasn't the reason for her being in Lee-on-the-Solent. "But I did remember the name. It's so very Scottish. When you spoke to Heather and said 'again' I wondered if it was the same man, and looked it up."

"I see."

"I know it must seem horrible to have people treating it like a mystery in a book or film, but…"

He sighed. "It's alright. I know people are interested – I wouldn't have a job if other people's lives didn't fascinate us, would I?"

"I suppose not."

"Look, I'm meeting the police next, and doing a news piece on Angus. I know you hoped to come into the studio, but if I'm on my own they might tell me things off the record. They won't do that if you're there."

"I understand." He didn't want her around and she didn't blame him.

"Can you amuse yourself in Southampton for a while?"

"No problem and I can get the bus back."

"If that's what you want."

"Not really…"

"You want to know what the police said?"

"Well, yes."

"I'll call you when I'm finished. Maybe together we can make some sense of all this?"

"Brilliant! I mean…"

"It's fine. You don't know him… You're a good person to talk to, Amelia. With Heather I have to be careful what I say, but with you I can be honest."

Southampton centre was a good place to keep Amelia occupied. Her main priority was to find gifts for Ava and Isla, but as that involved looking for an appropriate shop it also gave her a reason to explore. As well as all the usual shops and cafés, there was a medieval gatehouse, which had once been the main entrance to the old town. It was really impressive, and totally incongruous in the middle of a modern city centre.

Amelia rang Patrick, to ask what the girls might like. There was no reply, making her realise she'd called more to hear his voice than to make the enquiry. She bought two jigsaws of local scenes, and two children's puzzle books.

Should she eat? Would Sean get something at the studio, or want to go somewhere later? It didn't seem worth interrupting him to ask especially as, if he was interviewing the police or being filmed, he wouldn't reply. She settled for a sausage roll and coffee. That way she wouldn't have to leave before her order was cooked, could still eat something with Sean if he stopped for food, but wouldn't starve if he didn't.

A little research told her that parts of the city walls had survived. As she didn't know how long she'd have, she decided against searching for them and risk getting lost.

Instead she found her way back to where Sean had said he'd pick her up, in case that proved more difficult than she'd anticipated. She'd had no messages from either him or Patrick and began to worry her phone might not be working properly. It had been over two hours, should she call? To Patrick she sent a text simply saying 'Thinking of you x'.

She was still debating whether it would be more annoying to call Sean while he was still busy, or not to call if he was having trouble reaching her, when he rang to say he was on his way.

Sean didn't say anything when Amelia got in the car.

His expression spoke for him – he hadn't been given good news.

He drove for a while, then pulled into a layby. "I'm just so angry!"

"What's happened?"

"Nothing! Not a single damn thing that's any use."

"The police were no help?"

"They said he's an adult who has decided to leave home for a while, which isn't a crime, or in any way unusual."

"They got involved before."

"Only after a few days and because he sent the text we thought meant he was feeling suicidal. There hasn't been anything like that this time. And to them the fact he did it before and came back means he will again."

"Perhaps they're right?" Amelia suggested.

"I hope so, but this isn't like Angus. He's so sociable and friendly and open, usually. Something is badly wrong. Has been for a while."

"The drinking?"

"More the reasons for it. He'd got secretive, and became less reliable. He'd be in the wrong place at the wrong time, and even missed some commitments. If I wasn't sure he'd never do that to Heather, I'd have thought he was having an affair."

Amelia wondered if Sean was letting gratitude and friendship colour his judgement.

"The only thing the police seemed to care about was money!"

"Oh?"

"To do with the charity funding. It will be a mistake of some kind. Why are they looking into that and not the fact that Angus is missing, possibly suicidal?"

"I don't know." Amelia couldn't help thinking the police suspected, as she did, the two things could be linked. From what Nicole said, there was a lack of accuracy concerning the charity donations. That might not just be minor negligence.

"Argh!" Sean banged the steering wheel. "Because the police aren't interested in finding him, I had to fight to get it even mentioned on the lunchtime news. The only angle was the money, so to try to get someone, anyone, interested in finding my wonderful friend I had to go on air and make it sound like he's a crook!"

They talked for a while longer, but Sean's frustration and anger made it an unpleasant and unhelpful experience. She was relieved when he took her home.

"Thanks for today, Amelia. Sorry I've been so..." He sighed.

"It's fine. I understand."

"You've really helped – I needed to get it off my chest before I see Heather. Will you come with me tomorrow? We might have more information then."

It probably wouldn't be fun, but she was more than a little intrigued in the case and Sean was in need of someone to share his frustrations with. "Yes, OK."

Back at the B&B Amelia was desperate for pleasant conversation. She rang Patrick, but got no reply. She thought of ringing Nicole, but this wasn't an emergency and she didn't want to worry her friend.

Amelia checked her own phone. There were two texts. One was from Gabrielle saying she hoped she was having a good time. The other was from Jasper, 'Not missing you at all' and a photo of a handsome, dark skinned man holding up a huge and lavishly decorated cocktail in an inviting manner. They made her smile, but Amelia didn't feel like calling either of them and discovering they couldn't talk as they were working. No B&B guests were in. A conversation with her parents wasn't guaranteed to lift her spirits, and Amelia's mood wouldn't make them glad she'd called.

If she couldn't chat for her own pleasure, perhaps she could do so as a detection exercise? If she was an Agatha Christie character she'd get talking to a suspect and they'd reveal a clue. Amelia didn't have any suspects, but she slightly knew one of Nicole's near neighbours. The man with the waving dog and his friend had seemed nice, and they'd been concerned about her. Amelia checked the TV guide, walked down to the Co-op to buy a Red Velvet cake, and knocked on the door on her way back.

"Hi. I'm the person your friend helped the other day when I had a funny turn. He seemed concerned, so I just thought I'd let him know I'm OK."

"Come in and you can tell him yourself. And the offer of tea is still on."

"Thank you."

"Colin, we have a visitor!" he called as he led Amelia into a small and very yellow room.

"Well, put the kettle on then," Colin said.

"Your arms fallen off have they?" Her host's smile and the way he immediately left the room suggested that was a regular exchange.

"Don't mind, Brian. I recognise you, don't I?"

"Yes. I dropped pizza on you a few days ago and you were very kind."

"I remember."

Amelia looked round for the dog, and saw no sign of

one. "I thought you had a little dog?"

"Not ours, Brian's aunt's. We mind it for her sometimes."

Once tea was made and the men persuaded to share her cake, Amelia told Colin and Brian exactly why she'd been so affected by what she'd seen. They were delighted to have unwittingly helped her see both that Patrick hadn't got back with his ex, and that she really loved him.

"It would have been so sad if you were kept apart because of a misunderstanding," Brian said.

Amelia nodded. "Like that Scottish man the midday news said has gone missing."

"Angus McKellar?"

"His poor wife must be so worried," Amelia said.

"As are we."

"You know him?"

"We've met him. Lovely man."

"Not the sort to let people down," Colin added.

"I wonder if there's any more about it on the news?" Amelia prompted.

"It should be on any minute. Put the telly on, Brian."

Brian fetched the remote and presented it to Colin. "You can make yourself useful for a change."

They all watched Sean's report in silence. As he'd indicated to Amelia, it hinted heavily that financial irregularities connected with Salterns Support might account for Angus McKellar being out of contact. Sean mentioned the earlier unexplained disappearance, giving the impression Angus was unstable and unreliable.

"With friends like that," Colin said.

"You don't need enemies," Brian finished.

"He's his friend?" Amelia asked. A question can't be a

lie, can it?

"I can see why you're surprised, but then you don't know our Sean."

"Self-centred little pr… person."

Colin told her that both men ran marathons supposedly for the charity, but that Sean, as he did with everything else, used it to promote himself.

"He pretends to be caring and compassionate, Angus McKellar really is," Brian said.

"Some people judge others by their own standards. Because they're up to no good, they think others are."

"So you don't think Angus McKellar could be taking money from the charity he set up?" Amelia asked.

"We do not. He probably could get away with it, mind. One of the times we met him was to hand over the cash our club raised."

"We said it was a shame we'd not quite made it to a thousand."

"You got your name engraved on the window if you did."

"He asked how much we were short and he said… What did he say, Brian?"

"Dinnae fret about being such a wee bit under."

"That's it. He must have put in the rest himself."

"We know because we saw the club name go up, but if he'd helped himself to half of it, we'd never have known."

"That was nice of him," Amelia said.

"It was. Some say it's alright for him as he can afford it, but he puts in a lot of his own money. Thousands at least."

"That's just what's known about. I bet ours wasn't the only donation he added a bit to."

Amelia was reminded of Nicole's story about the donation which went up in value. How frustrating that she couldn't ask her about it until Sunday. There was no problem about talking to Brian and Colin. They were happy to discuss Angus McKellar, but other than confirming what she already knew, plus her initial impression of Sean, she learned little. It was easy to see why the men liked Angus and resented Sean speaking negatively of him, but they didn't know why he'd done that. They didn't know Angus at all well either.

When she got back she tried calling Patrick again. There was no reply, so she texted him. 'Happy to talk, anytime at all, if it will help. x'

Chapter 16

Amelia was ready with a little time to spare before Sean was due to pick her up on Friday. She texted him to ask if he'd collect her up the High Street instead of from the B&B. As that meant a slightly shorter journey for him, she wasn't surprised he agreed.

She went back into the Salterns Support charity shop, apparently to donate back her previous purchase and buy another book. She did want at least one, as she'd read those she brought with her and guessed she might have time to kill whilst Sean was working. What she wanted even more was to try to learn something about Angus McKellar or the charity's funding.

It was easy to get the assistant talking by mentioning the news report. Her reaction was much the same as that of Colin and Brian. Angus was a lovely man and she wasn't prepared to believe a word against him. "I don't know what can have happened to him, and Heather must be frantic, but I know there'll be an explanation."

Amelia selected three books.

"That's four fifty please."

Amelia gave her a fiver. "Keep the change. I'm sure the charity needs every penny it can get."

"It does, thanks." She took 50p from the till and dropped it into a collecting box.

"That sounds almost full."

"The chap hasn't been in to collect it."

"You don't pay it into the bank with the takings?"

"No, it's sealed up." She lifted it to make the point, and banged it back down.

Amelia didn't feel she could ask anything else, so changed the topic. "Looks like a lovely day to read a book on the beach."

"If you say so."

She had a point. Although it was sunny, there was a strong and very cold wind. Still, Amelia would rather be thought odd than leave the woman, who would most likely be an unpaid volunteer, feeling her honesty was in doubt.

"There's some good news," Sean said in reply to her question about Angus. "Heather checked their bank accounts and he's made withdrawals."

"That's great! They can find out where from."

"Hopefully. She's asked the bank. They can't tell her anything about his own accounts, but one is joint."

"When was this, do you know?"

"Every day, I think." He sounded worried.

"That's really good news, Sean. He's alive, and if he can get to a cashpoint and remember his PIN number he can't be too… upset. Maybe he really has just gone somewhere to think?"

"But about what? What can he have done that he can't talk to me about? Or to Heather?"

Embezzlement, an affair, or both. Amelia didn't think she needed to say so.

"Is he generally a worrier, would you say?" Amelia thought that sounded better than asking if he seemed the suicidal type.

"Angus?" Sean laughed. "No, he's really chilled out."

Amelia didn't see what was funny, but she was pleased Sean was now much less concerned about his friend.

Sean had a very busy day. Amelia spent a lot of time sitting in the car reading. As promised, he allowed her to watch him interviewing someone. He was doing his own filming, but only had to set it up and leave it running. Amelia was to stand by it and pretend to be his assistant.

The man talked about his postcard collection. Amelia could tell he found it fascinating. There were some aspects which might be interesting to others, but he did a pretty good job of hiding that. He had boxes of the things, those he'd been sent and others, both new and old, he'd bought himself. Those he considered the best of his collection were in albums, and it was these Sean concentrated on.

"Why is this one special?" Sean asked.

"My aunt Milly sent it to me. That's my dad's eldest sister. He had three. Susan, Louise and Milly. Her name was Mildred really, but everyone called her Milly."

There was a long pause between each sentence, as though he expected to be interrupted. Amelia could imagine that happened a lot.

"And you were particularly close to her?" Sean prompted.

"No, I wouldn't say that. I was fond of her, but I liked all my aunts. We're a close family. Aunt Susan is still with us and I visit her every week."

"But this card, sent by your Aunt Milly is special because…?"

"I was only six at the time. This was back in 1954, just after the rationing ended. I couldn't even read it."

Sean studied the back of the card. "It doesn't mention rationing."

"Why would she write about rationing to a six-year-old boy when it was already over?"

"Good point. So the reason this card is special, is because…?"

"It was the first one I ever got. Started off the whole thing, you see. I'd never been sent a postcard before and when I took it into school, I found I was the only boy who had one. It made me feel important like."

Amelia longed to escape. Being left to her own devices was far more entertaining – probably would have been even without the book. If only her phone would ring, she could slip out to answer it. Could she pretend she needed to do something technical and use that excuse to make her escape? Set fire to the boxes of cards? Stuff some in the man's mouth?

Eight and a half years, or perhaps only a couple of mind numbingly dull hours, later Sean wound things up with, "Thank you for that fascinating insight into something which clearly gives you a great deal of pleasure." He stood and offered his hand.

"You're going already? I have more in the loft."

"Alas I'm afraid we must."

"I don't envy whoever has to edit that!" Amelia said, when they eventually escaped.

"Should be quite simple. The pauses make it easy to cut and the repetitions will help with putting it together, so it flows smoothly."

"You were so patient with him."

"Have to be sometimes. I've got good at knowing when to ask direct questions, when to coax out information and when to just let people talk."

"A useful skill."

"It's not helping me find out much about where Angus is."

When they arrived at the destination for Sean's next

interview, Amelia said she'd wait in the car. "I'll make a list of what we know about Angus. Writing it all down might help somehow."

"Good idea. If I can forget it's my friend and just look at the bare facts, it might make more sense."

Amelia wrote out everything she knew, or rather everything Sean had told her or would otherwise expect her to know, in the order she believed events had happened. She left spaces for Sean to add anything else he could think of. Probably too many spaces, but there weren't many facts.

On his return, Sean suggested they get something to eat while they went through Amelia's timeline.

"That all looks right," he said as they sipped their coffee and waited for cheese toasties.

"When did you actually see him last?" Amelia asked.

"About four days before he went missing. I feel terrible about that. He called me a couple of times, but I was so busy with setting up the filming I didn't make time to talk to him properly. If I had…"

"You can't blame yourself. What about his wife? When did she see him last?"

"Sunday morning. He said he was playing golf with a friend and might be late back, so she didn't expect to see him the rest of the day. She hadn't really started to worry by the time he texted her about going to Scotland."

Amelia filled in some of the blanks.

"Was she surprised he'd go to Scotland?"

"No… That he'd just text her and go was out of character, but he'd been speaking to a cousin just a few days beforehand, who invited him up. That's who he said he would be staying with and as I say, he'd not been himself for a while."

Amelia made a note. "The golfing friend? Did he meet them?"

"Not as far as we know. He didn't say who it was, which Heather now thinks is odd. Usually he'd mention people by name and say whether he expected to beat them, things like that. She's called everyone she can think of. Nobody had arranged a game with him. I checked at the club and he hadn't booked a tee time."

"Do you have to do that?"

"At our club you do if you want a weekend game."

"Did he take his clubs?"

"Yes. It's possible he was intending to play somewhere else, but I think that was just to reassure Heather."

"Sounds like it. When was the next time anyone heard from him?"

"Sunday afternoon. He tried calling me a couple of times in the day, but I'd turned my phone off to do a run through for the film and forgot to switch it back on. I only realised when I went to switch it off for the real thing. I never forget to have my phone on. Why did it have to happen that day?"

"If he was already planning to go away, it wouldn't have made any difference."

"I could have… No, I wouldn't have had time to talk to him anyway." He sounded so dejected.

"You would, if you'd known he was really troubled."

"Of course I would! Thanks, Amelia. You're right, if he'd reached out, I'd have tried to help."

"He called again that night?" Angus going missing the evening they'd met felt like a bond between them, one that might help them discover what had happened.

"After I'd walked you home. He told me he was going

away to Scotland to think for a while. At first I wasn't at all worried. The first time he went missing he didn't say where he was going or why. He still has relatives in Scotland, and he'd mentioned his childhood a few times recently. He was quite nostalgic for those simpler times, so to me it made sense that he'd go there."

"You said he hadn't been the same since the first time he vanished?"

"He was definitely troubled. Not depressed I don't mean. I'd have tried to get him help if he was, but he had something on his mind which he wouldn't talk about."

"Not even to his wife?"

"No. Just fobbed us all off with saying he was worried about where he'd been in November."

"I suppose he would have been?"

"If he really didn't know. The more I think about it, the more sure I am that he does remember and wherever it was, he's gone back."

Patrick rang that afternoon, while Amelia was again sitting in Sean's car outside a house. "Sorry I've not returned your calls. Just after I spoke to you Isla was in so much pain we took her to hospital."

"Oh no! What happened?"

"They've operated. Meghan and I are taking it in turns to be with her. If I'm not in the hospital I've got Ava. I'm not sure if I can pick you up on Sunday. I don't want to leave you waiting and…"

"Patrick it's OK. I'll be fine. Tell me about Isla. Was it an accident?"

"No, the same problems she's been having for a while, but worse. We saw a different doctor, who had a hunch what was wrong. It's rare in children and doesn't usually progress so fast, but a biopsy proved him right."

"A biopsy? That's…" Cancer, but she couldn't bring herself to say it. There wasn't anything hopeful about rapidly advancing cancer.

"She urgently needs treatment, but they can't start until she heals from the operation. That could be weeks." He sobbed. "I don't think she'll ever be well again."

"Patrick…"

"Sorry, I have to go. Sorry about picking you up."

"Don't be. I can easily get a bus or a taxi. Look, don't worry about me at all. Just concentrate on Isla – Ava too, as she'll be needing you."

"Yeah, it's tough on her. She wants us to explain and tell her everything will be OK, but we can't."

"Give them both my love." She wanted to add that she loved him, but that didn't seem the occasion to say it for the first time.

Poor Patrick. It must be so awful knowing something was badly wrong, and not being able to do anything to help. That realisation should have made her more sympathetic to Sean, who was in a similar position, but Patrick's call did the opposite. He'd been primarily concerned with Isla of course, but also Ava and had even spared a thought for how Amelia would get home. No doubt he was also thinking of Meghan, and for once Amelia didn't begrudge the woman his support.

Sean's attitude was very different. He, as seemed usual for him, was thinking of himself. That became more irritating over the course of the afternoon. He was miffed Angus hadn't confided in him, seemed to think he could have made a difference.

"I'm going to have to do another news piece on him, suggesting he's doing something wrong. I hate doing that to a friend and it doesn't reflect well on me, either does it?"

The man really needed to learn that not everything was about him.

Of course he was upset, and she should make some allowances for that. Amelia didn't mind helping Sean and in any case, she very much wanted to learn more and perhaps play a part in solving the mystery. It was a welcome distraction too from worrying about Isla and Patrick. She'd rather be helping him, but there was nothing she could do from a distance.

Amelia and Sean went over the details of Angus's disappearance. It didn't feel they were making progress. Sean tried calling his friend again, receiving the message his phone was switched off. Amelia copied out her timeline, so Sean could have a tidy version and she had one for her case file, although she didn't tell Sean about that. They promised each other they'd get in touch if either of them thought of, or learned, anything else.

"It's a long shot, but keep an eye out in Falmouth when you get home. He was happy there. If he's subconsciously trying to get back to simpler times there's just a chance he'd go there," Sean said as he took her back to Lee-on-the-Solent.

Amelia asked to be dropped off in the High Street because she wanted to send another postcard to her downstairs neighbour. She wasn't anywhere near as boring to listen to as the collector Sean had interviewed, but might be just as pleased to receive one. From the interest she displayed in Amelia's post, she didn't get much herself.

"Good morning, Sunshine," Nicole said when Amelia

went down to the kitchen the next morning.

"Nicole!" They hugged. "Are you alright?" Amelia asked.

"Course. Why?"

"You're not due back until tonight."

"Incorrect. I always intended to come back last night."

"Then why tell me it was tonight?" Amelia asked.

"When are you due back at work?"

"Monday. I can try to get someone to swap, but…"

"Exactly! I'd have had five minutes with you and then you'd have been straight back to Falmouth. This way we get a day together."

"But what is it? What's wrong?"

"Nothing's wrong with me, you loon. I'm worried about you, all work and no life."

"It's not like that now." She explained the changes at The Fal View. "We work really long hours for three weeks and have one off. I'll be able to come down here, visit the parents, take holidays."

"Fab! Maybe you'll even get a life?"

"If you mean a man, I have one. Enough about me, how was your trip?"

"Man? What man."

"Uh uh. Come on, your go. Tell me all about your trip and the cousins."

"Do you mind if I don't, at least not just yet?"

"OK, but…?"

"Don't look so worried! I had a great time, fab food, drink, weather, scenery all that."

"Good, but…"

"There was something. Nothing bad. Good really. Yes, good… it's just, I need to think about it a bit first."

"There was a man?"

Nicole laughed. "There was, yes, but that's all I'm saying for now. Tell me what you've been doing."

Amelia could understand her friend not wanting to discuss either whatever she'd learned about her family or her new relationship, until she had it straight in her own mind, as she felt a bit that way about Patrick. Still, there was plenty else to talk about. "We'd better sort out the breakfasts first, there's a lot to tell."

"Sounds interesting!"

"A bit too interesting in a way."

After breakfast Amelia said there was so much she didn't know where to start.

"With the part about you having a man. Did you meet someone up here?"

"Yes, but not like that. I was wrong about Patrick and about Isla and about Angus McKellar actually."

"I've changed my mind. Start right at the beginning and go VERY slowly."

That was probably best. So much had happened she'd get them both confused if she wasn't logical. "Well, the first day I found my way to Portchester castle, and to a nice café for lunch, and then back here, all without getting lost."

"Impressive."

"I know. Maybe I should have quit while I was ahead, but I decided to go and look for your motte and bailey castle."

"Did you find it?"

"Yes, but not even my imagination could make that exciting. Don't send any guests you want to impress. It's just a tiny hill and really hard to find."

"You got lost?"

"I did. So lost I seemed to walk into an alternate reality."

"You were abducted by aliens?"

"No. The only alien in the area had already lured me up here to run her B&B so she could go off and conduct her icky experiments on humans in a different part of the planet."

"I didn't take my probes with me! Come on, what happened?"

"I was lost and it was getting dark, then I heard voices and saw strange lights."

"Aliens. I knew it!"

"No. Some people were filming. It was all dramatic lighting, leaping shadows and creepy blackness and they acted out a murder scene."

"Oh! You stumbled across one of your crime stories. Cool."

"Except that I didn't realise they were acting, and thought I'd seen a real murder. I screamed and ran off through the woods, with the murderer right behind me."

"No? Oh dear." Nicole might have been trying to look concerned, but she was doing no better at that than she was in hiding her laughter.

"Anyway, he caught up with me and explained. He's actually quite nice. He seemed it then anyway."

"You said that as though you think I'd doubt the niceness of a murderer chasing my friend through the woods in the dead of night."

"It was Sean Underhill."

"Oh!"

"I didn't recognise him at first, which I don't think went down well."

"I can imagine."

"Yeah, he does have an ego on him, but that kind of worked in my favour as he seemed to want to impress me. He felt bad about giving me a scare and made it up to me by taking me to the Royal Armouries, and wherever Calshot Castle is."

"It's at Calshot."

"That makes sense."

"So what, you've given up on the two-timing Patrick in favour of Sean and now I'll never get rid of you?"

"Patrick wasn't two-timing me. I saw the dog men and realised he hadn't been blowing kisses at Meghan, but to one of the girls."

"Dog men?"

"You said in order and I haven't got to that bit yet."

"But it's back on with you two?"

"I think so. He was going to pick me up at the station tomorrow and said we'd talk properly then, but his daughter is in hospital."

"What's happened?"

"I think it's cancer."

"Think?"

"We didn't talk for long and obviously he was upset, but Patrick mentioned a biopsy. That's cancer, isn't it?"

"Not always. It can be, but it's a test to see what, if anything, is wrong."

"There's definitely something wrong. She had an operation afterwards, but that sounded like the start of treatment, not the cure."

"Poor kid."

"I feel pretty bad. Remember I thought Meghan was exaggerating her illnesses?"

"Yep."

"Turns out they were all doing the opposite." She

explained some of what Patrick had told her.

"It sounds scary, but an operation and treatment are positive things, sweetie."

"You're right. And kids are resilient, aren't they?"

"Definitely. Come on then, tell me the rest."

Amelia knew Nicole was trying to distract her from her concern, and that she was right to do so. Worrying, when she didn't even know what there was to worry about, couldn't possibly help. Amelia tried to go through everything which had happened in order, but kept getting interrupted with questions, or remembering more details.

"By the way, Sean's got your mobile number. I had to give it to him to arrange being picked up but he doesn't know it isn't mine."

"You went out with him?"

"Not like dating, even without Patrick I wouldn't want to. It was worth it to find out more about Angus McKellar though."

"You make it sound like he's a criminal mastermind. Not that something like that would put you off – you'd be all over him."

"I would not. I'm interested in crime, I admit, but my only interest in criminals is seeing them brought to justice. Sean doesn't share that interest!" She explained about the shoplifting they'd witnessed.

"And he did nothing?"

"Nope. He did say that, because he's well known, getting involved is complicated, but he didn't have any dilemma over what to do, it just never occurred to him to take any action. He only came up with that after I said we should report it."

"It's as though he doesn't think things matter unless they're directly connected to him."

"Yes, that's it exactly!" Amelia agreed.

"What do you want to do, today? I gather that you wouldn't see Patrick or his little girl if you went back early?"

"No. At the risk of sounding like Sean, it would probably just complicate things if I tried."

"What about the mysteriously vanished man? Anything to be done there?"

"I don't think there is until someone hears something and I definitely don't want to hang around with Sean all day on the off chance of getting to learn about it slightly quicker. He did promise to ring me if he gets any news. I suppose I should give him my number?"

"You really don't like him, do you?"

"He's alright really, I just found him a bit unsettling the few times he turned his attention away from himself and on to me. He's very intense… and it's hard to get the image of him stabbing someone out of my head."

"So, there's nothing you can do about anything except worry?"

"Not really."

"In that case, let's try and have a fun day out together and see if we can forget about all the difficult stuff."

"Talking of which, Mum said to give you her best."

"I always was her favourite!"

"True! Seriously though, you're not going to interrogate me about Patrick and try to get me to work out if I really do want the happy ever after – if that's possible."

"No need as you've already told me. Looks like I'm going to have to spell it out to you though. You love the man and you love his kids."

There was no point in arguing with Nicole when she

was certain about anything. Amelia had not once proved her to be wrong. "What shall we do today then? You know better than me what's around here."

"We could start off with a bit of culture in the Gosport gallery. There's always something on. Some exhibitions are boring and some really good. It's free and indoors, so I always suggest it as a rainy day activity for guests. They've just put on something new, so I want to check it out."

"Lead on Mistress Tour Guide."

The best thing about the art display in the gallery were the pretentious descriptions of each exhibit. After a very quick look round they decided to get the ferry over to Portsmouth.

As they walked down Gosport High Street Amelia pointed to some graffiti. "See that there? It represents the artist's inner turmoil after being traumatised as a child, by seeing an off duty Santa rip the beard from his face."

"You can really feel his angst by the angle at which he held the spray can, keeping... No, sorry, I'm too overcome by emotion to go on."

"It is a powerful piece. What about that?"

"The dropped gum is a rebellion against consumerism and the throw-away society," Nicole said.

"Yes, I see that. The way it will entrap any unwary person who comes close to these shops... Talking of shops, I think that one sells chocolate and as we have a sea crossing coming up, we need supplies."

They selected a chocolate orange, to guard against scurvy, and ate a few segments whilst waiting for the ferry. On the top deck, Amelia described the lumpy bit in the middle as representing the way chocolate is the cog that holds friendships together.

"Is that right?" Nicole asked.

"Duh, yeah?"

"In that case the best friend gets it." She grabbed it.

"Oi!" Amelia exclaimed.

Nicole snapped it in two and gave Amelia the biggest piece.

"Aww. Thanks, mate."

Later in Gunwharf Quay they tried on clothes at the designer outlets. Amelia bought a dress with fringing on as it slightly reminded her of one of the flapper dresses Jasper had persuaded her to wear, and which Max Gold, aka Patrick, had been so complimentary about.

Over lunch, Amelia said, "I've worked it out you know."

"Worked what out?"

"What you're not telling me. You met a bloke out there, fell madly in love and are thinking of moving out there permanently. You didn't want to say anything to me yet as you don't know if anything will come of it, and you're trying not to even think about it at the moment. You want to cool off a bit, see how you feel about being back before trying to make any kind of decision."

"Yeah, that's pretty close."

"And there's the family connection."

"There is. I actually have quite a few relatives out there."

"That's great! It is, isn't it?"

"Yes it is, but it's taking a bit of getting used to."

"I can imagine. Something else you want to think about before talking about?"

"If you don't mind?"

"Of course not. I'll make up my own theories in the

meantime."

"Of course you will! Don't be too disappointed when I reveal I'm not royalty, will you?"

That wouldn't bother Amelia at all, but having Nicole move even further away would. She resolved to take more advantage of the fact she and Nicole were hundreds, not thousands of miles apart and both could provide accommodation for the other.

"Promise we'll get together again this summer?" Amelia said.

"It's a deal," Nicole agreed.

It was tactful of her to not mention that she'd regularly suggested it over the last couple of years and it was Amelia who'd always been too busy.

Chapter 17

On Sunday morning, as Nicole drove Amelia to the train station, she described her trip in the kind of gorgeous detail a travel brochure might use. Everything from black sand beaches, through rainforests and banana plantations, to volcanoes and the alien looking observatory were mentioned. She spoke of the sights and sounds, tastes and fragrances, but made it seem as though the only people she met were the waitress who brought plates of seafood and the driver who helped her explore the island.

Amelia let her get away with that while she was driving and then hugging her goodbye. Then, once on the train, she texted, 'Call me when you've finished doing the rooms. I want to know about your trip. x x x'.

"I told you this morning," Nicole said when she rang back an hour later.

"Not really. Just about the food and the weather and the scenery and the carnival."

"What more do you want?"

"Your cousins – you met them, they're nice?"

"Yes. It was slightly awkward. They don't all speak English and I don't speak anything else and we don't have much in common. I had a few meals with them and was shown around a bit, and we'll keep in touch."

"And you're happy with that?"

"Totally. I'm still getting used to the thought that I have family. It's going to take a while."

Amelia knew that meant Nicole still wasn't ready to talk about it.

"And the romance?"

"Stacks of it I expect. How could there not be on a heart shaped island?"

"I meant you."

"Did you?" Nicole's fake innocence had never been convincing.

"There was a man you said, but don't go thinking that's all you're going to say!"

"Alright. Remember I told you about going up through the clouds to the top of the mountain?"

"That was with him? Nice. And…?"

"And he took me to the carnival, and we sat up talking half the night under the clear starry sky."

"He speaks English then?"

"I said we were talking half the night."

"Oh. Actual talking? Fair enough. And…?"

"That's all you're getting for now."

"Tell me his name at least."

"Miguel."

Back at home, Amelia's downstairs neighbour greeted her in the hallway. Muriel wouldn't have been waiting there long, as she could see anyone approaching the flats from her lounge window, and had her seat positioned to make that easy.

"Thank you for the lovely postcard, dear. Really brightened my day getting that."

"You're welcome."

"I picked up all your post to keep it safe," she said. Apparently once, before Amelia had lived there, someone didn't get a letter they'd been expecting and thought it had been taken by someone else in the building. Muriel felt that justified her collecting the mail of anyone who was away. Although everyone knew it was just a way to feel useful and an excuse to have a chat on their return, nobody minded. Probably, like Amelia, they preferred to have one lady glance curiously at their post than to have it sat on public view for days.

In her own flat Amelia called Patrick to assure him she'd arrived home safely.

"Glad to hear it, though of course I never doubted you." He sounded far more upbeat than he had the last time she spoke to him – and the few times before that come to think of it.

"Because you know I keep caramels in the kitchen and can always find my way to them?"

"Thought never crossed my mind. Did you have a good time?"

"Very interesting. How's Isla?"

"Still really ill, but she's recovering well from the operation which means treatment will go ahead. There's hope she'll be a lot better soon. I'm just about to leave for the hospital."

"Oh, thank goodness. I'd better let you go then."

"I'll call you later. Maybe we can meet tomorrow?"

"I'd like that, but it will have to be after four. Will you have Ava with you?"

"Yes. Sorry but at the moment I can't…"

Amelia spoke over him. "I'll bring Bongo then. I expect she'd enjoy playing with him."

"She would. Poor kid's been having a boring time of it, as well as being worried, lately. Thank you, Amelia."

It was turning into another good day. A pleasant journey home with a good book, hopeful news for Isla and two people pleased Amelia was back. To continue with the theme she took Bongo for a quick run. His excited reaction to her return further boosted her mood.

Nothing could last forever though. Amelia phoned her parents.

"I'm just ringing to say I'm home," Amelia said, mentally cursing as she heard herself use the familiar opening words.

"How is Nicole?" Mum asked, without bothering to ask if Amelia had enjoyed herself, or how she was.

"Nicole is very well. Bongo is fine too, although he missed me."

The sarcasm was wasted. "I expect he did. Such a sweet little thing and so affectionate."

"Unlike, say a child?"

"Are you not getting on well with Patrick's children?"

Amelia had meant herself as a girl, but realised she was being petty and explained that Isla was in hospital.

"Oh dear. An accident?"

"No. She's been poorly for a while. The doctors couldn't work out what was wrong, but they must know now as she's starting treatment."

"It's so distressing to see a child ill. I remember when you had meningitis. It was awful not knowing what was wrong or how to help you."

"I don't really remember."

"Good. We tried so hard to hide our fears so as not to frighten you. It was much better once we knew what was wrong. We didn't feel so helpless then."

They'd felt like that about her? If it wasn't that Mum pretending to care was even more unlikely than it really happening, Amelia wouldn't have believed it.

"What's this, stocktaking?" Jasper asked.

"Sort of," Amelia said. "It's for September's murder

mystery. Part of it involves an art gallery. We're going to use the display boards we have for conferences and things. I'm just looking round to see if we could borrow any artwork." Sonia was perfectly willing to provide the required props, but there would be costs involved and they'd have to be stored somewhere in The Fal View, so it made sense to use whatever they already had.

"There's some art deco in…"

"That's the stuff you moved into the bar for last time?"

"Yes, it's perfect for the period."

"We're doing the sixties this time."

"You need to tell me these things, sweetie."

"Does it make a difference?"

"Of course it does!"

"I realise I can't have stuff that looks modern but…"

"Modern art is exactly what you do want. Think John Sparacio and Jackson Pollock."

"I think I've heard of Jackson Pollock. Doesn't he dress up as a weird looking girl?"

"That's Grayson Perry. He's too contemporary. You really don't know anything, do you?"

Amelia had to admit that, when it came to art, she didn't. Her idea had been to gather together any paintings which had, as far as she could tell, been done before 1960. Jasper was right in another way too. Work created during the decade would be more likely to be displayed in galleries than older things, and would add to the atmosphere for anyone who knew Perry from Pollock.

She did an internet search for Jackson Pollock and then got Jasper to spell Sparacio for her. "We don't have anything in the hotel that looks anything like those," she said. "Just as well, they'd give people nightmares."

"I was expecting you to say they look like children did

them."

"Not any children I know. Ava and Isla's work is much..." She stopped herself from saying better. "It displays a far more graphically accurate, yet simplified, representation of the world in which we live."

"Oh, very good!"

"I thought so. I think I'll write some of those little caption thingies for any paintings I find."

"Let me know if you want help. I can do pretentious."

"That I don't doubt." She also didn't doubt she'd have any trouble sourcing plenty of appropriate artwork.

As planned, Amelia brought Bongo when she met Patrick and Ava in Kimberley Park.

"Melia!" the little girl yelled at first sight of her. She let go of Patrick's hand, ran up and hugged Amelia briefly before turning all her attention to the dog.

Amelia was surprised how much she missed Isla's noisy air kisses, even though she'd have made a fuss of Bongo before noticing who had hold of the lead.

Patrick, who looked incredibly tired, hugged and kissed her. It was the first time he'd done more than kiss her cheek in front of his daughter. "I've missed you," he murmured.

"I missed you too." It wasn't the serious talk she'd expected, and they'd probably have later, but it left her in no doubt they were back together.

"Have they found out in hospital what's been wrong with Isla?" Amelia asked when Ava was running round with Bongo.

"Didn't I say? Sorry, I've thought and talked about almost nothing else and forget who I've told what."

He'd told Amelia very little. "You said she's being

treated?"

"Not yet. They've prepared her to start dialysis. She has kidney failure. Now it's diagnosed it seems they've been failing for years. By last week they were barely operating at ten per cent of normal and they'll only get worse."

Amelia didn't know what to say. She'd thought it was cancer, which would have been awful, but possibly curable. It didn't sound as though there was any hope of Isla's kidneys recovering, so although the dialysis would help, it wasn't a cure. She'd need a transplant for that and from what Amelia had heard, waiting lists were long.

"That must have been a shock," she managed.

"It was, even though that's one of the things they've been testing for. The biopsy confirmed it."

She hugged him and he held her tightly for a long time.

"Group hug!" Ava demanded and joined in. "Mummy said it makes things better," she said as she tried to include Bongo.

Amelia could feel Patrick stiffen beside her. Was he expecting Amelia to react badly to mention of Meghan? Probably. It was time to show her jealousy was no longer an issue.

"Your mummy must be very clever," Amelia said.

"She is. She said I should play with Bongo double, because he will have missed me and Isla so much. He did, didn't he?"

"He missed you ever so much. I bet he's been trying to remember all the tricks you taught him." That worked and Ava, aided by biscuits from Amelia's rainbow backpack, was soon engrossed in trying to get Bongo to bark, do a roly poly and waggle his ears.

"I know it's very serious, what's wrong with Isla, but you sound a bit more positive," Amelia said.

"We've been having counselling. I thought it was a terrible idea to leave my daughter's side and talk to a stranger, but it's really helped. We'll be having regular sessions. We… I have a better idea of what to expect now, and know all the options available to Isla, and can talk about it with her and Ava."

"And Meghan." Amelia said it gently and squeezed his hand to show that wasn't an accusation.

"Yes. We can make plans now, decide what's for the best. Help Isla. We were scaring each other silly, so stopped talking about it at all." He was quiet for a little while, then said, "I'm sorry. I'd sort of shut down. I know I've been a bit… distant lately."

"It was me who went two hundred miles away. You don't have anything to be sorry about. I'm the one who was jealous. That was silly."

He grinned. "Yes it was. I'd have thought that with your detective skills you could have worked out how I feel about you."

"Sometimes a girl needs to be told."

"I know. Amelia, you're wonderful…"

"Told *and* shown! I know you've got too much going on right now, but once things are… better, more settled, will you file for divorce?"

"Of course I will. In July."

"July? Why does the date matter?"

"It will be two years since Meghan and I agreed to split up. After two years we can get a simple divorce on the grounds the marriage has broken down. Before that it's much more complicated and unpleasant."

"You were always going to do that?"

"Yes. I admit that at first I'd hoped that if I moved out we'd realise we wanted to be together, but it didn't take me long to see how miserable we'd been making each other. And then Meghan met Stuart."

"Did you mind about that?"

"It was a relief in a way. It made things more definite and I was glad she'd be happy. He's a good bloke and the kids like him. I'm sorry, Amelia. I should have told you all this."

"Maybe." She'd not exactly encouraged conversations on the subject of his ex-wife.

"And I should have told you more about Isla, so you understood the situation."

"Why, Patrick? Why didn't you tell me the truth?" She spoke gently, hoping to encourage him to let go of some of his burdens.

"Partly because, like you said, I wanted to believe it wasn't as serious as I sometimes feared. I needed to have some fun and not think about it. And partly because I was beginning to realise she was terribly ill. My girls are very important to me, they'll always be a big part of my life."

"Of course they will."

"Not everyone would be able to accept that even if they were both well. I started to think you too might become a big part of my life and didn't want to put you off. And then I saw you were growing fond of them and… I've messed everything up."

"Is that why you said we should have a break? To spare me being upset?"

"Yes. No. Well, a little bit. I couldn't bear the thought of losing you and thought that if I put things on hold I could stop that happening."

"You did mess that bit up."

"I'm an idiot."

"I wouldn't say that."

"No?"

"No. I reckon you're a silly billy!" She increased the volume towards the end of the sentence.

"Why is Daddy a silly billy?" Ava asked.

"Because we're supposed to be having a picnic and he hasn't brought any cake."

"He might have thought you'd have some in your bag." She looked at it hopefully.

"What I've got in there are some presents for you and Isla."

"Thank you, Melia."

"You can look at those later when you don't have Bongo to play with. First we need cake."

"Lots and lots of cake!"

"Hey, I've had a really good idea," Patrick said. "Why don't I get us some cake and we can have a picnic!"

Ava laughed and Amelia hardly panicked at all when she realised Patrick going meant she'd be left alone with Ava for a little while. It had been fine when the two of them had climbed up Pendennis castle together, and on other occasions when Isla had been too tired to investigate something Ava wanted to see. All she needed was something for the child to be interested in.

"Oh look, someone has drawn numbers on the ground. I wonder what it means."

"That's a hopscotch, Melia."

"What's it for?"

"I'll show you."

Ava was excellent at the demonstration, and surprisingly good with the explanations. Bongo confused matters quite a lot though, so although Amelia gradually got better, she kept making the kind of mistakes Ava found hilarious. Finally, just as Patrick returned, she got the hang of it.

The picnic, composed mostly of caramel flavoured cake and biscuits, with a token sprinkling of foods with some nutritional value, was fun. Anyone seeing them would have taken them for a family. When Ava attempted a cartwheel and banged her elbow, it was Amelia she ran to.

"I broke my arm, Melia. Can you fix it?"

"Let me see."

"Does it need a plaster?"

"No, you're not bleeding. Can you move it?"

She could. After careful examination, Amelia realised it needed to be kissed better by Dr Bongo. A sprinkle of the last cake crumbs ensured treatment was swiftly administered.

"I'm all better now!"

"Good, but no more cartwheels. You need to rest it for thirty-seven and a half hours."

"When is that to?"

"Daddy will tell you when it's OK to try again."

"That's it, give me the blame," he said.

He was smiling though, really smiling. One of the first things which had drawn Amelia to him was the way his face seemed to show just what he was feeling. At the time she'd not known how genuine that was, nor how well she could read him. As they spent more time together and the way he looked at her changed, she'd thought she saw love on his face. Then, during the week or so before they rowed, it changed to sadness and worry. She'd told herself that eyebrows and a few creases in the skin couldn't tell her what was going on inside a person. Now she knew that in this case they could – and that for a short time she'd made him happy that day.

Before Patrick and Ava left, Amelia picked up Bongo. "Take a picture of him for Isla," she said and moved the dog's paw so he waved at the camera. As she put him back down she hoped one day both sisters would try to teach him to do that on his own.

"And Ava, you give her these." Amelia gave Ava two noisy air kisses. "And this is for you." She picked Ava up, swung her round and kissed her cheek. "Thank you for teaching me hopscotch."

Amelia gave Patrick the bag containing the puzzle books she'd bought his daughters. She'd thought the jigsaw would be too difficult to manage in hospital, so kept hold of both rather than give one girl more than the other. "I'll let you decide who gets which," she said.

Patrick hugged her and kissed her again. "Thank you so much."

She knew he wasn't referring to the gifts. Knew too that the worry would soon be back on his face. Amelia would do all she could to give him some respite, until the treatment Isla was receiving meant that wasn't needed. Please let that day come – even if it made her less necessary to him.

Chapter 18

When Nicole called that evening Amelia was able to report that things were looking more hopeful for Isla, and for Amelia's relationship with the girl's father.

"Now, what about you and Miguel? What's happening there?"

"We're still in touch."

"And that's it? You had me convinced you were going to sell up the B&B and move over there."

"I did have some vague thoughts about doing something like that, but it was no more than a day dream really. I hardly know him, do I?"

"No, suppose not. I'm glad you're not going, but it sounded as though you'd found someone special and I want that for you."

"He is special. In fact I'm thinking of inviting him over."

"Crikey." That sounded like a properly thought out decision, not the impulse of a holiday romance.

"Yes. Anyway, back to you. How are you feeling about the possibility of being a stepmother?"

Amelia knew better than to push before her friend was ready to talk. "Better. Ava taught me hopscotch."

"I think you'll find that was me. About… well, let's not worry how many years ago."

"As it turns out you were a rubbish teacher. I kept getting it wrong and making her laugh."

"Clever."

"I thought so. And it made me see something. I don't need to be her mother, she has one of those."

"Good point. You don't want to try and compete with Manky Meghan over the kids. You'd lose in a fair fight. Rightly so, I suppose."

"Yep."

"And with Patrick? Are you competing there?"

"I don't think so... But if I am, I won't be fighting fair!"

"You'll win. You're gorgeous and lovely. And what is she?"

Amelia laughed. "She's manky!" She doubted that was true. Isla and Ava were really pretty and didn't take after their father, and the glimpse Amelia had of Meghan's back view suggested she took trouble over her appearance. That didn't matter though. Amelia knew she was attractive, besides if Patrick couldn't see beyond looks then he wasn't the man for her. She wanted a relationship which would be just as strong after her glossy black hair turned grey, her tiny waist thickened and her laughter lines set into wrinkles.

"Seriously, Amelia, to know you is to love you. If it's what you want, then it'll work out somehow."

"It is what I want. Even before I spoke to him, I felt like I knew him. And then when we did speak, I wanted to know him a whole lot better."

"There you go then. You're a good judge of people. You didn't take to Sean Underhill did you? And you were right, he's odd."

"You thought so too," Amelia said.

"Now I know for sure. He phoned and clearly expected you to answer, and then for me to know who he was, which admittedly I did, but still."

"Sorry. I shouldn't have given him your number and let him think it was mine."

"Don't worry, it's public – he could easily have found it. That's not the problem. It was how he reacted when I said you'd gone home. He seemed to want you for something and wasn't at all happy he wasn't going to have his way. Aargh that man's ego! He asked what you'd told me about him, as though you'd only have wanted to see me so you could brag about meeting the wonderful Sean Underhill. Proper set my back up and I didn't tell him anything."

"Good. Not that he annoyed you, obvs."

"You don't want me to pass on your number then?"

"Not really. If he actually hears something about Angus McKellar I'd be interested. Have you heard anything about that?"

"No. Just the usual – concerns are growing and it seems the police are involved, but no actual information. I'll let you know if there is, you know that."

"I do. And I'm always pleased to hear from you even if there's no news."

"Well obvs. I'm just that fascinating!"

"You are, but I've heard quite enough about Sean Underhill, from the man himself, to last me for the entire rest of my life."

"OK, not to worry. I wasn't sure what to say, so pretended a guest had turned up to check in. If he calls back I'll offer to take his number to pass to you, but say I have a policy of not passing on guests' numbers without their permission – which of course I wouldn't do."

"He knows I wasn't just a guest."

"Oh. Does he know where you live and work?" Nicole asked.

"I'm not sure if I gave him the name of the hotel, but I expect I said enough that anyone could work it out if they were particularly interested. He does know it's in Falmouth."

"OK, if he asks I'll confirm that much, but no more."

As Amelia left work after the early shift, she almost bumped into Bianca who was rushing into the hotel.

"Something wrong?" she asked. Bianca had a fortnight's holiday booked and was driving up to meet friends in Wales that morning.

"I can't find my phone charger. I don't often use the car one, but we'll be camping some of the time. I was going to check the electricals box and see if there was one in there."

"Doubt it," Amelia said. They kept a variety of chargers and adapters on reception, to lend to guests as needed, but they were all for use in the building. "You can borrow mine if it fits."

They checked and it was suitable.

"You're sure you won't need it?" Bianca asked.

"I won't be making any long drives."

"Thanks then. I really appreciate it."

"Have a great time."

Amelia hadn't left the car park before her phone rang.

"Do you have any free time today? And if you do, how do you feel about going somewhere with me and Ava?"

It was tactful of Patrick to let her know he intended to bring Ava with him if she did admit to being free. "I don't have much planned, and nothing I can't put off."

"Great. It did us both a lot of good to have a break away from everything to do with hospitals and illness, and of course we enjoyed spending time with you. Sorry, I should have said that bit first."

"But it's so incredibly true you thought it almost went without saying?"

"That's the one."

"I do want to get out in the sunshine today and I suppose it wouldn't be too terrible to be with you for a while."

His chuckle told her she'd been right – the best way to help him was to provide a distraction. He had medical staff and counsellors to discuss Isla's condition with, and Meghan to worry with. Amelia might not be competing with her, but it wouldn't hurt that Patrick's memories of the two of them through this time were very different and that it was Amelia who made him happy.

Patrick suggested a walk. They'd all been spending too much time indoors and Ava especially often had to sit down and be quiet. She was a really good kid and tried, but it didn't come naturally.

"A walk it is then. I'll fetch Bongo and we'll see if we can tire them both out."

After arranging when Patrick would collect her, Amelia rang Gabrielle who she'd be taking over from at work that evening, and asked if she'd be able to stay on a bit later if that was needed.

"Is this about the sick little girl?"

"Her sister. She needs cheering up. We're going for a long walk and I don't want to have to cut it short if…"

"Take as long as you need. I assume you're taking Bongo, so not having to walk him when I get in will save me time."

"I'll make it up to you, I promise."

"Thank you for our books, Melia. Isla says thank you too."

"And so do I," Patrick added. "Perfect for little girls who have to stay still for a while."

The walk was fun and gave Amelia the chance to show off her still very limited bird knowledge. "You see that one with the black head and beady eye?" she asked Ava.

"He's watching us to see if we've got chips."

"I expect so. Do you know his name?"

"Dylan!"

"It might be, but what I meant is that he's a black headed gull."

"Called Dylan! There's a boy in my school called Dylan and he's always watching to see if there's anything to eat. That's why he's Isla's friend, so he can eat her lunch."

"Oh." She glanced at Patrick, who it seemed had only just learned why the school hadn't been particularly concerned about Isla's poor appetite.

"He won't be able to when she's better, because she'll want it all," Amelia said.

"She's not better yet, Melia. She needs lots of parrot and eel and we need to wash our hands and not do homework at home and then she will be better. Is that right, Daddy?"

"Yes, love."

"I see." As Ava seemed comforted by her own explanation Amelia decided to wait before asking Patrick for slightly more detailed information.

"What's that bird there?" Patrick pointed to a big gull, or tern, or whatever, which was pretty much the same light brown all over.

"Looks like a lesser spotted storm ousel," Amelia said with confidence.

"Thought so."

"He hasn't got spots," Ava pointed out.

"That's why he's a lesser spotted one. A greater spotted one has so many spots they're all joined together and you can't see anything else."

"Did Daddy tell you? Cos he's a silly billy and makes things up."

"Actually I made it up," Amelia confessed.

"Then you're a silly billy too!"

How odd, that felt exactly like a compliment. To earn it, Amelia joined in a three way competition to make up the silliest bird facts. Patrick won, by pointing out some black and white birds with long orange beaks. He informed them they were oyster catchers, which Amelia was fairly certain was true.

"Is it their job to catch oysters?" Ava asked.

"No. They do catch them and eat them for breakfast, but it's not their job."

"What is then?" Amelia asked.

"They farm traffic cones. See, they're all carrying little tiny ones? They grow them until they're big enough to go on the roads."

"Do they, Melia?"

"They might do. What do you think?"

"I'm going to ask Mummy. She's not a silly billy!"

That made Amelia even happier she was considered to be one, but wanted to prove she knew things too. She pointed out all the wildflowers she knew the names of – moon daisies, hogweed, seathrift.

"How do you know, Melia?"

"It's just like learning the names of people. Everyone is different... That one there is Valerian. That was easy to learn, because it's the name of a girl I was at school with."

"She's your friend?"

"I haven't seen her for a long time," Amelia said. That was true, although it didn't answer the question. Valerian had been put into the same children's home as Nicole when they were all about fourteen. Although she'd been a bit weird and intense, Nicole and Amelia had tried hard to be nice to her. It wasn't always easy and it wasn't enough for Valerian. She hadn't wanted to be a friend to the pair of them, but the best friend to one and for the other to be pushed aside. It hadn't seemed to matter which... Amelia wasn't going to spoil the lovely day with memories of that awkward time in her childhood, and looked round for more plants she recognised.

"That spiky bush is gorse. You're only allowed to kiss people when it's in flower."

"There's loads of flowers on it, Melia."

"Then we get lots of kisses!" She kissed both of Ava's cheeks, then did the same to Patrick.

Ava followed suit. "You know lots of things, Melia."

When she named red campion, which Ava correctly pointed out was pink, she was in danger of reverting to silly billy status, but the discovery of a white one rescued her.

"Do you do mixing up paints at school to get different colours?" she asked Ava.

"Yes. Yellow and blue make green and red and yellow make orange."

"And how do you get pink?"

"Red and white." It was sweet watching her start to work it out. "The pink ones are called red because they're more red than the white ones?"

"That's it exactly." The conversation reminded Amelia

of her plan to obtain suitable modern art for the next murder mystery weekend.

"I know Daddy has some paintings you and Isla did when you were younger. I was hoping I could have a look at them and maybe borrow some."

"What for, Melia?"

"We're going to be doing a special thing at work, where people pretend they are all living a long time ago."

"Like when you and Daddy met and he was two different peoples?"

"Yes, just like that." Had the girls asked how the relationship started? It was a nice thought they were interested in her enough to wonder. "This time there's going to be an art exhibition, and I think your paintings might be just right."

"We could do new ones. We're better now we're big."

"Yes, I expect you are." They'd be too good, in Amelia's opinion, but as Jasper had pointed out it was hardly an informed opinion. She wouldn't foist it on Ava, who seemed more than capable of deciding for herself what she liked and didn't like. "The thing is, I need a particular style of painting." She used her phone to show the little girl images of work by the two artists Jasper had mentioned.

"We could do things like that," Ava said with absolute confidence. "Don't worry, Melia. We'll help."

"It would be wonderful if you did." She wasn't sure if their paintings would really be something she could use, but they both loved to paint and draw, and Isla was going to need indoor activities which didn't exhaust her. "I'll get you the paper and paints of course." It would be nice to have an excuse to buy them things without feeling guilty for spoiling them.

"Oh look, that's a wild orchid," Amelia said a few moments later. Thankfully Ava didn't know there was more than one kind of orchid so didn't ask unanswerably searching questions. Early purple and common spotted were the only names Amelia knew. The one she found was a single plant in a very pale shade of mauve and in any case, how late in the year was considered early in orchid terms?

They had fun collecting fallen foxglove flowers and trying them on their fingers to see if they were foxes. Ava and Amelia were, Patrick wasn't.

"Can we pick flowers, Melia?"

"For Isla?"

"No, for Mummy. She's sad."

Of course she was. She'd be just as worried as Patrick. Ava who didn't understand all that was going on, was clearly still upset by their emotions.

"That's a really good idea, but let's wait until you're nearly going home, so they don't wilt."

Back at the car Amelia not only helped with the picking, but put some of the water she'd brought for Bongo into the plastic cup she'd brought for Ava to drink from, to act as a temporary vase.

"I love you, Melia," Ava said.

Amelia was too surprised, and too emotional to respond other than by picking her up and kissing her.

When she'd put his daughter down, Patrick pulled Amelia into his arms. "Thank you for today, it's really helped," he said, then gave her a quick kiss.

"It's been fun."

"You're supposed to say I love you!" Ava instructed.

"Oh, is that right?" Patrick answered.

"Yes. And you, Melia!"

Patrick nodded slightly in Bongo's direction and winked. Together he and Amelia crouched down, ruffled the dog's hair and told him they loved him loads and loads.

Ava giggled. "Two silly billies!" Then she joined in petting the dog. "I love you, Bongo! And Isla does too. Mwa mwa mwa!"

That evening Nicole rang to say Sean called back and had been fishing for information on Amelia. "I didn't want it to seem I wasn't being helpful, so I said I'd make sure you had his number, in case you wanted to contact him. I'll text it to you. I don't want to be a liar."

"You said you don't want to seem difficult, but I got the impression you wouldn't mind actually being difficult," Amelia said.

"He got my back up a bit. Rather too cocky, acting like he was doing me a favour talking to me. He wasn't, I wanted to get on and didn't fall for him wanting to do a TV piece on my place."

"He said that?"

"Hinted it. Who knows, maybe he does want to, but it would be for his benefit not mine. He'd seem all supportive of local business, but it would only go out locally, so not really draw in customers for me and anyway, I've got as much business as I can handle."

"You didn't like him any more off the TV than on, did you?" Amelia asked.

"Oh? Did it show? I'm used to having to be nice to my visitors all the time, which isn't difficult as almost all of them are lovely, but I do like the chance not to like someone now and again, if you see what I mean?"

"Absolutely I do. One of the hazards of being in the hospitality trade, I guess."

That wasn't why Amelia hadn't felt entirely comfortable with Sean though. Amelia rarely wanted to complain about people, but if she did then Jasper would listen and be entertainingly sympathetic, or she could talk to Gabrielle, Jorge or Charles.

Could Amelia's uneasiness over Sean be because she felt guilty for spending time with him? She and Patrick had kind of split up, but she knew she wouldn't like to learn he'd been taking a young woman to places of interest while she was away, just as she hadn't been happy about him taking Meghan to Llanhydrock. Of course taking the girls and the fact she was their mother made a difference. And that was before she realised how ill Isla was. It made sense they wanted to keep everything at home as familiar as possible and to reassure both girls.

Nicole's text arrived with Sean's number. Out of context it would seem Nicole wanted her to call him. What was it with phone calls? She again had a feeling there was something in her memory she should listen to. Something to do with Sean?

Amelia was reminded of his interview with the postcard collector. That wasn't what she was sure was lurking in her subconscious, but she was curious about how it turned out and looked for it in online. The final version made the hobby sound not fascinating exactly, but not deadly dull and Sean had come across as genuinely interested in the subject and the heavily edited stories he was told.

It didn't help. "There's something I need to remember. Something important."

During a break at work Amelia rang Nicole and told her how much closer she and Patrick had become in the two days since she'd returned from Lee-on-the-Solent.

"We've talked a bit about our relationship before and he even joked about me becoming Mrs Homes. Now we're not talking about that sort of thing, despite encouragement from Ava, but somehow we're saying more."

"Ava's encouraging that?"

"She's a great one for stories where people get married and live happily ever after. I don't think it's more than that, but she definitely likes me and she's adorable."

"I'm sure I said you can't have a favourite. You'd better buck up and get fond of the other one before you become their stepmum."

"I am. Admittedly I liked Ava more, but then with Isla being so ill she wouldn't have been at her best – but there's no guarantee I'll be their stepmother."

"Bet you a caramel flavoured wedding cake!"

"You're on."

"Hang on, someone at the door, I'll just see who it is." She was soon back. "Sean Underhill would you believe!"

"Crikey. What does he want?"

"Nothing I'm willing to offer!" Nicole laughed. "I'll get rid of him and call you back."

Amelia waited ten minutes for Nicole to call her back. Then she tried calling her. There was no response.

Chapter 19

Amelia's next 'date' with Patrick and Ava was a game of crazy golf followed by lunch. When he collected Amelia, Patrick returned the plastic cup which had contained the wildflowers. With it was a pretty card, saying 'To Amelia, Thank you' and signed by Meghan. It somehow felt like more than just politeness for Ava's sake.

Amelia was even worse at the golf game than she'd anticipated. Naturally Ava, who was considerably better, found that hilarious. Patrick did too. She couldn't tell if he was more amused before or after realising it wasn't put on for comic effect. However he did use that knowledge as an excuse to stand close and put his arms around Amelia as he coached her.

It felt like months not weeks since he'd last held her and she didn't need telling he missed their physical contact as much as she did. Probably it was for the best that it only took her a few tries, with Ava retrieving the ball each time, for Amelia to hit it over the little bridge, but she couldn't help being sorry that success meant he let go.

By the time they'd all got round the course, they were more than ready for lunch. After their burgers the three of them shared an enormous ice cream sundae.

"What flavour sauce would you like?" the waiter asked.

"Melia wants caramel," Ava said before the others thought to ask what the options were. "And Daddy wants chocolate and I want strawbererry."

The sundae arrived not only heaped with whipped cream, Maltesers, glacé cherries and chunks of something weirdly chewy, but drenched in the three sauces. An attempt to keep each to one third of the dessert had been made, but that didn't stop Ava from eating half of the chocolate and caramel segments as well as all of the part covered in strawberry sauce.

"I could of eated it all up myself, but didn't want to."

"Why not?" Amelia asked.

"It's not so much fun doing things on my own."

"You must miss your sister," said Amelia, who'd often wished she could spend all day every day with Nicole, rather than being left to entertain herself so much.

Ava nodded solemnly. "And she misses me even more. Poor Isla is chronololically bored in hospital."

No doubt she'd overheard an adult discussing her sister, but it was equally clear that she'd noticed and sympathised with what she'd misheard.

When it was time to go, Amelia said she had a present for Isla, to help her not be so bored. It was another puzzle book similar to the ones she'd bought in Southampton.

"That's kind," Patrick said. "You really don't have to, but I'm sure she'll be pleased."

Ava said nothing.

"And I have something for you too, Ava, as I bet you're bored sometimes, because you miss her."

Ava smiled brightly. "Thank you." She looked even happier when Amelia presented a gift wrapped package much larger than Isla's as it contained both jigsaws. "That's very ever so kind."

"It is," Patrick murmured. "Thank you."

Ava gave her both a regular kiss on the cheek and

noisy air kisses explaining, "These are from Isla." Then she added, "I love you, Melia!"

"I love you too, sweetie."

Ava made a kind of shooing gesture Amelia guessed was to encourage her and Patrick to declare their love. The child put her hands on her hips and sighed theatrically when the adults shook hands.

They both laughed, then shared a hug. Patrick's lips made contact with her cheek and lingered there. "Thank you for today. You've been wonderful again."

Now might not be the right time for her to say she loved him, but she could try to show it. She gave him a proper kiss and said, "I've had a great time, really. I'm here for you, OK?"

"Thank you."

As she waved them goodbye, Amelia reflected on how easy it had been to tell Ava she loved her. Easy because it was true. And she'd instinctively called her sweetie – the same nickname her two best friends sometimes used for her.

She needed to think up a good name for Isla too. Sugar? No, that seemed as sickly and empty as the substance. Caramel? It might help even out her favouritism to associate Isla with that, but it wouldn't be so easy to say. Oh well, sadly it seemed there was plenty of time to think about it as Isla was still far from well.

There had still been no word from Nicole and she didn't answer her mobile. Amelia had left one message on the landline's answering machine and was about to try calling that again, when Patrick rang with wonderful news. "Isla has recovered from the operation well enough to leave hospital temporarily. I'm bringing her home today."

"I'm so pleased!"

"She's still not ready to start treatment, but it won't be long. The doctors are confident they can get her stable with dialysis. That's not a complete answer, but there are several longer term options. For now what's important is that she'll be able to sleep in her own bed and eventually get up to mischief with Ava and go to school."

"You must be so relieved." He'd got his daughter back, and from his joyful tone she'd almost got her boyfriend back.

"I am. It's just felt so wrong without her. And it's good news for us too. We can have a proper date, just the two of us."

"I'd like that. Ava is lovely, but…"

"Exactly."

He surprised Amelia by suggesting dinner out. She'd expected to go to his place, or have him come to hers, and said she'd be happy to do that.

"I owe you a meal you don't have to cook and isn't a choice of either spag bol. or spaghetti with Bolognese sauce."

"Well, if your classic fish finger special isn't on offer, we may as well go out."

"I wasn't planning on letting you get away with never trying that, but not tonight."

"You want to go out tonight?"

"If you're free and want to."

"I am and I do."

"I'll stay with the girls until they're asleep. That should be about seven as Ava has school in the morning. Shall I aim to pick you up at eight?"

"Perfect." She didn't begrudge Meghan having his

company until then. It was right they spent some time together as a family – and it was Amelia he'd chosen to celebrate the good news with.

As Amelia was showering before dinner with Patrick, she received a voice mail message from Nicole's landline. "Sorry about not calling you back, but something too awful to talk about happened."

Amelia laughed and called her straight back. There was no reply. She tried her landline and got no reply to that either. Odd, but Nicole must be OK. If something awful really had happened she wouldn't break it like that, besides she'd definitely sounded like she was kidding.

It wasn't until Patrick buzzed the intercom and said, "Good evening, Miss Watson, may I come up?" that she realised her slight nervous feeling wasn't entirely due to her friend not answering the phone.

"Good evening, Mr Homes. Yes, you may."

When she opened her flat door to see he was very smartly dressed and clutching a bunch of multi-coloured daisies, Amelia knew his formality was only partly a joke. Somehow it felt almost as though she and Patrick were starting again.

Patrick was quiet on the drive to the restaurant.

"Everything OK with Isla?" Amelia asked.

"Delighted to be home, as are we all. I don't think the long-term implications have properly registered for any of us yet."

"Can I help? Do you want to talk about it?"

"I feel I've done nothing but talk about it. You can help best by providing a distraction."

"I'll do my best – and if there's anything else I can help with, just say. OK?"

"OK."

In the restaurant where they'd once witnessed a proposal, they ordered a glass of wine each. Patrick was driving and Amelia had the early shift in the morning, but they wanted to toast Isla's return from hospital. After they'd drunk to her good health Patrick said, "So tell me what's been going on in the real world. How was your trip?"

"Ha! I can answer one question or the other."

"Tell me about your friend then. Nicole isn't it?"

"I didn't see much of her. I was looking after the place so she could go away on a trip of her own."

"You were on your own? Sorry. You did say you were helping her out, but I didn't quite realise... Were you very bored?"

She was still a little hurt about the lack of notice he'd paid to anything she'd said in the days before they temporarily split up, but did understand. There was something she could tell him that might get his attention.

"I wouldn't consider witnessing a murder boring."

"What?!" He laughed. "OK, I deserved that for not listening. What really happened?"

She told him about her week, doing her best to make it funny, but not leaving out the fact she'd spent time with Sean after the murder. She didn't want to make Patrick overly jealous, just to be honest. And as she was being honest with him she was with herself too and acknowledged she wanted him to have some idea how she'd felt towards Meghan. It seemed to work. Patrick teased her about playing detective and she was confident he'd make every effort to come with her when she next went to Lee-on-the-Solent.

Patrick came up to her flat when he brought her home,

but only stepped inside the door. He kissed her long enough and passionately enough that she thought he might stay. When at last he stopped, he simply said, "Later," and left without another word. Initially there was no sound of footsteps after he gently closed her door. For a minute she thought he might change his mind, but no such luck. Knowing he'd been reluctant to leave wasn't really any consolation at all.

Amelia tried calling Nicole several times, getting no response. She'd started to worry something might actually be wrong by the time her friend rang back.

"Your Sean and my local mystery have gone national," she announced.

"He's not my Sean and I've not seen any mention of it on TV here." She was a bit miffed at Nicole for leaving that worrying message and not contacting her since.

"Have you been looking?"

"No," Amelia admitted. The disappearance of Angus McKellar seemed less important once she was home, had made up with Patrick, and knew what was wrong with Isla. She realised that, when she told Patrick, she'd given the impression any mystery was all in the past.

"You know some of the Salterns Support money has been taken?"

"I thought it was unaccounted for, rather than definitely stolen? I know Sean's earlier reports suggested it had been taken, but he'd been trying to make a bigger story out of the disappearance to make sure it was featured on the news."

"It's gone alright and we're talking hundreds of thousands. Apparently this came to light before Angus's second disappearance. He used to say charity begins at home and laugh like it was a big joke."

"Did he?" Amelia had seen nothing like that in the clips of him she'd seen.

"They're talking about it on a local Facebook group and someone put a clip up. I'll send you a link."

"Salterns Support is a local charity though – maybe he was just anti helping foreigners?" Which was actually quite horrible really. Fair enough to pick one charity and support that, but it wasn't nice to be pleased about not helping anyone else. "Do you think he was helping himself?"

"Had to have been, didn't he? Sean's been really careful what he says on the news, but he definitely thinks so."

"How do you know that, and why did you let me think you'd disappeared or had something terrible happen to you."

"It did. Oh sorry, you don't know! I couldn't get rid of Sean yesterday. He was really weird, like he was on drugs or something and said he needed you to prove he was innocent and asked what you'd said. Of course I said I had no idea what he was talking about. He calmed down a bit and asked if it was true you were interested in crime."

"I told him I was," Amelia said.

"I guessed you must have for him to ask, so said I thought it was. He asked if I thought you'd help him prove his innocence."

"What is it he's accused of?"

"Taking the charity money. He didn't say so then though and got really agitated. Then he snatched my phone and dropped it down the steps smashing it."

"He did what?"

"That bit was an accident. He wanted your number. I told him that was the only place I had it. He swore and then just when I thought things might get nasty he went."

"Awful for you."

"It wasn't nice at the time and it was a pain getting the phone sorted, but I'm starting to feel sorry for him."

"Because he broke your phone and it now looks as though he's involved in a crime?"

"It looks like he might be being framed over the missing money. And he was really sorry about the phone. He brought a huge bunch of flowers to apologise and offered to buy a new one."

"I hope you picked an expensive model."

"I'd already put in an insurance claim."

"So?"

"He said he'd had a lot on his mind lately and hadn't been thinking straight. Said he'd still like to hear from you."

"I'm still not sure I want to speak to him, but I'll watch the news report first."

"No, first you'll tell me how things are with you and Patrick, and with that little girl of his."

After Amelia had filled her in she added, "When I first realised things might get serious with us, I worried if I'd find it hard to accept he's a father."

"I know you did and I told you it would be OK, didn't I?"

"Probably. You did tell me I wanted kids, I didn't believe you but…"

"I was right as usual?"

"I reckon I'm already more loving to Patrick's children than my parents ever were to me."

"I'm sure they do love you, in their way. They're just

not great at showing it. Maybe there's a reason?"

"Maybe." Amelia didn't hide her doubts.

"Remember how you used to invent stories about why I was in the children's home? It always involved parents who loved me giving me up for my own good. I think that's often right. Not so much the bits about them having to return to their own planet, or being spies, but that thinking the baby would be better off without them. Depression can do that, or poverty."

"They had good jobs and even if Dad caught post natal depression from Mum, I think it usually wears off after a couple of decades."

"Yeah, it's not that, but there could be something. They were always welcoming to me. Making that effort to be nice to your friend shows they do care, doesn't it?"

"Good point." Because Nicole was in care, arranging for her to come round, or to take her out for the day, wasn't as simple as just phoning her parents to check it was OK. Would parents who didn't want one child have gone to so much trouble for a second, just to make the first one happy?

Amelia had come to realise that because she expected her parents to be cold and disinterested she sometimes caused that to happen. Who wanted a long friendly chat with someone who made it clear she'd called for a single reason and didn't expect the conversation to continue after that had been dealt with? Families were hard and people got hurt.

"I wonder if I shouldn't get so close to Isla and Ava?"

"Because she's so ill?"

"No! No. It will hurt like hell if anything more happens to her, but that's no reason to keep my distance."

"What then?"

"I don't know things will work out with Patrick."

"No, of course you don't. Nobody does. You know if you want it to though, and if you're prepared to work at it."

"That's true." And she knew the answer.

It was about the time the girls would be going to bed, so Amelia didn't disturb Patrick and instead turned her attention to something she didn't yet know enough about.

First she checked out the Facebook group Nicole had sent a link for. It was horrible. Half of those commenting 'knew' Angus was a liar, thief, adulterer and worse, and that those who disagreed were either stupid or just as bad themselves. Those who thought Angus could be innocent accused the others of judging people by their own standards. A lot of that was done with a great deal of swearing, too many capital letters, and very little punctuation.

There was quite a debate about his products. It began as a light-hearted discussion about personal favourites, but became heated when someone who considered giving sugar to children to be a form of child abuse joined in.

Amelia found the clip Nicole told her about. In it Angus did indeed say, "Charity begins at home," and then laugh. Underneath was a comment saying, 'You need the context to this. He's talking about a home he helped fund, where families of disabled kids can go for a break'. That had 37 likes. Below that someone had typed, 'CON IS RIGHT!!!' That had 82 likes.

Sean's latest reports about the disappearance were a little different from his earlier versions. They now mentioned that 'huge sums of money' were apparently missing from the Salterns Support charity Angus McKellar had set up, and had been taken over quite a long period. Sean did nothing at all to hint that Angus could possibly be involved – but the fact that man and money had both vanished without trace was enough to suggest that possibility.

The other main difference was that Sean had stopped using mention of Angus and the charity as an excuse to remind viewers what a wonderful person he was himself, for running marathons, helping to raise money and giving his time to Salterns Support. Instead he remarked on the way McKellar's confectionery had become such a huge brand since Angus opened his shop in Falmouth.

There was nothing in the reports to suggest Sean was involved in taking the money, which there wouldn't be as he was reporting. But if he'd been accused of anything, would he be allowed to do the reports? Clearly Sean wasn't under arrest.

Why had Nicole thought Sean was in trouble? Because he'd said he needed Amelia to help prove him innocent. That did sound as though he really was, but innocent of what and how did he think Amelia could help? She certainly wanted to try if there was really something she could do. Assisting Sean wasn't high on her list of priorities, but righting an injustice definitely was.

That a crime had taken place was not in doubt. As Nicole had said, Angus's disappearance along with that of the Salterns Support charity money was now being reported on the national news, and even Amelia's local news channels. Far more of their report was devoted to McKellar's confectionery than was the case with Outlook South, which understandably had concentrated more on his local charity activities. Only the local stations made a connection with Falmouth, and they milked it to the extent viewers must have been wondering why he ever left.

When it came to the disappearance of man and money, words such as 'allegedly', 'apparently' and 'speculation' were used so frequently on some channels it sounded as though the reporters knew Angus McKellar was guilty, but were legally prevented from saying so. Equally clear was that Angus wasn't the only trustee for the charity. The other was his close friend Sean Underhill. They played clips of Sean talking about Angus.

Amelia saw why Sean was worried. If Angus could have accessed the missing money on his own, then so could Sean. And if it needed both of them, then Sean was implicated.

It wasn't a nice thought, but Amelia had no trouble imagining Sean turning a blind eye to financial irregularities in order to cover up for his friend and benefactor – even if that did mean the children's respite centre they'd both supported lost out on much needed funding.

Chapter 20

As Amelia passed the bar area at work she heard a man say, "Nae bother, hen."

She had no reason to go into the bar for work and Jasper wasn't on duty, but she stopped walking – although she now preferred Irish, she'd always liked the Scottish accent, and that one was kind of familiar.

"Are you finished with this table the now?" she heard, and went back.

"That's braw. I didnae want to take the seat if you were coming back, you ken."

It was no good, she'd have to go in and see if he was wearing a kilt and Tam o' Shanter, drinking whisky and Irn Bru, and feeding porridge to his pet haggis.

Nobody in the bar was wearing tartan, sporting ginger hair or in any other way looking the slightest bit Scottish. Even so, Amelia had absolutely no doubt which of the drinkers she'd heard talking. That's because she was looking straight at Angus McKellar!

It couldn't be.

She looked again, but he was studying the bar snacks menu at very close range, so she couldn't see his face properly. Of course it couldn't be. True the accent had reminded her of him, but it was stronger than the one she'd heard in the TV news clips. For a moment in Lee-on-the-Solent she'd thought she'd seen him, just before discovering the truth about Patrick blowing kisses. It would have been unlikely for her to have stumbled across the man she was looking for so near to his home. Him turning up at her hotel while everyone was searching for him was impossible. OK, not absolutely impossible. Dead or alive the man must be somewhere, and he did have a connection to Falmouth.

A pity Jasper wasn't on duty. Amelia could have engaged him in a random conversation so she could keep watch and he'd have played along. With Zac, the barman who was working, she'd need to discuss work matters and couldn't do so for too long without the poor chap getting paranoid she thought he wasn't up to the job.

Amelia did her best to simultaneously conduct a normal conversation and surveillance on the customer, by use of the mirror behind the bar. The Scot had the same hair colour as Angus, but it wasn't so overly neat as usual. Although he wasn't wearing anything she recognised, he had the same terrible dress sense. He'd seemed a little taller than average on TV. He was sitting so it was hard to tell, but his head was a bit higher than several other occupants of the bar.

"There haven't been any complaints have there?" the junior barman asked.

"Not at all. I just feel… Well, I wanted to get to know you better."

"Right." That didn't seem to have helped at all. She'd have to get Jasper to say something to reassure him.

The Scot tugged at his ear, just as Amelia had noticed Angus doing. She remembered that although it was often considered to be a sign of a liar, she'd thought it could be nerves, as it happened when he was being praised on TV, and if he were a modest man then that could make him uncomfortable. Maybe she'd been both right and wrong and he was uncomfortable because he was lying about doing things for charity and actually spending the money himself? Could it be him?

McKellar's face had often seemed red and this man was pale, but Angus was often being interviewed after a marathon, or some other outdoor event, and on TV maybe he'd have make up on. This man seemed thinner, especially in the face. If he was on the run, or having a breakdown, or recovering from an alcoholic binge, he probably would look drawn.

Angus coming to Falmouth made a certain amount of sense. He might feel safer somewhere he knew, or still have contacts who could help him. But why would he hide out in her hotel? And if he was hiding, why not do more to disguise himself?

"Actually it's not you I'm checking up on," Amelia told young Zac. "See the man in the hideous yellow shirt and lurid green trousers?"

"I'm colour blind."

"Oh. Sorry." She almost said 'lucky you' but the horror of those clothes was more than compensated for by the beauty of wild flowers, medieval tapestries and the fabulous cocktails Jasper had almost certainly taught him to make. "In the far corner. Tallish."

"And Scottish?"

"That's him."

As though to prove the point, Amelia heard him say, "Careful there, hen," to a woman who'd just got up from her seat at a nearby table. Amelia hadn't spotted whatever caused his comment.

"What's he done?" the barman asked.

"Maybe nothing, but let me know if you notice anything odd, will you?"

"I don't know if it's odd, or just living up to his national stereotype, but he only buys the one drink and makes it last."

"He's been in before?"

"Every night since last Sunday. I've seen him once before now and Jasper mentioned him and his clothes. He wanted to have a word with him about them, but decided it might be better not to."

"Ordinarily I'd agree with that, but if either of you can get him talking, please do."

"Can I offer him a free whisky? He really should be drinking that, not lager even if it is McEwans."

"If you think it will help."

"What am I looking for?"

"I'd rather not say in case it colours your judgement." She winced inwardly at her mention of colour. "Please let me know anything you notice."

"Both times I've seen him he's grabbed that seat as soon as it's free. And he speaks a lot, but doesn't talk to people if you know what I mean?"

"Not really."

"It's like he's lonely, so wants to interact, but still wants to be alone."

"Thanks." If Amelia ever needed someone to study a suspect Zac would be the perfect person for the job.

Everything she'd seen and heard fitted with the yellow-shirted Scot being Angus McKellar, but Amelia was far from certain he was. It had been his clothes, actions and to a lesser extent his voice which had made him distinctive. Otherwise there was little to set him apart from many other white middle-aged men, and there were always plenty of those in The Fal View. Amelia was pleased though with the analytical way she'd studied him and would enjoy trying to rule out the possibility that she'd found the missing man. Someone, another Scot she thought, had said that ruling out the wrong answers was as important as finding the right ones. Or a step in that direction at any rate.

Later Amelia checked the hotel register. Not surprisingly there was no Angus McKellar listed, nor any other name she knew. There was a man with the initial A booked in. Amelia amused herself by calling his room. "Good evening, sir. Housekeeping here, just calling to check you have sufficient towels."

His, "I sure do, Honey," swiftly eliminated him.

Amelia rang Patrick who actually answered. "Sorry, I've not been ignoring you, honestly."

"I know that. Was Isla able to start treatment today?"

"She was and it went well. The doctors were very pleased and Isla's biggest complaint is that it's boring."

"I can imagine it would be. Will she have to go back to hospital for every session?" Amelia had looked up dialysis on the internet, but as there were different kinds and as Patrick hadn't specified she wasn't absolutely sure which Isla would have.

"Only until Meghan and I've had the training and we can get the kit for her to have it at home. We'll have to be really careful about infections and things especially at first, but eventually she'll be able to go back to school."

"That's great. So it's peritoneal dialysis she's having?" She'd guessed that, based on Ava's reference to parrot and eel treatments and the fact her internet browsing suggested it was usually the best option for a child.

"Correct, detective."

"She'll be out of hospital again soon, then?"

"Everything is looking good for that. She'll still be ill, but she'll be recovering, and not having to go into hospital all the time will make things easier on all of us."

"And Ava? She OK?"

"Fine. She's getting bored. She's been really good but it's been difficult for her and sometimes she plays up to get attention."

Amelia could understand that. She was feeling a bit neglected herself. What made it worse was she now had the free time she'd lacked when they first met. She was a grown up though, so wouldn't add to Patrick's problems by complaining.

When he asked what she was doing, Amelia replied, "Solving another mystery."

"No hotels guests been murdered I hope?"

"Not quite as exciting as that... Have you seen on the news about Angus McKellar stealing charity money and going missing?"

"Can't remember the last time I watched anything but kids' TV."

"Well he's missing and I think he might be staying at The Fal View."

"Why would he do that?"

"I don't know, but he did live near here once, it looks like him and he's Scottish and acting odd."

"Better keep an eye on him then."

"That's my plan."

He'd been humouring her, but Amelia wouldn't let his dismissive attitude put her off. She completely understood why Patrick wasn't spending much time with her, and was distracted when he did, but she needed something to keep her amused and occupied. In that situation she often played detectives and this wasn't going to be an exception.

Amelia asked Jasper about his mystery customer,

confiding her suspicion he could be the missing Angus McKellar.

"Is that what it is? Zac said you were keeping an eye on him and we've been building up a case!"

"Excellent. So what do you know?"

"He's not staying in the hotel, but comes in for a drink every night. Sometimes people do come in just for a drink, or more than one, but then it's usually cocktails, not beer. They can get that much cheaper elsewhere. This guy has been in every night for over a week and has one pint each time. Very weird."

"Same time?"

"No. He always stays about an hour though."

"Does he meet anyone?"

"No, but the first time I thought he'd been stood up. He looks up whenever anyone comes in, and always picks a seat where he can see most of the room."

"If it's Angus, he used to live in Falmouth. He might still have contacts here."

"He might, but I no longer think he was waiting for someone – nobody would put up with that eight days in a row would they?"

"Not without a good reason."

Neither of them could think of a convincing explanation for being told where to meet but not at what time, or why a date or any other kind of meeting would need to be cancelled so many times, but still seem likely to happen.

"Maybe he was trying to avoid being seen?" Amelia suggested.

"If he is your missing man then that would make sense. Something about him doesn't ring true."

"Zac said he seemed lonely, but not as though he

wanted to get to know anyone. From what I've seen of Angus McKellar he was very sociable. Would someone like that take a risk in order not to be alone?"

"Perhaps. I can't imagine voluntarily being lonely," Jasper said.

"A big hotel like The Fal View might seem a good place to be anonymous?"

"Yeah. I had noticed him, but would soon have forgotten if you hadn't asked about him."

"Let me know if he comes in tonight or any other time I'm on duty."

"You're not doing a double shift?"

"No, thankfully those days are long gone. I've got nothing on tonight though."

"Aw, sweetie, I thought those days were long gone too."

"It's just because little Isla is so sick. All Patrick's attention is taken up with the girls at the moment."

"You don't see him at all?"

"Yeah, I do."

"Then I'll find you a dress for next time, and get him thinking about making new babies!"

She pretended to be shocked, but knew that if Jasper found something as suitable as the flapper outfits he'd sourced for the murder mystery weekend then she'd try it on – and there was an excellent chance Patrick would take it off her.

About four, an hour and a half before Amelia's shift was due to finish, Jasper called. "He's here."

"Patrick?"

"No, sweetie, sorry. Your bonny chieftain of the pudding race."

"Is that a new drink?"

"No." He sounded disappointed.

Bonny was a Scottish term, wasn't it? Bonny Prince Charlie and all that. "Oh! It's a code. I'm on my way."

Amelia walked around the bar area in what hopefully looked like a casual check from management. She did that for real often enough to be convincing.

The mystery man, this time wearing an orange shirt and turquoise trousers, was studying the bar snacks menu again. If they suddenly lost every copy and the computer file they printed them from, he'd be able to reproduce it from memory.

Amelia approached Jasper at the bar.

"What will it be?" he asked.

"I don't want a drink."

"The dress."

As Jasper talked about bias cuts, and draped necklines Amelia watched her quarry in the mirror. He didn't lose interest in his menu, except to visit the gents. Despite the bar being almost empty, he almost bumped into someone.

"Excuse me, hen," he said far more loudly than seemed necessary.

"Is he drunk?" Amelia asked.

"Would I have served him if he was?"

"Sorry, of course not."

"Don't worry, sweetie, I see why you asked. I'd stake my job that he never has a drink before the pint he buys here, and I doubt he has one after."

If it was the missing man Amelia should report seeing him, but she wasn't positive and as he'd been there over a week it didn't seem urgent, so she'd rather try to find out more first. She was due to finish soon, so maybe she could follow him and find out where he was staying.

That would help the police far more than a sighting which might not be repeated.

When Gabrielle arrived in good time for her shift Amelia said, "There's not much happening and I've noted everything you need to know. Would you mind if I left a bit early?"

"Of course not. You have to grab whatever time you can with that handsome Irishman of yours."

It would take too long to explain she was actually planning to be close to, but not with, an unattractive Scot, so Amelia just thanked her and got ready to leave.

Amelia then realised she couldn't follow him out the hotel without it being obvious. She needed to already be outside, just ahead of him to make it seem like coincidence. She didn't know if he'd be on foot, but she couldn't follow him if he was in a car and she was walking. If he was on foot then she could drive by a few times and at least narrow down where he went.

Amelia raced to her car and drove round in circles repeatedly passing all the possible exits from the hotel, but didn't see him once. She called Jasper to confirm he'd left.

"Not ten minutes after you."

She'd almost definitely have seen him if he'd been walking; that orange and turquoise combination was pretty unmissable. Even if he'd gone into a shop she'd driven round long enough to see him afterwards. So he was in a car.

What now? Should she report him, or hope he came back again the following day? Both seemed a real anti-climax. She took Bongo for a good long walk while trying to make up her mind. She was still out with him when Patrick called.

"There are two young ladies here who miss you so much they can't possibly sleep unless they say good night to you."

"Isla's home?"

"Not quite yet, but she and Ava like to have their bedtime story read together. I've done that, but they won't feel sleepy without talking to you."

The couple of treatment sessions she'd had must have really perked Isla up if she was well enough to want to delay bedtime. "In that case you'd better hand them the phone."

"What are you doing, Melia?"

"I'm taking Bongo for a walk," she said, and put the call on loudspeaker at their request.

They both told Bongo how much they missed him and from the way his tail wagged Amelia felt fully justified in saying he felt the same way. "And I miss you both too."

"We miss you lots and lots and lots."

"Thank you for my presents, Amelia."

"You're very welcome, Isla. I'm glad you're starting to get better."

"I have a special tube that fills up my tummy with cleaning fluid and when it's emptied again the bad stuff goes with it and makes my blood good."

"That's excellent."

"It's a parrot and eel dialalysis, Melia."

"Sounds very clever."

"Will we see you soon?"

"I'd like that. When you're both asleep Daddy can call me back to arrange it."

"Yay!"

There was a double lot of noisy air kissing and then

the phone was passed back to Patrick. "I'll take you up on that, because I miss you too."

Weirdly the call had made her miss her parents, so after cooking and eating her supper and reading a couple of chapters of her book, she called them. The phone was already ringing when she realised how late it was. Calling them just as they were going to bed wasn't a great idea. Hanging up leaving them to wonder who it was and if they'd try again was probably worse.

"Sorry it's so late," she apologised, explaining she hadn't realised until after dialling.

"It's fine. I was just thinking of making some Ovaltine. Is everything alright?"

"Fine." She followed her customary "I just called," with "for a chat."

"How nice," Mum surprised her by saying. "It's good that having more staff at work gives you the time."

"It is. I'd almost forgotten what it was like to have time on my hands."

"Do you still read detective stories? I remember you always had your head in one of those unless Nicole was with you."

There was no reproach in Mum's voice, but still Amelia wondered if she'd ignored her parents at times.

"Yes, I still do. And actually I'm doing it for real, sort of." She told them a little about trying to investigate Angus McKellar.

"The man on the news?"

"Yes. There's someone a bit like him who comes into the hotel."

Amelia heard her mum talking to her dad, who then came on the line. "Have you told the police?" he asked.

"Not yet. How's the garden, Dad?"

"Looking good. You should see the tomatoes." He described the progress of his vegetables before handing the phone back to his wife.

"How's the pilates, Mum?"

"I'm getting better, I think. My instructor said so anyway." There was a mumble in the background. "Your father says I'm getting better at coffee and cake with the girls afterwards."

They chatted for a few more minutes, then as the pauses where each was thinking of what else to say lengthened, Amelia said, "It's been lovely to chat, but I really must go."

"Of course. Thank you for calling. Your father is waving."

"Tell him I'm waving back."

When Amelia ended the call, she saw both that her battery level was low and Jasper had made three attempts to contact her. She rang him straight back.

"Sconcey face is back," he hissed.

"What?"

"Honestly, do you know nothing? Your hideously dressed Scot. Aubergine and taupe now!"

"I'm coming. Keep him talking if he tries to leave."

"What are you up to?"

"I can't explain now."

She drove straight down to The Fal View and parked in the customer car park where she scrunched herself low in the seat and called Jasper.

"He's still here. About an inch of beer to go."

"Thanks." Then, to preserve battery life, said she'd explain later. She'd watched enough films to know that making your most daring move just as your phone died was a really bad idea. Knowing Bianca had her car charger, Amelia should have taken extra care to keep it charged in case of emergencies. A better detective would have done.

As she waited in the dark, Amelia's back got stiff and she decided it would look really obvious what she was doing if she suddenly sprang upright and started up her car to follow him, especially as at that time of night almost all the cars would belong to guests staying overnight. She sat more normally, ready to start her engine whenever he came out. She'd make a hash of getting out from the tight parking space and so naturally leave the car park right behind him. She was very pleased with that plan.

Amelia was less pleased the mystery man was such a slow drinker. It seemed like forever and she started to get nervous. If it really was Angus and he didn't want to be found then he wouldn't be happy to know she was stalking him. She clicked on the central locking and put her phone in the cup holder so she could grab it quickly, should she need to call for help.

Someone came out. Amelia started her engine, realised it wasn't him and fumbled about in her glove box in order to look busy. The other man headed for a Range Rover. Just as Amelia realised she didn't have to worry about drawing his attention to herself, she found her notebook and pen. She jotted down all the registration numbers she could see. Thanks to the floodlit car park, that was all but a few which were at the wrong angle, and one she could only see part of. Then her target appeared and she marked the ones which were in the direction he was headed and began her manoeuvring. She was far too good at her impression of someone who couldn't manoeuvre out of the parking space and both vehicles had left the car park before she got out. Fortunately they'd both turned in the same direction and as only one was a car, she was able to work out which was which.

Tailing him wasn't as easy as she'd hoped. When she'd thought of it, she'd imagined the hardest bit would be not making it obvious she was following if he went down a quiet side road, or a track or something. Actually even with just a few cars about it was hard to keep up with him. Traffic lights didn't always work in her favour, and they seemed to be going round in circles. Was he trying to make sure he wasn't followed? Amelia tried not to worry that, as well as the possibility of losing him, she was getting lost herself.

He pulled over into an unlit bus stop. Without thinking, she pulled in behind him. As soon as his car door opened, she realised that was a big mistake.

Chapter 21

Amelia didn't want a confrontation with a man who was on the run and potentially desperate. Nor did she want to explain to a stranger, late at night and alone, that she suspected them of being such a person.

She could just imagine how that conversation might go.

'Oh, sorry for tailing you as though you're a criminal, but I fancy myself as a detective and thought you could be one?'

'And what made you think that?'

'You're wearing an aubergine jumper and have an accent.'

'And how could you tell that from looking at my car?'

'Oh, I didn't. I had my bar staff watch you for days before I decided to tail you.'

No, that wouldn't go down well and might result in a complaint and bad publicity for the hotel. She quickly pulled out of the bus stop, then continued as slowly as she dared, dividing her attention between the road and the man who might be Angus McKellar. When she passed, he seemed to be taking off a hat, but she couldn't be sure as another car drove up behind Amelia's, blocking her view, and forcing her to speed up.

Amelia was by then in a residential area, with cars parked all down the road, so couldn't pull in anywhere and wait. She'd have to try to loop back and hope to be behind him again when he left the bus stop – even so late at night she doubted he'd park his car there for long.

Should she risk trying to find her way without help, or

use up power and time by finding an online map? "I will always keep my phone fully charged from now on," she promised herself.

She spotted a road sign for something Crescent. If she was lucky, that would take her back round to the other side of the bus stop. It did! Nicole wouldn't believe it when Amelia gloated about her brilliant bit of navigation.

There was still a car in the bus stop. As she drove slowly by she thought it looked about as big and flashy as the one she'd been following. It pulled out not long after she went by. When she stopped at traffic lights Amelia's quarry was right behind her. At least, she thought it was him. It was hard to tell just from the silhouette, especially as she'd seen him taking something off his head. If it was him, that something wasn't a hat. He hadn't been wearing one earlier. He was too close for her to read the number plate, even if she had memorised them all.

Amelia continued to drive slowly, hoping he'd overtake. He didn't, but she saw him indicate and stop outside a small B&B. She parked as soon as she could find a space and walked back, taking her notebook with her. Sea Mist wasn't the sort of place where she could go in for a drink, just a largish house with rooms to let. There was nothing to stop her walking into the car park, which was just a few tarmac covered bays between the road and building.

The first half of the number plate corresponded with the partial registration she'd noted earlier. Feeling like a proper detective she put her hand on the bonnet. It was warm. There was no doubt in her mind that this car was the same as that driven out of The Fal View car park, by the man who resembled the missing Angus McKellar.

She felt along the front of the car and, using the flashlight of her mobile phone very briefly, investigated the number plate. It was broken off, explaining why she'd only seen part of it earlier. The car had a big dent too. How had that happened? Although Jasper had been confident the man never arrived at the pub drunk he didn't know where he went or what he did afterwards. Sean said Angus had started drinking more since the first disappearance, and he had come in for a pint that afternoon, as well as the later one. Maybe he'd really needed that drink?

Amelia risked another few seconds from her phone torch to note the car's make and colour. She couldn't get behind the car as he'd reversed it up to Sea Mist's front wall, but she did spot a sticker on the rear window for the Salterns Support charity. "It must belong to Angus McKellar." She should call the police – but it would be so much better if she could say it was, rather than it might be, the missing man. Amelia shone her phone torch inside the car. In the time before it died there was no sign of anything the man could have taken off his head, nor any further clues to the identity of the driver. She left hoping there were no car thefts that night and no CCTV cameras, or she'd have some very awkward explaining to do.

On the plus side, she recognised where she was and was able to drive home without incident. On the way Amelia tried to think of ways to confirm who the car belonged to, and to learn more about him. She didn't know anyone who could trace the registration number. She could ring the B&B, but if he was in hiding he wouldn't be using his real name and she doubted the owner would give out any information to a random enquiry about 'the Scot with the terrible trousers'.

It was no good, she was going to have to call the police with a 'might be', not a definite identification. On the face of things it must be him, but then she definitely saw Patrick blowing kisses at Meghan, and she definitely saw Sean stab a man, but had still been wrong. Suppose Sean hadn't caught up with her. She'd have called the police, wasted their time and caused a lot of fuss for everyone.

"Sean! Of course." He'd asked her to call and he'd know what model of car Angus drove. He might be able to think of other ways to help identify Angus too. It was very late, but he'd definitely be interested to hear from her. Waiting to call the police until she'd spoken to him couldn't make any difference.

As soon as she got home, Amelia put her phone on charge and made herself a cup of caramel flavoured hot chocolate. Once the phone had enough charge she texted Sean. 'Amelia here. I think I may have seen Angus McKellar'.

Sean rang her back after only a few minutes.

"Thanks so much for getting in touch, Amelia."

"I wanted to ask about his car. Do you…"

Sean spoke over her. "How did he seem? Is he OK?"

She'd almost forgotten Angus McKellar was a friend Sean was deeply concerned about, not just an interesting case as he was to her. "He's fine. That's if it is him. I'm not absolutely sure. He doesn't look like quite how he did on TV."

"In what way?"

"He's thinner and his hair is different." She wondered then if he could have been wearing a wig. If so, why choose one so similar to his own hair? Unless that too was a wig and he'd not taken it with him, or had lost it somewhere.

"That's not surprising if he's trying to be hidden and presumably he's worried."

That made sense to Amelia, except that Angus wasn't making a great job of hiding himself. Unless…

"Is he colour blind?" Amelia asked.

"Not that I know of. Why?"

"Just a thought. He's wearing bright clothes, but normal ones – not tracksuits and things. I wondered if he didn't realise he stood out."

"I see what you mean… He did know his tracksuits were bright, but Heather could have told him that, or even bought them. He said he liked his sponsors to be able to see him when he ran. Where did you see him? In the hotel where you work?"

"Yeah, but he's not staying there. It's weird. Almost as though he's two people – one wanting to get caught, one not."

"Like Jekyll and Hyde, sort of? Makes sense. He's a good man. I'm sure of that, but there's no doubt he's also stolen the money. The two sides of him could be battling it out. Poor man."

"I wonder why he came here?"

"No idea."

"He lived here, didn't he?"

"Yes, but that was years ago. It's quite a coincidence, unless… No, that wouldn't make any sense."

"What wouldn't?"

"Nothing. Like I said a coincidence."

Sean was annoying her. Angus had lived in Falmouth, so although it was by no means certain that he'd go back there, it was a bit more than pure coincidence that he had. "What is it, Sean?"

"It's just that he helped out a young woman who worked for him, when she got pregnant."

"You told me about that."

"Did I? I'm sure there was nothing funny in it. He always helped people out. It's just odd that she moved just before he went off the first time. I don't know where exactly, but he said the west country."

"Interesting." If the woman was no more to Angus than an unfortunate employee, would he have talked to Sean about her?

"But no help. He's not staying with her, is he?" Sean pointed out. "That's if it is him. What made you think it could be?"

Amelia thought back to when she'd first thought she may have found Mr McKellar. Really she'd had very little to go on. Just bright clothes, accent and similar height. "He's Scottish."

Had she convinced herself, because she wanted to solve the mystery? No. The man had behaved strangely, and there was the charity sticker. She started to tell Sean she was certain it was more than wishful thinking, but he spoke over her.

"OK. So he looks and sounds like Angus."

"A bit. He seems different from when I saw him on TV, but then so do you."

"I do?"

"Yes, like one is the real you and one a kind of imitation."

"What are you trying to say, Amelia?"

Oh dear, she'd offended him. Still, it had taken a surprisingly long time before his ego came into play, and it didn't mean he wasn't worried. "Just that people have a private and public side. I'm always cheery to guests, even if I'm not happy or they're annoying. You have to seem interested in people you interview even if they're boring."

He laughed. "True. They cut all the boring bits, so I have to look like that's already happened. And you're right, Angus wasn't always quite as he seemed on TV. If he's on the run he'll be behaving even less like that. Any idea where he could be hiding out?"

"Oh yes. I followed him to the Sea Mist B&B."

"Proper detective you!"

"I felt like one. Tailing a car isn't easy."

"Car? What kind of car?"

"Sorry, I should have started with that." She read out the make and partial number plate. "It's a deep blue."

"Same make, same colour."

"It must be him then, mustn't it?"

"You should call the police, Amelia."

"You're right."

"You don't sound sure."

It wasn't phoning the police she was unsure about. She didn't know what was prickling in her mind, but it wasn't that. Or maybe it was. OK they wouldn't just arrest a man late at night based on her uncertain identification, but she'd hate to be wrong the very first time she gave evidence to real police about a real crime.

"I'm not sure. About it being him I mean. I know it seems like it must be, but…"

"Yeah, you don't want to get it wrong and raise hopes. And you probably don't want to be giving statements at this time of night. Tell you what, call me tomorrow and in the meantime I'll think of little things he says and does, see if any of that rings any bells."

"Great. Thanks."

That was a good compromise. After the excitement of what was almost a car chase, her adrenaline levels had crashed and she was exhausted. As Sean suggested, tiredness was probably partly why she was reluctant to contact the police. She could call early, so Angus would still be at the B&B and she'd be alert enough to give accurate information, and do so with confidence.

The next morning Amelia woke before seven. Probably too early to call Sean, considering how late she'd spoken to him the night before. Too early for guests to be checking out of B&Bs, but Nicole would be awake and having a coffee before getting breakfasts ready.

Amelia wanted to say she'd found Angus, but was now even less certain than before speaking to Sean and she'd had doubts all along. Despite longing for it to be true, she couldn't quite believe she'd solved the mystery.

She asked if Nicole had heard any more about Angus's disappearance.

"No, it's getting quite a bit of coverage, but nothing new," Nicole said.

"Did it come to light what had happened to him before?"

"I'd have told you."

"Yeah, you would if you knew anything. I'd like to go over it though."

"As far as I know there's no clue at all to where he's been. He always said he didn't know."

"Was he much of a drinker?"

"Not that I know of. If he'd got so drunk he blacked out for days you'd think someone would have said something, wouldn't you?"

"Yes, I would," Amelia said. "That never seemed likely to me, I'm sure there was more to it than that."

Nicole laughed. "That's the kind of thing you would be sure of."

"Maybe, and you might say I'm being fanciful now, but… Do you think he'd come back to Falmouth?"

"Don't tell me you've found him!"

"OK, I won't. Come on, Nicole, think. Does he have any reason to come here?" Nicole had mentioned other rumours about him. If she'd heard he had a mistress who'd moved near to Amelia she wasn't likely to have kept that to herself, but as it happened before his first disappearance she could have forgotten.

"I don't know enough about the man to say."

"You have things in common with him. You both moved to Lee-on-the-Solent from somewhere else and started a business there. If you needed to get away would you come to Falmouth?"

"Of course I would."

"To see me…"

"Obvs. Angus might still be in contact with people from when he lived there, and he's got a boat hasn't he? He could have sailed to Falmouth."

"Not this time, but being on a boat would be a good way to disappear. Maybe that's where he was the first time he went missing? I wonder how long it would take to sail from Lee-on-the-Solent and back."

"You really do think you've found him, don't you?"

"I've seen a man who broadly matches his description. He has a Scottish accent and is driving a car of the right colour and make."

"You have to tell the police!"

"Thing is, I don't know that it really is him."

"You don't have to know. They'll investigate and find out for sure."

"You're right. I will."

Next question was which number to call. Not 999. This wasn't an emergency. 101 didn't seem right either. Was that surprising? Amelia had got so many things wrong when she'd been positive about the evidence of her own eyes.

This time she wasn't at all sure of what she'd seen. She definitely had seen a man, who did look a lot like Angus and was behaving oddly. Maybe it really would be better to wait until she was a bit more sure. She called Sean. "Sorry, I know it's early, but…"

"No problem. I was just wondering if it was too early to call you, so we can work out if it really is Angus. His poor wife is worried sick, and the sooner he's found the better for her, and Angus himself."

"I don't want to give her false hope if it isn't him, or waste police time."

"Heather needs hope right now and the police have asked for any information or possible sightings."

"True."

"I've checked Angus's car registration; it was registered with the golf club." He gave it to her. "Is that the same?"

"Yes, well mostly. It was broken."

"Had he had an accident, do you think?"

"That's possible," Amelia said.

"How did he seem? Was he well?"

She again did her best to reassure Sean that physically Angus looked fine. "He came into the hotel bar for a pint several times."

"Beer? He hasn't drunk that in ages... I'm wondering... Could he have partially lost his memory? You know how people with Alzheimer's kind of go back to their past?"

"Maybe. He did seem to be acting oddly. The bar in the hotel isn't an obvious place for a drink if you're not staying there. Do you know where he lived in Falmouth?"

"Over the shop. He and Heather often speak fondly of that time."

"So it's likely he'd want to come back?"

"I bet that's it. I've been trying to figure out how he could have done everything he did. The only thing I can think of is that he's got confused. He's returned to Falmouth, not remembering he left. He hasn't called Heather because he can't remember her and maybe he thought having his name on the charity's accounts meant it was his money?"

"Perhaps," she said, although that sounded like clutching at straws to Amelia. But then she knew nothing about dementia or mental illness. He could have had some kind of breakdown before or after taking the money.

"Whatever the reason, I really do think you should call the police."

She should already have done that. "I'll do it now."

"Good. And we'll keep in touch. I'm so glad to have your help with this. It's really important to me to find out what's happened."

Amelia was quite touched by his deep level of concern, until she recalled him getting so upset with Nicole. As a trustee for Salterns Support he'd felt under suspicion himself with regard to the missing money, and considered that whoever took it had left him to take the blame. At the time Amelia thought he might have turned a blind eye to his friend misappropriating the funds. That seemed far less likely now, but he might have been too trusting and not checked the finances thoroughly enough. Considering what the cash was for, that would be enough to bring on an attack of guilt.

As soon as he'd rung off Amelia looked online for a news report, to see if that gave the correct police number to call. It did, and she discovered the car's registration details had been made public. If she'd done the right thing and called them as soon as she'd had suspicions then she'd have known that. Oh well, she wouldn't waste any more time.

She called and gave brief information, then was put through to someone else and had to repeat it all. Then she had to give an embarrassing explanation of why a person working in the hotel where the man had been drinking, also knew which B&B he'd driven to straight afterwards. She sounded like a crackpot to herself and was impressed how the police officer managed to treat her politely, especially when she admitted the first possible sighting had been several days previously.

The officer thanked her for calling, requested she call back immediately if she saw the man again and said they may be in touch for a statement. She felt daft for having admitted to tailing the man, and not having called when she first suspected him, but knew that at last she'd done the right thing.

Amelia carefully updated her Angus McKellar case file with complete details of everything which had happened, including as much as she could recall of the different telephone calls. She felt much happier after doing that. Having done her duty by helping the police investigation she was now free to enjoy her own unofficial one. And she'd gained an ally in Sean. Although she hadn't really taken to him in person, he was more than tolerable on the phone and there was no doubt that having someone with personal insight into the situation could be useful.

On her way into work, Amelia detoured past the Sea Mist B&B. The car she'd followed was no longer parked in one of the bays outside reserved for guests, but a police car was. She so wanted to go in, but couldn't think of a single thing she could add to her statement. Without that she'd just be in the way and further convince them her interest in the case wasn't normal.

At work, after a quick handover from Charles, Amelia headed straight to Jorge's office to inform him about what she'd reported to the police and how it involved the hotel.

"It could be good publicity if we handle it right. We'd better work on a press release," Jorge said.

They worked together to produce something that was half a statement of the way members of staff had given useful information to the police and half an advert for The Fal View. The comfortable, extensively stocked bar which was popular with locals, guests, and other tourists in the area was mentioned, as were the murder mystery weekends the hotel was famous for.

"That's a bit of an exaggeration."

"It won't be if we make the national news."

"I suppose not. Shall I call Sonia and see if we can set up another for early next year?"

"Good idea."

Once the statement said everything they wanted it to, they spent a few minutes shortening it as much as they possibly could, to increase the chances of it being used.

"I'll put it up on our website and send copies to BBC Focus, Devon News, Falmouth Wave and everyone else I can think of," Jorge said.

"We'd better check with the police first, in case we accidentally interfere with their enquiry."

"You said they were at the B&B, they'll have arrested him by now."

"Probably, but his car wasn't there. He could have got away."

"You're right. I'll check it's OK first. I'll ask their advice for answering questions from the press too. Do you want to talk to reporters if they arrive while you're on duty?"

"Not unless you particularly want me to." It had been bad enough explaining to the police why she'd tailed Angus instead of calling them immediately. If Jorge handled the press it would be much easier for him to deflect awkward questions.

Explaining to him had been easy. "You know what I'm like," had done it. Jorge who'd previously been roped into her slightly elaborate plans to find out such things as why the cardboard recycling bins had been empty three weeks in a row, who had sent the chef a Valentine's card and why the checking out queues were frequently longer on Tuesdays, admitted he did.

Back in the duty manager's office, Amelia found a large, flat cardboard box waiting for her. It was very light and definitely not new. There were several address labels, 'handle with care' notices and courier company stickers. One new looking label read, 'Amelia Watson.

Yours until Friday'.

"Yes!" She was so looking forward to putting the contents to use.

Amelia called her parents, this time not worrying that it was, "Just to let you know I might be mentioned on the news". She gave a brief explanation then called Patrick. From him she learned that Isla was doing well and he'd just about caught up with the work he'd missed due to her hospital stays. "I'd love to see you, but I can't guarantee I won't fall asleep on you."

"Don't worry about that. Are you free this evening?"

"Yes."

"Then come round to mine as soon as the girls are asleep. I have a case I need your help with."

"The missing Scot?"

"Nothing to do with him, hospitals, illness, murder or… Actually that's it for clues. Bring your toothbrush and stuff in case you really do fall asleep."

"That sounds promising."

Angus McKellar hadn't shown up in the hotel by the time Gabrielle arrived in the office for her handover at four-thirty. That wasn't at all surprising, as the lunchtime news had reported he was believed to have been staying in Falmouth, but to have moved on. An attempt to interview the owner of the hotel where he'd been staying was made. The man declared he never watched the news, so had no idea his guest was a wanted man. His unwillingness to tell the reporter anything else made his lack of interest in the television entirely convincing.

Gabrielle's mother had seen the news report, which saved a lot of explanations, but still left Amelia with questions to answer. She was quite relieved to get to a minor problem with the laundry, and a chambermaid who would only be doing light duties as she was pregnant. Maybe an inkling of how many times she'd have to explain herself had been at the back of Amelia's mind before she'd called the police and added to her reluctance to do it?

Just to be thorough, Amelia drove home via the Sea Mist B&B. The parking bay was full, but not with any vehicles she recognised.

"Hope I'm not too early, Watson?" Patrick said when she answered the buzzer in her flat.

"Not at all, come up." He was earlier than she'd expected, but she was ready. She opened her front door, then retreated to her bedroom.

"Amelia?" he called.

"In here!"

"What's this case... Oh, wow!"

"Could you help me with the zip?" she asked in her most seductive voice. The red silk dress Jasper had left boxed up in her office fitted perfectly, and looked as good as she'd hoped, but that didn't mean she couldn't give it a helping hand.

Patrick strode across the room and pulled her into his arms for a lingering kiss. If he hadn't been holding her firmly her legs might have given way causing her to sink onto the bed. The way his hand caressed the bare skin of her back went some way towards making up for the fact he was keeping her upright.

"This zip, is it going up or down?" he asked.

"Your decision entirely."

He made the right one and the dress slithered gracefully to the floor.

Chapter 22

"I'm sorry about falling asleep so early last night," Patrick said when she brought him a cup of tea.

He'd warned her he might, and stayed awake long enough to make love and eat the meal she'd prepared for them, so Amelia decided to be forgiving. "That's OK, you can make it up to me now," she said and got back into bed.

Over breakfast, an hour later, Amelia mentioned reporting her sighting of Angus McKellar to the police.

"It really was him then?"

"Yep, I gave the police a statement and it was on the news."

"I'm sorry I ever doubted you."

"I should think so."

"Will you be on TV? The girls would love to see you."

"Probably not. I like the detecting part, but I wouldn't want to be a famous detective."

"Amelia the anonymous sleuth?"

"Something like that. I was wondering, can you tell how long someone has lived somewhere, even if you hadn't sold the place?"

"If they bought it, that's easy. It's on the government website."

"Really? Can you check the flat above McKellar's sweetshop?"

"Anything for you, Watson." Patrick searched for the address. "It was sold five years ago, but somewhere like that is probably rented out, so the tenants may not have been there that long. Sorry I couldn't help."

"You have." Angus hadn't retained ownership of the flat, and hadn't recently bought it for his mistress or anyone else. "Can you search for properties a particular person bought?"

"Just the date and the price. Sorry."

"Don't worry about it. You mentioned the girls would like to see me. Could I visit Isla in hospital?"

"She'd like that. I'll check up on the best times."

"Please do. It would be best either when you're there or she doesn't have any other visitors." Amelia guessed Meghan would be there whenever Patrick wasn't. "Will she be in much longer?"

"Only until we can get the dialysis machine for her at home. Meghan and I have started the training on how to use it already."

"And then she'll be OK?"

"She'll be far better than she is now, but it's not a cure, just a treatment to replicate as close as possible what her kidneys should be doing."

"And she'll have to have it forever?"

"Until she can have a transplant. Thankfully Meghan and I are both the right blood group, so there's an excellent chance of one of us being a good match."

"They'd take one of your kidneys? Would you be OK with just one?"

"Better than I will with two and only one daughter."

She didn't doubt that, but it still seemed very drastic.

"It's not that uncommon," Patrick said. "People can cope really well with just one; both the donor and recipient. It's much better for her if the kidney comes from someone who is a close match, a live donor gives a much better chance of it working, and it's likely to work for years longer than one from a dead donor. That's partly because it can happen sooner. People can wait years for a suitable match."

He'd obviously learned a lot about it and made his decision. Meghan too by the sound of it. Would her parents do that for her? Actually Amelia thought they might, they just wouldn't give her a reassuring hug before surgery. Or was she being unfair to them? Probably.

"I'm not working today, maybe I could come with you to collect Ava from school?"

"I was going to suggest that."

"How about I bring Bongo and we go for a nice long walk? It might be good for Ava to get some attention that's just for her."

"Great idea. You're going to be a… You're really good with the girls. I do appreciate that. I know you found the whole idea difficult."

"I did, but that was before I met them. It's getting much easier." She almost said it would be no trouble at all once Isla was well, but she suspected there would often be times when even such lovely girls caused trouble of one kind or another. And Isla might not be well for a long time – Amelia wanted to be part of Patrick's life sooner rather than later.

"By the way, Watson, you said you wanted my help with a case. Was that just a sneaky ruse to lure me here?"

"Do I need one?"

"No."

"Then I think we can consider the case of the disappearing boyfriend to be closed."

Angus was briefly mentioned on the national news at

lunchtime as well as there being more detailed coverage on BBC Spotlight. The presenter reported from outside the Falmouth branch of McKellar's confectionery. All reports said Mr McKellar had allegedly syphoned off hundreds of thousands of pounds and was reported to have been seen in Falmouth, but no longer there.

"There are fears for his safety," the reporter said.

That was the phrase used the first time he'd vanished and sent a text to his wife saying he was sorry. Heather McKellar, Sean, and the police had believed at the time it had signalled a suicide attempt. It sounded to Amelia as though something must have happened this time to suggest he would try again, or perhaps already had. Surely the fact he'd been seen alive and well the previous day would otherwise have reassured everyone to some extent?

Sean wasn't reporting on Outlook South. She'd not seen him on television when she'd checked that channel the previous day either. She texted to reassure him of her continued support.

Amelia called Nicole, who'd seen the news but didn't know anything more.

"You're the one with all the inside information!" Nicole claimed.

"I wish I was. I only know what I saw and what Sean's told me. That's sometimes a bit confused. I'd have thought him fairly unshakeable, but he's taken this badly."

"Yeah, I remember the state he was in when he came here. Whatever is behind it, it seems his friend isn't the person he'd always thought him to be."

Amelia could only imagine how shocked and upset she'd be to discover Nicole had a dark side she knew nothing about, and didn't really share the views and principles she'd always thought they had in common. That would be as distressing as the thought of her being in physical danger.

"Enough about your partner in crime, how's it going with your potential partner in life?"

"Funny you should say that. Patrick said how good I was with the girls and I'm sure he almost said I'd be a good stepmother."

"Of course you would!"

"I hope so, but do you think he was hinting we might get married?" She tried to recall the exact conversation, but Nicole cut her off.

"He's been hinting that for months – unless you think him saying he'd like you to be Mrs Homes meant he wants to fix you up with one of his brothers?"

"Probably not."

"There you go then. And how are your future stepdaughters?"

Amelia shared her hopes and fears for the girls and her relationship with them.

Sean called and apologised for not having been in touch. "Have you seen the news?"

"Yes. I guess something has happened since I saw him here?"

"You know he took the charity's money?"

As far as Amelia was aware that hadn't been confirmed. But the chances of both the man and cash going missing at the same time without there being any connection was very slight. "I thought you didn't believe it?"

"I can't, not really, but he's confessed."

"He's been found?"

"If only. No. He sent texts to me and others involved in the charity saying he was sorry. Then to Heather he sent one admitting his guilt and saying he couldn't ask her to forgive him as he'd never forgive himself. It ended, 'remember I loved you and try to be happy.' "

"Oh." That did sound like a suicide note.

"I just can't understand it. He's a good man, there must be an explanation. No way would he have done this to the children he did so much to help, and to Heather too."

"She must be so worried."

"Of course, there's that too. If we took longer playing a round of golf than usual he'd call and tell her he'd be a bit late home. He wouldn't just vanish... but he has. Twice."

Amelia had that prickling sensation in her head again. What had she missed?

"Sean, did you mean he stole money from his wife?"

"Not technically as the accounts are all in his name, or joint ones, but he's made the maximum withdrawals each day."

"Every day since he went missing?"

"And before. Was that not on the news? I've lost track of who knows what. I haven't been able to work – I'm too close to it to be objective."

Sean rambled a bit, saying he couldn't think why Angus had taken the money, but there must have been a good reason. Perhaps he was in some kind of trouble, even being blackmailed, although he was such a good man, Sean didn't see how he could have anything to hide. "There has to have been a mistake of some kind."

Amelia thought that if he was 'such a good man' and did steal the money, which he must have if it was really gone, then perhaps he couldn't live with what he'd done. That would fit with when she saw him. He seemed half to want to get caught – maybe he'd been trying to decide what to do and suicide seemed the only answer.

Why had it come to this? If he'd given into temptation on impulse surely he could have returned the money... No, it wasn't a single moment of weakness. His earlier disappearance, and repeated withdrawals, showed that.

"It's tragic," Amelia said when she realised Sean was waiting for a response.

"Thanks, Amelia. Other than Heather you're the only one who believes me."

Amelia wasn't even sure what it was he wanted her to believe, but did feel sympathy for him being so upset over his friend and for the man's wife. "I'll do anything I can to help."

"Thank you. If you remember anything or think of anything then let me know and I'll pass on anything I find out. We'll work this out together. Thanks, Amelia."

"Sean," she said quickly, before he hung up. "Did you find out anything about his... employee? The one who got pregnant?"

Sean sighed. "I don't think she can have any connection to this."

"She probably doesn't, but it's good to rule things out."

"I'm so pleased to hear you say that, as it's exactly what I thought myself. I've made enquiries. Maybe you could go and see her? Like I said, I don't see how she could be connected, but he saw a lot of her before and after the birth. It's possible he confided in her, or something."

"You have her address?"

"Yeah, it's... 124 the High Street, Bissom, Penwith,

Cornwall."

"Are you sure?"

"I know it's a big coincidence her being in the same general area as he was seen. Or maybe if I'm right about him getting confused then her address was something he remembered? Of course if it's too far for you to travel…"

"It's just up the road, but it's not that. Bissom is a tiny place." She was going to say she doubted if it had a high street, but if it did it wouldn't have 124 houses on it. She should check though. And there was a Bissom Road. Maybe that was it. "Do you have her name?"

"Ellie Roebuck."

"Like the footballer?"

"Who?"

"Isn't that the name of the England goalkeeper? I don't mean it's actually her of course."

"Shouldn't think so."

Of course it wasn't. A professional sportswoman wouldn't be working for Angus McKellar. "I assume people have tried calling Angus?"

"Yes, he's had lots of calls."

"What? What does he say?"

"Missed calls I mean. His phone is always off."

"He must turn it on to text… Can the police trace it?"

"Probably, but they know where he's been."

"But not where he is now. He sent those texts after he left Falmouth, didn't he?"

"After he left the B&B he was staying in anyway. Good point. That might show where he was headed. I'll see what I can find out."

When Amelia met Patrick and Ava she was presented with two drawings – one from each girl.

"How wonderful! Thank you so much." She was very pleased they'd taken the trouble to create something for her.

"Which is best, Melia?"

Amelia who wasn't sure who did which drawing said they were both really good, and both had chosen excellent subjects. She was almost certain one was of Bongo as a pirate captain aboard his ship, and the other was of brave dog Bongo rescuing a family of six people. Was one of them supposed to be her?

"Yes, but which is best?" Ava demanded.

"This one is the most colourful."

"Oh, does that make it best?" She didn't seem keen on the amount of colour being a deciding factor.

"This one is more lively and vigorous." It had certainly been created with a great deal of enthusiasm. There were fewer individual colours, but each was present in greater abundance.

"Is that good?"

"Definitely."

"That's mine! Mine is the bestest."

"They're both really, really good," said Amelia. She wouldn't want Isla to think her efforts weren't appreciated.

"I won't tell Isla you like mine best. It would make her sad."

"That's kind of you."

"I'm very kind and good, aren't I, Daddy?"

"You certainly are, Ava love."

"Are you coming to tea with us, Melia?"

"Not today. We're going to go for a nice long walk and then I have to take Bongo back to his other mummy."

"Bongo is lucky to have two mummies, and for me and Isla to be his friends."

"That's very true."

"Does he have any daddies?"

"No." Oh crikey, please don't let this turn into a biology lesson!

"A girl at school has two mummies. They're librarians."

"Oh."

"Have you got any treats for Bongo? It's time for his lesson."

Amelia gave Ava a handful of dog biscuits and watched as she got the dog confused but enthused, by giving multiple instructions and rewards in quick succession.

"We're hoping Isla will leave hospital this week," Patrick said.

"That's brilliant!"

"It is, yes. But it's going to be difficult too. We've got to be ultra careful about infections."

"Ava said something about hand washing, I guessed that was part of getting her prepared for that."

"You are good at working things out. Everything will have to be kept very clean. Ava won't be able to bring anything home from school. After we've been out we'll get changed before we go into Isla's room. She'll come into contact with as few people as possible…"

"Best for me not to see her in hospital then?"

"Sorry." He sounded far more apologetic than was needed. Although she missed Isla and it felt right to visit her in hospital, not being able to wasn't a massive disappointment if the girl would be out soon.

"There's something else?"

He looked concerned. "We have to set up the equipment and have more training on how to use it, and there's counselling for us all and…"

His comments about limited contact began to sink in. "I'm not going to see any of you for a while?"

"It's not that I don't want to see you or the girls don't want to."

"OK."

"If it helps Stuart, Meghan's new partner, is staying away too, and our families."

That did help a bit. "Isla's health comes before anything else."

"Thank you for understanding."

"Do what you need to for Isla, stay in touch and see me whenever you possibly can, OK?"

"I promise."

Amelia, determined not to spoil what time they had together played a mad game of 'What's the time, Mr Wolf?' which Bongo won, on account of having the hairiest ears. Patrick came last on account of not knowing that both ear hairiness and hopping on all your legs at once were part of the rules.

When it was time to say goodbye, Amelia kissed Ava and gave her air kisses to pass on to Isla, before giving their father the kind of kiss she hoped would make sure he was thinking about her even while they were apart.

Amelia thought about Patrick's comment that it had felt wrong without Isla about. Of course it had. Amelia's parents must have found it strange when she'd gone straight from college and living with them, to a live in job hundreds of miles away. She'd been fine, as she was sharing a room with Nicole – they were as close as the sisters she'd always wanted them to be. It must have been a shock for her parents though. At the time she'd been hurt they'd let her go without any kind of protest, but perhaps they'd done it because they'd thought it was best for her?

She called, but not to ask them about that. How could she? Instead she called just to hear their voices. At least that was her plan. When she'd told Mum about Isla being in hospital and that she might not see any of them for a while, Mum said, "You'll miss them so much, but you're doing the right thing."

"I don't have any choice, do I?"

"No. But… you know that saying, about how if you love something you have to let it go?"

"Yeah. I suppose that's what I'm doing."

"It won't be long. I'm sure Patrick will call you and see you when he can."

"You're right, Mum. Thank you, you've made me feel better." And she had. The reassurance about Patrick was welcome, but it wasn't just that. Her parents had let her go because they thought it was best for her. Because they loved her.

"Mum, when I left home… I'm sorry I didn't come back or call much."

"That was a long time ago, Amelia and you were very young."

"I'm still sorry. Tell Dad will you?"

"I'll do that."

Partly to keep herself busy, and partly so she could take time off when Isla was stronger, Amelia took on extra shifts at work. In the limited free time between them she busied herself playing detective with an impressive lack of factual result, but a ton of speculation.

As she'd guessed there was no High Street in Bissom and nowhere else which seemed at all likely to be the real address of the woman who had just possibly been Angus McKellar's mistress. That was starting to seem ever more unlikely. The man's disappearance had been reported in the tabloids and they would have made the very most of the slightest hint of anything in that line. But if there was nothing to hide, why had Sean been given a false address? And who had given it to him?

Amelia obtained the phone number of the Salterns Support charity shop in Lee-on-the-Solent and called. Her request to speak to Ellie Roebuck was met with, "Sorry, never heard of her." The same thing happened when she rang the respite centre, and the head office of McKellar's Confectionery.

As Ellie wasn't still employed by Angus, that didn't prove much. Besides, if she'd given a false address to whoever Sean spoke to, she probably hadn't given the real one to any of her former colleagues. You'd only lie about your address if you didn't want to be found. That made two of them with her and Angus – three if you counted the illegitimate child he'd done so much to support. Could he still be doing that with the charity's funds?

Angus's home phone number wasn't listed.

Amelia did learn something when she visited the Falmouth B&B Angus McKellar had stayed in – that she was an interfering little madam who should keep her nose out of other people's business. She added the man's name to her case file, as possibly being in league with Angus and Ellie over the fraud. That wasn't because she believed it, but to make her feel better about his rude outburst to her perfectly polite question.

"It's hardly my fault he's had every TV channel and newspaper in the country hounding him," she said as she drove home. A little voice in her head told her that actually it was.

Patrick spent one night with Amelia, met her a couple of times for lunch and they walked Ava home from school whenever Amelia's shifts allowed. She went almost to Meghan's door and called greetings to Isla who replied from her bedroom window. The first time it felt so odd to be there – even more so as she long distance air kissed Isla goodbye. Soon though it became almost normal.

It was brilliant she was able to see the sick girl's improvement for herself. She was still much thinner, paler and quieter than Avid Ava, but Isla's improvement was undeniable.

Patrick called frequently and always assured her of the same thing. Both girls often joined in the conversations, and the lively chatter and almost continuous giggling and silliness from the pair of them backed that up. Isla and Ava also thanked her for the cards she sent them both, and the photos of Bongo and her silly billy friend. That was Jasper who did the daftest bird impressions ever, while she videoed him.

Those conversations always ended the same way.

"I love you, Melia!"

"I love you too, Ava sweetie."

"I love you, Amelia!"

"And I love you, Isla treacle."

Neither Patrick nor Amelia expressed their love for each other using the word, but the longing in his voice when he said they'd be together soon told her what she wanted to know. She was sure her comments, that the wait would be worth it, gave him a fair idea of her own feelings.

TV news reports on the Angus McKellar disappearance claimed money had been removed 'over an extended period' from the account of the Salterns Support charity he'd set up to help the Salterns respite centre. They were careful not to say he was responsible, but did say this had begun just days before his first, still unexplained, disappearance.

There were frequent reminders of the few facts known about both times he'd gone missing. These were presented with a definite bias. They started with the reporter mentioning Angus's yacht and cars and ended with him staying 'in the Sea Mist boutique hotel in the popular resort of Falmouth'. Some reports stated, 'He was seen regularly visiting the cocktail bar of the upmarket Fal View Hotel'.

The boss and Jorge would be pleased with that description. Possibly the owner of the Sea Mist would have been pleased with how his small premises were portrayed, if he made an exception and watched the news.

Angus's wife, Heather McKellar, gave an appeal for any information about her husband. She began by reading a prepared statement, then added, "I'm certain my husband did not take that money. I'd have known if he was doing anything like that, and wouldn't have been a party to it, or helped cover it up. It would be a sin and Angus is a good man."

Amelia had no doubt Heather McKellar was completely innocent. That should have made it seem less likely Angus was guilty, but coming after the biased report, it gave the impression she was a naive woman, duped by her swindler of a husband.

Mrs McKellar also stated she didn't believe her husband would kill himself. That sounded like a brave attempt to convince herself.

Amelia didn't know what to think. Was it just her dislike of the way the media were manipulating viewer opinion which made her want to discover Angus was innocent? Or was it that both his wife and close friend agreed that stealing money and causing so much anxiety were completely out of character? It wasn't just them either. Nicole, the two 'dog men' Colin and Brian, and the charity shop worker had all said what a lovely man he was.

It was possible that his generosity to Ellie Roebuck was just kindness and the girl had covered her tracks for some reason completely unconnected with Angus McKellar. Although it seemed an odd coincidence that she'd claimed to be going to near where Angus was seen, it would be wrong to assume that everything Amelia discovered was connected to the case. In fact it would be wrong to make any assumptions at all.

Had the man she'd seen been totally innocent of all wrongdoing? That was hard to believe. Surely he'd have assured his wife he was alive, protested against the accusations and wanted to help discover what had really happened to the missing money. Was he a tortured soul, wracked with guilt? Possibly. His behaviour was definitely unusual and not consistent with someone trying to hide. He certainly hadn't been carefree and joyfully living the high life on stolen money as some TV reports suggested.

Amelia's phone rang about quarter past seven one evening. She initially assumed it was Patrick calling after getting the girls to sleep, but it was an unknown number.

"Is that Amelia?"

"Yes, who is this?"

"I'm Meghan. Meghan Homes. Patrick gave me your number, just in case of emergencies."

Chapter 23

"What's happened? Is Patrick OK? The girls?"

"They're fine. I'm sorry, I didn't mean to give you a shock."

What had the stupid woman imagined would happen when she rang up talking of emergencies? "How can I help you?" Amelia knew she sounded curt.

"I wanted to suggest that you come here to see Isla and Ava after school tomorrow."

"Oh."

"They've been pestering for a long time, and Isla is much stronger now."

Amelia did want to see Isla and it had already occurred to her that going into the house was the only way to achieve that in the near future. And she'd known she'd encounter Meghan eventually. She wanted that to happen on her terms though, not be summoned. As she was working later than usual the next day, it wasn't a great choice.

Or was it? She'd arrive shortly before the girls' bedtime. Making it a quick meeting might be best all round. "I'm working tomorrow, I won't finish until six."

"That would be perfect. We're gradually easing them both back into normality, so a short visit might be best the first time."

"OK, right." She loved the thought that her spending time with Isla and Ava was part of their normality. If Meghan could accept that and invite her into her home, then surely Amelia could cope with meeting the woman?

"You know you have to take some precautions, to

avoid infections. Take off your shoes and wash your hands…"

"Patrick said. Actually Ava did too. I'm fine with all that, I'll do whatever's needed."

"I know it's slightly weird to meet the ex, but try to think of me as a friend of Patrick's."

Meghan wasn't stupid then – she'd worked out what Amelia was less fine with.

"I'll try."

"They're extremely fond of you. It will do Isla good to have you visit."

"Right. Just after six then."

Amelia decided against buying more gifts for the girls in her lunch break. She didn't want to seem to be buying their affection. Nor did she want to watch Meghan decontaminate her offerings. To keep herself fully occupied at work she devised menus and entertainment for the third murder mystery weekend planned for November. There were nearly five months to go, but already enough places had been booked to ensure it would happen. The coach company who'd unsuccessfully tried to book onto the September one, had made a block booking.

Amelia and Sonia had decided to have the sixties theme for both forthcoming weekends, as they could re-use some props and the age of many of those who'd attended last year's one meant they'd be nostalgic for that time. The plot would be different for each, so it wouldn't matter if any guests came to both.

"We can play some great music," Sonia had said.

Since Jasper learned that, he'd been trying to decide between a Beatles look or flower power for himself, but he'd assured Amelia he had no doubts about her outfit.

"A huge floppy hat and teeny tiny skirt?"

"You won't find out until there's no time left to think of excuses not to wear it."

Amelia briefly considered asking Jasper to mix her a sample sixties themed cocktail to give her some courage before going to Meghan's home, but wisely called Nicole for a pep talk instead.

"It will be fine," Nicole said at length and in multiple ways, until she'd just about brainwashed Amelia into believing that. Or at least convinced her it might just possibly be something close to fine.

Amelia texted Patrick to say she was almost there, and was pleased to see him waiting outside the house for her. That was a huge relief, as she'd been dreading him and Meghan greeting her together, like the married couple they still technically were.

Patrick hugged her. "Thanks for coming."

"You know I've missed Isla." If she pretended this was no big deal, maybe it really would be fine.

"Come on then." He took her hand and they walked up the path and in through the front door together.

Inside the house they removed their shoes, which made Amelia realise Patrick put his on just so she hadn't needed to walk in alone. When Amelia emerged from the bathroom, after the required thorough hand washing, he took her into the lounge and introduced her to his ex.

Meghan was a stunningly good looking, petite yet curvaceous blonde. Having seen her daughters, and the back view of the woman, that wasn't exactly a surprise, but it was kind of a relief. She looked so different from Amelia they couldn't be compared one with the other.

"Hello, Meghan," was Amelia's carefully thought out greeting.

"It's nice to meet you, and the girls are really looking forward to seeing you again. Do you want to go right up?"

"Yes. Thank you."

She was rewarded by a smile and the sight of Meghan picking up a book.

As they climbed the stairs, Patrick explained that both girls would be in Ava's room. "They spend most of their time together when Ava's not at school. Isla just goes back to her own room if she needs a nap, and at night, to sleep and have her dialysis."

As he opened the door, both girls hurtled towards her, calling her name. She hugged them both.

"I missed you, Amelia."

"I've missed you too, Treacle."

"I know what treacle is now," Isla said. "It's like syrup, but it's more natural. Mummy told me and she got me a treacle tart and I ate a big bit."

"And I ate the rest, Melia. It was sweet like me!"

"Nothing is as sweet as you two," Amelia said.

"Except caramels?" Patrick suggested.

"True. And cake."

"Biscuits."

"Chocolate."

"Ice cream."

"Daddy, Melia, stop it! You know me and Isla are the sweetest everer."

"Of course we do," Amelia said.

"How are you, Isla? You look much better."

"I am. Do you want to know why?"

"Yes I do," she said, mainly because Isla seemed keen

to tell her.

"I have treatments when I'm asleep to make me get better. It's called peritoneal dialysis. I'm poorly because my kidneys don't work properly so there's horrid stuff in my blood that I can't wee out like most people. I have a special machine…"

"I told Melia about the parrot and eel and the stuff in your tummy, didn't I, Melia?"

"Yes you did, which was clever of you, but now Isla is telling me a bit more." She hoped Isla did have a bit more and Ava hadn't cut her off completely.

"It's called an exchange when the bad stuff goes out, and soon I will be able to go back to school and play with my friends and Bongo and we can have picnics and be princesses in a castle. And then I'll get a new kidney and I won't even need the dialysis."

"That's wonderful," Amelia said. It was heartbreaking though that a child so young was in a position to have to know so much about the inner workings of her body.

"Yes and I'm clever too. I can spell dialysis." She proved the point.

"What clever girls you both are!"

They both attempted to impress her with their spelling abilities and were successful. Isla because she could spell a lot of difficult words and Ava because she was able to incorporate so many extra letters. With a bit of prompting they got through their times tables too. Amelia was surprised by how much more advanced Isla was, until she remembered she was two years older. She wondered if she'd grow more now she was receiving treatment, but thought it better not to ask.

"Will you read us a story, please, Amelia?"

"OK. How about this one?" she said picking up what

looked like a fun book from the shelf near Ava's bed.

"Yay!"

The girls acted out the words as she spoke, and said some with her. After a while she asked if they'd heard the story before.

Patrick explained it was part of a series and that the main character tended to repeat his actions and had several catchphrases.

"They're my favourite stories," Isla said.

"Are they your favourites too, Ava?"

"No, this one is." She held up a picture book.

"I'll read both then," Amelia promised, and not just because it would delay her having to be sociable with Meghan.

Amelia loved being part of their extended bedtime routine and thought how lucky she was they'd taken to her so well. Then when Patrick picked the sleepy Isla up to take her to her own room, her pyjama top rode up exposing just how painfully thin she was. Being involved with that little girl was going to be hard, just not in the way she'd feared. It would be easier if she didn't love the little mite.

Amelia cared about Patrick just as much. There was plenty of potential for heartbreak in the whole situation. It wasn't just her overactive imagination creating the possibility of disaster. This was real. But so was the potential for happiness. She was willing to take the risk. Actually she didn't feel she had any choice.

When they left the girls and went back downstairs Amelia tried to follow Meghan's suggestion of seeing her just as a friend of Patrick's, so accepted a cup of tea and attempted to have a normal conversation. It was strained, but not unbearable.

Amelia and Patrick left together and went out for dinner.

As they waited for their food, Amelia asked Patrick, about Meghan. "You clearly get on well, especially when it comes to the girls. Why did you spilt up?"

"I suppose because we should never have married. We've been friends since junior school. We never dated each other, but often went out as a foursome with whoever we were both seeing at the time. Or just three when one of us was single. Then there was a time we'd both split up from quite serious relationships. Consoling each other led to a brief fling. Very brief and we'd already gone back to just being friends, when Meghan realised she was pregnant."

"Isla."

"Exactly. Getting married seemed logical. We got on well, and both wanted her to have the baby. It was OK for a few years, but not enough. Meghan accepted that sooner than I did. I think somehow I told myself if we could make the marriage work then we'd make Isla healthy too. I just made things worse by insisting we keep trying."

"Patrick, you didn't make Isla ill."

"No. I do see that now, but it felt like it at one time. And I caused all of us far more pain than I should have. I've learned from it though."

"Oh?"

"I understand my feelings better now. I love my girls, love being a family. I suppose in a way I do love Meghan, but that's as my long term friend and the mother of my daughters. I don't feel about her in the way I feel about you."

Amelia understood – Patrick loved her, but this time

he wasn't going to commit to a more permanent relationship without being as sure as he possibly could be, that it was the right decision. They held hands without saying anything else, until their meal arrived.

As the waiter walked away, Amelia said, "I love you too. Now eat before it gets cold."

Later that evening she repeated her offer to do anything she could to help with the girls. "I was thinking, maybe I could meet Ava's teachers or whatever is required so I could pick her up from school if it would be difficult because of looking after Isla."

"That's a great idea and there are definitely times it would help. I'll speak to Meghan."

Clearly he did, as Meghan called Amelia the following day.

"Thanks for your offer to pick up Ava from school if needed. That could be really useful." She said it in much the same way Gabrielle responded if Amelia offered to wait in for a delivery before taking Bongo out.

"No problem," Amelia responded, just as she would have done in that situation.

"You don't strictly need to go to the school first, I can just have them add your name to the list and give you a password. I'll sort that out today, but I was thinking it might be good if we went together next time your shifts allow. I understand you've never gone to the school gate and if you were on your own the first time, that might worry Ava."

It made sense. Plus, although Amelia knew where the school was, she wasn't sure exactly where she'd have to wait. It would be awful if she got it wrong and made Ava think nobody had come for her.

"I could come this afternoon. I was planning to walk

my dog about then anyway."

"Do bring him. The girls have said so much about Bongo I'd like to meet him myself."

Amelia fretted about her arrival time at the school. She couldn't be late and have it seem she was unreliable, but she didn't want to be alone with Meghan longer than needed. It was taken out of her hands when Meghan approached from an unexpected angle.

Amelia crossed over to meet her.

"Hi. Isla is having a lesson at home, so I took the opportunity to do a bit of shopping." She waved a canvas shopping bag.

"Her teachers come to the house?"

"No. They send work for her and she has a private tutor. She has for a while as she was missing so much school. He's my partner Stuart. It's how we met."

"Ah." Patrick had said something about him being great with the girls, but because it involved Meghan she hadn't paid full attention.

"So, this is the famous Bongo? Is it OK...?"

"Yeah, you can stroke him."

Amelia was rather pleased Bongo's reaction was polite, but not effusive. She tried not to be pleased that Ava's was and that she called, "Melia!" as she ran towards them.

Then both Meghan and Amelia laughed when Ava threw herself at Bongo and told him how much she loved and missed him. Eventually she let him go, and hugged her mother and Amelia.

"Are we taking Bongo for a walk, Melia?"

"If that's OK with your mum."

"Yes, it is," Meghan said.

Amelia didn't know if she should invite Meghan to

come too.

"But first Mummy needs to see Bongo's tricks. He's ever so clever. Me and Isla and Melia trained him."

They walked to the grassy area where Amelia had often sat with Patrick while one or both of the girls played with the dog. Ava was too excited to get the best out of Bongo, but the little dog very clearly demonstrated his tolerance of children and the pleasure he gave Ava.

"Shall we say about an hour for the walk?" Meghan suggested. "I expect you'll all be ready for a drink and snack by then."

It felt oddly like it had when Amelia's parents allowed her out to play with Nicole and made it clear her friend was welcome to come home with her.

"Sounds good. Thanks."

From then on Amelia stopped thinking of Meghan as a rival. She was, just as she'd said, an old friend of Patrick's. She was also the mother of two little girls Amelia loved, and was generously making it easy for her to have a part in their lives.

By the time Patrick told her they'd started the divorce proceedings it felt to Amelia like nothing more than a paperwork exercise confirming what had already happened. It might mean more to Patrick, who'd tried hard to make the marriage work.

"Are you OK about it?" she asked him.

"Of course. This is what we agreed. It's definitely the right thing to do, for Meghan and Stuart as well as us."

"It is, yes. It's OK not to be feeling in a party mood over it though."

Patrick hugged her. "Thank you for understanding

that. It is kind of sad. I suppose it's a little like people who are sad to leave their old home, even though they're moving to somewhere better or more suited to their needs."

Over the next few weeks Amelia often called at Meghan's home. Usually with Patrick, or when he was already there, but sometimes on her own. She shared Sunday lunch with the whole family, including Meghan's partner Stuart.

Amelia had offered to provide the dessert and brought with her a pear and caramel tart, which she'd baked herself.

"I confess," she said after receiving lavish praise, "I had some help. Chef at work made the base and sauce. I just put it all together and stuck it in the oven."

"That's not fair!" Meghan protested. "Now I'm going to have to own up to buying the gravy, and that the Yorkshire's were only so good because Stuart made those."

"I did wonder how you'd suddenly become such a good cook," Patrick said.

Amelia grinned. She was pleased that his reference to his earlier life with Meghan caused her no pain, and smug that Patrick, Ava and Isla had claimed the monster Yorkshire puddings she'd once served them were 'the bestest in the world ever' and got through them all and every drop of gravy.

Occasionally Amelia collected Ava from school, and then both girls. If Isla felt well enough they'd go for a walk, if not they took the shortest route to the girls' home. The most recent of those times had been when Patrick was in hospital for an afternoon undergoing the start of testing to determine whether he was a suitable transplant donor for Isla.

He hadn't wanted to celebrate the end of is marriage, but he did when he got the news that he'd be cut open and his kidney removed. "Of course what I'm happiest about is that Isla has the chance to be healthy, but it feels good that I'll be the one giving her that chance."

On the twelfth of July, Amelia's birthday, Patrick took her and the girls to the beach where they had a delicious but small picnic lunch. The highlight was a cake made by both girls. Ava and Isla were so desperate for her to try it and so eager for her to open their gift to her that several minutes were spent deliberating which to do first.

"Let's eat," Patrick said. "Poor Bongo is drooling."

"It's truly amazing," Amelia was able to honestly declare about the cake. Having been primed by Patrick she was also able to see that it represented a princess's crown jewels which had been stolen by a pirate, rescued by brave Sir Bongo and stored in the castle, while the naughty pirate had to clean out the dungeons.

That was a lot to get onto one six inch cake, but they'd done an excellent job. It had been decorated without the slightest trace of restraint. Presumably Patrick had cut back on the savoury items to compensate for the inches of icing, chocolate, jelly sweets, meringue nests, brandy snaps and Flakes.

After the food, Amelia opened her presents.

"Mine first, girls. After Amelia's seen what you have for her, she'll forget all about this."

"That's true."

"OK, Daddy."

Patrick gave her the most beautiful heart shaped locket.

"Thank you. It's lovely." She kissed him.

"Are you going to put Daddy's picture in it, Melia?"

"Yes, I am. And yours and Treacle's. Maybe we could go and get one of us all together later on today?"

"And Bongo!"

"Well, maybe."

"Great idea," Patrick said. "I know just the place."

"Ours now!" Ava said, pushing the gift towards Amelia.

Ava and Isla had made her a picture book, telling the story allegedly depicted on her cake. It was decorated just as lavishly, although thankfully without any sugar. Every word was carefully handwritten and spelled correctly. The story seemed to include elements of every silly game she'd ever played with the girls. Every page was neatly trimmed and laced to the others with thin ribbons. Every sticker, cut out image and sprinkle of glitter was carefully fixed into place.

"Why are you crying, Melia?"

"You do like books, don't you Amelia?"

"I do, but I don't like this one."

"Oh!"

"Melia!"

"I absolutely and totally adore it. This is the best book I've ever seen in my whole life. It's so good, it's very nearly as lovely as you two."

"Yay!"

"Group hug!"

The girl's gift didn't quite make Amelia forget about the locket Patrick gave her, but it did come as a slight surprise when not long after they'd buried him in the sand, got Bongo to search for him and then rescued him, he suggested they go and have the photo taken to go in it. Nobody, not even Isla, was too tired to have stayed out a bit longer. Strangely, when he suggested they take Bongo home first, the girls didn't object. She was grateful as she wanted a proper photo of Patrick, and one of Ava and Isla for her locket. Taking some silly ones with the dog would have been OK, had he been allowed in the photo booth, but it would have been hard to get anything else.

It was a bigger and far less welcome surprise when, after successfully getting her pictures, plus some lovely ones of the four of them together, she got a text from work, saying she was needed urgently.

With some exasperation she told Patrick what it said and called back. "Can't it wait? It's my birthday and I'm having a day out."

"Oh. Happy birthday," Bianca said. "Sorry about that, but it's really urgent and won't take long."

"What's happened?"

"It'll take ages to explain. Please, just come in and take a look."

Amelia knew that if she refused she'd spoil the rest of the day wondering what had gone wrong, and she was only a few minutes' walk away. She sighed. "Alright. I'll come, but only for a minute."

Chapter 24

As Amelia strode into the lobby, Bianca came to meet her. "Follow me."

"I'll be back as soon as I can," Amelia said to Patrick and the girls. She followed the receptionist to the Pendennis room.

Bianca opened the door and gestured for Amelia to go in.

"Surprise!" the assembled people yelled.

Ava and Isla rushed past her and started everyone singing 'Happy Birthday'. Jasper was there as well as her other friends from work. Even the boss had come in. And Mum and Dad!

"How did you do this? Who did this?" She remembered the ease with which Patrick had persuaded Ava and Isla to leave the beach, relinquish Bongo and have their photos taken with relatively little messing about. "You two! You knew and didn't tell me! I thought you were my friends."

"No, mate, I'm your friend," Nicole said.

"Nicole! Did you do this?"

"Nope. Wasn't even my idea."

"Then who?"

"Your mum and dad. They called me and said they thought you'd like to see me today, and I remembered I had Patrick's number on my phone from when you came up. They remembered Jasper... it just all came together."

After her colleagues had toasted her health and presented her with a card signed by them all, they retreated. Amelia started the introductions by telling

Patrick and the girls, "This is my best friend, Nicole."

"We're your best friends too, Melia."

"Yes you are. What I meant is Nicole is my oldest friend."

"Is she older than you, Melia?"

"Oh yes, days and days." And she'd only sent her a joke card and a gift voucher. Nicole had put her business on hold and travelled hundreds of miles.

"And this is my mum and dad."

"Hello Melia's mummy and daddy. I'm Ava sweetie."

"And I'm Isla treacle."

"We're very pleased to meet you both," Mum said. "And you, Patrick."

"Yes indeed," Dad added.

"Likewise," Patrick said, shaking hands.

Patrick and the girls had no trouble chatting with the three people they'd not previously met and seemed to win instant approval. That wasn't surprising – Nicole liked the same kind of people Amelia did, and her parents were always polite.

Dad asked about the estate agency and Amelia had a sudden image of him taking Patrick aside and asking if his attentions were honourable. She was saved from explaining her suppressed giggle by Jorge appearing. He ushered Amelia, her parents, Nicole, Patrick, Isla and Ava into the dining room for an afternoon tea.

When the huge tiered stand of sandwiches and cakes was brought out, Ava and Isla informed her they'd had such a tea before, in the same restaurant.

"It was with Granny and Granddad," Isla said.

Of course. It was because of that association Patrick had been so eager to book into the Fal View.

"Granny and Granddad are Daddy's mummy and

daddy," Ava explained. "Does that mean your mummy and daddy are our granny and granddad too?"

"Not precisely," Amelia said.

"Course not, silly billy. Amelia and Daddy have to get married first. Isn't that right?"

"More tea, anyone?" Mum asked.

Later, when Amelia excused herself to go to the bathroom, Mum came with her.

"Those two are delightful. I quite see why you're so fond of them."

"And Patrick, what do you think of him?"

"He seems very nice, and clearly cares very deeply about you."

"An improvement on James?"

"Very much so!"

"Mum, you never said one word against him."

"Perhaps I should have done."

"You weren't to know what would happen."

"I didn't know, but I was uneasy…"

"That's in the past, Mum. Now tell me what you think about being a granny to Ava and Isla."

"I think it's entirely up to you."

"You've said that a lot, Mum."

"Too often perhaps, but there is a reason. I've been thinking… since we talked about you leaving home… Where to start? Your father and I were childhood sweethearts."

"But you didn't get married until you were in your thirties." Was Mum warning her against rushing things with Patrick? She didn't think she could be accused of that.

"No, because our parents kept us apart. I wasn't good enough for your father's lot, and his family were too

Catholic for mine."

"I had no idea." Amelia had seen very little of any of her grandparents and always assumed that was because her parents were on the cool and distant side.

"It's not something we like to think or talk about."

"I suppose not. But you got back together?"

"Yes, and in time they reluctantly accepted we would marry. For a long time we thought we wouldn't have a child. When you came along we were determined not to repeat the mistakes which had kept us apart for too long. Not to interfere too much in your life. Not to make your decisions for you. I don't know now that we were right."

"You were, Mum." Perhaps what they'd done wasn't always best for Amelia, but they had acted for the right reason – they loved her.

"I'm not sure. James hurt you so badly. If I'd spoken against the wedding…"

"I wouldn't have listened, or I'd have blamed you when it didn't happen. You did your best, you and Dad. I can only hope I do as well with Ava and Isla, if I get the chance."

"I hope you do. I'd love to be granny to that cheeky pair."

Meghan and Stuart came at seven to wish Amelia a happy birthday and collect the girls. Amelia was touched when they gave her a card and an enamelled bookmark decorated with rainbows, very like the pattern on her bag. She was also slightly pleased it was a lot harder to get Ava and Isla to go home than it had been to persuade them to leave the beach. Amelia knew it was as much a wish to stay up a bit later than to snatch a few more minutes with her, but felt sure they were sorry to be leaving her company.

Ava and Isla were back at The Fal View the following day. They claimed they needed to see where their paintings would hang in order to make a really good job of creating suitable artwork for the murder mystery. This was despite them having made an enthusiastic start, based on examples Patrick had printed for them.

"And I expect having another cake and milkshake while you're there will help?"

"It will, Melia!"

"I think so as well," Isla had said.

"Perhaps you're right." It wouldn't hurt to put up a display and email Sonia to show her what she'd be working with, and the girls deserved a reward for their efforts. They'd been incredibly industrious, having created a dozen large artworks, in various mediums, as well as the fabulous book they'd given Amelia for her birthday.

Amelia had made up labels using both the girls' real names and the pseudonyms of A. Sweetie and I. Treacle in large letters, which pleased them.

"What does the rest say?" Isla asked. "It's too high for me to read."

"This piece represents the naivety of youth," Patrick read. "And the longing to break free from the past into a sugar filled future."

None of them seemed to understand Amelia's reference to the collage featuring brightly coloured wrappers from confectionery which hadn't been produced until long after the 60s. "Honestly, do you know nothing about art?" she asked the painters and their creative director.

"And you do?" Patrick asked, while his eyebrows

made clear he very much doubted that.

"If you take this thoughtful piece in a dual monotone, I think you'll clearly see the influence of John Sparacio, whereas this one by Ms Treacle is very much in the style of Pollock."

Patrick, after a quick internet search, declared himself impressed.

"Come on, let's see what's the cake of the day," Amelia suggested before he had time to remember she'd told him which artists she wanted the girls to imitate.

Nicole rang two days after Amelia's birthday party. "Are you watching the news?"

"No, what's happened?"

"Angus McKellar has been found – dead."

"What?"

It wasn't that it had happened which surprised her so much as the realisation she'd hardly thought about the case in the last few days. It was as though it was a mystery in a book which she could put down and nothing would happen until she picked it up again. She explained that to Nicole.

"I know what you mean. I noticed a lot of police about this morning, but it still doesn't seem like something which could happen here. People still talk about the time a dead whale got washed up and that happened more than a decade before I moved here."

"Angus got washed up on the beach?"

"Yep."

"Where?"

"Right near the children's splash park and play area opposite the High Street. A dog walker found him really early. Good job too."

"I'll say!" Amelia had seen for herself how busy that area was in the fairly cool May weather. Now it was warmer there would be even more families. How awful if a child had discovered the body, not that it would be much more pleasant for an adult.

"Patrick was right, he said dog walkers always find the body. They're sure it is him, are they?"

"Yeah. The person who found him recognised him."

"Must have been a horrible shock."

"Just from TV I think, not because he was a friend. Anyway, the news are now saying it was him, none of that 'believed to be' stuff, so it must have been confirmed."

"So he's been alive all this time?"

"I don't know about that."

"If his body had been in the water more than a few days it would… It would take more than a quick look to know it was him."

"Urgh. Yeah, see what you mean. I wonder where he was? He didn't go home. His wife has made a few more appeals for information and I can't believe she knew anything. Plus the press keep hanging around, and the police have been in and out the house."

"Was it suicide, have they said?"

"Suspicious, is how it's been described."

They talked for a while about the case, but soon moved on to Amelia's relationship with Patrick and the girls. Nicole said that's what had pushed thoughts of crime from Amelia's mind. "And a good thing too."

"It's definitely a good thing that I've been thinking of them and not about a missing man, but you can't blame me for being a bit interested again now."

"You wouldn't be you if you weren't. You'd better get

yourself up here and investigate, hadn't you?"

"I might take you up on that."

"I'm counting on it. Feel free to bring the family."

"I might bring Patrick. He's been promising me a murder mystery weekend that I don't have to organise."

"Then tell him I've laid one on."

Amelia didn't know whether to call Sean. He hadn't been in touch for a while. After Amelia reported his lead about Ellie Roebuck had been a dead-end she hadn't been surprised his calls, and apparently his interest in finding Angus, had dwindled away. He'd assumed his friend was dead. Amelia had too. She'd still wanted to know the truth, but it became less important and far less urgent as the days passed and she got on with her life.

She wasn't a close enough acquaintance to feel her condolences would mean anything to Sean. She had no new information to offer and even if she had it wouldn't bring Angus back. She settled for sending a text saying she'd seen the news and was sorry. That might be her last contact with him, which frankly wouldn't bother her at all. Amelia shivered as she recalled her first meeting with Sean had involved an unreal death which seemed so real. Her contact with him had, or soon would, come to an end because of another death, and this one was genuine.

Obviously Amelia still wanted to know the story behind Angus's disappearances, but the police would work that out and make it public. Despite what she'd said to Nicole, Amelia on her own, and without knowing the people involved, wasn't likely to be able to learn anything more.

Despite his previous connection to the area, she was

lucky Angus had chosen to hide away where she lived, and even more fortunate, from a solving part of the mystery point of view, that he'd chosen to drink in The Fal View. Without that and the coincidence of meeting Sean in Lee-on-the-Solent she'd have known no more than anyone else just watching it unfold on TV.

Amelia used iPlayer to watch the news, and searched online for further reports. There was lots of coverage, but very little more information than Nicole had supplied. The only additional fact which came to light was that Angus's boat, which had remained moored up since he'd gone missing in May, appeared to have been used just prior to when his body was discovered. There were 'signs it may have been occupied'.

Surely he couldn't have been living on it for months in his home town without anyone noticing?

Angus's wife made another appeal, supported by Sean who was there as a friend, not to conduct an interview. Heather McKellar had aged dramatically since the last time Amelia had seen her on TV. The widow stated she couldn't believe Angus could have an accident at sea. He always wore a lifejacket. Besides, his boat had been moored up the whole time. To Amelia and probably anyone else, it sounded like he'd committed suicide and Heather, understandably, was unwilling to accept the fact.

There was no mention of Angus's car. Did that mean it hadn't been found, or wasn't considered important as it wasn't connected with his death? Amelia knew he had his car with him in Falmouth. She'd made the police aware of that, but it hadn't been made public.

Sean rang back whilst Amelia was still trying to make sense of the little she knew.

"That's it then, it was all true," he said, sounding very despondent. "He took the money and couldn't live with what he'd done."

"Sorry, it does look like that."

"He was such a good man, he really was. How could this have happened?"

"I don't know."

"It makes no sense."

"No, a lot of it doesn't. Do you know what happened to his car?"

"Car? What does that matter now?"

"I suppose it doesn't. I just wondered if it had been found. It wasn't mentioned on the news, but if he drove back to his boat in Lee-on-the-Solent you'd expect it to be somewhere local."

"You only saw part of the number plate, maybe it wasn't really his car you saw?"

She'd definitely seen him driving though. "Even if it wasn't, his is still missing."

"True. It doesn't matter though, does it?"

"Not the car, no, but you asked for my help in finding out what happened. I know the news must have been a horrible shock, but... Do you still want to know?"

"Yes, of course." His voice said the opposite.

"There'll be an inquest, won't there?" Amelia asked.

"Almost certainly."

"I'll come up for that."

"No need. They'll just open and adjourn it. Anyway, I can tell you whatever is said."

"Right. OK." She was going, but as he clearly didn't like the idea of her continuing to play detective, she wouldn't mention it until much nearer the time. Then, once she knew the date, she could say that coincidentally that's when she'd arranged to visit Nicole. As they'd agreed Amelia would stay whenever the inquest was held, that was the truth and made her seem less like a ghoulish spectator. She hoped that wasn't what she actually was.

Amelia still had the number of the police officer she'd reported her sighting of Angus McKellar to. She'd been given it in case she could provide any more information, but Amelia didn't let that stop her calling and trying to obtain some from the officer.

"Will there be an inquest?" she asked.

"Yes, but don't worry, it's not likely you'll be called as a witness."

"Oh." She wasn't sure whether to be relieved or disappointed.

"He was seen in the guest house after you last saw him, and the owner spoke to him, so might be able to give some idea of his state of mind."

Amelia couldn't do that. Zac or Jasper would make better witnesses than she would.

"Can I go anyway?"

"Inquests are public," the officer said. "Most likely though it will be opened and then adjourned."

That's what Sean had said. Even so… "Do you know when it will be?"

The officer gave her the most likely date.

Amelia arranged time off work and her visit to Nicole's, in both cases allowing two days either side and giving the dates as provisional. She also told Patrick and asked if he'd come with her.

"I'll pencil it in," he said and made a note of the dates.

"I know it's difficult for you to say until you know the

definite dates and it looks like it will be in the school holidays." She didn't want to put too much pressure on him at that early stage, but she was definitely going herself and very much hoped he'd join her.

Amelia remembered that, when she'd talked about her week in Lee-on-the-Solent, she'd thought what she'd said about Sean might have made Patrick slightly jealous and intent on accompanying her on future visits. She didn't remind him. It was one thing to coerce clients thanking her instead of complaining, or doing something to make Ava and Isla laugh rather than squabble, but quite another to manipulate the man she loved into doing something against his wishes.

She now understood the reasons behind their one and only row and didn't intend to throw it in his face every time she didn't immediately get her way. He had tried to take her away a couple of times and it wasn't his fault it hadn't happened – once it was because of Isla and once because of Amelia's job. Lastly, she knew how horrible it felt to be jealous and she wouldn't deliberately do anything to cause him pain.

That night Amelia had a nightmare about when she'd first met Sean. In her dream she was searching for him and found him stabbing someone while his accomplice held the man still. She screamed and tried to get away. When she awoke it was her quilt not brambles restraining her legs. And it was Patrick, not Sean, who held her.

"Shh, you're OK. It was just a dream."

"It was real, I saw it."

"Amelia, you're safe here with me. Watch your eyes, I'll turn on the light." He held her and stroked her back. "I've got you. You're safe."

"I know. I'm OK now. But it was real. Well not real, but not my imagination. I saw Sean with a knife. And Angus McKellar is really dead."

"Tell me about the dream."

After she'd described it, Patrick said, "That Sean Underhill is thoroughly irresponsible." It sounded as though he had other less favourable opinions of the man.

"It wasn't his fault. He didn't mean to scare me and wasn't to know anyone would see him."

"Didn't you say it happened by a road?"

"Not a proper one, just a track really. And if I'd been on that instead of completely lost I wouldn't have seen anything but the backs of the vehicles and… oh."

"What?"

"I've seen it in my mind so many times, but I've only just realised there was more than one vehicle."

"You keep having these dreams?"

"Not as bad as tonight, but I can't forget it."

"It's probably happening now because you're going back there and there's the inquest and everything."

"I suppose so."

"Tell you what, when we go back up we'll find the place where they were doing the filming. Maybe seeing it in daylight will help?"

"You'll come with me?"

"Of course I will."

Chapter 25

The police officer's estimate of the inquest date was just one day out, meaning Amelia and Patrick had three days together at Nicole's beforehand and, as they'd decided to stay for a whole week, three after. To make up for their short absence, they'd promised Ava and Isla they'd take them camping later in the school holidays. Patrick had booked them into a nearby site for two days mid-week.

"That's not much of a trip," Amelia said.

"Maybe I'm being over cautious, but I don't want to take Isla far from hospital, and doctors who know her."

"I didn't mean that. Nicole and I used to camp in the garden and that was an adventure. It just doesn't seem long."

"Not now it doesn't. Trust me, it will by the end."

"You're probably right. Come to think of it, when we were little Mum and Dad probably got more peace when we were indoors than when we were down the garden."

Knowing Sean would attend the inquest, as a reporter if nothing else, Amelia texted him as they drove up.

'Hi Sean. I'm coming up to Lee-on-the-Solent to stay with my friend. Heard Angus McKellar's inquest is Tuesday, so thought I'd go. Just wanted to let you know.'

He replied about an hour later, 'It will be nice to see you. You been to an inquest before?'

'No. It's only because I feel sort of involved that I think I should.' She really did feel that way. There was no need to add she actually wanted to.

'Let me know when you get here and maybe we can

go for a coffee. I can tell you what to expect on the day.'

That would be useful in helping her understand the proceedings, and seeing Sean again under friendly circumstances should help put an end to the nightmares which still sometimes jolted her awake. Having Patrick with her would also be a big help. She should probably let Sean know about that. Even though he'd not seemed interested in her that way, his ego might mean he had the wrong impression about her.

'Patrick and I would like that'.

Sean responded with a thumbs up emoji.

Nicole came out to the little car park behind her Wight View B&B and hugged Patrick before he'd even got their bags out of the car. "So lovely to see you again, even if you did bring the dippy detective with you!"

"Had to. She's not safe out on her own, is she?" Patrick said.

"Ah, I see you've worked out why I've been her friend all these years. Keeping an eye on her is my civic duty."

"Oi!" Amelia said.

"Oh, hello, sweetie. I didn't see you there. Lovely to see you." Nicole hugged Amelia. "Now, do you think you can find your way inside? It's three paces to the left, one straight ahead and through that white door there."

"I can probably manage to find my way, but only if you carry my bags." She proved herself able not only to navigate into the building, but also to locate the fridge. By the time Patrick and Nicole brought in everything from the car, Amelia had poured three glasses of wine.

They talked about the journey, weather, things Amelia and Patrick planned to do while they were up in Lee-on-the-Solent and Nicole's business over the first half glass of wine.

"And how are the little imps?" Nicole asked.

"We're taking them camping in a fortnight. Patrick assures me I'll know them a whole lot better after that."

"I don't doubt it! So Isla's well enough for that? Of course she is, or you wouldn't take her. I'm just surprised she can travel. I thought she had dialysis every night?"

"She does," Patrick said. "The machine is portable. It's a bit of a faff, but she can have it done anywhere. She's already had a night at her grandparents and it was fine."

"She's as well as I've ever known her," Amelia said. "And as well as she'll get without the transplant."

"And that's going to be when, January?"

"If all goes to plan, yes," Patrick said.

"It's brave of you to have an operation that doesn't benefit you," Nicole said.

"But it does. Helping my kids is helping me." Then he splashed a bit more wine into Nicole's glass. "Now to what I really came for – dish the dirt on all Amelia's embarrassing secrets."

"No, Nicole. Don't do that."

"Absolutely not. What do you take me for? No way will I ever tell anyone about the great chocolate robbery, nearly getting expelled for stalking our maths teacher, or the thing with the hair. As for the time she got so lost she ended up in another country, that's something I never, ever, even mention."

"Shame," Patrick said.

"Unless I've had a second glass of wine of course. Sadly this bottle is nearly empty."

"Oh well, it was a good try. You might not be willing to talk to me, but I know you and Amelia will want to chat. Why don't you point me towards a decent take away and I'll go get us some food?"

Nicole produced a selection of menus and she and Amelia placed their orders.

"See you in a bit," Patrick said.

"He's going to buy more wine, I just know it," Amelia said.

"Don't worry about that."

"Really? You won't drink it and tell all?"

"What I meant was, there's a couple more bottles in the fridge, so I'll be drinking and talking anyway."

"I used to like you."

"Yeah. But now you've got Patrick, Ava and Isla to love and you'll forget all about me and live happily ever after with them."

"I hope so."

"Oh cheers, mate."

"You know I'd never forget about you or stop being your friend."

"Not with what I've got on you!"

"That works both ways you know. Talking of which, when do I get to meet Miguel?"

"I'll bring him to your wedding."

"You're just trying to distract me."

"Yep. And it's working." She hummed the Wedding March.

"Do you really think…?"

"We've been through this. You really are a terrible detective when it comes to things which are happening right in front of you! Would he be up here this week, instead of home with his girls, if he didn't love you?"

"Probably not."

"And would he let the girls grow to love you if he wasn't expecting you to feature in their future?"

"Definitely not."

Amelia had another nightmare about Sean's action scene. In the morning Patrick said the first thing they should do was to visit the spot it had happened. "So you can see it how it looks now, not how you remember it."

"Good idea."

"As you're going to have to rely on Amelia's navigation, I won't come with you," Nicole said. "I have plans for Christmas."

"I totally understand, but I was rather hoping you might be able to supply me with a map."

Nicole did, and pointed out a few landmarks for him. Amelia tried to protest that she knew where she was going but, as she didn't, wasn't surprised they doubted her.

It was pleasant walking round the nature reserve, especially in the shaded areas. They did manage to find the little bridge she'd crossed and the motte and bailey castle. They also found some tracks, any one of which might have been the one Sean and his actor friends had used to bring in their equipment.

"We might have already walked over where it happened," Amelia said. "I don't think I'll ever know for sure where it was, but that's good. I see now there's nothing to see. If I do remember what happened, I can remind myself it looks like this now. Long grass instead of long shadows. And moon daisies and butterflies and birds singing."

"I'm glad." He kissed her.

"What now?"

"I'll phone Sean and say I'm here. Seeing him other than at the inquest might be good too."

"OK."

She did that, and Sean said he'd be in touch to arrange a time to meet them.

Patrick gestured for her to pass him the phone. He introduced himself and explained about Amelia's nightmares. After a pause he said, "I'm sure if she saw the finished thing, it would help." Another pause and he said, "OK, until then."

He returned the phone to his pocket. "He sounds really sorry about scaring you."

"He was at the time."

Patrick handed her the map. "Come on then, Columbus. Which way back?"

Amelia studied it. "Probably the way Sean took me is quickest, but I've had enough thinking about that night. Let's go another way and walk along the seafront." Then remembering that's where Angus McKellar washed up, "But not near the High Street."

"OK. So along here?" He indicated a route.

"Yes."

"You don't know do you?"

Actually she was fairly certain he was right, but that wasn't the point. "I do know – that I can trust you not to lead me astray."

As they walked along the shingle beach, back towards Nicole's B&B they saw several boats and ships. Amelia told Patrick about the ferries to the Isle of Wight and across the channel, container and cruise ships at Southampton and Royal Navy vessels in Portsmouth harbour, all of which could be seen at different times in the Solent. "It's a great place for ship spotters, but not for train spotters as Gosport is the largest UK town with no railway station."

"You're as good as a tour guide."

"Nicole told me." She didn't tell him that much of the shipping information had come from Sean, but did remember he'd lectured her practically into a coma, prompting her to think Patrick would have made it fun.

"That's a container ship," she said pointing at something in the distance which looked about right. "What do you think is on it?"

"Swearing parrots!" He flapped his arms as Amelia had done when impersonating talking pirate parrots for Isla and Ava. "Bum, fart, big wobbly thingies!" They both laughed.

"What precisely is a big wobbly thingy?" Amelia asked.

"No idea. You're better at this than me. Anyway, what do you think is on the ship? Treasure?"

She sighed. "Probably a load of plastic rubbish for pound shops."

"Sadly I expect you're right about some of it – but there must be other things too. Maybe a bulk consignment of caramel?"

"By bulk, you mean how much?"

"Maybe enough to last you a week. Let me do the maths… How big are those containers?"

"A lorry load."

"And how many containers per ship?"

Sean had thrown a lot of numbers at her, gross tonnage, maximum draft and a lot of other stuff she'd forgotten, but she did recall one detail. "The biggest one in the world has about twenty-four thousand."

"Wow! There'd be smaller here I suppose?"

"Apparently not."

"That's a lot of caramel. Maybe each one holds a

different flavour?"

"Go on then, name twenty-four thousand flavours of caramel."

"That's easy."

"It is?"

"Yep. Loving you means I've done my research. There's chocolate coated, brazil nut, brazil nut with chocolate coating, plain caramel, banana caramel, mint caramel, mint caramel with chocolate coating…"

Amelia wasn't listening. Patrick loved her! She'd known that really, but hearing him saying it was better than a whole shipment of anything.

"… Cherry caramel, white chocolate coated cherry caramel, dark chocolate coated cherry caramel."

"One more and I think you've done it," Amelia said.

"Lemon and mint raspberry ripple caramel."

"Bad luck. You said that one earlier. I win."

"I'll get you some caramel as a prize. Caramel sauce perhaps?"

"And what would I put that on?"

"Come on, Miss Watson. Use your imagination."

They went back to Nicole's for lunch. During the meal, Sean rang to suggest meeting that evening. "Do you have transport?" he asked.

"Yes, we drove up."

"In that case, considering how much you like castles, how about the Castle In The Air pub?"

"That sounds great. What time?"

"Nine? I'm going to see Corey first."

"Corey?" The name vaguely rang a bell.

"He was in the film with me and Tony. He's making a copy for you."

"Brilliant. Thank you."

"I'll drive you, if you like," Nicole said. "Just to prove to Patrick I'm not a complete lush."

"It's fine. I only plan to stay for one drink. That'll be enough of Sean's company. Do come though if you like."

"You're OK. I get more than enough of him on TV."

"I thought you'd come round to him?"

"I felt sorry for him when he was so upset over Angus and it seemed he was being set up for taking the money, but I'm not exactly his biggest fan."

"Nor am I," Patrick said.

"Oh, you didn't hear. He's bringing the film with him."

"The one you saw him making?" Nicole asked.

"Patrick told him about my nightmares and asked him to get it."

"Good thinking. Talking of which, what do we reckon really happened to Angus McKellar?"

Amelia fetched the case file and they went through the facts as they knew them.

"Angus vanished, reappeared and vanished again, along with the charity money. He turned up in Falmouth, vanished again and turned up dead," Nicole summarised.

"There's a lot more to it than that," Amelia protested. "Ellie Roebuck for example and…"

"Hey, I know him!" Nicole said, pulling out a newspaper clipping. "He used to own a B&B."

"He still does. The Sea Mist."

"In Falmouth? He had one here before."

"You sure it's him? George Williams isn't exactly an unusual name."

"George Williams's who look like that and hate publicity are. We have business networking meetings here for everyone connected with tourism, which is why

I recognise him. The press came to one and he refused to be interviewed. Said he didn't hold any truck with the TV or papers."

"That's exactly what he said to me, and not very politely," Amelia said.

"He let Angus McKellar, registered under his own name, hide out for a week," Patrick said. "Even if he didn't buy a paper himself his guests probably do, and he'd have heard local people talking about it."

"You think he was helping Angus?" Amelia asked.

"He must have had a reason to come to Falmouth."

"He knew the area."

"From a long time ago."

"What about Ellie Roebuck?" Nicole suggested. "She disappeared just before Angus went missing the first time, didn't she?"

"I only know what Sean told me, but that sounds right. Except... She wasn't in Falmouth, was she? It was a false address?"

"Maybe Sean got it wrong? Or whoever told him?"

"I think we need to look at it from a different angle," Patrick said. "Angus McKellar took the money, right?"

"Right," Nicole said.

"We don't actually know that," Amelia pointed out.

"How much was it?" Patrick asked.

"Nearly three hundred thousand," Nicole said.

"How much is his house worth?"

"A million? Oh! I see what you mean," Amelia said. "Nicole, there wasn't any hint he was in financial trouble, was there?"

"None."

"So he didn't need the money?"

"OK, I'm with you," Nicole said. "He stole the money,

planning to run off with Ellie and the baby, which we assume is his. She and George Williams helped him somehow, but he felt bad about what he'd done and killed himself."

"Or those two double-crossed and killed him?" Patrick suggested.

"I don't think so. It's all so complicated," Amelia said.

"You're the one who said there was more to it than him and the money going missing."

"I know. But everyone said what a lovely man he was. They're still saying it, most of them. His wife, friends and colleagues, even people at the charity." Amelia pointed to the sheets of tributes she'd printed out. "If so many people think that, it's probably true."

"You think he's innocent?" Nicole asked.

"Maybe. I admit there are a lot of things I can't explain and for a long time I've felt there's something I'm missing. A lot of it could be coincidence though, couldn't it? Or maybe Sean was right and Angus wasn't well. Alzheimer's or something? Those closest to him might not notice a gradual change."

"Maybe."

"The weekend I met Amelia, she got me to help write out her theory for the mystery weekend. She said if she didn't commit to one, she'd think she'd got it right as she'd suspected everyone in turn. That's sort of what we're doing now."

"OK then, I say he's guilty of taking the money, and felt bad and killed himself," Nicole said.

"What I meant was we don't... Oh, alright. He was set up by Ellie and George somehow. They duped him into taking the money and killed him for it."

"Angus is innocent," Amelia declared. "If only I could

get hold of what makes me think that."

"We have it covered anyhow. He either took the money and killed himself, took it and was killed or didn't take it," Patrick said.

Sean texted to say, 'Can we make it nine-thirty?' Even so he wasn't in the Castle In The Air when Amelia and Patrick arrived. He turned up not long after they'd ordered. He got his own pint and joined them.

"To Angus," he said and took a sip.

"To Angus," Amelia and Patrick repeated, rather dismally.

"Sorry," Sean said. "I meant to show it's OK to talk about him, not to get all morbid. I bet Amelia here has some theories about what happened?"

"We were talking about it earlier," Amelia admitted. "It seems horrible, but we were playing detective."

"It's OK really. You did tell me about your tendency to do that. Come on then, what's your answer?"

They repeated their theories.

"I reckon Amelia was in on it," Sean said after listening to them all. "She's obsessed by crime right?"

"Hmm," Patrick tentatively agreed.

"That's just her cover! It gave her an excuse to come up here. She stalked Angus at his home, distracted me while he escaped, didn't report seeing him in Falmouth until he was able to leave…"

Amelia stared at him. How did he know she'd been to the McKellar home? Admittedly that, and the time it took her to contact the police after first suspecting Angus was drinking in The Fal View did sound a little suspicious, but Sean couldn't really believe she was involved in the crime – could he?

Chapter 26

Sean laughed. "Don't worry, I know you didn't do it."

Amelia forced a smile. It was nice of him to try to put them at ease when talking about Angus, but making jokes seemed a bit heartless. Or did she just think that because it was at her expense?

"I've got something to show you which explains where Angus went. It's on his boat, where there's also a dvd player so I can show you the film you came across us making."

"How long will that take?" Patrick asked. He sounded reluctant.

"The film is less than ten minutes and the boat is moored down in Gosport, so not very long. Will you come?"

"Of course," Amelia said. No way was she missing out on seeing any evidence connected with the case. "I love boats, and I'd have looked round Angus's before if I'd had the chance," she confessed. "And the sooner I see that film, the sooner I'll stop having nightmares."

That last bit seemed to convince Patrick.

"Great." Sean gave complicated directions to the marina, then swiftly downed the rest of his pint. "I'll meet you on the boat. The code for the gate is 2110N, take the left pontoon. The boat is the seventh along. Even you can't miss it, Amelia. It has the name painted on it in letters this big."

"Do you want me to drive?" Patrick asked as they finished their drinks.

"No. You navigate. I'm so bad at finding my way I

might miss the sea!"

"He really got to you, didn't he?"

"You laughed."

"Sorry."

"You're forgiven. Not Sean though."

"Did you really stalk Angus?"

"Not technically."

"And the technicality is…?"

"He must have already been gone by then." She described taking Jehovah's Witness leaflets to the empty house and taking a peep round the back. "I didn't tell Sean. Angus's wife must have seen it on CCTV. Perhaps I should let Sean off making fun of me, because he must have explained that away. Can you imagine what the police would think if they knew about that, as well as all the rest? It would sound suspicious."

"A bit, yes. Is that why you didn't try to get on his boat?"

"No. I'd have tried if I thought there was a chance, but didn't know where it was moored and was pretty sure I wouldn't have been able to get aboard even if I did."

In the car, Amelia took her phone from her bag. "I'll just text Nicole."

"I can do that."

Amelia handed over the phone and started the engine. "Back the way we came to start with?"

"Yep. What do you want me to say to Nicole?"

"Just tell her we're meeting Sean on Angus's boat, so might be a bit later than we thought. Oh and put three little kisses with a gap between each, at the bottom. It's our secret code, so she knows it's me."

"Not very secret."

"You're the only other person who knows." There it

was again, that little prickle of something hidden in her mind. Something to do with secrets? There had to be some involved with the case, but everything she knew was public knowledge, wasn't it?

No. George Williams, the owner of the Sea Mist, having previously lived in Lee-on-the-Solent wasn't. Nobody seemed to know much about Ellie Roebuck either. But she'd had that feeling before learning about either.

What could Sean have to show them? Did Angus have something like the AIS used by ships, which would show where the yacht had been? Amelia couldn't see how it would help even if he had, but then if it was obvious the police would have worked it out long ago.

One thing which would help was the short film Sean and his friends had made. Even if it still looked horribly realistic, knowing it was a film would be reassuring. Some of the thrillers she watched had graphic scenes and those never gave her nightmares. And if Sean had kept his promise and included her in the credits she wanted to see that.

"Just here on the left," Patrick said.

There was no sign of Sean when they arrived, so they parked, followed his instructions and found the boat. They could see a light and it sounded as though the engine was running.

"Sean?"

"Welcome aboard!" He helped Amelia step up onto the side of the boat and climb over the safety wire around the deck.

Even in the dusk she could see tell the boat's polished woodwork and stainless steel trim were high quality. The Fal View's fixtures and fittings were classy, but they weren't up to this standard.

"Patrick, undo that rope and chuck it across, will you?" Sean said.

"We're going out?" Amelia asked. She'd never been on a boat in the dark before, it should be an interesting experience.

"Just a little way."

"Why?" Patrick asked, as he stepped aboard.

"Amelia deserves to know the truth now and this is the only way I can really show her."

"You think you know what happened to Angus?" Amelia asked.

"I do know." His calm confidence was convincing.

Sean manoeuvred the boat away from its mooring.

"Amelia, you remember I told you about AIS?"

She felt pleased with herself for guessing that could be involved. Pity she hadn't shared the theory with Patrick. Never mind, she could impress him with her specialist knowledge. "Yes. That's the transmitter thing which shows where ships and boats are. You had an app for it on your phone."

"Give me yours a minute."

She switched it on and handed it over.

"There you go, I've installed the app. Look there's a ferry." He showed them. "And there's us." He lodged the phone on the helm. "Normally the AIS transmitter is on all the time, even when the boat is moored. But it can be disconnected." He reached down and pressed a switch. "It refreshes about every fifteen minutes. When it does, it will look like we've vanished."

"Are you saying Angus was on his boat when he disappeared?" Amelia asked. She knew that wasn't the case for the entire period.

"Some of the time. You've seen how easy it is to take the boat out without anyone paying attention."

"There's CCTV," Patrick said.

"Yes, but it's not monitored. It would only be checked if someone reported a problem."

"That doesn't explain the money, or how he died, or..." As far as Amelia could tell it didn't really solve anything. There had to be more to Sean's theory than that.

"I know. I wanted to demonstrate something easy to explain first, because the rest is harder... I have to tell you though. I think you'll understand and you'll help me. You will, won't you, Amelia?"

"I think maybe you'd better just tell us," Patrick said.

Amelia agreed. She wanted answers, not to be told how this was all about Sean.

"Just tell you?" He sighed, then lifted his hands in a gesture of acceptance. "OK then. Angus took the charity money. As a trustee myself I gradually realised what he was doing. At first I didn't want to believe it, hoped I'd misunderstood the paperwork, then I thought he must have a reason. And I was right."

"There's no good reason for stealing from the charity," Amelia said.

"His reasons weren't all bad. He'd made a terrible mistake over Ellie."

"An affair?"

"Yes, and the baby was his. The affair was over, but he felt guilty for how he'd treated both her and his wife. He bought Ellie a house. He intended to pay for it himself, but there wasn't time to do it and keep it hidden from Heather, so he used the charity funds."

"Why didn't you tell the police?" Patrick asked.

"He made me swear not to tell anyone about the affair. That's why I hoped you'd find her and uncover the truth, Amelia. And he'd agreed to give it back."

The story was believable, including the part about Sean manipulating her into revealing the facts. He could have called the police the moment she'd told him Angus was at the Sea Mist B&B, but he'd left it to her. Unfortunately by the time she had, it had been too late. Even so, it wasn't the complete story.

"None of that explains where Angus has been all this time or why he died."

Sean took a step away from the controls and turned his back on Amelia and Patrick. "He said he had a way to make everything right and asked me to meet him. We drove to the Alver Valley Country park, where you saw me. I thought he was going to return the money and perhaps get me to sign something to cover up what he'd done. Instead he attacked me. You really did see me stab him, but it was in self-defence."

Sean killed him? No. What he said didn't match what she saw. And she'd seen Angus alive weeks after that. Did he think it was funny, to keep making up stupid stories?

"Your friend was holding him," Amelia pointed out.

Sean returned to his position at the controls and adjusted the boat's course. "He's no friend of mine. He was in on the scam with Angus. Not just that, either. He worked for Salterns Support. Part of his job was to collect the charity boxes and donations and he skimmed some off."

That part she did believe. It fitted with what Nicole and the lady in the charity shop had said, and it had always seemed odd that Angus could have just withdrawn the charity's money himself. It was far more likely he had help.

"So why was he holding Angus?" Patrick asked.

"To stop him killing me. He wasn't worried about taking the money, but that was too much."

"You should have told the police all this!"

"I know, but I didn't want to admit even to myself how wrong I'd been about a man I'd admired so much and... Look, you need to see the whole film, you'll understand then. Amelia, as you're so keen on boats, would you steer while Patrick helps me set up the player and screen? It's awkward for one person to do."

"What do I have to do?" Amelia asked. Despite the rather weird situation she couldn't help being a tiny bit excited that she was getting the chance to steer this fabulous boat.

"Just turn this like a steering wheel. See that light ahead?"

"Yes."

"It's a marker buoy, just keep heading for that."

"OK."

As he was instructing Patrick on how to access the companionway to the lower deck, Amelia remembered the AIS transmitter was still disconnected. She bent down and flipped it back on.

There was a loud thud.

"Careful!" Sean yelled.

Amelia turned to look, but it wasn't her he was shouting at.

"Patrick? Are you OK?" Sean called.

"What's happened? Patrick?"

"The boat moved and he fell. I'll go and see…"

"No, you drive. I'm first aid trained." She climbed

down to Patrick. "Can you hear me?" she asked, trying to keep panic out of her voice.

He mumbled something she didn't understand.

A lot of things weren't making sense. Sean's story for a start, and why did they need to be on the boat to hear it? She must have caused the boat to move while switching the AIS transmitter back on, but in that case why didn't she feel anything? None of that was as important as Patrick.

She felt his pulse, which wasn't as strong or steady as she'd have liked. Amelia carefully checked Patrick over for injuries. He had a cut on his head, which hopefully looked worse than it really was. "Patrick, can you hear me?" She still couldn't make out what he was trying to say, or even if he was aware she was with him.

He had to be OK. She loved him, needed him. His girls needed him. Isla needed his kidney. He'd be fine, of course he would. He was the hero and although things sometimes looked dark, the hero always made it through.

"I'm going to put you in the recovery position." As she manoeuvred him, she murmured, "I've no idea what's going on, but getting back to land seems a really good idea." It was a lot more important than that, but she didn't want to scare Patrick if he could hear her. Keeping him calm and comfortable until they could get medical help was her top priority. The boat seemed to have sped up, which she hoped meant Sean was racing back to the marina.

She found Patrick's phone, thankfully not damaged in the fall, and dialled 999.

"Emergency, which service do you require?"

Who could reach them at sea? Air ambulance, the RNLI, navy? "We're on a boat and someone has been knocked out..."

"Putting you through to the coastguard."

Once connected, Amelia began explaining the situation, but the call-taker kept interrupting. That happened a couple of times before Amelia realised her panicked account wasn't making sense. More calmly, and with prompts, she described Patrick's condition and gave what information she could about their location, adding, "The boat has an AIS tracker."

Patrick opened his eyes as she was speaking.

"I think he's coming round. Patrick? Can you hear me?"

"Amelia?"

"Yes, I'm here. Do you know what happened?"

"It's all wrong. Need to get off the boat." He sounded so tired and it seemed he had trouble focussing on her face.

"I know." To the coastguard she said, "He's just about conscious. I'm going to speak to Sean who's driving the boat."

Amelia left the phone with Patrick and climbed back to Sean.

"He's bleeding pretty badly and barely conscious. He needs to get to hospital straight away."

"I'll call the coastguard."

Amelia didn't say she already had. Her account was garbled and she hadn't known where they were. Sean would give the right information to the right people. As he spoke Amelia tried to understand what was happening, but all she could think of was Patrick, lying almost unresponsive on the deck below. He looked so much like he had when playing dead as Max Gould at the murder mystery weekend. Same clammy skin and livid wound.

"I've been advised to head for Southampton," Sean said. "A boat will be sent out to meet us and take Patrick straight to hospital."

Thank goodness Sean had called. She'd thought they were much nearer to Portsmouth than Southampton, and had said so.

They were moving at an incredible speed. The rush of cold air cleared her head, or perhaps it was the knowledge that Patrick would soon have help. Even so, she couldn't make sense of Sean's story.

"Why did you say you killed Angus?"

"Why do you think?"

"I don't know." She reached for her phone, which was still lodged on the helm.

"Who are you going to call?" He asked as though he found the idea amusing.

"Nicole. To tell her what's happened." Maybe doing that would help her understand it herself?

"No need. Check your call history."

She did and found a text. 'Won't be back tonight. Will explain all later x x x'

That sounded exactly like a text from her. As Patrick said, their code wasn't very secret. It would be very easy to impersonate her after a quick look at other texts she'd sent Nicole. That was it! The thing she hadn't quite seen.

Both times Angus had gone missing, he'd communicated only via text. If someone had his phone it would be easy to fake those, especially if the person knew him well. Think, Amelia, think. What did she actually know? Nicole had said, "Angus vanished, reappeared and vanished again, along with the charity money. He turned up in Falmouth, vanished again and turned up dead."

The first and last bits were true, she was certain. It was just possible the money going missing at the same time was coincidence. But it could be connected in some way other than Angus having stolen it. And she knew Angus had appeared in Falmouth because she'd seen him.

Sean slid her phone from her hand and chucked it in the sea.

This was getting bizarre – and scary. Why would he get rid of her phone? The obvious answer was he didn't want her calling anyone. Not a reassuring thought. He'd said he killed Angus. The most likely reason for doing that was because it was true.

She was on a boat with a killer! No, that couldn't be right. This was real life, not a film or mystery weekend at The Fal View. But Angus McKellar's death was all too real.

Even if it had been self-defence, which seemed doubtful, Sean had covered it up. And he'd given Nicole a false message which would stop her expecting Amelia and Patrick to return until the next day. Throwing Amelia's phone into the sea hadn't been an accident. Most likely Patrick's fall wasn't either. She knew it wasn't.

No, she couldn't believe that or she'd be even more terrified than when she'd seen him with the knife, and this time there was nowhere to run. She didn't know anything. Sean was just playing some weird game, creating a puzzle for her. He hadn't killed Angus and hadn't hurt Patrick. That was just makeup on his head, like she'd seen before. She'd go back down to him and together they'd work it all out and this nightmare would end.

"No you don't." Sean grabbed her arm and yanked her towards him.

It was no use trying to fight. He was far stronger than her. But that didn't matter as it wasn't real. She couldn't let herself believe it was.

In this game, she needed to keep Sean talking until help arrived. How long would that take? She now doubted Sean had called the coastguard. They were travelling incredibly fast. Even if the vague location she'd given had been correct at the time, it no longer was.

This story must have a happy ending. She just needed to see the clues which would allow that to happen. Some glimmer of hope.

There weren't many boats out at night, and she'd given its name. If they had enough time, rescuers could track it on AIS or find them some other way. Sean liked to explain how clever he was. If she could just get him started…

"Who did I see in Falmouth?" Amelia asked, almost at random.

"Ah, the little detective is finally getting it, is she? Took you long enough considering it all happened right in front of you."

"You said I deserved to know. I think I do too, but I won't unless you explain." Was his ego big enough, and his tendency to mansplain strong enough, for that to work? Of course it would be, the killer always explains himself to the detective.

"You deserve something alright, for the trouble you caused me!"

"I don't understand."

"You will. It was Corey you saw."

"The man who held Angus while you stabbed him?"

"That's right. Angus gave a few last twitches after I stabbed him, but I wasn't sure it would convince you he was fine, so I prompted Corey to speak for him then. He's a good actor."

He was. The way he'd turned away to attend to what she'd assumed was the camera equipment had done nearly as much to convince her it really was a film scene, as had hearing the victim speak.

"He sometimes impersonated Angus when he returned from the first disappearance, didn't he? That's why people thought they'd seen him in odd places, or acting strangely."

"That's right," Sean confirmed. "It wasn't Angus acting, but Corey. And I was directing it all."

To give the impression Angus wasn't the honest, reliable man everyone knew him to be. "Then, when I saw you kill him, you did it again so I'd think he was still alive?"

"The opportunity to turn the one witness against us to someone working to prove my innocence was too good to miss."

"What would you have done if I hadn't seen you kill him?"

"Taken him out to sea and run over him with the boat. The damage from the propellers would have disguised the stab wound."

Amelia shuddered. A horrible death for an innocent man wasn't a good fit for the cosy mystery she was telling herself she'd got involved in.

"Oh, don't worry. All you did was delay things a bit and that allowed us to get more money from his accounts. As a reward I'll answer three more questions."

She didn't want to know why it was only three or what would happen next, but she had to keep him talking. What would take a lot of explaining?

"How could you withdraw money from his account?"

"Easy when I had his wallet and he'd used the marina's entrance code as his PIN."

"Oh." Amelia used the numbers in her car registration. If she got out of this alive she'd change it. First though, she had a bigger problem. "The first time Angus went missing, back in November, was that because of you?"

"Of course it was."

Too short an answer. She needed better questions. "How? Why?" She hoped he wasn't keeping count.

"It's easy to get people to do what you want if you slip rohypnol into their drink. We just kept him on that for a few days, giving him a little food and water between doses to keep him going. Then we dumped him in the New Forest with a bottle of whisky, making sure he'd be good and thirsty when he came round. It worked like a charm. He was blind drunk when he was found and couldn't remember a thing."

"That's how, and I think I know why. You wanted to discredit him, so people would believe he'd stolen the money or had a secret to hide. And after you'd killed him, it would seem he'd chosen to go away again. And then me thinking I'd seen him in Falmouth made that seem even more likely."

Sean was looking pleased with himself. Amelia could use that. "You had me completely fooled, and managed to make more money at the same time! It was a very clever plan."

"Got my revenge on that stupid George Williams too."

"You knew him?"

"Refused to give me an interview when I was starting out. He'd witnessed a car crash which killed three kids. Big scoop it would have been for me, but he said it was disgusting the way I was snooping round, trying to benefit from someone else's tragedy."

"He wasn't very nice to me either. I'm glad you got revenge on him. How did you do it?"

"Called in a few anonymous tips, saying he had celebrities staying there. He got so fed up with the press camping out on his doorstep he moved."

"So it was because of him Angus... No, Corey, went to Falmouth?"

"That was just a bonus."

"What about Ellie Roebuck?"

"A footballer, I think you said." He laughed.

"You made her up? So it was only because of me you picked Falmouth?"

"Of course it was. And you played your part beautifully, Amelia. You saw exactly what you, and we, wanted you to see, even if like now you took your time about it."

"I still don't understand all of it."

"All you need to know is that you've become so obsessed with the crime you persuaded your boyfriend to help you steal Angus's boat and then had a terrible accident."

He was going to kill them too? Of course he was, why else had he taken them out to sea? And that's why he'd arranged it so they arrived without him and let themselves into the marina. With the things he'd mentioned in the pub, and the message to Nicole, it might seem as though she'd taken her investigations too far and got herself and Patrick killed. Aargh! That's exactly what she had done!

Except it would be no accident. Sean would be their killer – and he'd still be on the boat. How would he explain that? Amelia wanted to say he wouldn't get away with it but decided against repeating Angus McKellar's dying words. "Won't it look odd that the boat gets safely back?"

"No, because that won't happen." Sean brought the boat to a sudden, silent stop. "See those lights?"

She nodded. This was it – he'd tie up the loose ends for her, the credits would roll and she and Patrick would live happily ever after.

"That's not anyone coming to rescue you, but my mate Corey. He's going to help me put Patrick in the water, but I can manage you myself."

No more pretending. Something grabbed her and held her rigid – fear. There was nothing Amelia could do to help herself, but she had to warn Patrick. Give him a chance. She screamed.

Sean grabbed her leg and sent her sprawling over the safety wire around the boat's upper deck. As she fell towards the water, Amelia clamped a hand over her nose and mouth.

The water was so cold she couldn't help a gasp. Thanks to having covered her airways she swallowed only a little water.

The sea seemed to be dragging her down. She tried to stay calm, but wasted energy frantically kicking off her shoes and trying to remove her jacket. Amelia knew she was still underwater, but she couldn't stop her body trying to breathe. She felt the sting of salt hitting her lungs. Then nothing.

Chapter 27

Amelia was so, so tired. She just wanted to sleep, to forget the agony of running out of air and breathing in salty water. They wouldn't let her.

Whatever she was lying on was rocking. She must be back on the boat. Had Sean changed his mind and rescued her? What about Patrick? She tried to call his name, but her raw throat wouldn't cooperate. The attempt made her cough convulsively and she didn't have the strength to try again.

"It's OK, love. We'll have you both in hospital soon."

That wasn't Sean.

She forced her eyes open. It wasn't Angus's boat. A man in uniform was by her side. The coastguard had found them!

Amelia threw up on her saviour.

People spoke to her. They moved her and did all kinds of things. She knew they were trying to help, but wished they'd just leave her alone.

They wouldn't let her travel to the hospital with Patrick, or see him when she got there. She didn't have her phone to call Nicole, wasn't sure her request she be contacted was understood.

Sometime later, minutes or hours, Amelia was examined and told she was OK, but would need to be kept under observation. They said the same about Patrick. Maybe it was true?

"Amelia?"
"Nicole?"

Her friend kissed her cheek. "I'm your sister, OK? They called to say you were here, but I thought they might not let me in unless I was a relative."

"It's nearly true." It was hard to speak and hurt to breathe.

"Are you OK? They said you were."

"Hurts."

"I know, sweetie. You breathed in water. That's not a good thing to do. You had to be revived and you're going to feel terrible for a while. There's no sign of brain damage though, or any other complications. I'm going to stay here until I can take you home. If they kick me off the ward I'll wait in the corridor. I'm not leaving this hospital without you."

Amelia tried to find the courage to ask the most important question. She needed to be brave, because Nicole wouldn't lie to her. "Patrick?"

"He's OK."

"You... saw him?"

"I haven't seen him myself, but he is OK."

"Please."

"I don't think they'll let me see him, sweetie. It's three in the morning and they're not going to believe we're triplets."

"Please."

"I'll try."

It seemed a long time until Nicole came back. Amelia must have slept because a nurse checked her. "Your sister said to tell you she'll be back soon. She shouldn't really be here, but I could tell she wasn't going to leave you."

"Patrick?"

"I'm sure he's just fine. You rest."

Now they wanted her to sleep she needed to stay awake and find out if Patrick was OK.

"Amelia?" It was Nicole. "Patrick is asleep, but he's definitely breathing. He has three stitches in his head, a massive bruise and looks even worse than you do. He's going to be fine."

Amelia slept on and off until the morning. Whenever she woke Nicole was there and told her she was OK. In the morning Amelia dressed in the clothes Nicole had brought for her and asked to see Patrick.

"The doctor will be round to see you soon so she can discharge you. Perhaps you can see him after that," a nurse said.

Amelia looked at Nicole. "Please."

Nicole stood and turned to face the man. "Nurse, my sister and her fiancé nearly died last night. She's desperately worried about him." She put her hands on her hips and spoke firmly. "All night I've been told over and over that she needs to be kept calm and quiet. Seeing that he's alright is the only way that's going to happen."

"The night shift told me about you. Whatever you do, don't wait until I'm not looking, put your friend in that chair over there and wheel her down for a very quick look. And for pity's sake get her back here before the doctor arrives."

Patrick looked exactly as Nicole had described, except he was awake.

"Stay in the chair and shut up," Nicole ordered.

Amelia obeyed, and reached out to hold Patrick's hand. He gently squeezed hers.

"Are you OK?" he asked.

"Patrick, it hurts her to talk, but she's fine and will be discharged this morning. I'll bring her back then, but she couldn't wait to see you. She loves you loads and all that stuff. Now you say the same and I'll take her back before the doctor comes and she misses the chance to be discharged or that nurse gets the sack for conspiracy to kidnap."

"Amelia, I love you loads and all that stuff."

It was a jokey way to say it, but she didn't doubt he meant it. "Love you," Amelia croaked. Her effort was rewarded by seeing the pain and worry temporarily vanish from his face, to be replaced by an expression which told her everything was going to be just fine. She'd nearly got him killed, and he still loved her!

"Right, come on, sis." Nicole wheeled her back to the ward.

Two police officers and the, by then, harassed looking nurse were waiting for them on their return.

"We'd like to ask you a few questions, if you feel up to it?" a female police officer said.

Amelia nodded. If she'd said she wasn't, perhaps she wouldn't be considered fit enough for discharge and wouldn't be allowed to return to Patrick.

Nicole explained about her difficulty in talking. "I'm staying with her."

"Is that what you want?"

Amelia nodded.

Nicole answered as many of the questions as she knew the answers to. Amelia was able to give a fairly complete account of what she knew by one word replies, or written answers to the officers' questions. She wanted answers herself, but it was hard to ask and they told her it was still being investigated.

Finally they thanked her, and said they or someone else would be in touch. Nicole provided her contact details.

"Tell Mum and Dad," Amelia said once they'd gone. If they were to hear anything about the night's events on the news they'd be so worried.

Nicole rang and said that Amelia was OK, but had spent the night in hospital. After a pause she said, "Honestly she's fine. We're just waiting for her to be discharged." To Amelia she said, "They want to come down."

Amelia shook her head, and tried to mime that she'd see them soon.

"I think she's trying to say she'll come to you." A moment later Nicole said, "She really is OK, I swear. It's just that she finds it really hard to talk. I'll put you on speakerphone and she'll be able to hear you."

It was comforting to hear their voices and touching how concerned they were. Both of them were so sweet and, unlike the police, didn't ask any questions which made her feel stupid for having got into such a dangerous situation. They were obviously deeply worried.

"Mum, Dad... I'm OK," she managed to say. After that she let Nicole do the talking.

Nicole sounded reassuring and convincing, even when she said she couldn't switch to a video call, allowing them to see Amelia was OK, because of rules on patient confidentiality. Perhaps that was true? It was certainly a good thing Mum and Dad couldn't see her. If she looked halfway as bad as she felt, they'd have been even more concerned.

"Are you sure you don't want us to come down?" Mum asked Amelia, after hearing as much as Nicole could tell her.

Amelia tried her mime again.

"She says she will come to you soon." Nicole explained Amelia would have to speak to the police again, and they didn't yet know how long Patrick would need to stay in hospital. "I promise to take good care of her."

"Thank you, Nicole. Amelia, when, if, you do want us then just say. We'll come right away."

Amelia couldn't thank them. It wasn't just her injured lungs and sore throat stopping her speak, it was emotion too. Her parents loved her and wanted to be with her. She'd go up to them soon. She was surprised by how much that thought pleased her.

There was someone else who needed to be told what had happened. "Meghan," Amelia croaked.

"She knows. Patrick got me to text her, and his family, to say he was OK and would be in touch soon."

Eventually the doctor came and after a brief examination said Amelia could leave the hospital. Nicole took her, in the wheelchair, straight to see Patrick. He was dressed and out of bed.

The police officers who'd spoken to Amelia were with him. At first they asked her to wait outside, then the male one came to fetch them, at Patrick's request. "He said he wants you to hear."

"So, Sean asked you to help with something on the lower deck? What happened when you went down?"

"I didn't climb down. I started to and he shouted for me to look out and I lost my footing. I'm not sure if he pushed me and I banged my head as I fell, or if he hit me with something."

"You're certain you didn't slip?"

"Positive."

"Thank you. So, you were on the lower deck, with a head injury?"

"Yes. Amelia came down. I tried to tell her I didn't fall, but I was pretty much out of it then. She put me in the recovery position and called the emergency services. She left the phone with me. By then I was thinking more clearly. The operator stayed on the line and I told her what was happening."

"Could you go through that now, please?"

"I said I thought I'd been pushed and suspected Sean was up to no good. The operator probably thought I was concussed. I couldn't hear what Sean and Amelia were talking about, but started to get worried when she didn't come back down. I knew she'd have come to check on me and reassure me Sean was taking us back to land if that was the case. I told the operator and she said the boat was being tracked, and help was on the way. I'm sure she'd started to believe me that it wasn't just a simple accident."

The policeman wrote that down. "You couldn't hear what was happening on the deck above?"

"The engine was too loud most of the time. But I could when he stopped. He said his friend was coming to help put me in the sea, but that he could manage Amelia on his own. There was a struggle, scream and a splash." Patrick had to stop speaking to wipe his eyes and blow his nose. "I thought they'd throw me in too and I wouldn't be able to help her."

Amelia wanted to tell him that he had helped, by convincing the operator both their lives were in danger. She'd got them into that danger, despite her instincts having warned her against Sean – but she too had helped save them, by activating the AIS and keeping him talking.

The police officers gave Patrick a moment to compose himself. "And you were on the phone to the operator all this time?"

"Yes, and I told her everything I heard. Aren't the calls recorded?"

"They are, but we need to hear it all from your perspective too." The officer then got Patrick to go through the arrival of the rescue service and police marine unit. "I don't really know what happened after that. Did you arrest Sean?"

"Yes. We've had to add assault on police officers to the list of charges, but there was nowhere for him to go."

"And his friend, Corey? Was he really coming to help kill us and take Sean back to land?"

"He was, and we've arrested him too."

After a few minutes more the police left and Amelia was in Patrick's arms. She clung to him as he said he loved her and that everything was going to be OK. She believed him then, but not when he said he should have done more to protect her.

"No. It…" She coughed.

"Shh, don't try to speak. There will be time for that later." He kissed her.

"Are they letting you out of hospital today?" Nicole asked.

"I don't know. A doctor is coming soon."

"I think she's already here."

Amelia turned to see the doctor who'd discharged her was approaching.

"If you could just wait outside while I examine him, I'll be able to tell him that," she said in reply to Nicole's question.

Amelia wasn't aware of much on the drive back to Nicole's. All she knew, and all that seemed to matter, was that Patrick was with her. At one point he phoned Meghan asking her to explain to the girls in case they heard something and were worried. It was clear from his replies that Meghan was concerned herself and that she asked after Amelia too.

Both Amelia and Patrick slept for a while after they got back. Nicole woke them to say the police would like to ask more questions.

"I'll say no if you like, but I suppose you'll have to do it sometime, and if you get up for a while, you'll sleep better tonight."

The next two days were spent resting, talking to the police, being cosseted by Nicole, and short walks along the seafront. As her voice improved, Amelia had several telephone calls with her parents and Isla and Ava. Everyone missed and loved her. Mum and Dad sent flowers and a huge pack of caramels. Meghan texted photos of get well cards the girls had made. 'Sorry, couldn't get envelopes big enough' she typed.

"I feel well enough to go to the inquest," Amelia said on the third day.

"Pity it was yesterday," Nicole said.

"No!" She'd lost track of time and didn't have her phone to check the date. "No, it's today." Nicole was probably just trying to protect her.

"Sorry, but you didn't miss much. As expected it was opened and adjourned pending further investigations."

"We still don't know what happened then?"

"Pretty much, don't we?" Nicole fetched the case file she'd made for Amelia back in May, and which would no longer close as Amelia had frequently updated it and Nicole had added to the contents in the time Amelia and Patrick had been recovering.

"Sean stole the money and tried to frame Angus. I don't know what he said to get him to meet him the night he killed him. Maybe Angus didn't know by then?"

"Back up a bit," Patrick said. "What about the first disappearance?"

"It was an attempt to discredit Angus," Amelia said. "They drugged him, Sean admitted it. Like I said before, everyone who knew him said what a lovely man he was. People wouldn't have believed he would just take the money and go, at least not without good reason. Sean spread rumours too, easy to do in his job I expect."

"And it worked," Nicole said. "We and lots of others had all kinds of theories about why and where he went, but nobody thought it wasn't either by choice or because he'd had a breakdown or something."

"The person he was supposed to meet both times before he went missing was Sean? Or something he arranged?" Amelia said. "Yes, must have been. And he sent those texts making it seem as though Angus was alive. Probably he was going to anyway, but after me seeing the stabbing it was even more important for it to seem he was still alive."

"Yeah. When his body was found, the initial reports said he was thought to have been in the water a couple of days. Sean had been all over the TV those two days, and did a couple of volunteer stints at the respite centre."

"Giving himself an alibi," Patrick said. "Quite clever."

"But where was Angus? We know now it wasn't him I saw in Falmouth, but Sean's accomplice Corey dressed up. Like Sean said, I saw what I wanted to see," Amelia said bitterly.

"That wasn't your fault," Patrick said.

"Sean also said Corey was taking donation money. That bit was true, I think, except they were in it together."

"And they withdrew a lot of cash from the McKellar accounts. There's his car too, bet they sold it. They must have got away with a lot more than the three hundred thousand. And they stole his boat…"

"They haven't got away with it, Amelia. They've been arrested, the police assured me there's no chance of bail, and there's plenty of evidence."

"Where did Angus go, do you have a theory, Nicole?" Patrick asked.

"Nowhere. He was dead, wasn't he?"

"But his body stayed… fresh," Amelia pointed out. "No one would have recognised him on sight otherwise."

"That's because it was in a freezer."

"That could account for it," Patrick said.

"It's a fact. While the police were waiting to question you, I asked some of my own. I didn't get much from them, but they did say the body had been frozen. It still partly was when they started the autopsy."

Shortly afterwards, a news report confirmed that, and added the fact the deep freeze was at Corey's home.

"Nice place for an out of work actor," Nicole said as the camera panned back to show the property.

"No!" Amelia gasped. "That's one of the houses I sat outside while I was waiting for Sean. I thought he was interviewing someone boring and stayed in the car trying to work out what had happened to Angus. If I'd gone inside… "

"You wouldn't be here now," Patrick said.

"I suppose you're right."

"Of course he is," Nicole said.

"Oh crikey, I've just remembered. When I asked what sort of person Angus was, Sean said he was chilled out."

Nicole sent Patrick out to buy fish and chips. "I've done nothing but slave for you two for two days straight, it's the least you can do."

"Couldn't agree more," he said.

"What's up?" Amelia asked as soon as he'd left. "You obviously got him out the way for a reason."

"And I thought I'd been so subtle."

"Come on then, spill."

"Manky Meghan called."

"We don't call her that anymore. What did she want?"

"To bring Ava and Isla up here. They want to see that you and Patrick are OK."

"That would be brilliant!"

"It would?"

"Of course. We talked about going straight back, but there was the police stuff and neither of us was up to the drive."

"I wouldn't have let you try."

"There's that too! Then we thought it might be better to wait until after the weekend as we'd planned, so we were totally recovered and Patrick's stitches were out. We've both got another week off work, so were going to pick the girls up and take them up to Mum and Dad's to prove I'm OK."

"That'll be fun."

"You know, I think it will, especially with the girls there. Patrick seemed quite keen on the idea."

"Hmmm, wonder why?"

"Don't start that, I'm totally done with mysteries."

"Of course you are."

"I am."

"Right."

It was wonderful to see Ava and Isla again. Just hearing, "Melia!" yelled as they clambered out of the car almost made her cry. When the girls hugged her and Patrick the tears really did fall.

"Don't cry, Melia."

"It means she's happy," Isla said.

"She's a silly billy!"

After Meghan and Stuart had unloaded their bags and sorted out Isla's dialysis machine, they all, Nicole included, went to a local pub for an early dinner. After the meal, Nicole, Amelia and Patrick walked the girls home, leaving Meghan and Stuart to have another drink and come back later.

"We can all stay," Ava suggested.

"I can't," Nicole said. "I need to get up early to make your breakfast."

"And the rest of us need to sleep too, so we'll be ready to go somewhere special tomorrow," Patrick said.

"Really, really, special?"

"Yes."

"Where, Daddy?"

"Not telling you."

"Where is it, Melia?"

"I can't tell you because I don't know."

Patrick pulled her close and whispered, "Portchester castle, if that's OK?"

"It is."

"Where, Melia?"

"Where are we going, Amelia?"

"Let's see if you can guess before we get back to Nicole's shall we?"

It didn't take long for them to suggest a castle. It took a lot longer to get the girls settled. They weren't naughty, just excited to be somewhere different and to have a castle visit to look forward to.

Amelia recalled thinking, on her first visit to Portchester castle, that it would be more fun with the girls. She was right. She hadn't at that time admitted to herself she'd also wanted Patrick with her, but deep down she'd known it was true. Of course she hadn't known he'd join in with Ava rolling down the partial dry moat.

Amelia laughed at the pair of them, then noticed Isla watching wistfully. Although reasonably well and strong now, with the catheter in place for her dialysis such a physical game might not be sensible.

"They're a pair of silly billies, aren't they?" Amelia said.

"Yes they are."

"Let's teach them a lesson. Come on, let's hide!" She grabbed Isla's hand and ran with her through the huge doorway in the castle's curtain wall.

Once inside there was nowhere obvious to go. Amelia didn't want the others to have a long search, so she suggested they snuggle in behind the wall. "When they come through we can jump out and go boo!"

They waited, giggling together until they heard Patrick say, "They must have come through here. Can you see them, Ava?"

"Shh," Amelia said to Isla.

Ava ran past them. 'Melia! Isla! We can see you!

Daddy, where did they go?"

"I don't know."

"Now," Amelia whispered and she and Isla shouted 'boo!' and ran up to the others.

"You are silly billies!" Ava declared.

"No, you are more silly," Isla retorted.

"You are!"

"No, me and Amelia are the silliest." Patrick grinned at Amelia. "Come on, let's give them our swearing parrots." He and Amelia both flapped their wings and shouted various mildly rude words until all four of them were laughing helplessly. Each time some of them recovered either one of the others, or the reactions of people passing by, set them off again.

Later as they were exploring the castle, Isla read to them from one of the information panels. Patrick helped a little, but she did really well considering how many of the words must be unfamiliar to her.

"She's not really silly, she's clever," Ava told Amelia.

"Yes she is, and so are you."

"And you and Daddy, but he really is a silly billy!"

Amelia laughed. "That's true!"

As they moved away from the sign, an elderly lady said, "Excuse me, I just wanted to say what a lovely family you are."

"Thank you," Patrick said. "I'm very lucky."

Amelia couldn't say anything, but she was sure the smile on her face was answer enough.

When they were outside again, Patrick suggested the girls make daisy chains. He took Amelia's hand and walked a few steps away from the girls.

"I've been thinking," he said. "What that lady said, about us being a nice family, and Nicole claiming we're engaged… how would you feel about making it official?"

It wasn't the most romantic of proposals, but she wouldn't let a little detail like that stop her accepting. "As long as Ava and Isla are OK about it, that sounds like a really good idea."

"They'll be delighted. We had a talk about it."

That must have been before they left for Lee-on-the-Solent, he hadn't spent any time alone with them since they arrived the previous day. "You've been thinking about this for a while then?"

"I have. Amelia," he dropped down onto one knee and held out a diamond ring engraved in the same pattern as the locket he'd given her for her birthday. "Will you marry me?"

"Yes! Yes, I will!"

They kissed until Amelia felt little hands tugging at her. "Melia, can we be bridesmaids?"

"We'd be really good, look."

Amelia watched as the two girls put circlets of daisies on each other's heads, then held hands, curtsied and gave angelic smiles.

"Of course you can. You'll be the prettiest and nicest bridesmaids in the world."

"And Bongo?"

"I don't think so."

"Oh please, Melia."

"Please, please, please."

With special thanks to Fiona Loud at Kidney Care UK, who kindly took time to help me with the medical details.

Thank you for reading this book. I hope you enjoyed it. If you did, I'd really appreciate it if you could spare the time to leave a short review on Amazon and/or Goodreads.

To learn more about my writing life, hear about new releases and get a free short story, sign up to my newsletter – https://mailchi.mp/677f65e1ee8f/sign-up or you can find the link on my website patsycollins.uk

More books by Patsy Collins

Novels –

Firestarter
Escape To The Country
A Year And A Day
Paint Me A Picture
Leave Nothing But Footprints

Short story collections –

Over The Garden Fence
Up The Garden Path
Through The Garden Gate
In The Garden Air

No Family Secrets
Can't Choose Your Family
Keep It In The Family
Family Feeling
Happy Families

All That Love Stuff
With Love And Kisses
Lots Of Love
Love Is The Answer

Slightly Spooky Stories I
Slightly Spooky Stories II
Slightly Spooky Stories III
Slightly Spooky Stories IV

Just A Job
Perfect Timing
A Way With Words
Dressed To Impress
Coffee & Cake
Criminal Intent
Not A Drop To Drink

Non-fiction –

From Story Idea To Reader
(co-written with Rosemary J. Kind)

A Year Of Ideas:
365 sets of writing prompts and exercises

Lightning Source UK Ltd.
Milton Keynes UK
UKHW021842181121
394140UK00007B/506